PLAN D . . .

To Pam
with best regards
from
Michael Seymour

PLAN D . . .

a Love Story

MICHAEL SEYMOUR

authorHOUSE®

AuthorHouse™ *UK Ltd.*
1663 Liberty Drive
Bloomington, IN 47403 USA
www.authorhouse.co.uk
Phone: 0800.197.4150

Published by AuthorHouse   07 / 23 / 2013

ISBN: 978-1-4817-9770-2 (sc)
ISBN: 978-1-4817-9771-9 (e)

Reference: Much of the material used in this book is drawn from Palestinian and Israeli sources, as well as other
independent records.
There is also a certain amount of autobiographical material, woven into the story.

For Linda

Chapter 1

We met first at art school, in those early days. Simon was tall, thin, and rather gangling, with unruly curly brown hair, and very blue eyes. He seemed to be rather shy and reserved, almost aloof.

As time went by though we became close friends. We shared many of the same interests: A wide range of reading and music, artists and painters, and long distance walking. We also shared the same iconoclastic and esoteric humour, triggering each other off into more absurdities, until we cried with laughter and drew closer together. We often spent whole days at the weekends walking in the Purbeck hills, marvelling at the panoramic skies, looking down on Poole Harbour with its bird sanctuary on Brownsea Island in the middle, with little white sailed yachts and dinghies in respectful attendance.

Tea at Corfe, with strawberry jam and scones, clotted cream and thick cups of strong tea, and us, replete in the sun at the foot of the ancient castle. Then the long walk back over the hills to Studland, down the straight road and across the entrance to the harbour for the last ferry. As we walked, we talked, of everything and nothing. Michelangelo and Proust, Degas and dreams, Rubens and Rococo, the meaning of life, the past and the future, love and despair. All religions discussed, all discarded.

There was a certain idyllic quality to these times, rather like Brideshead Revisited which we had both read, without the homosexual undertones. We were unquestionably heterosexual, vying with one another as to which of us would reach the promised land first. Simon won by a short head having had his first experience under a beach hut on the cliffs in the freezing cold. I followed later, rather prosaically on a sofa, in the warmth, when my girlfriend's parents were out for the evening. There followed much discussion between Simon and me, of D H Lawrence and whether it was as mystic as he made it out to be.

We progressed through art school, taking first the Intermediate, then the National Diploma in painting. We were now dedicated artists, with our eyes set on a garret in Paris.

Then the day came when we received our call-up papers, the inescapable National Service. I received mine a couple of months before Simon, as I was slightly older. We had both anticipated this with dread and resentment, two years of our lives taken away from us! I went away for my basic training, somewhere in Wiltshire. Simon saw me off at the station and we shook hands rather formally, something we had never done before. We promised to write to one another. I waved to his receding figure, until the swirl of steam hid him from sight.

When I finished my basic training, and had a 48 hour pass before being posted to Aldershot, I went back home. Simon had gone to Catterick in Yorkshire to do his basic training.

I was posted to Aldershot and remained there, apart from short periods of leave and weekend passes, for the remainder of my service. It suited me very well as I had no desire to go abroad and wanted to be close to home so I could see my parents and my girlfriend.

When Simon finished his basic training, he went to a training camp near Loughborough, where he remained, doing an intensive course, until he was finally posted to Cyprus.

Cyprus at that time was in the throes of freeing itself from British rule. Eoka and Enosis were mentioned daily in the news, Makarios was vilified and sent into exile. Bombings of camps and convoys, soldiers killed by snipers, were almost a daily occurrence. It sounded dangerous to me, and I did write several times to Simon, but received no replies. I was still in contact with his parents and they assured me that he had written to say that he was quite safe. He had not revealed what he was actually doing, but his mother hinted darkly that she thought that he was engaged in some sort of intelligence work.

Eventually the great day came and I was demobbed. It was at the end of August, two years to the day since I had been called up. I immediately began getting work together in order to apply for a place at the Royal College of Art, that pinnacle of art schools in Britain, to which we aspired. Not long after I arrived back I heard from Simon's parents that he was returning from Egypt on a troopship. Egypt? . . . I thought he was in Cyprus.

I looked forward with excitement to seeing Simon again, but had to wait for the troopship to make its slow way through the Mediterranean and then via the Bay of Biscay up to Southampton, where it docked one beautiful sunny September afternoon. I was there on the quayside with Simon's parents as it drew alongside. There were over 900 soldiers on board, a sea of khaki lining the rail. I searched in vain for Simon's face in this crowd, but couldn't see him, neither could his parents. We were told to wait in the customs shed, as those with people to greet them would be allowed ashore for half an hour. We waited with other eager parents, watching as they greeted their sons, some with tears, others with laughter and smiles. Eventually we were told that he couldn't come ashore as he had to travel the next day up to Chester, for some sort of debriefing. I thought . . . all that way up there and here he was only 30 miles from his home! His mother plainly felt the same

He didn't return for over two weeks. When he finally appeared he seemed much changed. He was even thinner than before. His face was tanned and very gaunt. There were lines around his eyes showing white against his tan, no doubt from squinting in the sun. He seemed to have become more introverted again, hesitant in his greeting, as if he didn't know me. His eyes shifting away from my face . . . a mumbled greeting. I had an absurd desire to put my arms around him. I put my hand out as if to touch him, and he flinched away.

Over the next few weeks we gradually revived our friendship. I felt I had to be very careful with him, as if he was fragile and could be easily broken. One day I asked him what he had been doing in Cyprus. He thought for a moment, then replied rather brusquely, 'I was attached to that oxymoron, Military Intelligence.'

He didn't seem inclined to elaborate, and I felt that this was not the time to ask him what exactly he was doing.

At first he too seemed keen to apply for the Royal College. One day he and I were having coffee in a café we frequented when I asked if I could see some of his drawings. He had his sketchbook with him, on the table. I picked it up. He had managed to do quite a lot of drawing while he was in Cyprus, rather delicate pen and ink drawings of orange groves. Some sketches of people inside a rather simple bar. A man with a dark moustache was pictured sitting very upright, a shepherd perhaps. There were two women with their heads shrouded in black shawls. A young girl was asleep with her head on the table. He had done drawings also of buildings and houses, in what I suppose was Famagusta, with tiny figures of people sitting at tables outside their houses. There was a minaret and part of a mosque, olive trees, a thistle. Then turning a page I saw drawings of men with what looked like hoods over

3

their heads, their hands tied behind their backs. Before I could examine them properly Simon snatched the book away from me. 'What were those?' I asked.

'Nothing' he said, 'just fantasies.'

I didn't pursue it further. Simon had a strange look on his face, hard and opaque, I knew better than to try.

I was doing well getting a portfolio of work together to send to the Royal College, it had to be sent before the end of March. Apart from a folder of drawings and sketches we were allowed to send three paintings no larger than 20 inches by 30. I had two already and I was working on a third. Simon didn't seem to be doing any more work to send in. He had a couple of older paintings which he had done before we went into the army, but appeared to have done nothing more. He was becoming increasingly morose and sometimes I wouldn't see him for several days at a time.

One day I had a call from Simon's mother. She asked me if we could meet for tea one afternoon, suggesting Fuller's, a rather genteel teashop on the Westover Road, not a place that us grubby art students usually patronised. We arranged an afternoon, and out of respect for Simon's mother, I put on a jacket and a clean shirt, with a pair of grey flannels and reasonably clean shoes.

I was intrigued at this suggested meeting; it was not something that I had ever done before. I liked her well enough and she had always been kind to me, but our social paths had never crossed before.

I was exquisitely punctual, but when I arrived at Fuller's, she was already there, sitting neatly, with her spectacles perched on her nose, reading the menu. I sat down and she immediately suggested several cakes I might like, and ordered a pot of Earl Grey tea for two. I didn't like to say that I didn't care for Earl Grey, much preferring straight English breakfast tea. She asked me how I was, and how I was getting on with my work for the Royal College. When the tea and cakes arrived she poured us a cup each and offered me the plate of cakes to choose from.

Once we were eating and sipping our tea she said,

'Christopher, tell me about Simon, how do you think he is?'

I was disconcerted by this direct question. I was not certain how to answer it, on the one hand I was concerned about Simon, on the other, as a close friend, I wanted to protect him from prying, even though she was his mother.

I was guarded in my reply, 'I think he's still suffering from a reaction to two unwelcome years in the army.'

'Yes,' she said thoughtfully. 'Tell me has he ever discussed with you what he was doing in Cyprus and later in Egypt?'

'No, he doesn't seem to want to speak about it'.

She was lost in thought for a few minutes, her gaze abstracted and inward looking. Her look reminded me very much of Simon at certain moments. She said, 'you know that he's drinking too much? . . . His father's afraid he may be becoming an alcoholic.'

I shook my head, 'I didn't know.' It was the truth; he hadn't had a drink with me since he had got back.

Then she said, 'I think something bad happened to him, while he was there, and he doesn't want to talk about it.'

I was inclined to agree with her and I thought of those drawings, which I had seen briefly in his sketchbook, before he snatched it away from me. I was certainly not going to mention them to her.

She then changed the subject and asked me how my girlfriend June was and did I have plans to marry her? If so how would that fit in with me going to the Royal College, if I got in? She also asked about my parents, who she had met. I answered as best I could, saying that getting married was far from my mind at the moment, that my father was now retired and seemed to be enjoying it. Indeed this was true: he was now able to devote more time to the local opera company, where he sang in the chorus.

She insisted on paying the bill and we parted. Her last remark to me was rather touching. 'You know that you are Simon's closest friend . . . in fact I suspect you are his only friend . . . please do your best to help him.'

We then said goodbye and I watched her small neat figure walking off down the Westover Road, looking occasionally in shop windows. Somehow this made me feel rather sad.

Her remark about Simon drinking too much explained a lot of things, his frequent absences for days at a time, when I would not see him, his moroseness, his sometimes haggard looks, his bloodshot eyes. He had never been a particularly heavy drinker before. Yes we had occasionally got rather drunk in our earlier days, like most young people we experimented with things like that, more to know what it was about than to really enjoy it. Fortunately it seemed that neither of us had addictive personalities.

I was determined to find out more about this. I wondered where he did his drinking. The town was not very large at that time, and I knew most of the pubs, if not by experience at least by sight.

I remembered a small pub, called The Bell, which we did at one time frequent, rather for its ambience than for the beer. It had retained that slightly Edwardian look which was fast disappearing at the time, as many pubs were being turned into bars, with Formica-topped bar counters.

One evening I made my way there and sure enough, tucked in a corner, by himself, was Simon. There was an empty glass on the table and an unopened book; Simon was staring into space, deep in thought. He was startled when I appeared, and his look was almost resentful.

'What are you doing here?' He asked rather brusquely.

'I might say the same to you,' I answered, 'anyway, do you want a drink?' He thought for a moment, then asked for a Scotch.

I went to the bar and ordered the Scotch and a half a pint of bitter for me, and brought them back. I noticed that the book on the table was Voltaire's "Candide", an old favourite of ours.

Simon made a deliberate effort to be more sociable, I didn't ask him why he had never suggested that we had a drink together, since he had returned. I asked him if he had done any more work for the Royal College entrance, he shook his head. 'I've decided that I'm not going to do it.' This startled me, I had assumed that, if we could, we would be there together.

'No,' Simon said, 'I've decided, no more art school, its time I entered the real world and got on with life.' I was deeply disappointed; I had looked forward to us experiencing London together.

We stayed for the rest of the evening, matching drink for drink, my half of bitter, his small Scotch. We seemed to revive our old spirit of friendship, talking and laughing and telling funny stories, some of our experiences in the army. I noticed though that Simon's stories were related to the early part of his training, before he went to Cyprus, any attempt on my part to draw anything out of him about the time he was abroad, received no response. Towards the end of the evening he became more morose, more angry, with something inside himself, something as yet unrevealed.

When the pub closed we set off in different directions. As I walked away I turned and watched him going down the road. He was a little unsteady, weaving slightly, a little drunk perhaps, but then so was I.

A couple of weeks later Simon suddenly had some good fortune, an uncle had died and left him a small amount of money. He used some of it to buy a second hand Landrover. He had been taught to drive in the army, something which I envied very much, I would have loved to be able to drive. It became his pride and joy; his spirit was much lightened by this. He began to add things to it, a towing bracket at the back, as well as two brackets to take jerry cans, a winch on the front and a luggage rack on the roof. It came with a radio already fitted. He would sometimes go off with it and find some environment to try out the 4-wheel drive and lower gear range, usually somewhere in the New Forest, which was close by. He would return with his eyes bright with excitement, the Landrover covered in mud. He would then clean it meticulously.

One day he said,'Come on, let's go for a drive.'

We set off, skirting Poole, then Wareham, we headed for Corfe, our old haunt. The teashop was still there and we had our tea, still strong, in those thick white cups, with scones, strawberry jam and clotted cream. Afterwards Simon suggested that we went for a walk up in the hills. It was like old times. We reached the top and rested, gazing down on Poole harbour. It was late afternoon and dusk was approaching. Simon had gone quiet and was sitting with his back to a stonewall, surveying the scene.

Suddenly he said, 'You want to know what I was doing in Cyprus and Egypt?'

I was taken by surprise. I hadn't asked that question since he once answered with a rather brusque statement about the Intelligence Corps.

I was silent for a while, then said, 'It's up to you.'

He was quiet for a moment, 'When you were in the army, did you ever encounter the FS?'

I vaguely remembered some incident where they were called in and everyone from the CO downwards became very nervous.

'Isn't that what they call Field Security?'

'Yes.'

'So what about it?

He paused again. He appeared hesitant, then . . . 'When I first arrived in Cyprus, I was attached to the Intelligence Corps. I was in the Signals Intelligence Section. We were monitoring the Russians, tracking their radar stations on the Black Sea, Odessa, Tashkent and other places. We were also tracking their aircraft movements.'

'That must have been interesting.'

He didn't seem to hear. He went on, 'When the troubles began and things got more serious I was moved over to Field Security. He paused again as if seeking the right words. 'We were picking up a number of Cyps at the time, suspected of having links with Eoka. Part of FS is involved with interrogation.

'Questioning them?'

'You could put it like that . . . more like beating the shit out of them until they confessed.'

This startled me, I'd never heard anyone use that descriptive language before, particularly Simon who, though capable of strong arguments, and since he'd been in the army, strong language, had always been a fundamentally gentle person.

'I see' I said, rather ineffectually.'Did you do this?'

He shut his eyes for a moment as if trying to recall something. 'No, I didn't do the physical stuff, my job was to be there and record whatever came out of it. Take notes.'

'Why did you end up in Egypt?'

Another pause. Another hesitation. He seemed to be mentally taking a deep breath. 'We weren't getting the results that we hoped for. In other words, we were too soft. So it was decided that certain suspects would be taken to Egypt. As you know, we still had a strong military presence there, and also there was a big MCE at Moascar.'

'What's an MCE?'

'Military Corrective Establishment, or, as we call them, a glasshouse, a military prison, like Colchester or Shepton Mallet, ideal to set up an interrogation unit there. I was one of the people detailed to escort them, then stay and take notes.'

'Were the FS interrogators tougher there?'

'What they did was pull in a unit of Egyptian police interrogators . . . to do it for them . . . they were experts . . . no qualms there.'

'What did they do?'

I don't know why I asked that question, I really didn't want to know, I suppose I needed to try to understand what had so damaged Simon.

He went completely silent this time and shut his eyes, leaning hack against the wall. He was silent so long that I thought he had finished. He didn't want to talk about it any more. I was just about to say 'OK, let's go', when he opened his eyes again.

'They were very thorough. They started with a general beating, very violent. If that didn't produce results, they moved on to lighted cigarettes, applied to the most sensitive parts of the body. After that, they got more technical, electrodes attached to the genitals and other parts, sleep deprivation of course, finally the water tortures, simulating drowning.' He paused again. 'Have you ever heard a man screaming when you run an electric current through his testicles? It gets up into the high octaves, almost like a schoolgirl's'.

His voice shook and I swear I could see tears running down his cheeks.

'By this time they'd confess to anything, giving lists of friends, acquaintances, relations, implicating them all in the same fictitious activities'. He fell silent again, but not for long, he got abruptly to his feet. 'Let's go, let's get out of here'.

He set off at a fast pace. It was now nearly dark as we descended the path, back down the hill to his Landrover, waiting patiently at the bottom. We drove back most of the way in silence. I was completely shocked by what I heard. Simon had gone somewhere inside himself, his brows furrowed, his face grim. He didn't drive dangerously but he drove fast, concentrating on what he could see in the headlights.

As we reached the outskirts of the town he suddenly said, 'You remember when I came back on that troopship? You and my parents were there to meet me.' I nodded.

'The reason I didn't come ashore to meet you was because I was under arrest and being escorted back. They were taking me up to Chester, there was a likelihood I was going to be court-martialed.'

'Court-martialed! Whatever for?'

'Disobeying orders. About a month before I was due to come back I refused to attend any more of those interrogations. I was given a direct order by my OC to continue, to attend and take notes. I refused.'

'What happened then?'

'I was put on a charge, I forget which section of the Army Act it was, something to do with disobeying a direct order when on active service. In wartime you used to be shot for that.'

I was aghast at this, 'But it wasn't wartime!'

He laughed, it was more like a bark. 'Listen, the army can do what it likes with you, they can interpret it any way that suits them.'

He continued, 'It was decided as I was due to return to England anyway, to ship me back and sort it out at Chester.'

He paused to navigate a roundabout.

'They decided not to go through the process of court-martialing me; it could be embarrassing for them, the revelation that they were torturing civilians. So they gave me a serious reprimand and told me that it would go on my military record. As if I cared . . . I didn't want to be in the bloody army anyway. Then I was discharged'.

By now we were in the centre of town.

I said, 'You can drop me here, I'll walk, it's not far . . . do me good.'

He found a place to let me out. Just before I got out he said, 'Everything I've told you is covered by the Official Secrets Act. If you talk about it, not only will I be vulnerable . . . so will you'.

He briefly touched my arm. I got out and with a wave he drove off. I walked home, my mind dark with the memories of what he had told me.

A few days passed and I didn't see him. I thought he might be avoiding me, conscious perhaps that I would make some judgment about his involvement with these interrogations. In fact I felt pity and concern for him, carrying that burden of knowledge must have been almost intolerable for him.

When the few days extended into a couple of weeks I became concerned and went searching for him. I first thought that I would find him at the pub, but he wasn't there. The people behind the bar said that they hadn't seen him since the time we were both there.

Then one day he called me and suggested that we meet, again at The Bell. He was there when I arrived. Rather as before he was in a corner, an empty glass before him. The book this time was Henry Miller's, 'The Colossus of Maroussi'.

In reply to my question, what did he want to drink? He said, 'Half of bitter.'

I returned to the table with the drinks and sat down. We talked for a while, he asked me how my stuff for the application was going, and I replied that I had done the best I could and was sending it the following week.

He was listening to me but I felt that his mind was elsewhere. He suddenly said, 'Let's go for a walk.' Without waiting for a reply he put on his dark blue donkey jacket, which was hanging on the back of the chair, and got to his feet. We left the pub and began walking towards a small park nearby.

It had been raining, but had now stopped, the sky was clearing and a few stars were beginning to show. There was a flight of steps at the end of the park, where it sloped up. We climbed to a flat area at the top and sat down on a park bench. Simon reached inside his jacket and produced a bulky envelope, which he handed to me. 'I want you to take care of this.' Seeing my hesitation he said, 'It's OK, there is a small package of photographs and a notebook.'

He gazed up at the stars, which were now showing more clearly.

'If anything should happen to me I want you to send it to the person I have named on the outside, send it to him via the Manchester Guardian. He's a feature writer and will find it interesting.'

'What do you mean, 'If anything should happen to you?''

He continued looking at the stars. 'Oh I don't know . . . some accident maybe.'

We sat for a while in silence, and then still gazing at the sky, he said, 'I'm going away for a time.'

'Where?'

'I don't know, I'll travel for a bit . . . see what's out there . . . maybe find a peaceful place . . . start painting again. I'll write to you sometime . . . when I find it.'

It was getting cold sitting there and after a few more minutes of silence we set off back down the steps and into the lights of the town.

Just before we parted, he said, 'Keep that package in a safe place, there may be other people interested in it.'

His Landrover was parked near the pub; he offered me a lift, which I declined. I preferred to walk. Just before he climbed back in he came over to me and put his arms around me. 'Take care of yourself.' Then he was gone.

Chapter 2

A year passed. I had gained entry to the Royal College and was in the midst of my first year when I received a letter from Simon, passed on by my parents. I had almost despaired of hearing from him. About three months after he had departed I had received a postcard from Trieste saying that he was OK, but there was no address on it and I had no further communication from him until this letter arrived. It was postmarked Athens but again had no address. I was intrigued that he was now in Greece, a place we had thought of visiting in our efforts to understand the meaning of democracy. He wrote,

> Dear Chris,
>
> Long time I know but I think I have found the place. It's a little village, very un-touristy, just goat and sheep herders and several tavernas. It's right beside the sea, with a tiny unspoilt cove and a little beach. Every day I swim in the sea. Nearby, on a headland, there is a Greek temple dedicated to Poseidon. Apparently Byron went there and carved his name somewhere. I found it one day, **BYRON**, beautifully carved at the base of one of the columns. If he did carve it he must have (A) been an excellent stone carver and (B) carried a set of stone carving implements around with him!

I am regarded as an eccentric curiosity in the village, a sort of television substitute (they don't have TV yet in Greece). I go to my local taverna every Saturday night, get drunk on retsina and dance to Greek songs on the jukebox. They love it, I'm a sort of free floor show. They ply me with half litres of retsina to encourage me. I'm drawing a lot and doing some second rate paintings. There is a gallery in Athens that likes my work and sells it. There is also another one in Hydra. So I survive OK on some earnings from these. I draw water up from a well in front of my house with a bucket on the end of a rope.

I have a lovely French lady called Claudine living with me and we seem to be very happy, but who knows, things change.

I have the only motor vehicle in the village so my Landrover is much in demand for ferrying sick people to the nearest doctor in a town about 7 miles away, or taking my friend Georgios, who runs the local taverna, into the same town, once a week, to pick up his supplies. I don't charge anyone for this, but I am liberally paid with eggs, feta and yoghurt by the local people and frequent free suppers from Georgios.

Once a day a bus comes down from Athens, 45 miles away, otherwise I am the only transport.

Just after I moved here I was woken early one morning by an explosion. I thought for a moment I was back in Cyprus, but later discovered that it was Georgios, out in the bay, dynamiting fish! After we became friends it was a signal for his 12 year old son Stavros, to come up during the morning and say, 'Seemon, my father says come to supper tonight, there is fish!"

Anyway life seems good here, simple but just right. Long may it last! Hope you are OK, I will write again sometime.

Your friend,
Simon

I was relieved to get this letter but frustrated that I had no address to reply to. I did contemplate finding a map of Greece and figure out, from clues in the letter, which village it might be, but after some thought I came to the conclusion that he didn't want to be traced yet and I should leave him alone.

College was occupying me fully during the day and I had a job in the evenings as a stagehand at a local theatre. It was also coming to the end of my first year in the painting school and at that time if students didn't appear to be making progress they could be asked to leave. I adopted a policy of doing as much work as I could, to confuse them with quantity if not quality.

I had found somewhere to live in Clapham, a basement flat. It had one room and a kitchen, I shared the bathroom with the owners of the house. My grant, subsidised by my evening job, was just sufficient to pay the rent and gave me a little money to eat in the college canteen as well as making use of the pub next to the theatre. Once a week, usually a Sunday, I would call my parents, using a call-box on the street, and reverse the charges. Then later, having got together sufficient change, I would call my girlfriend June.

One Sunday I called my parents and it was immediately apparent that my mother was very agitated about something. It transpired that they had been burgled. When I asked her what had been stolen she said that as far as they could tell nothing had been taken. She did add that they seemed to concentrate on my room, which had been reduced to even more of a shambles than it usually was. They had left it as it was, so that I could check it out myself to see if there was anything missing.

I was very upset by this and said that I would come down as soon as possible. I managed to get someone to stand in for me at the theatre and the next day I took a train home to see for myself what had happened.

My mother met me at the station and we went home together on the bus. She seemed calmer now, and once she realised that as far as she could see nothing had been stolen, it had been relegated to an outraged conversational piece, which she made much of with her friends and neighbours. The most shocking thing for her was that it had happened at all, in this quiet suburb of a seaside town.

As soon as I got home I went to my room, which was indeed in chaos. Drawers had been pulled out and the contents had been scattered on the floor, books had been taken from the bookshelves and had been opened as if someone had been searching through the pages, then thrown face downwards on the floor. All my sketchbooks and folders of drawings had received the same treatment. My small collection of records had the covers ripped off them and the records were lying on the floor, several were broken, as if someone had accidentally trodden on them. It seemed to me that whoever had done this had been searching for something.

I began the process of tidying up, my mother helped me. As we put the books back in the bookshelves and the sketches and drawings back in their folders, she chatted to me about the reaction of the neighbours.

Then she said 'June called and asked you to call her as soon as you could. I didn't tell you while you were still in London, I thought you would want to do it down here, I know that making calls from London is very expensive.'

When we had finished tidying the room I went downstairs to the telephone, which sat on the windowsill, by the front door. I picked the 'phone up and listened for a moment. At that time getting a telephone installed was still quite difficult and usually involved a long wait until a line became available. One of the ways to expedite this was to agree to share a line with a neighbour, this was known as a 'party line'. In order not to infringe on our neighbour's calls, it was necessary to check to see if they were on the 'phone. It appeared that the line was free, so I dialled the operator who put me through to June's number. It was answered by her mother, who recognised my voice. Before I could ask to speak to June she started telling me about how they had just been burgled. She was so anxious to tell me about it that several minutes passed before she said that she would pass me over to June. She asked me to wait while she went off to call her.

As I was waiting for June to come to the telephone I heard a click and thought that it was perhaps our neighbours picking up the 'phone. 'Hello? I'm on a call,' I said.

There was no reply and I didn't hear the sound of a receiver being replaced. I came to the conclusion that I had misheard.

June was much less excited than her mother. Once she had ascertained that nothing had been stolen as far as she could tell, she was angry about the mess that had been made of her room. We agreed to meet later that evening in a café we frequented near the centre of the town.

After I had finished this call I went down to the shed at the bottom of the garden. When I was young, before I discovered art, I had fancied myself as a carpenter. The shed, which had been used by the former owner, had been fitted out with a very long workbench, with a vice at one end. I'd managed, with my pocket money, to acquire various tools, like chisels, saws, smoothing planes and sundry other useful and necessary tools for my prospective career as a master carpenter. I was in fact a very poor craftsman and inflicted many wobbly coffee tables and shelf units on my mother, who duly admired them and did her best to use them.

The shed seemed undisturbed since the last time I had been down there. Under the bench, concealed from view by various boxes with tins of paint, was a loose floorboard. Removing the boxes I lifted the board and felt underneath it. The package which Simon had left in my care was still there, wrapped up in an old paint rag.

I met up with June that evening. She was still puzzled about why the burglar hadn't taken anything. I'd not revealed anything about Simon's package and I had no intention of doing so now. I told her that we too had been burgled. In a way she seemed to find this rather consoling, as if we had been part of an epidemic which had now passed. The fact is that my mother had said that no one she knew had been burgled, and although June had been, they had also only concentrated on her room.

We began to talk of other things, then she asked me how I was getting on at the Royal College and how I liked living in London.

'I've been thinking,' she said, 'my department head said that I could apply for a transfer to their Head Office in London.' She looked at me brightly, waiting for my enthusiastic response.

I was completely taken by surprise, I had very mixed feelings about this. I was very fond of her and we got on well together, but I was beginning to relish my independence in London. Having June live with me, which is what it would inevitably mean, suggested a permanence to our relationship, which is not what I was inclined to want at this period in my life.

Some of these thoughts must have shown on my face for she said rather impatiently, 'Well, don't you want me to be with you?'

'Yes of course,' I said hurriedly, 'It's just that I wonder if this is the right time. I am still a student trying to live on a very low grant and a part time job, in a tiny flat.'

'That's all right, I'll have my job and income to help and we can look for a larger place.'

I tried to dissuade her, but she seemed very determined, so I left it for the time being, having given the appearance of being rather excited at the idea.

The next day I returned to London and resumed my time at the College as well as my evening work at the theatre. I knew that I must give June a call and explain why I didn't think it was a good idea, her coming to London in order to live with me. I tried to think of some convincing excuses, but I knew she would be unconvinced by whatever I made up. Finally I decided that honesty would be the best course, although I knew she would be hurt and angry, but it had to be done. That weekend I called her again, and without many preliminaries I told her that I didn't want us to live together at this time. Predictably she was outraged.

'You mean that you don't love me?'

'I didn't say that,' I replied lamely.

'Yes but that's what you mean!'

I could hear that she was on the edge of tears.'Of course I love you. It's just that I am not ready for marriage.'

She was silent for a moment, then, 'You don't love me, you don't want me!'

This last was delivered with the sound of tears in her voice, there was a pause and I could hear her sobbing. 'I hate you!' Then the 'phone was slammed down.

I felt bad for a while, but this passed and suddenly I felt a great relief, I'd done it.

I heard no more from her, no letters, no sudden appearances, nothing. I was sorry to have hurt her, we had been together a long time, and indeed I would miss her, but I didn't see us spending our lives together, in some suburb, having children, trying to continue painting, gradually giving up, surrendering to anonymity.

I plunged back into life at the College and at the theatre. Weeks, then months passed. I had managed to survive my first year. The long summer vacation passed, almost unnoticed as I came and went, working at the theatre and at weekends, as well as going into the College, where I worked at my paintings. Those of us who did stay in London were allowed to go there and use the almost empty studios.

Again I heard nothing more from Simon. I had no means of contacting him, as I had no address. The second year at College began; I felt euphoric. I had survived the first year, failing an accident I would be there for two more years. I applied myself diligently to painting, trying to find a way to make my work significant.

One afternoon I was in an upstairs studio, drawing one of the many models available to us, when a fellow student that I knew came in and walked up to me. 'There's a girl downstairs, by the registry office, she wants to talk to you. They won't let her come up . . . you have to go down'.

I went down the stairs and as I looked I could see a slim, dark haired girl, standing by the window of the registry office. I went up to her and said, 'Hello, I hear you wanted to talk to me?'

'You are Christopher?' She had a distinctly French accent, I nodded.

'My name is Claudine.'

I knew immediately who she was. 'Have you a message from Simon?'

She looked around, the staircase was busy with students, mostly on their way to have lunch in the common room. 'Is there somewhere we could talk privately?'

I had been intending to have lunch at the common room, where it was 'cheap and cheerful'. It was hardly the place one could talk quietly. I thought a moment and then decided to take her to another place nearby. It was a small, early wine bar type of café which also had a modest menu.

We walked quite quickly there, without having any further conversation. Once we were seated, and had ordered our food, I said, 'First tell how you knew where to find me?'

'He told me that if anything happened to him I was to contact you, he gave me your home address, but suggested that I first tried to find you at the Royal College.'

'Has something happened to him?'

She thought for a minute then, 'He disappeared . . . I think he's been kidnapped.'

'Disappeared? When? Where?'

'In Greece . . . nearly three weeks ago.'

She then told me about how they lived in this small village by the sea, about 45 miles down the coast from Athens. It was a very simple, the inhabitants were just peasants, who worked the land, and herded the sheep and goats from one sparse pasture to another. In the summer, one or two people who owned small houses there, came down for two or three weeks, to holiday in the summer. Otherwise it was only occupied by the peasant people, until a couple of weeks in the autumn, when migrating birds came through there and were shot at by Athenian business men who came down for the sport, returning in the evenings to Athens. She and Simon had lived there happily for over a year.

The last she saw of Simon was one afternoon, three weeks ago, when he had walked down to the beach for his daily afternoon swim. She had been washing clothes and hanging them up around their verandah. She could see down to the beach from there and saw Simon talking to two men by a car parked at the side of the coastal road. She thought nothing of it, as people quite often stopped there to admire the view out to sea, and occasionally to ask for directions. She went inside to do some writing, she was a journalist and was now writing a book. When two hours had passed and Simon had still not returned, she decided to walk down to the beach and find him. On occasions he had dozed off on the beach, after his swim.

When she got to the beach there was no sign of him, in fact it was completely deserted its whole length. She was still not concerned, Simon, who loved walking, would sometimes wander off on long walks in the hills around.

She went back to the house and began preparing their supper. When it started getting dark she did begin to worry. She finally decided to walk down to their local taverna and either find Simon there, or at least ask Georgios, who owned it, if he had seen Simon, but he had not.

She spent a restless night, hoping to hear Simon's footsteps returning.

In the morning she went again to Georgios's tavern and explained she was worried about Simon. She asked him if he had any strangers visit his taverna yesterday. He thought for a moment, and then said that there had been two men in a car who had stopped nearby and come in for lunch. Now he remembered that they had asked if there were any English people living in the village. He had mentioned Simon, describing him as an artist. They didn't seem particularly interested, more amused that an English artist would be living there.

'What nationality were they?' I asked

'He thought one was Greek, with a funny accent, he may have been a Cypriot.'

'And the other?'

'He didn't say much, but he had the impression he was English.'

No one it seems had noticed the car. The visitors had paid for their lunch and left soon afterwards. She had asked what time it was, it sounded like they had left just before Simon had decided to walk down to the beach.

The next day, with still no sign of Simon, she decided to go up to Athens. It seems that Simon had registered at the British Embassy when he had first arrived in Greece

Before she set off to Athens she went again to the taverna, to tell Georgios where she was going, in case Simon came back. Georgios was setting out the tables and chairs in front of his little taverna. He asked if she would like some coffee before she left. When he brought it he sat down opposite her.'I have something to tell you Claudine'.

He spoke to her in Greek, which she understood well enough, having been living there for a year.'You know Andreas the shepherd?'She nodded.

'Yesterday he was in the hills with his herd, and he looked down to the road by the beach, where he saw Simon talking to two strangers by a car. They seemed to be arguing. Suddenly they were struggling with Simon, then, they dragged him to the car and forced him inside and drove off towards Athens. He was too far away to be of any help.'Claudine was shocked. She asked Georgios whether Andreas had remembered anything about the car.

Georgios thought for a moment then, 'It was pale blue I think, quite big, maybe a Mercedes.'

She drove Simon's Landrover up to Athens, her mind whirling with what she had just heard. She found somewhere to park near the Embassy, then went to the Consular section and reported Simon missing. The first thing they did was to give her a form to fill in. She filled in the form, giving Simon's full name, her name, where they were from, their home addresses and various other details. The clerk, who seemed to be presiding there, took the form off to some interior destination, asking Claudine to wait.

He returned after what seemed like half an hour and asked her to accompany him. They walked along a corridor to a door at the far end, where the clerk knocked and waited. After an interval the door was opened by a man of about fifty with short cropped hair, he beckoned Claudine in. She entered on her own, the door was closed in the face of the man who had brought her there.

There were two other men, already seated at a table. There were three chairs on their side of the table, and one chair on the side facing them. The man who had brought her in led her over to the table and indicated the single chair facing the others. She sat down, while the other man sat at the remaining chair on the side facing her.

They studied her in silence for a moment or two, then the man sitting in the middle, a younger man than the others, also with short cropped hair, blonde in this instance, with distinct blue eyes, started to speak, 'Miss . . .' he turned to the notes in front of him, 'Miss Claudine Doucet?' He asked. She nodded. 'What is your occupation Miss Doucet?'

'I'm a journalist.'

'Where do you normally work?'

'I'm a freelance journalist, so I work wherever I happen to be.'

'What are you working on now?'

She began to have the distinct impression she was being interrogated.

'What has this got to do with Simon's disappearance?'

'Answer the question Miss Doucet.'

His tone was suddenly intimidating. Reluctantly she answered,

'As I said I'm a freelance journalist, I'm also endeavouring to write a book, which is what I have been doing down in Legrena. It's peaceful there . . . or has been.'

'You are a French citizen?'

'Yes.'

'Have you worked in North Africa, Algeria for instance?'

'Yes.'

'The Middle East, Egypt, Jordan, Israel, Syria?'

'I don't like this interrogation! I need to call the French Embassy!'

His tone became more conciliatory. 'You don't need to do that Miss Doucet, we just want your help in finding out what has happened to Simon, and who the people were who may have taken him away.'

She was slightly mollified by his tone, but was still deeply suspicious of his line of questioning. She told me that as a journalist she had done several articles, which had appeared in various left wing papers in France, about the interrogation of prisoners in Algeria by the occupying French army. She had begun to specialise in articles about interrogation methods.

'Were you aware that Simon did military service in Cyprus and Egypt?'

This last question came from one of the other men, he was older than the others and she had the impression he had more authority than them.

'Yes.'

'Did he speak about what he did?'

'Only that he was a trained wireless operator.'

'Nothing else?'

'No, he told me that he was bound by the Official Secrets Act and could not speak about it. I didn't question him any further.'

The man frowned, 'It seems strange to me that you had an . . . an intimate relationship with this man for over a year, and you didn't discuss it in more detail.'

'Not really, he is a very private man, as well as being bound by the Official Secrets Act.'

'What is the subject of the book you are writing now?'

Claudine had become very unhappy with these questions. 'That is my business. Now I've had enough of this and I need to go, I have other things to do while I'm in Athens . . . will you please inform me when and if you have discovered what has happened to Simon'. She stood up.

They conferred for a minute, speaking quietly to one another.'How will we contact you?'

'I will give you my agent's address in Paris, also his 'phone number'.

'In the meantime you will be in the village where you have been living?'

'Yes.'

'Please let us know if you think of leaving.'

She wrote her agent's address on the piece of paper they passed to her. The man, who had opened the door, let her out and accompanied her down the corridor to the entrance. As she was about to leave he said,

'Miss Doucet, if I were you I would leave quite soon, I think you are vulnerable down there.'

She thanked him and left. She already had every intention of leaving, as soon as she was able to arrange what to do with the little house they had rented, in the village.

She drove back to the village. There was still no news about Simon at the taverna. Georgios insisted that she had supper down there in the evening. The villagers were very kind and concerned. They asked what she was going to do. She told them she had reported Simon's disappearance to the Embassy. She didn't elaborate any further. She told them that she needed to go to England and report what had happened, to Simon's family. She asked them to keep an eye on their little house and notice if anyone came asking about her. To tell them they didn't know where she had gone, but that she would be back. If Simon should return they should explain to him that she would be back and that she had left the Landrover with his friend in Plaka, Athens. She didn't give them a name but she knew whom she was going to leave it with, and she was sure that Simon would know also.

That night she locked all the doors in the house. Then she gathered up all her papers, notes and the manuscript of her book, also Simon's sketchbooks and notes, packed them ready to leave first thing in the morning. She looked for Simon's passport, but was unable to find it. She thought that was odd, he would hardly have taken it down to the beach with him. He must have hidden it somewhere.

She slept fitfully, conscious of every sound. First light she was up and after packing everything important into the Landrover she drove off quietly, heading along the deserted road to Athens.

She was just passing through Anavassos, with its heaps of salt from the salt mine, about ten miles up the road to Athens from their village, when she saw a blue Mercedes driving towards her, as it passed she was able to see two men in front, one looked as if he could be Greek, the other with short cropped blonde hair, was of uncertain identity. She watched carefully in her rear view mirror, but it didn't slow down, and although she continued to watch her mirror, there was no sign of it following her.

When she reached Athens she went straight to Plaka, where their friend Alexi lived. He was a writer who had made a quite successful living writing novels based on espionage. He had a house with a garage and a forecourt to his house. He was happy to keep the Landrover, and didn't ask any questions when she told him that Simon was away and that she had to make a quick trip to somewhere unspecified.

She then took a taxi to Monastraki, where the owners of their house in the village ran a shop. They were always delightfully friendly and seemed unconcerned when she told them that she and Simon were going to be away for a couple of weeks.

She then took another taxi to Heraklion Airport, purchased a one way ticket to London for a BEA flight leaving in two hours. She waited in the departure lounge, taking up a position where she could observe the entry doors.

The flight was called, as she made her way on to the 'plane she saw two men questioning the hostess at the departure desk, the hostess was shaking her head.

As soon as she arrived in London, she called a friend who lived in Earl's Court and then made her way there, and had been staying there for the last few days.

'Then I came to find you.'

I had listened to her story with rapt attention. I was very concerned by what she was telling me. As she spoke I watched the way she used her hands, her animated gestures, so uncharacteristic of the British. Although she was not beautiful, nor could she be described as pretty, when she spoke, her animation made her shine. Her eyes in particular were very striking, dark with natural long eyelashes, they shone with intelligence, her hair was long and black, with a wavy quality, she wore it tied back in a pony tail. She seemed slim but as she wore a loose dress, it was not possible to really ascertain her figure. I found her very attractive and could see what Simon saw in her.

'Do you have any idea why this has happened?'

She thought for a moment, then, 'I'm sure you know that Simon was very troubled about what he had witnessed, when he was in the military.'

I nodded.

'I thought he had left some information with you?'

I thought for a moment, then said, 'Only a couple of sketchbooks, drawings he had done in Cyprus, nothing more'.

She looked at me carefully again, 'Nothing more?'

I shook my head. She seemed disappointed.

We finished our lunch, she said she was going back to her friends in Earls Court, they had a telephone and she needed to make some calls, especially to Paris, to speak to her agent and other unspecified people. I offered to walk with her to Earls Court, but she shook her head. She suggested that we met again that evening. I explained to her that I worked at the theatre in Sloane Square, she agreed to meet me after the show in the pub next door. She left, and I watched her cross the road and turn the corner, she waved just before she disappeared. A man who had been looking in the window of the art shop opposite turned and walked in the same direction.

I stayed for a while, thinking about what she had told me about Simon and her journey to London. I had hesitated to tell her about the notes and drawings that Simon had left with me. I didn't know her, and there was some mystery here, which she might be part of.

I went back to the College and tried to concentrate on my painting, but my mind was distracted by what I had just heard about Simon. What could have happened to him? Who were the people who had struggled with him before pushing him into the car? Was he OK? My thoughts went round and round. Who was this French woman? Could I trust her with what Simon had asked me to hold for him?

That evening I was at the pub, where I had agreed to meet Claudine. I waited, nursing a small glass of bitter. I was short of money, so I had to eke things out, I would not be paid by the theatre until the end of the week. Eventually she arrived, she seemed excited about something. Before I could offer, she asked me what I would like to drink. I said, another half of bitter, and she went straight to the bar, returning with my bitter and a single brandy for her. I was surprised at the brandy, she explained that they didn't serve wine and this was the nearest she could get.

We sat for a few seconds sipping our drinks, then she said, 'I heard from Simon!'.

Before I could ask, she continued, 'He called my agent in Paris, and left a message.'

'What did he say?'

'He wants you to come to Paris at the weekend, he needs to talk to you, he will call on my home 'phone.'

'Paris!' I was aghast.

'Its OK, I can get you a weekend return ticket, they're quite cheap. You do have a passport?

I nodded. Although I still had not been abroad, I had got a passport the previous year, when I had planned to go to Paris for the first time. In the end I didn't go, the friend I was going to travel with fell ill at the last moment, and I didn't want to go on my own.

'Alright, I'll get you on an evening flight this Friday, I will be going in the morning that day anyway, as I need to see some people there before you arrive. I'll meet you off the flight at Orly.'

I was still in shock at the idea of suddenly travelling to Paris. Part of me loved the thought of going to that city, the other part of me was nervous, I had never been abroad, nor had I ever flown. She was watching me as these thoughts went through my head, I felt foolish.

Eventually I blurted it out, 'I've never been abroad!' The fact was I was also concerned about traveling to Paris, why could he not come here. It seemed to me that he may have got himself in some dangerous situation.

She looked at me with some amusement, 'Poor Christopher! Don't worry, I will look after you, we are quite civilized in Paris you know.' She reached out and touched my hand briefly, 'You will come won't you? Simon was insistent that he talked to you there, he needs you.' Whatever doubts I entertained were completely assuaged by that statement. He needed me, which was enough.

Chapter 3

On the Friday evening I made my way to Heathrow. I had collected my ticket from the Air France agency in Bond Street, as Claudine had instructed me, the flight was due to depart at 7.30 pm. I then boarded an Air France coach at Victoria coach station to take me to the airport. I was very nervous, not only had I never been abroad before but I also had never flown.

I found the Air France departure area, after a certain amount of confused wandering around, largely thanks to a smartly dressed air hostess, who spotted me looking totally lost and taking me in hand led me to the departure desks. I had no luggage, just a shoulder bag with a few essentials in it, so I was quickly processed and directed to the passport control area, where my passport was stamped at the British passport desk. I shuffled along obediently with a small crowd of people who were plainly taking the same flight.

The flight was not very full, so I managed to secure a seat by a window. I had hesitated at first, as I had a poor head for heights, but in the end I decided that I must try and overcome this, as it was a new adventure, and gaze out of the window.

It was still light when we took off, although dusk was fast approaching. The 'plane raced down the runway, its propellers whirring, its wheels bumping on the uneven surface, would it make it? Or was I going to be part of tomorrow's headlines?

Faster and faster it went, I could see the end of the runway approaching, I held my breath, and suddenly the bumping ceased, the engine note changed and we were flying!

We rose up through the scattered clouds, and finally clearing the top of them we came out into broad sunlight. It was magical. I gazed down through openings in the clouds at this toy landscape with tiny houses and buildings, miniature cars raced along ribbon-like roads, some with their headlights already on in the growing twilight, while we were still in the bright sunny uplands.

I remained entranced as we headed south for the coast, the patchwork quilt of the fields below us, gradually disappearing in the fading light. We crossed the coastline and in the distance I could see twinkling lights of what must be France. I still went on gazing out of the window, watching the slow descent of the sun behind the horizon.

A pretty hostess came round pushing a small trolley with drinks. She asked me what I wanted, her French accent charmed me, I said I was sorry but I had no French money, she said there was no need, it was complimentary, and offered me a small bottle of champagne, which held enough for two glasses. I nodded and she deftly opened the bottle, there was no 'pop', just a gentle hiss. She provided a glass and a bag of nuts and showed me how to pull down the little shelf on the back of the seat in front of me.

I sipped the champagne and lay back. It felt wonderful. This is the life, I thought, I want to spend the rest of my life like this, flying and sipping champagne, and gazing out of the window on the world below.

It was all darkness when we crossed the French coastline, with the occasional sprinkling of lights, and sudden clusters of what were presumably small villages and townships.

Then began the outskirts of Paris, and soon it was possible to view the whole of the city, like a great box overflowing with glittering jewels. I was glued to the window, holding my breath at the sheer beauty of it. I could see the Seine, winding its way through it, like a great lazy serpent. We swung south, over the edge of the city, and then swung back again. I saw ahead of me the lights and runway of what must be Orly.

We came lower and lower, the ground rushing up to meet us, I began to see individual houses, with little gardens, we seemed to be passing literally over their fences, I could see in their windows. Then suddenly we were over the runway, where we seemed to hang for a moment, then touched down with a slight bump and were rushing along at decreasing speed. Buildings flashed past us and airport vehicles, until we slowed to a mere walking pace, turning off finally on an exit road from the main runway eventually halting near a long low building, with what I assumed was a control tower at the end.

The engine noise died down, the propellers fluttered to a halt, and there was the clattering sound of safety belts being released.

Everyone rose to their feet, bags and luggage were pulled down from the overhead lockers. I stood up as well and pulled down my shoulder bag. Gradually we shuffled down the 'plane. There were steps drawn up outside and we made our way down and boarded a waiting bus, which took us to the terminal building, where we went through immigration, my passport was stamped again, then to customs, where, with my small shoulder bag I was waved through.

Emerging into the arrival area I looked round, there was no sign of Claudine. I waited, growing increasingly anxious. I had no French money, and only a small amount of English money, my French was abysmal, I was quite bewildered.

Suddenly I heard my name being called, looking up I saw Claudine pushing her way though the crowd.

'I'm so sorry! I got held up.'

I was so relieved; she kissed me on both cheeks. This startled me, it was not something we did in England, I was yet to learn what a common practice it is on the continent.

'Do you have any luggage?'

I shook my head and showed her my shoulder bag.'Good, let's get out of here.' There was a line of taxis outside the terminal. A small group of people shuffled forward as each one drew up and then sped away, with often only a single passenger.

We were soon at the head of the group, Claudine and I crammed ourselves into the back. Claudine leaned forward and said, 'S' il vous plait, La Coupole.' The driver nodded. Claudine turned to me, 'How was your journey, did you eat anything?'

'Only a bag of nuts, but they did give me champagne.'

'I'll take you somewhere where we can eat. I also need to meet up with someone, who may be there.'

I was quite overwhelmed by what was happening. Here I was, in Paris! I had flown in a 'plane, I already had two stamps in my passport. I was being taken out to dinner in Paris! I gazed out of the window, seeing buildings and houses, which were very different from England. My head buzzed slightly with the after effects of the champagne and flying.

I looked at Claudine, 'When will Simon call?'

'Tomorrow, in the evening.'

'Where is he?'She shrugged, 'I only know what my agent told me, that he will call tomorrow evening at 8pm.'

For the rest of the journey into Paris I was completely preoccupied with gazing out of the window at houses and buildings, many seemed very different from buildings in London.

Claudine did her best to answer some of my questions about what I was seeing, but after her initial amusement at my naive questioning, she began to show signs of impatience, so I stopped asking her. We plunged into the suburbs of the city. The buildings, the lights, and the occasional bursts of music, the people and the signs in French entranced me.

We eventually reached an area which teemed with restaurants and small cafes,'Where is this?'

'It's an area known as Montparnasse, there's a great railway terminal here.'

Soon we passed the station, with its magnificent façade and broad steps leading down to the road. Not long afterwards we drew up outside a large restaurant, the sign over the entrance said 'La Coupole'.'Nous sommes arrivés.' Claudine said.

She paid the taxi driver and we started to walk towards the entrance. I hung back.

'Claudine, I have hardly any money with me, and it's still in English pounds.'

'It's alright, Simon is aware of this, he told me to take care of everything.'

'I can't just let you pay for everything!

'Its alright, just relax, I have money, I earn a lot with what I do as a journalist, Simon and I have an agreement.'We entered the restaurant, or brasserie as I was later told. The noise was deafening, there were chairs, tables and banquettes wherever we looked. Smoke filled the air. They all seemed to be full with groups of people, arguing, chatting, much waving of arms to illustrate a point. Waiters in white aprons carrying trays scurried back and forth. There seemed no place for us to sit down. Claudine gazed around, scanning the tables, eventually spotting a hand and arm raised, in a distant banquette, beckoning us towards it.

We reached the table, there was a young, dark haired man with a beard, who stood up as we approached and embraced Claudine, kissing her on both cheeks, then turned to me holding out his hand.'Ca, va?'

I must have looked confused. Claudine said, 'He is greeting you, "ça, va" is 'how are you', you just say "ça, va" back.'

I hesitated, then I said, 'Ca, va?' and we shook hands.

We sat down and Claudine put her hand on the young man's arm, 'This is Sayyd.'She turned to Sayyid and said, 'C'est Christopher, un ami de Simon.'

Sayyd smiled, and turning to Claudine, broke into a torrent of French, occasionally nodding at me.

A waiter came by and she turned to me and asked what I would like to eat, in French. 'Avez-vous fait votre choix?'

I must have looked confused again. She laughed and turned to the waiter.

'Un croque-monsieur, pour mon ami, et deux verres de vin rouge.' She ordered. The waiter scurried away.

Claudine continued their discussion in French. Then Sayyd said something in a language, which was not French, and Claudine replied in what seemed to be the same language. I couldn't tell what it was, it had sometimes a rather bubbling sound.

Whatever he said, Claudine suddenly lapsed back into French, 'Merde!' The word just slipped out. Even I knew what it meant.

They continued their discussion vehemently, in this other language, with frequent glances at me.

My food arrived, as well as two glasses of red wine. Claudine took one and pushed the other towards me. I glanced at Sayyd. She said quickly, 'He doesn't drink alcohol, it's against his religion.' I noticed that he had a glass of water in front of him as well as an empty coffee cup.

I ate my food while they continued their conversation in French. It was a sort of 'glorified Welsh rarebit', with ham. I was ravenous and it went down very well.

I sipped my wine cautiously, it was not something easily available in Britain. I gazed around, overwhelmed by the noise and chatter. There were many young women there, sometimes with groups of men, sometimes with just a man, and occasionally just a group of women at a table, talking vehemently with frequent arm waving and puffing of Gauloise. People arrived and departed, there was much kissing of cheeks. Waiters endlessly scurrying. It was so exhilarating, so different from what I knew.

They seemed to have finished their conversation and Sayyd got up, he was obviously leaving. He shook my hand again, smiling, and said 'A bientôt', à demain.' He kissed Claudine again, and waved goodbye.

Claudine sat for a moment in silence.'Things have changed, Simon will not be calling on my number tomorrow, there is another arrangement.'

'What has happened?'

'It's difficult to talk here, Let's wait until we are on our way back to my place.

'Where is Simon? Is he here in Paris?'

'Yes.'

'Where? Why didn't he come here?'

'I will explain everything later, as we walk back to my apartment.' She saw my rather dejected face. She put her hand on my arm, 'Poor Christopher, you came all this way and now we have thrown you into confusion. It's all right, everything will be explained, I will tell you some of it and Simon will tell you more.'

I was curious, 'What was that other language you were speaking?'

'Arabic.'

'You speak Arabic?

'I was born in Algeria, my father was an administrator there, I am what is called a 'pied noir'. I learned Arabic at the same time I learned French.

'Pied noir?'

'Literally it means 'black foot', a deprecating term, we are rather looked down on by French people born in France. We are considered second class citizens.'

She smiled at me and patted my arm, 'Let's have another glass of wine, then we will go back to my apartment.' You must be tired after all this excitement. How was the food?'

'It was perfect, just what I wanted, I was actually very hungry.'

We sat and talked over our glass of wine. She asked me questions about my life in London. 'You know Simon is very fond of you, he said you were the only person he could really trust.'

I felt myself blushing, Simon and I had never talked about our feelings for one another. To hear this compliment from a stranger was somehow very moving. She paid the bill and we left the brasserie. I still felt very uncomfortable about her paying for everything; it was not something I felt was right. Again she assured me that Simon wanted her to take care of me, that I would be able to repay in other ways.

She took my arm as we walked, 'I am so glad you came, and so is Simon.'

We walked in silence for a few moments. Then she said, 'The reason Simon doesn't want to 'phone my apartment is because Sayyid found out that the French Intelligence Agency, the SDECE, are bugging my 'phone. Indeed they may be bugging my whole apartment.'

'Bugging?'

'Listening in to my 'phone calls.'

To say I was shocked was an understatement. Suddenly I started to wonder what I was getting myself into.

'So' she continued, 'I don't think we should talk about anything to do with Simon while we are in my apartment.'

We didn't have to walk far before we came to the street where she lived. It was mainly small shops with dwellings above, built probably about mid-nineteenth century the French equivalent to our Victorian period. There was an entrance between what appeared to be a baker's shop, a boulangerie, according to the sign over the window, and a general grocery store. We went through into a small courtyard, then through another door to a staircase, where we climbed up to the second floor. Claudine produced a key and opened the door into a small apartment, and switched on a light. The room we entered was plainly the living room, sparsely furnished with a couch, a low table, two small chairs, a rug with a Moroccan design on it, some framed photographs on one of the white painted walls, the opposite wall had bookshelves from floor to ceiling, crammed with books and files, a telephone on a side table, a small folding table, with a chair in front of the window, and very little else. The window faced on to the street, with a blind of some sort of thin reed.

'This is my pied à terre in Paris, it's rather bleak and simple I'm afraid, but as you know, I've been living mainly in Greece. I only come to Paris as part of my journalistic life.'

She led me across the room, where there were two doors. She pointed to one on the left, 'That one is my bedroom, very small, just about takes the bed.' She opened the door to show me. It was indeed true, it contained a double bed, a small wardrobe, set into the wall, and very little else.

She opened the other door, revealing an even tinier bathroom, a shower, a plastic curtain, with pictures of the Eiffel Tower on it, a tiny washbasin, with a glass shelf, strewn with toiletries, and a toilet. There was no window, but it looked as if there was an extractor fan set in the wall, with a cord hanging from it, which doubtless switched it on and off.

That's it. You can sleep on the couch, I've got some blankets and a sleeping bag, if you prefer it.' There was a small curtained off area on one side of the main room. Claudine pushed the curtain to one side, revealing a kitchen sink with a draining board, and a kitchen cupboard. She opened the cupboard and took out a bottle of red wine and two tumbler shaped glasses. Taking them over to the sofa she put the glasses and bottle down on the low table, then sat on the sofa. She patted the space next to her and said, 'Come and sit down and we'll talk about what to do tomorrow.'

I did what I was told, and she poured us glasses of wine.

'So, as this is your first time in Paris I will show you some of the nicest areas, we can talk as we walk. Did you bring a camera?'

I kicked myself for not bringing my camera. The last couple of years, when I discovered that I could make use of a darkroom at the College, I had become a keen photographer.

No, I'm afraid I didn't think to. I did bring a sketchbook though, maybe I could find time to do some drawing?'

'Yes of course. About 2 pm I need to see my agent, I could leave you somewhere, which you might like to draw, and come back about two hours later to collect you.'

This sounded good to me, so it was agreed. Claudine then made some suggestions for our 'tour' of Paris, walking. 'We'll talk about it again tomorrow.'

We drank our wine and talked a little longer. Then she got up and taking the wine glasses and the now empty bottle over to the sink area, she washed the glasses and put the empty bottle in a rubbish bag.

'I'll get some blankets for you, if you don't mind I will use the bathroom first, then it's all yours.'

While she was in the bathroom I got up and went over to the wall with the photographs and examined them. There was one that looked like a Russian workers' canteen, some people were dancing, watched by a beautiful girl with her hair in a babushka leaning against a pillar, at the top of which was some sort of notice in what looked like Russian.

Another was a group of rather overweight people, with their backs to the camera, picnicking by a river, there is a boat moored in front of them, a man in the left foreground is pouring wine into a glass, he is wearing a black hat. On the right is a fat woman with a slip tucked into her skirt, she seems to be contemplating a chicken bone she is eating.

The next one was of a rather cheeky-looking boy, with a large bottle of wine under each arm, grinning at the photographer.

Further along was a photograph of an elderly looking man sitting in what looked like a dressing gown, holding a white dove in his hand, in the right foreground is a large birdcage with three doves sitting on top. There is another large birdcage behind the seated man. He is wearing a kind of nightcap on his head.

Finally there was a photograph of a group of children playing in what look like ruins. There is a boy in the foreground of the group on crutches. The photograph was taken through a hole in a wall, which has been blasted through. There are bullet holes on the right hand side of the opening.

Claudine came out of the bathroom, she was wearing a sort of Chinese robe and was obviously naked underneath.

'These are great photographs!'

'Yes, they are taken by Cartier-Bresson, I took them out of a book and had them framed. He is a wonderful photographer.'

These entranced me, they were like paintings in the way they were composed. It was then I first began to truly realise that photography was an art form.'I'll show you more tomorrow. There is an exhibition of some of his work in a small gallery in Passy, we could go there. I'm going to bed now, but I will be up by eight.'

She turned towards her bedroom door. As she was going through she turned again, 'Christopher, I usually sleep naked, so if I need to go to the bathroom in the middle of the night I don't bother to put my robe on.' She laughed, 'I don't want to shock you

'Don't worry,' I said, 'I spend my life at the moment drawing naked women. It is not new to me.' Anyway I am sure I will be dead asleep, I'm exhausted now.'I did not add that I also sleep naked.

I fell asleep very quickly, and must have continued to sleep for several hours, until I was woken by the sound of activity in the street outside. I groped for my watch, which I had laid on the floor by the couch. It was only just after 6am, but being summer time it was already light. I badly needed to go to the bathroom. I put my shirt on, in case Claudine should appear, and crept across the floor to the bathroom. I could hear no sound within, so I pushed the door open, only to be regaled by the sight of Claudine, naked, bending over the sink cleaning her teeth. She didn't seem to have heard me. I hastily retreated, but not before I had a chance to regard her nakedness. She was slender, with a slight broadening of hips, the two dimples, above the cleavage of her neatly rounded buttocks, quite marked. Her legs were also slender and tapered to small feet, which had bright red painted toenails. There were bikini marks from when she must have sunbathed in Greece.

I quickly returned to the couch where I laid down again, pulling the blanket up to my chin and closing my eyes. Still retaining the image of the naked form I had just seen. It's true, I spend my time drawing naked men and women almost every day at the Royal College. Nevertheless this has not made me blasé. Rather something of a connoisseur.

I heard Claudine leave the bathroom and after a few minutes I got up and went there myself. It was still very early; after I returned to my couch I lay for a while, listening to the sounds of the street below. I was wide-awake now and would have loved to go out for a walk. I wondered if Claudine was still awake. I listened, and after a while thought I heard the sound of a typewriter coming from her bedroom. I got up and dressed, then went to the door of the bedroom. There was definitely the sound of a typewriter. I tapped on the door.

'Oui?'

'It's me.'

'Come in, come in. I am decent.'

I pushed the door open, Claudine was sitting on the edge of her bed with a portable typewriter in her lap, she was wearing the Chinese robe I had seen her in the night before.

'I know its 6.30 in the morning, but I am awake and I thought I would go out for awalk around.'

Claudine glanced at her watch.'You are wrong Christopher, it's 7.30, you didn't change your watch, we are an hour ahead of Britain here. I tell you what, I have about another hour's work here, then I'll get dressed and meet you at 9am. There is a café a little way along the road on the left, it's called "Le Chat Noir", I'll meet you there at 9 o'clock.

She blew me a kiss, and I set off on my first adventure on my own in Paris. I made my way down stairs, then across the little courtyard to the street door. Before I reached it a woman appeared from a doorway to one side of the entrance, which I hadn't noticed the night before. She was middle-aged, with her dark hair tied back in a bun, showing a few grey hairs. She was wearing an apron and carried a broom. She looked at me as I approached her. She nodded.'Bonjour Monsieur.'

I was about to say 'Good morning' when I suddenly mustered my minimal French and replied, 'Bonjour Madame,' Then as an inspired after thought I added, 'Ca va?' 'Ca va, monsieur'. She watched me step out into the street. As I walked away I turned my head and saw her peeping out after me.

Was this my first encounter with the SDECE? Was I under surveillance?

In the best tradition of spy stories and counter espionage, I kept stopping and looking in shop windows, nervously examining the reflection for anyone following me.

After a while I got bored with doing this and cautiously accepted the idea that I was being followed. I even found the thought rather exhilarating, what a thrill to be able to recount this experience to my friends at the College, when I got back.

It was a lovely, sunny summer day in Paris, still relatively cool because of the early hour. I walked around several blocks, keeping in mind my route so that I would be able to find my way back. It was all wonderful, small shops, patisseries, boulangeries, épiceries, tabacs. A shop with a picture of a horse's head hung outside, called a 'Bouchier de Chevaline' and thought, I must ask Claudine what that meant. Then there were the smells, fresh ground coffee, baking bread, flowers, and something else, underlying all the other smells, something reminiscent of warm sewage. Everywhere I looked, it was like a Utrillo painting. Shopkeepers were washing down the pavement in front of their shops. I had never seen that in London, or anywhere else in England. The sound of French voices talking, calling to one another. Many people greeting each other with kisses on cheeks and handshakes. At one point, when I was attempting to cross the road, I was nearly run down, as I had forgotten that they drove on the right. In spite of that it was all a delight to me. I sauntered along in the warm sunlight feeling wonderful. I was in Paris at last!

Soon it was 9 o'clock, I had altered my watch. I retraced my route to the street where Claudine's apartment was, and soon found the café 'Le Chat Noir'.

Claudine was already there, seated at a table outside, reading a newspaper. She greeted me with, 'Bonjour, ça va?'

'Bien, ça va?'

She smiled at me, 'I see your French is already improving.'

She had not yet ordered. When a waiter appeared she said 'Deux crème, et deux tartine.'

She turned to me, 'I hope that's OK, I ordered you a coffee with milk and French bread and butter?'

I nodded, 'Excellent!'

'Was it good, your walk?'

'Wonderful, it was like being in a series of Impressionist paintings.'

I told her about the woman in the courtyard and how I thought I was being followed by the SDECE, because of this encounter.

She burst out laughing, 'That was Madame Racine, she is the concierge, its part of her function to be suspicious of everyone, until she knows you.' She laughed again, 'Madame Racine will be delighted to hear that someone thought she was part of the Intelligence services, I think I'll tell her.'

We sat and had our coffee and 'pain et beurre' in the warm sunlight. The long French bread was delicious. I had never found anything like it in London. Then we went to the St. Germain area and walked through the little streets of the Left Bank. After that down to the river where there were book stalls, along the side of the river wall. I browsed there for a while. It was all as I had hoped it would be. We walked until we could see the Notre Dame, towering massively over the nearby buildings, we crossed over the bridge and stood in front of the great cathedral. I gazed up at the soaring facade. I thought of Charles Laughton clambering down it, as the hunchback of Notre Dame. We walked around the cathedral and crossed the river over the Pont D'Arcole to the Right Bank, as I was informed by Claudine. We walked on and passed by a large store.

'That's the Bazaar de Hotel de Ville, or as we call it, the BHV. It's the equivalent of your Harrods, maybe not so grand. It's the main big store in Paris.'

Reaching the Rue de Rivoli we turned left and began a long walk towards the Place de La Concorde. After a while we passed near a large building, set back in a large courtyard, with steps leading up to the entrance.

'That's the Louvre', Claudine said, 'We'll go there tomorrow'.

Not long afterwards we passed another building. The sign outside proclaimed it as 'Le Musee de l'Art Decoratif'.'We'll go there too, if we have the time.'

She turned into a park which stretched along by the river.

'This is the Tuileries Gardens. How are you feeling?'

'I love it all, but I feel like something to eat, what about you?'

'Good, I was hoping you would say that, let's cross over on the Pont Royal and find somewhere to eat on the Left Bank.

We crossed over the bridge, and as we did I saw where I would like to sit drawing after lunch.

We found a small bistro in one of the little squares off the Quai Voltaire, as the road, which ran along by the river, was called. Again we managed to find a table outside. We sat in the sun eating our small lunch, Claudine ordered me something which sounded like 'lentille aux lardon' with a small side salad. I liked it, I had heard about lentils in England, but I had never eaten them. We also shared a carafe of red wine. My wine intake had escalated exponentially. We talked more about Simon. It seems that whatever happened down there in Greece, he had managed to escape and make his way back to France. For some reason he appeared to be hiding out in Paris. I was so relieved to hear he was safe.

'Sayyid is going to pick you up this evening with his car and take you to meet Simon, somewhere in the 15th arrondissement, near the river.'

'Aren't you coming too?'

'No, Simon wants to meet you on your own. Sayyid will leave you there, you can get a taxi back, I'll give you the money.'

I had given up protesting about her paying for everything. We had passed several 'bureau de change', and I was determined that while Claudine was busy this afternoon, I would change the small amount of English money I had brought with me. We finished our lunch. Claudine glanced at her watch.

'Its nearly time for me to go and meet my agent. Where do you think you will be?'

'I'll be on the bridge we just crossed, I saw where I want to do a drawing, when we were crossing the river.'

'OK, let's meet in a café.' She pointed to the other side of the little square we were in.

'There's a café over there, we'll meet there at 1 o'clock. Is that alright?'I nodded, 'Perfect, I'll see you then.'

I walked back to the bridge. I was carrying my sketchbook in my shoulder bag, having emptied it of my change of clothing and toiletries at Claudine's apartment. Standing on the bridge and looking at the view, I realised that I needed to get a bit closer to the L'Ilé de la Citie. I could see that there were two more bridges which were closer. I decided to walk along towards them. En route I saw a bureau de change. I went in and changed the £10 I had brought with me. This represented nearly two weeks' pay for my work at the theatre.

As I left the 'bureau' I accidentally bumped into a young man who was coming in. He was tall with a beard and was wearing the long dark robes and a white skull cap affected by men of Islamic origin. He was wearing dark glasses. I had seen many like him during our walk; far more than I had ever seen in London, where it was more likely that we saw people of Indian or Pakastani origin.

I apologised, 'Sorry', quickly amending it to 'pardon, excusez moi'. I hoped I was demonstrating my newly acquired efforts in the French language.

'Pas de problem.' He replied.

I guessed that meant something like, 'No problem'.

I walked on, heading for the next bridge. When I reached it I was pleased to find that it was a pedestrian bridge, so no traffic. The bridge was called, appropriately, 'Pont des Arts). I found somewhere to sit. Getting my sketchbook out I started drawing. As it was a pedestrian bridge there were quite a few people walking across it. Inevitably many of them glanced curiously at my drawing; a few stopped beside me and peered over my shoulder. Over the years I had become accustomed to this and no longer found it disturbing. I became absorbed in the process of drawing. At one point though I became conscious of someone standing beside me for longer than usual. I glanced up, and saw that it was the same Muslim man who I had bumped into at the 'bureau de change'. He continued to study my drawing, then with a 'Très bien,' he walked off. Curious I thought, it must be an accident, he just happened to be going the same way that I had been going.

I worked away steadily for nearly two hours. Then conscious that I had gone further than the bridge I told Claudine I was going to, I hurried back to the little square with the café. Claudine was already there, sitting outside the café.'I thought you might have got lost!'

I explained to her that I had walked on to a bridge nearer the 'Ilé de la Citie'. It was now getting on for 4.30pm. Claudine suggested that we took the Metro to Montparnasse, as Sayyid was going to pick me up at 6pm. We walked up to St. Germaine and got on the Metro there. I was as excited again by this new experience as I had been by everything else we had done that day. It seemed that the trains ran on rubber wheels, and were remarkably quiet, so different from the Underground in London. As we travelled I asked Claudine how Simon was looking after his ordeal.

'I've not physically seen him, he has only communicated with me over the 'phone.

'I was astonished at this. 'Surely you want to see him?'

'I do, I really do, I miss him so much, but he thinks it's not very safe for us to meet at the moment.'

She seemed almost tearful. I put my arm around her and for a brief few moments she leant against me. I knew how strong her feelings were for Simon. I knew too how difficult he could be.

We got back to Claudine's apartment in time, just before Sayyid was due. As we crossed the courtyard Madame Racine appeared and I was introduced to her formally, as a friend from London. She chattered with Claudine for a while then we went up to the apartment. Claudine wanted to give me money for a taxi to bring me back, but I refused, telling her that I had changed some money, adding that I wanted to take her out to dinner tonight.

Sayyd arrived. He seemed to be in a hurry to start, explaining that he had to meet up with someone later on, after he had connected me with Simon.

We set off in Sayyid's 'Deux Chevaux', a rather battered little car, with one wing badly crumpled, the other a completely different colour from the rest of the car, which was a sort of nondescript grey green. Sayyd drove hunched over the wheel, staring ahead, swerving his way in and out of the traffic, sometimes with hair raising misses. He kept up a continual stream of muttered abuse at other drivers, in French, and what I assume was Arabic. Certainly Parisian drivers drove with fierce panache, daring one to occupy a part of the road in which they wanted to be, which as far as I could see, was all of it.

After about fifteen minutes of this 'life shortening' drive, we arrived in a quiet area, away from any main road. It seemed to be a rather poorer than the one we had left, with run down buildings, looking as if they had not been painted since before the war. There were a few shops, some of which had been boarded up, interspersed with cafés and bistros, some with signs in Arabic.

We eventually pulled up outside what was called 'Café Bagdad'. Sayyd parked the Deux Chevaux in what seemed to be an impossibly small space between two other cars, by dint of 'bumping' the car in front and the one behind, so that the space was enlarged enough to enable Sayyd to park. The whole event had the characteristics of fairground tactics.

We entered the café. My first impression was that it was entirely occupied by people of Muslim origin. Many were bearded, some with beards so long that they reached their chests, others more like Sayyd's, comparatively short and well trimmed. A few were in long dark robes, with those white crocheted skull caps, which I had noticed before. Some of the tables had groups of 4 or 5, others, just two people. Occasionally there were solitary men. What was clear was that there were only men here. I had the distinct impression that I had been transposed to somewhere in the Middle East.

Sayyd was obviously known here, several people called out to him and he would pause and greet them with something that sounded like, 'Asalamo alikom'. It seemed to have the same connotations and usage as the French 'Ca va?' There was much kissing of bearded cheeks. Sayyd didn't introduce me, although a number of people glanced at me curiously.

We found an empty table and sat down. A waiter came by and we ordered coffee.

I gazed round the café, there were a few non-Muslim people, but they were distinctly a minority. I turned to Sayyd, 'Are most of the people here also from Algeria?' He shook his head, 'No, the majority are from Palestine . . . as I am.'

I was quite disturbed by this. I had assumed that as Claudine was a 'pied noir' from Algeria, Sayyd would also be from there. All I knew about Palestinians was that they were 'terrorists', committed to the destruction of the nascent country of Israel. Although I was not particularly political in my thinking, I and my fellow students were steeped in sympathy for the Israelis, or should I say, the Jewish people. We all had an international feeling of guilt after the Holocaust, which was still in the very recent past.

So, here I was, sitting in a café in Paris full of potential 'terrorists', with someone who might also be one. No wonder the SDECE were possibly aware, maybe we were all under surveillance.

After a while a young man came in, he was also wearing Muslim attire. He glanced around, then came and sat at the next table to us. He was carrying a book and after ordering coffee he settled down to read it. I noticed he had dark tinted glasses. Suddenly, with a shock I realised it was the man who I had bumped into at the 'bureau de change'.

Sayyd, who was becoming increasingly restless, and kept glancing at his watch suddenly said, 'I must go, I'm late.'

He called the waiter and paid for the coffee. As he was leaving he turned to me. 'I'm sure Simon will be here very soon.'

Suddenly I was on my own, in a café filled with potential terrorists. I watched the door nervously, praying that Simon would arrive.

The man at the next table shut the book, and suddenly passed it to me. 'Have you read this Christopher?'

I was just finishing my coffee, wondering if I should order another. I literally choked. I turned towards the man, and as I did so he lifted his glasses briefly, there was no mistaking those blue eyes.

'Simon . . . !'

He put his fingers to his lips, 'Not now, let's go for a walk'.

He got up and headed for the door.

I struggled to my feet, still clutching the book. I glanced at it briefly, it was Arthur Koestler's 'Thieves in the Night'.

I stumbled out of the café, where Simon was already waiting. Before I could say anything he jerked his head to the left, 'Let's walk this way, it will take us down to the river.'

He set off briskly, striding along at a familiar pace. I had so many questions to ask I didn't know where to start. Have you become a Muslim? How long have you been in Paris? How did you escape? How did you get to France?

In the end I settled for, 'I am so pleased to see you again.'

He stopped and turned to me, 'I can't tell you how much I have missed you. I have so much to tell you.'

I was enormously touched by this. I had been afraid that he would have retired inside himself, rather like he had when he came out of the army. How it took weeks before he became more like the person I knew.

'Have you become a Muslim?

He laughed, 'Certainly not, I'm still as committed an agnostic as I always was, more so in fact. No, this outfit is useful sometimes in certain company, it's also a form of disguise.' He laughed again and added, 'It fooled you didn't it, at the 'bureau de change' and later on the bridge. The beard's real though.'

'What happened when you were kidnapped in Greece, who did it, and how did you get away?'

'It's a long story, I'll tell you later.'

All this was very intriguing. Kidnapping, intelligence surveillance? This was a different world to my quiet life in London.

We walked along, towards the river. As we did so he briefly outlined what had happened to him after he left England, over two years ago. How he had first made his way to Paris, where quite quickly he had found a room that he could rent cheaply. It was on the Left Bank, in that area of small streets off St. Germaine, through which I had walked with Claudine that afternoon. The room was in a rather large sprawling apartment, not far from the 'Ecole des Beaux-Arts', in Rue Visconti. The rest of the rooms were occupied mainly by students and young artists.

'I had it in mind to try and enroll at L'Ecole des Beaux-Arts myself. As you may remember I was quite good at French.'

I did indeed remember this; I had once found Simon reading a Gide novel in French. He seemed to be one of those people who could pick up languages quite quickly, living in a French city had obviously helped him a lot.

'I became friends with several of the students. They were all very political, they would go to meetings and I would go with them. Through them I learned about the appalling crimes carried out by the French in their efforts to thwart the call for independence in Algeria. How they had called them to arms during the Second World War, where they had fought bravely alongside the French army in the battles for the liberation of France, then afterwards were abandoned by them.'

We had reached the river by then and turned right to walk along by the boulevard, which separated us from the actual riverbank. Quite soon we reached a little green area, hardly big enough to be called a park. There were several seats facing the river, we sat down at one.

'At one of these meetings I met Claudine. She seemed very involved with the politics of that time. I found out that she was a journalist, and had spent time in Algeria during the time of the war for Independence. She talked a lot about the interrogation methods that were used at that time.'

He paused and thought for a moment, then, 'I told her about what I was involved in Cyprus and Egypt.'

He spoke as if it was something that was ten years ago, but which in actual fact was only four at the most.

'What I didn't tell you was that while I was in Egypt, I met a man who was a refugee from Palestine. Through him I began to learn about the deliberate policy of 'ethnic cleansing' which the Israelis had been implementing since 1947. At first I didn't believe it, but quite soon after I came back to France I began to research it more and I realised the full extent of what the Israelis had done, and were continuing to do. It was then that I became pro-Palestinian.'

I was aghast at this, 'You can't be! The poor Israelis are desperately trying to survive, surrounded by hostile Arabs, after all they suffered through the Holocaust. How can you be against them!'

'I didn't say I was against them, what I am against is what they are doing to the Palestinians.'

'It seems to me that they are asking for it, all these unprovoked terrorist attacks. The Israelis are just defending themselves.'

Simon turned to me, 'Unprovoked! Unprovoked!'

He was very agitated, almost angry. He didn't say anything for a few moments, he appeared to be calming himself down. Then, 'Christopher, have you ever heard of Al Nakbar?'

I shook my head. I was very politically unaware, especially about events abroad. Like many people at that time I had been enthusiastic about the establishment of the state of Israel. It seemed that some sort justice had been created for the Jewish people. The opposition of the Palestinians was incomprehensible to me, especially as my knowledge of that area was limited to much reading of 'The Seven Pillars of Wisdom', and little beyond that period of time.

Simon seemed to have calmed down.

'Al Nakbar was the massive ethnic cleansing of the Palestinians in 1948, by intimidation, violence and massacres. Seven hundred and twenty-six thousand Palestinians were evicted from their own country, to become refugees, denied the right to return by the Israelis. Over five hundred Palestinian towns and villages were destroyed.'

'I've never heard about this!'

'No, it was very played down in the press. Before the end of the British Mandate, we had done a lot to favour the Israelis, the United Nations concluded the job. As soon as Israel was established we began supplying them with military equipment, in a covert way. There was a profit motive there.'

'I still find it difficult to believe, I'm sure some of this is wrong, misconstrued in some way.'

He thought for a moment, then, 'I'm going to give you some stuff to read. When are you going back?'

'Tomorrow evening.'

'OK, let's meet up and have lunch or something. I will bring you an envelope with copies of stuff I have collected . . . research. Take it back with you, read it and I will contact you in a week.'

We talked more, he asked me questions about my life. He knew that I had got into the Royal College of Art. I told him about the burglary, also that June's house had been burgled.

He thought about this, and then asked me if anything else suspicious had happened. I told him not since this had happened, nearly a year ago.

'Nothing permanent, a few brief affairs, no ties.'

We watched a long tourist boat pass on the river.

'When do you begin the summer vacation?'

'Three weeks' time.'

'Fancy a trip?'

'With you?'

'Sort of.'

'Don't know if I can afford it. What do you mean sort of?'

'I may be able to organise something, where you'll get paid, like a sort of summer job. What do you think?

'Where?'

'I'll tell you tomorrow.'

He got up, 'I need to go; I have to meet someone later. You won't get a taxi here. I'll walk with you back the way we came, there's a taxi rank further up that road.'

We set off. I was intrigued by the idea of doing a trip with Simon, but where? He refused to tell me, saying it would all be revealed the following day. He asked me what my plans were. I told him that Claudine had suggested that we visit the Louvre, then maybe go to the Cartier-Bresson exhibition in Passy. He made a face.

'The Louvre doesn't open until 11 o'clock on Sunday mornings. If you go there you won't get out in less than two hours, maybe three. Then if we have lunch, by the time we finish it will be getting on for four in the afternoon. I suggest you skip Passy. There are bound to be other Cartier-Bresson exhibitions. Leave it until you come back again. Let's meet somewhere in St. Germaine. How about 'Le Deux Magot'? It's a bit pricey, but you should have the experience, it's a legendary place. Let's meet there at 2 o'clock.'

'How about Claudine?'

He thought for a minute, 'Look, there are things I want to discuss with you, which are just between you and I. She doesn't need to be involved in this, I'll explain things to her later.'

'So what am I going to say to her?'

We crossed the road; I could see the taxi rank ahead.

'Tell her that we just need to catch up some more, not having seen each other for over two years, and why doesn't she come along a bit later, say 3.30.'

'She's not stupid, she knows that you wanted to meet me urgently about something, which is why I came to Paris.'

'Well, think of something . . . use your best diplomatic skills.'

With that, he turned down a side street. He waved and said, 'See you tomorrow.'

I was quite angry about this cavalier attitude he seemed to have towards Claudine. There was a taxi waiting there, so I got in, I gave the man Claudine's address in my halting French, then fumed quietly about Simon casually leaving me with the problem of putting her off until later.

The problem was resolved for me by Claudine herself. I told her that after going to the Louvre in the morning I was going to meet Simon for lunch at 'Les Deux Margot' at 2 o'clock.

'Merde,' she said, 'I have to meet someone else for lunch. I do so want to see Simon! Maybe I can join you later?'

'Perfect, let's say 3.30 then?'

'I should be able to make it by then.'

We went out for supper to a small bistro near where she lived. What I would describe as 'cheap and cheerful'. It had long tables with benches either side. It was busy, with a lively atmosphere, lots of smoke, carafes of cheap but good red wine, much chatter and laughter. Everyone was French, except me.

We talked, mainly about Simon. She asked me how he was, how did he escape from his kidnappers, did he still have a beard, where was he living. I answered as best I could, reassuring her that he seemed in good health. I realized that Simon hadn't answered my question about his apparent kidnapping.

She told me something about their life in Greece. Although they were together a lot of the time, she had to make frequent trips to Paris and sometimes Algeria. Simon also went off a couple of times, once he was away for two months. She didn't know where he went exactly, they didnt pry into each other's activities, but when they were together they were very close.

'I fell in love with him. We had so much in common. We are both passionate about the same things. I hope he loves me too.' Again I could see that she was rather tearful.

This touched me. I had assumed that they were both in love, but I knew how remote Simon could be.

We finished our meal and I made sure that I paid the bill.

That night I slept rather restlessly, my mind was active with thoughts about what Simon was up to.

In the morning Claudine and I had breakfast together, she had managed to get some croissants. She made a big pot of coffee and poured it into two large bowls. We sat on the sofa, using the long low table to put our coffee and croissants on. She also provided two small plates and knives as well as butter. I was astonished to see that she dipped her croissant into the coffee. Something which I had never seen an English person do. My mother would have frowned severely if she had caught me doing it. I quickly realized that it was a French custom, and so I began to do it myself.

It was another beautiful day and we strolled down to the river again, crossing over the bridge and arriving at the Louvre just before it opened. There was already a considerable crowd of people waiting to get in, mostly tourists.

To my surprise we had to pay to go in. It would have been free in London. The idea of having to pay to get into National Gallery or the Tate would have been a total anathema to us.

I of course made straight to where the Mona Lisa was, along with about twenty other people. It was so much smaller than it appeared in all the reproductions in books. She was rather lovely in an enigmatic way, with her closed lip smile. Unkind people had said that she only smiled with her lips shut because her teeth were bad.

We made our way to the section where there was more recent and contemporary work: the Impressionists and Post-Impressionists, then Picasso and Braque, the Manets and the Monets. While I wallowed in all this, Claudine went off to look at other things. I found her in the Egyptian collection. In no time at all it was 1.30pm. We both said simultaneously that we had to get going to our separate appointments. Claudine decided to take a taxi to her destination. We found a taxi rank nearby and as it was now getting on towards 2 o'clock I did the same. I arrived outside 'Le Deux Margot' just after 2 o'clock. Simon was already there, sitting languidly at a table outside, in the sun. He was no longer dressed as a Muslim. With jeans and a short-sleeved shirt, and a sweater around his shoulders he looked a typical student. He had even trimmed his beard.

He stood up when I arrived and shook my hand, 'Ca va?' He was doing an impersonation of a Frenchman, thank God he didn't try to kiss me on both cheeks.

'Simon', I said, 'you don't have to put on that performance for me.'

He just grinned and sat down.

'OK, let's get something to eat, how about a bottle of wine as well?'

He seemed to be in the most ebullient mood, more like the old Simon I knew.

'This is not really a restaurant, but we can get some small stuff, I think you'll like it. He signaled a waiter, who arrived with a couple of menus, 'Si'l vous plait, un bouteille de Chablis,' He turned to me, 'you OK with white wine?'

Frankly I was OK with anything. We studied the brief menu as we basked in the sun. I felt as if I was back to the time before we had to do our military service, when life seemed simpler and we had romantic dreams of the future. I suddenly remembered Claudine.

'Claudine is going to try and join us about 3.30'.

'Right, then we had better get the serious stuff over first.' He reached in his bag, which was under his chair and pulled out a bulky envelope.

'Here's your homework.' Take it with you and read it thoroughly, we'll talk next week.'

'Talk where?'

'You must know someone with a 'phone?'

I thought for a minute, 'Well there's Andy, he lives in a flat where they share a 'phone. I could talk to him.'

'Know the number?'

I rummaged in my shoulder bag and found a rather battered, pocket-sized black sketchbook, which I used for making quick impromptu sketches, sometimes writing odd telephone numbers in it.

I flicked through the pages,' Here it is, PAR 6059, it's a London number.'

'PAR?'

'Its short for Park. It's Notting Hill, a run down area, north of Kensington Gardens. Lots of students find rooms there, it's cheap.'

'Right, I'll call next Friday, 6 pm your time. That'll give you time to digest all that, he indicated the envelope. Put it away now and don't show it to anyone else.'

The wine arrived, closely followed by the food. I had chosen an 'omelette aux champignon'. Simon had some unidentifiable concoction.

Simon poured the wine. It was the first white wine I had tasted. It went well with a summer day. We began eating.

'Now about this trip, we can't travel together but I can arrange we meet up there.'

'Where Simon? Where?'

'Oh, didn't I say? . . . . Palestine and Israel.'

I seemed to be constantly choking over my food. When I had recovered enough to speak I said, 'My God Simon, that's the Middle East!'

'Well sort of.'

'It is! According to my atlas! I can't afford this . . . its impossible!'

'Don't worry. I've arranged it all. You are invited by an art group in Tel Aviv, called 'New Horizons'. They are primarily a group of Israeli artists, but they have decided that it would be a good idea to invite someone from outside the country to travel round doing drawings and paintings, to record their beautiful new country for the outside world. They'll pay for everything, air fare, hotels, someone to drive you when you need, and a reasonable allowance. What do you think?'

'You didn't arrange all that since last evening?'

'No, I've been arranging it for the last three months.'

'You mean you assumed that I would be willing to do it?'

'Yes.'

I was furious, Simon had just taken me for granted. I felt manipulated.

'I don't like being taken for granted, you think you can order me around and I'll do anything you say!'

'Christopher, think, we can have an adventure together, you are the one person I can really trust. Think of the stories we can tell later.'

He hesitated, 'Christopher, you are my only real friend, it would be wonderful to do this with you.'

He was getting to me, I could feel it, I was softening and calming down. It was true, what an adventure, what stories to tell, what drawings and paintings I could do.

'What about you? Are you invited by them as well?'

'Not by the same organisation, I am under the auspices of the 'Palestine Aid Organisation.'

'What!'

'Yes, I'm an observer, I volunteered.'

I suddenly noticed Claudine at the other side of Boulevard St. Germaine. She was about to cross over.

'Simon, Claudine's coming.'

We watched Claudine cross the Boulevard, always a hazardous operation on any Paris street, I was beginning to realise.

As she approached we stood up, like two well brought up English boys. She went first to Simon, kissing him on both cheeks, then putting her arms round him she rested her head on his shoulder and I heard her say something softly in his ear. It sounded like 'Je t'aime.'

After that she turned to me and kissed me on both cheeks, no embrace though.

We sat down. Claudine had already eaten, but she accepted a glass of wine. Simon ordered another bottle. I could see that I was going to be rather 'sloshed' when I went to the airport.

Simon lay back in his seat, basking in the sun.

'Christopher and I have been going down memory lane, reviving stories of our misspent youth.'

He then began to recount several incidents, most of them about me, some embarrassing. We began to laugh together as we developed and embroidered the stories, much like we did when we were younger, until we became almost hysterical with laughter. Claudine joined in the laughter when she could follow the references, but mostly she gazed at us with quiet affection.

At one point she got up to go to the toilet. Whilst she was away Simon said quickly, 'Christopher, you must learn to drive. Can you do a quick crash course over the next four weeks?'

'Yes I expect so . . . . but I can't afford it.'

'Can't you borrow the money temporarily from your parents?'

'Maybe . . . . I'll try.'

I wondered about all this secrecy from Claudine. What was the problem? He had been more or less living with her for at least a year. Surely she must know what he was doing.

'Simon, I will write to you when I get back to London. This meeting has been too short. I have so many questions to ask you, so many things I need to know. Let me have an address. I'll give you mine.'

I tore a single sheet from my pocket sketchbook, wrote my London address on it and passed it to him. I then passed him the sketchbook and he hastily wrote his. I could see Claudine returning.

It was getting quite late in the afternoon. I needed to go back to Claudine's apartment and collect my stuff, prior to going to the airport.

Simon insisted on paying for our meal and the wine. I didn't question him about where his money was coming from. I was pretty sure that he had gone through all that was left of his uncle's money, after buying his Landrover. Maybe he had made more money in Greece selling his drawings and paintings than I had realised.

Claudine and Simon agreed to meet later at a bistro in the Marais area. I was not sure where in Paris that was.

We got up to leave. Simon put his arm round my shoulders, 'It's great seeing you again, I'll call you. Do your homework! We'll discuss it by letter. See you next time.'

Claudine and I made our way back to her apartment. She was very happy at seeing Simon again. She volunteered to come to the airport with me, but I decided that it was time that I learned to take care of myself. It looked like I was going to be doing a lot of serious travelling in more distant places than Paris.

I packed my meager belongings, took one last look at the Cartier-Bresson photographs, kissed Claudine goodbye, thanking her for putting me up.

I made my way along the street to where I had seen a taxi rank. I looked around, taking in once more the atmosphere of Paris, the shops, the signs, the sounds, the people, the music, the chatter of French voices. I felt confident that I would come here again, hopefully many times.

Chapter 4

I managed to find the Air France check-in without much difficulty. Already I was feeling like a seasoned traveller, Aanother stamp in my passport. When we boarded, I again managed to find a window seat. After we had taken off and circled round Paris, we headed north towards the coast. It was already getting dark. I got out the envelope with the material which Simon had given me and started to read. There was a smaller, sealed envelope inside, on it Simon had written, *Read this after you have read the other stuff! Only if you are with me, if not DESTROY IT!*

Simon's becoming quite theatrical, verging on the eccentric, I thought.

I became so absorbed in the other material, that I hardly noticed when the pretty stewardess came by, pushing her trolley with drinks. I shook my head when she asked me if I would like anything. I was still feeling the effects of the wine I had been drinking with Simon.

I was still reading when I became aware that we were coming in to land. The seat belt light came on and the stewardess came round again, checking to see if we were all belted in.

I took the airport bus to Victoria, and then made my way home to Clapham. I stayed up, continuing to read the contents of the envelope until late at night. I was aghast at what I learned from this. How had this been hardly reported, why were we kept virtually unaware of this? Why were we fed the idea that all Palestinians were terrorists, that the Israelis were the innocent party?

The information contained was very explicit, starting with a quote from David Ben Gurion.

> "We must expel the Arabs and take their places."—*David Ben Gurion, 1937*

Followed by a vast amount of researched information on the Israeli plans, master minded by Ben Gurion, for how to implement the programme of 'ethnic cleansing'. Starting in 1947, before the end of the British Mandate, and before the United Nations officially recognised the formation of the Israeli state. It detailed the organised Israeli attacks on Arab villages and small towns. The violent expulsions by the Haganah and Stern gang, of countless Palestinians, men, women and children, with massacres and rape were laid bare, causing 250,000 people driven to become refugees in other Arab countries. The careful planning of the next phase, Plan C, which entailed:

> *Killing the Palestinian political leadership.*
> *Killing the Palestinian inciters and their financial supporters.*
> *Killing Palestinians who acted against Jews.*
> *Killing Palestinian officers and officials.*
> *Damaging Palestinian transportation.*
> *Damaging the sources of Palestinian livelihoods: water wells, mills etc.*
> *Attacking nearby Palestinian villages likely to assist in future attacks.*
> *Attacking Palestinian clubs, coffee houses, meeting places etc.*

This was followed by Plan D, 'Plan Dalet', which was the 'final solution' implemented as soon as Israel became officially a nation. This involved 'the systematic expulsion from their homeland' of the Palestinians. When this was completed in 1948, a further 726,000 Palestinians had been driven from their homes and into refugee camps in other countries. The Israelis then occupied their lands and started cultivating them as their own.

In1956 Ben Gurion's final quote was:

> "If I was an Arab leader I would never make terms with Israel. That is natural: we have taken their country. Sure, God promised it to us, but what does that matter to them? Our God is not theirs. We come from Israel, it's true, but two thousand years ago, and what is that to them? There has been anti-Semitism, the Nazis, Hitler, Auschwitz, but was that

their fault? They only see one thing: we have come here and <u>stolen</u> their country. Why should they accept that? They may perhaps forget in one or two generations' time, but for the moment there is no chance. So it's simple: we have to stay strong and maintain a powerful army. Our whole policy is there. Otherwise the Arabs will wipe us out".

It was 2am before I finished going through all the other research. My head ached, my mouth was dry and I needed to get some sleep. I picked up Simon's envelope and decided to open it in the morning, when I had slept and my head was clearer. I drank two glasses of water, cleaned my teeth, examined my red eyes in the mirror, then undressed and fell into bed.

In spite of being so late to bed I was wide awake by 7am. I got up, shaved, got dressed, made myself some tea and toast and sat down to read Simon's letter. Whatever . . . . I was with him.

Dear Christopher,

So you've read all that? Terrible isn't it? How has all this seemingly escaped the notice of the majority of people, certainly in Britain and, as I know, in France? It seems there is a conspiracy of silence. Well there are reasons for this. Both Britain and France were the first to start supplying arms to Israel. France went even further, in 1956 they started helping the Israelis develop a nuclear programme in the Negev at Dimona. All this was very covert, and remains so. The US, who in 1948 were very unenthusiastic about the United Nations resolution on the formation of the state of Israel, did a quick 'volte face' in 1949 and became solid supporters of Israel, no doubt seeing Israel as an ally in the Middle East in the future. They too began supplying Israel with arms and financial support on a large scale. You should also realise that there is a powerful Jewish lobby in Washington.

So, because of this, we should be very aware that there are several intelligence services who are likely to be guarding these secrets, and if we're not very careful we may find ourselves under surveillance by some, if not all of them. These could include SDECE, the French Intelligence Service, MI6 and MI5, CIA and more dangerously, (if that's possible) Mossad.

Having said all that, assuming now you are with me, this is my plan. You will be going to Israel under the auspices of 'New Horizons', an Israeli group of artists, so through them you may be able to get access to information from their side. I on the other hand am going as part of Palestine Aid, an international charitable organisation, at the moment tolerated by the Israelis. Through them I can get more information from the Palestinian side. What I want you to do is try and visit as many sites of villages and small towns destroyed by the Israelis, and their inhabitants either massacred or 'ethnically cleansed' as you can. You can't possibly cover them all, there were 531 altogether. Do some paintings and drawings of as many of theses sites as you can, and take as many photographs as you can as well. I will give you a list of the most important ones. Let me tell you something about 'New Horizons'. They are primarily a group of artists/painters. As artists they are liberal thinkers and because of this, many are outraged by what the Zionists are doing in their name, and thoroughly disapprove of it. You will find some very sympathetic people amongst them, but be careful, some are not.

I, in the meantime, will try and find more information on the sources of the material, which I have covered in this letter. Hopefully I will find out more.

I love the idea that we are going to do this together. Speak to you on Friday.

Your very best friend,
Simon

I sat back, overwhelmed by what Simon was proposing. Had I really agreed to get into all this? I looked at my watch, I needed to leave to go to the College.

I decided not to cycle and took the bus. This gave me time to think. I had to make a list of the stuff to do. First, I must call my parents and see if I could borrow the money for driving lessons. If I didn't get on with that now I wouldn't make it in time before I went. I guess I would have to tell them where I was going. I wonder what their reaction was going to be. There was the theatre to tell, saying I was going to be away for maybe two months, find a substitute, and hope I get my job back when I returned. Check at the Israeli consulate and see if I needed a visa. Get sketchbooks and materials together. Buy film for camera. Speak to my tutor. What clothes would I need? It will be very hot in July and August in Palestine.

Also there was another person I needed to talk to. I hadn't been entirely truthful with Simon when he asked me if I had any other relationships, after my breakup with June. During the last few months I had been spending a lot of time with a girl who was still in her first year at the College, her name was Sylvia. I had first noticed her at one of our College dances. We had them two or three times a term, they were usually referred to as 'hops'. They were very popular with other art schools in the London area, many of their students came to them. They were noisy affairs with a lot of loud music. We also had a small bar.

I had tried my hand at dancing, but I was very un-relaxed and rather stiff, I usually loosened up with a few drinks, so on this occasion I went to the bar. I ordered a drink and having paid for it I went and sat in a corner, watching other people. Quite soon I noticed a girl, also sitting by herself, near me. She was gazing round rather nervously. She was small and slightly built, with dark hair, which came down to her shoulders. She seemed to be alone. She looked incredibly young for someone to be at the Royal College. Maybe she came from one of the other art schools in London. I wondered what she doing here on her own? I was summoning up enough courage to speak to her, when she suddenly rose to her feet, picked up her coat and left. I stayed for a while, and then decided to leave myself.

A few days later I was wandering round the studios, looking to see what other people were doing, when, in a corner, I saw the girl again. She was doing a small painting, as far as I could see using oil paints. I couldn't get behind her to see what she was painting. I waited until lunchtime, when everyone had left for lunch, and then I walked round to look at her painting.

I found it quite disturbing, there seemed to be a hint of darkness there, a cross between Munch and Fuseli, so out of keeping with her young, almost childlike demeanour. It was mostly a flat red landscape, overcast with streaks of black clouds. There were flashes of lightning, and a girl in a red dress running in the foreground, her mouth was open, as if she was screaming. In the distance behind her were two men in pursuit. It was filled with dread, it made me want to know more about her.

Not long afterwards the first year students had to do their exhibitions. In every studio they were busy framing their paintings, with simple frames and mounting their drawings and sketches on stiff white card. I remembered how anxious I was, doing this the year before, everything depended on how one presented the work if one would be able to stay on a further two years, or asked to leave as not being suitable.

I walked around with my friend Andy, seeing how they were getting on. When we reached the studio the girl was in, we found her sitting disconsolate on the floor, surrounded by unframed and un-mounted paintings and drawings. She seemed not to know how to begin. We decided to take charge of her, and during the next few hours we worked away, mounting the drawings, framing the paintings and finally arranging them on the wall. She watched us helplessly, she seemed unable to do anything. We had to make a small sign with her name on it, so I asked her what her name was, 'Sylvia Haugas' she replied, in almost a whisper. I noticed that she had a slight accent, I couldn't identify it.

Over the next few weeks, I gradually began to get to know her. At first she hardly responded to my overtures, almost as if she was frightened of me, but after a while she seemed to know that I was no threat to her, and began to accept me. I asked her about herself. She was rather reticent at first, but gradually she began to open up. It appeared that she was a refugee from Latvia. She and her parents had managed to make their way to Britain, where they had been granted asylum status. Quite what had occurred to make them refugees was still not clear. Her father had been a doctor in Latvia, and her mother a teacher. Her father was trying to take his medical exams again in order to practice medicine in England. I found out that Sylvia was actually 23 years old and when they had escaped from Latvia she had been 16 years old. There was something very vulnerable about her, she had been damaged in some way, and it was showing in her paintings. We were not having a relationship in a physical sense, I wouldn't have dreamed of making a move in that direction. She seemed too sensitive, too easy to damage still further. Every now and then though, she would take my arm as we walked, and sometimes she would hold my hand. Although I was more or less the same age as her, I felt very much that somehow she was still a child.

All these thoughts were jumbled in my head as the bus crossed over Battersea Bridge and headed for Sloane Square. I jumped off there and headed for the Underground station, it was better to go that way as I could get off at South Kensington and walk through the long tunnel to the Science Museum exit, where all I needed to do was cross the road and go straight to the Painting School entrance at the side of the Victoria and Albert Museum.

I signed in at the front desk, something we were required to do to show our continued attendance. Although I knew that after that we could just go if we wanted to. I climbed the stairs to the top studios, my friend Andy was already there. He was an old friend from my previous art school. We hadn't known each other very well there, but as we had both managed to get into the Royal College we had developed a friendship. He had a good sense of humour, not quite as dry as Simon's, but we got on very well together. He was as tall as me, he had dark straight hair, rather piercing grey blue eyes and a slightly hooked nose, apparently like his father, who was in the army. Andy didn't get on with his father, an officer in the army who had risen through the ranks and who couldn't come to terms with the fact that Andy had chosen to go to art school. In his mind that made Andy a 'pansy' and he concealed the fact from his fellow soldiers.

Andy immediately asked me how my weekend in Paris had gone. I told him I would give him a full description at morning break. I looked around but couldn't see Sylvia anywhere. I was not concerned about this, as she may well be in one of the studios down stairs.

I turned to the painting I was doing before I left. It was of a nearby square, based on a series of sketches I'd done from a window in the Victoria and Albert Museum, which was right next door to the Painting School. I tried to continue with it, but my mind was distracted by all the thoughts brought on by Simon's letter and the material he had given me to read. I sat down and began to make a list. I decided to call my parents that evening and ask them if they could loan me the money for the driving lessons. In the meantime I could apply for a provisional licence and set a date for a driving test. I must also find my tutor, to tell him about this unexpected invitation to spend time in Palestine and Israel. I know he would approve, I just needed to produce a convincing story as to why I had been invited. I would ask Andy about using the 'phone where he was living, at 6 pm on Friday. In a way I was quite excited about this venture. In another way I was terrified.

About 11 o'clock we decided to go and get our daily coffee. Andy and I usually went to the V and A café. There was a back entrance from the College, which led us straight into the main Museum.

We walked through the galleries, varying it almost every day, one day the main hall with its Michelangelo 'David', another day through the costume department, with its sixteenth-, seventeenth- and eighteenth-century costumes, another day its jewellery department, with glove rings from the time of Henry VIII. Occasionally we took a diversion through the plaster cast replica department, which included a full sized cast of the Trajan column, as well as a cast of part of the facade of the Notre Dame, which I had seen only two days before in Paris. It was an educational approach to a rather ordinary museum café, where we usually queued for indifferent coffee or tea, and an Eccles cake, a throwback to my army days in the NAAFI. Today, after experiencing real coffee and croissants in Paris, I settled for well-stewed tea instead, and a bun.

We found a table and sat down. Andy was eager to hear about my weekend in Paris. He knew about the fact that Simon had been kidnapped, and had then mysteriously reappeared in Paris.

I gave him an edited version, glossing over the fact that I had stayed on my own in Claudine's apartment, giving the impression that Simon was there as well. I invented a story about how Simon had escaped from his kidnappers. Although Simon had still not explained it to me. I avoided any mention of the Israel and Palestine situation. I made the fact that Simon had been anxious to have me come over to meet him as just a renewal of our friendship. I then told him that Simon was organising a trip for us during the summer vacation, to

Palestine, and that he was going to call about this on Friday evening, at Andy's number.

He was not stupid either, I could see that he was suspicious of some of the gaps in my story and began asking me probing questions. I avoided them by changing the subject and asking him if he could stand in for me at the theatre during the summer vacation months.

I wondered why I was concealing so much information from him, I suppose I had been influenced by Simon's need for some sort of secrecy, even from Claudine. Perhaps I liked this role of a covert life.

While I was talking to Andy, I noticed that Sylvia had entered the café. Although I was sure that she had seen us, she had got her tea and went and sat by herself at another table, not far away.

We eventually got up to return to the studios. As we were leaving I said to Andy, 'You go ahead, I will be along shortly'. He glanced back and saw Sylvia sitting by herself.

'OK.'

I went over to Sylvia's table and sat down. Her eyes were cast down, looking at the table. I saw that she had been crying. I reached across the table and took her hand.

'Sylvia, what's the matter?'

She lifted her eyes, I could see they were still swimming with tears. Her hand was limp in mine. She shook her head.

I pulled her hand towards me, and kissed it gently, 'Tell me, what's thematter?'

She looked at me again, her hand tightened on mine.

'I had this terrible dream, I dreamt you were dead!'

This rather shocked me. I kissed her hand again, 'Well as you can see, I'm not dead.'

'I saw it so clearly . . . . this big truck . . . . so terrible!'

I thought she was going to start to cry again.

'Sylvia, it's alright . . . . I'm here . . . . unharmed . . . . don't cry!

She gradually calmed down. I bought her another tea. When she finished it we made our way back to the studios. She was very quiet, although she held my hand as we walked, she was somehow retiring inside herself again, as she had been when I first met her. I went with her to the studio she was working in. There was another painting on her easel, she didn't invite me to see it. She had not asked me anything about my trip to Paris.

That evening I called my parents. My mother was full of exciting news. Apparently my father had received a late bonus from the company he'd worked for, and with some of it he had bought me a scooter! A Lambretta. I'd always hankered after one, I much preferred the Lambrettas to the other popular scooter, the Vespa. I realised that I could hardly ask them for driving lessons as well. I would just have to drain my modest saving account. I told her that I was delighted, which I was, and spoke to my father, thanking him profusely and promised to come down late Saturday evening after I had finished at the theatre.

I also spoke to my tutor and told him about the trip to Palestine. He was delighted for me. He had served in the army during the war as an official war artist, and at one time found himself in North Africa, particularly Libya and Algeria. He had been there at the time of the battle of El Alamein, the turning point of the war in North Africa. As a result of this he had become very interested in Arab culture, as well as the Middle East in general, he later brought in some of his drawings to show me. I was very pleased to see them, I very much wanted to draw as well as he did. He suggested that I did a lot of pen and ink drawings and used water-colour paints on them.

'You can always work them up as oil paintings after you get back, if you want to.'

I booked myself a driving test in three weeks' time, and went to a BSM (British School of Motoring) shop and organised an intensive series of lessons. They were very helpful about me financing it by paying week by week, they even gave me a discount. I drew out enough from my meager savings account to pay the first week. I had my first lesson, as early in the morning as I could, on the Wednesday. I'd managed to get a provisional driving licence on the Tuesday.

All of this took up a lot of my time and I was concerned about keeping up with my painting at the College. I managed to make progress with my 'Thurloe Square' painting, but little else. However I consoled myself with the thought that I would be doing a lot of drawing and painting during the long vacation.

I saw very little of Sylvia because of all this, when I did she seemed to have withdrawn inside herself again and hardly responded to my efforts to make conversation with her.

I worried about her, especially after she had told me about her dream, or nightmare. I hesitated to tell her that I was going away for the whole of the summer vacation. She lived with her parents in London and originally I'd hoped to see her during that time. I felt an unexpected tenderness and concern for her.

The driving lessons went well, especially after the first two or three. It was quite hair-raising at first, learning to drive in the busy London streets. I was much encouraged when the instructor said I was a 'natural'. I was determined to pass my test first time.

Friday came and I went round to where Andy lived, to wait for that 'phone call from Simon.

The house that Andy lived in was some way up a road, which led north from the underground station at Notting Hill. It was in a long terrace of mid-Victorian houses. They were of the period when the architecture of these houses still had echoes of an earlier Georgian architectural style, with porticos supported by pillars and steps leading up to panelled front doors. They were three and four stories with basement areas, painted stucco, which had once been white, but was now a sort of dull grey, with much chipped and peeling paint, smoke-stained by the coal fires of a hundred years. Once this area had plainly been prosperous, but was now sadly neglected. Some windows were boarded up. Others had rather ragged and dirty curtains. The whole area was now a slum.

When I reached the house in which Andy lived, I climbed the steps to the front door. There seemed to be a myriad of names on the various bell pushes. With difficulty I located the name 'Andrews' and pushed the bell. Before I got a response the door opened and a large black man came out. 'You visiting, man?' He enquired, I nodded and pointed to the name on the bell push. He held the door open for me, just as I heard Andy's voice on the door 'phone.

'Its OK, I'm in.'

I thanked the man for holding the door open.

He's on the third floor.' He said, as he slipped past me.

I waited in the hallway, I could hear Andy coming down the stairs.

'Hi.' he said, 'The 'phone's there.' He pointed to the wall near the staircase. It was in fact a pay 'phone, doubtless because of the number of people living in the house and the difficulty of dividing up the bill. He sat down on the third stair, waiting with me for the 'phone to ring. I hoped he wouldn't stick around when Simon called, I was concerned that he didn't hear too much.

I looked around the hallway, it was very shabby, rather like the exterior of the house, it seemed as if it had not been painted since before the war. What paintwork there was could have been originally cream, but was now a rather dirty grey. A large section of plaster had fallen off one wall, leaving brickwork exposed. There were pipes and wires exposed, running along the top of the walls. A large fuse box and electricity meter was visible at the top of one wall. There was also that unidentifiable smell, made up of various forms of cooking over a long period of time. Perhaps the most pervasive smell, which overlaid all, was fish, which had been cooked or fried.

Andy watched me gazing around with a certain amusement.

'Not quite up to your standard, eh?' Andy had been to where I lived. Although it was in Clapham, south of the river, in a rather poor area, it was in a tiny crescent of small, late-Georgian houses, they were a bit shabby, but not like this. A married couple that lived there owned the house, I was their only tenant, living in the basement. They were a nice couple that owned it, and they kept the inside of the house immaculately. The only reason I could afford to live there on my own was because I supplemented my small grant with working in the theatre.

'Yes, well it's a bit different.'

'When you finish your 'phone call come up and see where I live, there are four of us who share, we're all students.'

'OK, I will, but I don't have much time, I need to get to the theatre by 7.15 latest.'

At that moment the 'phone rang. I picked it up, there was a crackling sound with various voices speaking to one another. I heard a French operator, then an English operator, finally Simon's voice, rather distant, with a sort of echo, and lots of crackling, also the sound of music.

'Christopher?'

'Yes.'

Andy took his cue and started upstairs, he gestured to me to come up afterwards.

'Christopher, I don't have much time, I'm making this call from a pay 'phone in a café in the Marais. I have a pile of 'jetons' here, but they won't last long on an international call. Tell me how you're doing? You are coming aren't you?'

'Jetons?' I thought, 'Yes, yes, I'm with you.'

'Great!'

I quickly told him what I was doing, driving lessons, the arrangement for a driving test. My plans for checking at the Israeli Embassy about a visa, informing the theatre that I was going to be away, asking Andy to stand in for me, getting materials together. I also told him about the scooter which my father had bought for me.

This latter gave him pause for thought, then, 'That's a great idea, learn to drive it, there are lots in Israel, I'm sure you'll be able to rent one.'

Oh shit, I thought, now I am going to have to take a test on the scooter.

'When do you finish the term at College?'

'The 15th of August'

'OK, can you come here on the 22nd? That will give you a week to get your stuff together.'

'I can manage that.'

'Alright, I'll organise a ticket for you to Paris on the 22nd, then we'll have a couple of days to talk about things, then El Al have opened flights from here to Tel Aviv, so I'll get you on a flight there on the 24th.'

'El Al?'

'It's the new Israeli Airline . . . actually it's not that new, it really began in a small way in 1948, but now it is becoming a full blown airline. Listen I'm running out of jetons, I'll write to you.'

'OK, I'll write you back.'

'Bye!'

The line went dead, I hung up. Well, I thought, now I am committed, I'll have to get everything together as soon as possible.

I made my way up the stairs until I reached the third floor, which was also the top floor. There was one door there and I knocked on it. Andy opened the door immediately, he was obviously expecting me.

'Come in.'

I followed him in. The first room appeared to be a communal living room. There were several upright dining-room chairs, none of them matching. There was a small two-seater sofa, a rather battered arm chair, a basket chair with a couple of cushions with rather unlikely floral patterns, that looked as if they had been brought from somebody's home. A threadbare carpet covered the centre of the floor, with imitation parquet linoleum surrounding it. There was a coffee table of sorts, heaped with magazines and elderly newspapers, and the remains of someone's meal, with traces of egg still sticking to the plate. I took in all this rather quickly, as I was anxious to get on my way. It was plain that this was a 'student flat'.

'Very nice.' I said.

Andy laughed, 'Nice is not how I would describe it, but we like it. Come and see the other rooms.'

There were three small bedrooms, Andy had the largest, with what looked like a double bed, neatly made up to my surprise, it also had a small chest of drawers. The other two were smaller with single beds and very little else, boys clothes scattered everywhere. There was one bathroom. A line of socks and pants were drying on a line strung over the bath, and, to my surprise, a brassiere, and two pairs of female panties. I looked at Andy enquiringly.

'Oh, they're Sarah's.'

'Sarah?'

Yeah, there are two other guys and Sarah.'

I decided not to question him any further then, as I was in a hurry to get on my way, it could wait until I saw Andy tomorrow at the College. We went back to the living-room.

'Where is everyone?

'Ron and Steve are down at the pub I expect, and Sarah's got a job as a waitress in the evenings.'

I needed to get on my way to the theatre.

'Thanks a lot for the 'phone, I'll see you tomorrow.'

'OK, you can find your way out?'

'Yes, of course.'

I hurried downstairs, then up the road back to the Underground station.

On the way to Sloane Square where the theatre was, I thought about Simon's call. I could just about get everything together by those dates. A lot depended on whether I could get my driving tests successfully. I must check tomorrow, when I could get a test for the scooter as well.

That evening, after working at the theatre I took the late train to visit my parents. I had asked at the theatre if I could take Saturday off, Peter the lighting consultant was working the switchboard, so I was mainly helping the stagehands. It was a really slow train, it stopped at every small town on the way, it was known as the 'milk train'. It eventually arrived at 2.15 in the morning. I had told my mother I would be late, and that I would make my way home on my own. From the station it was a three mile walk and usually took me about 40 minutes. When I got there and found the key under the doormat, I let myself in. Typical of my mother, who never believed that I had enough to eat, there was a tray with some food on the hall table. I balanced the tray carefully and crept upstairs, without putting a light on, anxious not to wake anyone. I might as well have not bothered, inevitably as I reached the door of my bedroom, she called out, 'Are you alright dear?'

'Yes mother.' I replied patiently. I was twenty-three years old and my mother seemed incapable of coming to terms with the fact that I was not a child anymore.

In spite of arriving so late I was up early next morning. My mother was preparing breakfast and my father was in the bathroom.

This was a good opportunity for me to tell my mother about the trip to Palestine. She was taken aback at first, worrying about whether it would be safe, but after I explained that it was quite an honour for me to be chosen by New Horizons, she came round to the idea. Anything that I did in the area of art gave her great pleasure, as she liked to think that all my 'artistic abilities' came from her.

My father came down and we sat down to breakfast. I thought he was looking much older, and he seemed to have lost some of his height, he was also losing his hair. He was very cheerful though and thought that the trip to Palestine was a great opportunity. He told me with some pleasure about the scooter he had bought for me, and I was effusive in my thanks. He said that the dealer was holding it for me and that we should go along after breakfast and collect it. They asked me questions about Paris and I gave them the same expurgated version that I had given Andy. My parents came from an era when travelling abroad was regarded as a luxury, only available to the very rich. They had been once to Paris and my mother never forgot a visit to the 'Galeries Lafayette' a large store, again rather like Harrods in London. To her, that was the most significant event in the whole of her visit to Paris. Her first question to me was, 'Did you go to the Galeries Lafayette?' I had to confess that I hadn't. Their time in Paris had been of very short duration and not long after that the Second World War occurred, so there was no longer any possibility of visiting the Continent. Now their income, my father's pension, was so small that there was no likelihood of that sort of travel.

After we finished our breakfast my father and I made our way to the scooter dealer, which was quite close to where we lived, so we were able to walk there. It was not often that my father and I spent time alone together and he was unusually talkative. Now he was retired he was enjoying life far more than when he worked for the tobacco factory, where he had been a 'middle manager'. He talked about his involvement with the local opera company, how much he enjoyed the singing, the voluntary, unpaid work he did for them as a business manager. How he also did small paid jobs for the local council, like taking part in a traffic census, or organising a polling station when there was an election, either national or for the local council. I was very touched by this sudden closeness from my father. He had always been working during my growing up years, I knew much more of my mother's life than his.

The scooter, when we arrived at the dealer's, was already standing in the forecourt. It was just what I wanted, it was a very light grey, almost off-white. It had a windscreen already fitted and the dealer had affixed L-plates to show that I was a learner. I sat astride it and kick started it. A friend of mine at the College had one very similar, he had shown me where the clutch was, how to change gear, where the brakes were, how to switch on the lights, and other details, including what sort of fuel it required, which consisted of a mixture of petrol and oil. He had also allowed me to drive a few yards on his. The controls were in fact very simple. I was delighted with it.

My father watched me drive it around the forecourt, then, seeing that I seemed to know what I was doing, suggested that I drove it back home, while he collected the purchase documents from the dealer. He would walk back, as I couldn't take him as a passenger as I was still a learner. I drove off, and with a few wobbly moments, arrived back home. My mother came out to admire the scooter and instruct me to be careful.

Before my father returned she sat me down in the kitchen while she made a pot of tea.

'There is something I need to tell you before your father comes back.'

I waited expectantly while she made the tea. She then sat down with me at the kitchen table.

'I think you should know that your father is not well. He went to the doctor a couple of weeks ago and he sent him to the hospital for tests. It seems that he has a rather bad heart condition, I am worried about him.'

I was startled to hear this, somehow, like most of us, I assumed that my parents would be there for ever, the idea of one of them dying had never occurred to me.

'Is there anything that can be done?'

'He is taking some medication, which seems to help, and is careful about his diet, no more fatty foods, and he must take more exercise, not too strenuous though.'

I looked at my mother, she suddenly looked older. I got up and put my arm round her.

'Don't worry mother, I'm sure if he take his medication and is careful he will be OK.'

She rested her head against my shoulder for a moment. We heard my father coming in, so I hastily returned to my seat.

My father came and joined us at the kitchen table.

How did you find the scooter?'

'Its wonderful Dad, just what I wanted, I can't thank you enough.'

He looked pleased at this, 'Well that should mean you won't be hitchhiking up and down from London anymore.'

Hitchhiking everywhere was a preferred way of travelling since my days in the Army.

'Yes, I suppose so.'

Actually I had always rather enjoyed that method of travelling, I had met many very interesting people doing this.

My mother suddenly interrupted, 'Christopher I have some news for you. June is getting married.'

She looked at me expectantly, hoping no doubt that I would look sad about this. In fact I felt a great relief, I had not forgotten June and felt bad about the fact that I had hurt her feelings.

'Great,' I said, 'Who is she marrying?'

'A nice young man, he works in a bank.'

Perfect I thought, she needs someone like that, not some itinerant artist like me, she wanted solid security. I wondered what she would think about the trip to Palestine that I was about to do.

That evening I called June and congratulated her. She asked me how I was getting on at the Royal College. I told her that I was doing OK. She asked me if I had a new girlfriend.

'No not really.' I would not call Sylvia a girlfriend, in the sense she meant, she was someone I cared about at that time in the most Platonic way.

She went on to talk about their marriage plans, when they planned the wedding, where they were going to live. Finally she said, 'Do you ever think about me?'

'Yes of course.'

There was a silence for a moment, then, 'I loved you Christopher. I will always miss you.' Then she hung up.

I stood with the 'phone in my hand and wondered whether I should call her back. I realised that if I did I would be drawn into the opening up of our relationship again. I put the 'phone down.

The next day I told my parents that I was going to ride the scooter back to London. I had been practicing on it around town, and a short trip out into the country. I now felt reasonably confident that I could make the journey back to London, although I intended to do it as carefully and as slowly as possible.

I decided to leave quite early in the afternoon, anxious to get back to London before it was dark.

I said goodbye to my parents and promised to ring them when I arrived back to London, to assure them that I was safe and sound. The trip went well, the only time I was nervous was when I began to enter London traffic, as at that time it was busy with returning weekend traffic. I made my way to my flat in Clapham, parking outside. When I opened the door and went inside I found a letter, which had obviously been delivered by hand. I didn't recognise the handwriting. Before I read it I went out to a 'phone box nearby and called my parents. They were relieved to hear that I got back safely. I promised to come down again before I made my trip to Palestine.

When I got back to the flat I sat down and opened the letter. It was a very short note from Sylvia.

> *Dear Christopher,*
>
> *I have not spoken to you for a while and I'm sorry. I am staying home for a few days as I have not been well, my father is delivering this to you. Please come and see me.*
>
> *Sylvia*

There was an address in Putney at the top, and a telephone number. I decided I would call the next day.

In the morning I went out and prepared to start the scooter. As I sat astride it the man who owned the house came out of his front door, obviously on his way to work.

'That looks very nice', he said.

'Yes it is, my father gave it to me.'

'Lucky you, I was thinking of getting one myself.'

He set off down the road as I kick started the scooter. As I passed him he waved. The journey to College was quite demanding as I had to deal with the early morning traffic, but I could feel myself growing in confidence with each journey I made. When I got to College I parked in the entryway to the Painting School, alongside the other one owned by Jim, the friend who had given me instructions. I went up to the studios, but found that Andy was not in yet, I looked forward to showing him my new acquisition.

During the course of the day I managed to arrange a test for the scooter. It was before the driving test for the car. Jim had told me that it would be quite easy as long as I read the Highway Code booklet I had been given, and abide by all the instructions. Later in the afternoon I found a 'phone box and called Sylvia's number. A man's voice answered, it had a very strong accent and I assumed that it was Sylvia's father. He was pleased that I had called and gave me some instructions on how to get to where they lived. I said I would be there at about 4.30 the following afternoon.

When Andy had come in, rather late for him, as he was normally a very 'early bird', we went to have our regular morning break at the V and A café. I had time now to question him about Sarah. He reluctantly admitted that Sarah was sharing his bed. I was rather pleased for him, as I had begun to wonder if he would ever have a girlfriend. It seems that it had started at some party he went to, initially it was simply lust on both their parts, but now it had grown into a strong relationship.

She was in the Textile Design School, which was based in another building not far away. There were a number of schools grouped under the title of Royal College of Art. These included the School of Sculpture, The School of Engraving and Illustration, The School of Ceramics, The School of Interior Design, The School of Fashion, The School of Industrial Design. Recently another one had been added, The School of Stained Glass. This latter was largely due to the considerable destruction of churches and their windows during the German 'blitz' in the war. The School of Painting, which Andy and I were in, was regarded as the 'cream' of the Royal College.

The next day I went to College on the bus and tube. The rest of the day I spent working on my painting and doing some 'life' drawing. At 4 o'clock I set off for Putney, which was south of the river. I had decided to take the Underground, rather than go by scooter. I found the address without much difficulty, largely due to Sylvia's father's instructions. It was a small, rather modest late-Victorian house, more red brick than the houses where Andy lived. There was no portico or pillars and the downstairs front room was bow fronted. It was identical to the other houses in the road.

I rang the bell and the door was opened by what I assumed was man, presumably Sylvia's father. He was probably in his 50's, quite short with a round face. He had a small greying moustache, and was going bald. He smiled at me.

'So, you are Christopher? Come in, come in.'

He led me into the small front room. It was furnished with a comfortable sofa and two armchairs. There was a fireplace with a 'fire guard' in front of it, and a very polished brass fender. On the mantelpiece there were some framed photographs, one of which showed a couple with a small child. I could see that it was Sylvia's father, much younger, with a pretty woman, who I assumed was Sylvia's mother, the child was Sylvia, probably about eight years old. They were all laughing at the camera.

'Can I get you some tea? My wife is at work at the moment, but she will be back soon.'

'Should I not see Sylvia first?'

'Yes of course, I'm afraid she is still in bed, she has had a bad case of the 'flu, but she is getting better. Let me go and tell her that you are coming up to see her.'

He left me in the room and I had time to examine it in more detail. There was a small bookcase against one wall. Most of the book titles were in a foreign language, but some of them were in English. There was one very large book, which I examined, it was an omnibus edition of all George Bernard Shaw's plays. When I was about 14, I had, like Sylvia, a bad case of 'flu, and when I was recovering I had read, in a similar edition, nearly all of his plays.

We went upstairs, Sylvia's bedroom was at the back of the house. We went in and I saw Sylvia sitting up in bed. She looked very pale and I could see that she was still recovering from the illness. She was wearing what I assumed was her schoolgirl 'nightie', with what looked like tiny bunches of 'forget-me knots' sprinkled across it. Round her shoulders was a pink cardigan, with crochet flowers around the collar. She looked so small, and more like a child than ever.

'Here he is,' said her father. He turned to me, 'I'll leave you here, would you both like some tea?' We both said yes. After he was gone Sylvia patted the bed, 'Sit here.' I sat down.

'Thank you for coming.'

'I wanted to see you, I didn't know you were ill.'

She asked me what I had been doing and I described my visit home and how my father had given me a scooter. I told her that I was taking driving lessons and that I had driving tests arranged in about two weeks' time. Her father reappeared with two cups of tea. I helped her sit more upright in the bed, so that she could drink the tea. When I put my arm round her shoulders to do this I could feel how thin she was. She listened to everything I said but I could see that she was distracted about something.

She suddenly took my hand, 'Christopher, I had that dream again . . . it was so real!' Her voice shook and I saw tears running down her cheeks. I put my arm around her again. She pressed her face against my shoulder, I could feel her tears warm through my shirt.

'Sylvia, it's only a dream, it's because you have been ill, that you have had a nightmare, nothing is going to happen to me,'

After a moment she sat up again and searched under her pillow. 'I wrote you a letter.' She produced a rather crumpled envelope, which she passed to me. 'Don't open it now, read it later.'

She found a small handkerchief in the bedclothes and blew her nose, quite noisily for a little girl. 'I'm sorry, I keep crying when I see you, I just . . .' She did not finish her sentence, she smiled at me 'I'm so pleased to see you, I didn't mean to spoil it.'

I looked round the room, it was quite large for a bedroom, there was a drawing board and a small easel and a table with a palette, a jar with brushes sticking out and several paint tubes, scattered about. There was also another table with piles of what looked like drawings. It was obviously her workspace, as well as her bedroom. She saw me looking round the room.

'My parents are very kind, they wanted me to have my own studio so they gave me the biggest bedroom.'

There was a small bookshelf, laden with what looked like 'art books'. I went across to look at them. They were mostly monographs of various artists, Chagall, Odile Redon, Gustave Moreau, Fuseli, Hieronymus Bosch, Richard Dadd, Gwen John, Van Gogh, Munch, and a small book on an artist called Balthus. There was also a book called, *The World through Blunted Vision,* an interesting book by Patrick Trevor-Roper, which I had read, about the physical and psychological impairments of some artists, which may have contributed to their creative abilities.

Mostly they were the darker fantasy artists, apart from Gwen John and Balthus, although the latter I did not know. Richard Dadd had actually gone mad and murdered his father, spending his later days in the newly built Broadmoor, a hospital for the criminally insane, where he did some of his finest paintings.

Sylvia began coughing, I went back to her, she was struggling to get her breath, I put my arm around her as she coughed and choked. Eventually the coughing subsided.

'I'm sorry, I thought I was past this, but it keeps coming back, I think I am still not very well.' She managed a rather pathetic smile. 'I'm not much fun am I?'

I felt so sorry for her, she looked so frail, I wanted to gather her up in my arms. I resisted this though, it was probably something she would have been shocked by. Anyway I had no intention of encouraging anything that could be interpreted as an overture to love. I had enough problems already.

I patted her hand, 'You must stay in bed for a few more days and recover properly. I'll come and visit you again soon.' I sounded like a doctor delivering an opinion. 'I have to leave now, otherwise I'll be late for the theatre.'

She nodded, 'Please come again, soon'. I kissed her on the forehead. As I left she raised her hand to me in a farewell gesture.

I went downstairs. Her father was waiting for me in the front room.

'I'm sorry, I have to go.' I explained to him about my job at the theatre. He asked me if I was walking to the station at Putney. When I said I was, he asked me if he could accompany me.

At first we walked in silence, then he suddenly asked me how I thought Sylvia was doing.

'Well, she certainly still looks weak, and she still has a very bad cough, but I would have thought that after a few more days she will begin to get better.'

'No I didn't mean about her 'flu. I meant in general, at the College and with other people.'

This was an interesting question for me, how should I answer? Shall I tell the truth, about her reclusive manner, her dark and unresponsive moments, her seeming separation from any everyday contact? Should I prevaricate and say that she seemed fine, and that she was doing very well, I felt somehow he needed to hear the truth.

'She seems to have swings in her mood, sometimes she's quite happy and full of energy, then another day she retires into herself and hardly responds when I speak to her. It's almost like a darkness has descended on her.'

'Yes, yes, that is how she is, increasingly so, we are very concerned about her. Does she have other friends at the College?

'No, to be quite honest I have never seen her talking with anyone else.' We walked on in silence for a while, then, 'She has become very fond of you; I have never known her talk so positively about a boy. She said that you and your friend helped her enormously with her first year exhibition.'

'It's nothing, we just remembered how important it was at the end of our first year.'

We were getting near the station. He was pondering something, then, just as we reached the station he said, 'Could we meet again? I would like to talk to you more about Sylvia, there are some things I think you should know.'

I told him I would call him in the next couple of days.

As I travelled back towards Sloane Square and the theatre, I thought about what he had said about Sylvia, especially in relationship to me. Of course I was aware that my concern for her could be interpreted as something more intimate. I didn't want to withdraw from her, especially as I was very conscious of her vulnerability. In truth I was very attracted to her, but at the same time I knew that any physical approach by me or anyone else would terrify her. How I knew this was not clear, I somehow just knew it. She had been damaged in the past and in my clumsy and as yet still inexperienced way, I was afraid I might damage her further. Perhaps it was eveidence that I was growing up, or at least having some regard for other people.

I suddenly remembered the letter Sylvia had passed to me, It was rather sweet and touching.

> *Dear Christopher,*
>
> *I think about you and your kindness to me very often. Apart from my parents I never had anyone be so kind and thoughtful to me. I know I am not a very interesting person now, and I have these very dark moments, where I want to hide from everyone, but I really don't want to hide from you. Be patient with me, I need your support. Don't give up on me.*
>
> *Very affectionately,*
> *Sylvia. X*

Poor Sylvia I thought, she seems so frail, I mustn't lead her on, or even think of abandoning her.

My time was becoming increasingly crowded, there were only two weeks left before I was due to fly to Paris. I was still taking driving lessons, and when I used the scooter I paid particular attention to the rules in the Highway Code booklet, which I had acquired. Both tests were occurring in the last week before I was due to leave, the first was the scooter, then two days later the car. I needed to make another visit to my father and mother. I had asked Andy to come to the theatre so that I could explain to him how to deal with the lighting switchboard. This would take several visits. I was running out of money as well.

Another letter from Simon arrived.

> *Dear Christopher,*
>
> *How are you doing? How do you find the scooter? The more I think about it, the more I think it would be ideal for what you will be doing. Still, try and get your car driving licence as well.*
>
> *Good news from 'New Horizons', they have sent me an'official letter' welcoming you to Israel and looking forward to your work recording their beautiful new country. They are going to supply you with someone to travel around with you and act as an interpreter, who will also know the country and the areas you may need to go to. They don't say who that will be*

yet but it will probably be someone who speaks English and Hebrew, also hopefully some Arabic as well.

Your main contact at 'New Horizons' will be a man called Yurem Ben Ami. I've met him. He's OK, a good painter and also something of an organiser, which being a bunch of opinionated artists they badly need. I must tell you, Israelis love to argue when it comes to doing anything as a group. As I said, Yurem is basically a good guy, but he is also a passionate Zionist, so avoid expressing any opinion about the things we discussed.

They have booked your flight on El Al, should be good trip as it is on one of their newly acquired Boeing 707's, a jet! They have made some basic accommodation available to you in Tel Aviv, which will be good to use as a base. They will also supply you with some living expenses and refund you for any other accommodation you get while travelling. All good eh?

It's good that you will have base in Tel Aviv, as I will be based in Jaffa, which is very close by, practically a suburb.

I've asked Sayyid to pick you up at Orly. You are booked on the 7.30 evening Air France flight. This time you are staying with me, one of the guys in this apartment is going to be away, in the south of France, so you can have his room.

I will fill you in with more stuff when you come over. Oh and get yourself a few more Passport photos, you may need them for other documents.

This is our first adventure together!!!

Your friend, Simon

Great! I thought, passport photographs, another thing to do. I would have to go to some photographer and have them done. Then I remembered those kiosks, which were beginning to sprout at every Underground station in London. You sat inside facing a mirror, put your money in and waited. About every ten seconds there was a flash and your photograph was taken. When it was finished you went outside, after a while through a slot came four passport sized photographs. It was a bit hit or miss, if you kept absolutely still and didn't blink they were usually OK, but often there was at least one where your eyes were half shut, or you had some idiotic expression on your face. The following evening I found a kiosk at Sloane Square station, and after two attempts succeeded in getting four reasonable photographs.

The weekend coming up was a big changeover of the play. The theatre was run a bit like a repertory theatre, plays ran for six weeks, and then we got another play. As stagehands, and in my case also as a stage electrician, it was a long, busy weekend for us. We did a matinee and evening performance on the Saturday, then as soon as the curtain came down and the audience cleared we started 'striking' the set. This took us until about three in the morning. We took the scenery down, then had to get it out and loaded onto a waiting van. We then took a break until the scenery for the next play arrived.

When it was unloaded we began to stand it up. Round about six in the morning we were given about three hours to go to our homes to clean up and have some breakfast, then we returned to the theatre about nine to nine thirty. We were ready to set up the scenery for the first act of the new play. During the course of that Sunday we worked all day, setting up the scenery for each act in turn. In amongst this I was also involved, with the lighting director, in setting up the lighting for the whole play. This continued all day, until quite late in the evening, when we went to our homes and had some sleep. The Monday was designated as a public rehearsal, so we worked all day, setting the scenery up for each act, so the actors could rehearse and we could continue with the lighting process. Then in the evening the public was allowed in to watch the play.

As a result of this we all earned a relatively large amount of money in overtime, which I very much needed.

There was one week left before the end of our summer term. I worked away, drawing and painting as much as I could. I had several conversations with my tutor about my trip. He was still very enthusiastic about it, and gave me several tips about what materials to take.

I called Sylvia's father and we arranged to meet early the next evening, in the pub next to the theatre. It was a good time for both of us, he was doing some training work in the evenings at a hospital quite near the area the theatre was in.

That evening I arrived early at the pub, to my surprise he was already there, sitting quietly in a corner. He looked up as I approached and smiled, he rose to his feet, and shook my hand. I was not used to such courtesy from an older man. He immediately said, 'Let me get you a drink?'

I had been going to get him one, but he would not hear of it. When he returned with my half of bitter, he sat down and offered me a toast in what I assume was Latvian, we touched glasses.

'How is Sylvia?'

'She is definitely getting better, your visit somehow put new heart in her, you were obviously a tonic.'

'Please give her my best regards.'

He shook his head, 'I'm afraid that I didn't tell her I was meeting you.'

I didn't ask why not.

'You know she is very fragile?'

'Yes I realise that, I am very conscious that she could be easily damaged.'

He was thoughtful for a moment.

'I expect she told you that we are refugees from Latvia.'

I nodded.

'You may want to know why?'

I shook my head, 'Only if you think it's important.'

'Yes I think it is. I was a member of a dissident group, we campaigned to have the Russians leave our country. The Latvian government, such as it was, was dominated by people who did very well out of their relationship with Russia. They had dacha's made available to them, they were allocated Zim cars with chauffeurs, they attended banquets hosted by Russians, they had access to good schools for their children, there were special stores where they could buy good food and clothing. So my voice, along with others, was not welcome to them. We would not desist from our campaigning, so in the end many of us were arrested. My wife continued to campaign, she also was arrested. We were beaten and tortured many times.'

I was horrified to hear this, 'What about Sylvia?'

He bowed his head and studied his hands and was silent for a few minutes. When he looked up I could see what looked like tears in his eyes.

'Christopher, I am going to tell you something which I have never told any other person. I beg of you not to tell anyone else.' He looked at me beseechingly.

'Of course, of course, please believe me.'

He looked at his hands again, then, began to speak without raising his head.

'Her aunt, my wife's sister, took her in, she was only fourteen at the time. Sylvia was very worried, she knew we had been arrested, she had no idea though that we were being tortured and beaten. Her aunt, who knew what was happening, concealed it from her.' He paused again, then, still studying his hands, he continued, 'One day she was returning on her own from school, when she encountered three Russian soldiers. They were drunk. They dragged her into some nearby woods and took it in turns to rape her.'

I felt as if I had been hit in the face by a club, I must have cried out, I could see people turning their heads, I covered my face with my hands, tears flooded from my eyes, between my fingers. I felt myself rocking backwards and forwards. I was shaken with sobs.

He touched my arm.

'Christopher, I'm so sorry, I should not have told you now, here in this public place.'

I shook my head, groping with one hand in my pocket for a handkerchief. I tried to calm myself. When I could, I said, my voice choking with emotion, 'That's so terrible, how could anyone do that to a child!'

'Sadly Christopher, there are many who could.'

I sat there shaken, unable to think properly, without asking me, he got up and went to the bar, returning with a brandy, which he insisted that I drank.

'I needed to tell you, I know you are fond of her, how much I'm not sure, but I also realised that you knew that she is fragile, but now you must realise how much.

We sat for a while, the brandy worked, I calmed down. Inside I was aching with the pain of what had happened to her, and perhaps always would, but for now I had to get on with what I was doing.

'Dr. Haugas,' I began.

'Please,' he said, 'Call me George.'

With his accent, which had suddenly become more noticeable to me, it sounded like 'Jorge.'

'George', I began again, rather awkwardly, it was difficult for me to address an older man, who was a father of someone I knew, by his first name. 'I need to tell Sylvia that I will be away almost the whole of the summer, I have had an offer to do some work abroad, it's rather like a travelling scholarship, it will require me to do a lot of drawing and painting. I know that we are not, or I am not having a relationship with her other than one of friendship, but I have become concerned about her seeming to depend on this friendship, and I don't want to hurt her. Especially now that you have told me about this terrible thing that happened to her.'

I could feel myself getting emotional again.

'Don't worry, I know she still looks like a child, but in many things she is quite grown up. Just tell her how enthusiastic you are about this and she will understand and be pleased for you.'

I was relieved to hear this.

'I will call tomorrow and ask her if she would like me to come again.'

He smiled, 'I don't think there is any doubt that, she will be pleased to see you.'

I looked at the clock, 'I must go, I have to be at the theatre by 7pm.'

'Yes, so must I, I have to be at the hospital by 7.30.'

We left the pub, the theatre was right next door. Before we parted I said, 'I must apologise for my very emotional response . . . you must have been embarrassed.'

He gripped my arm, 'Your response was nothing to mine, when I heard what had happened.' He looked at me, 'You have a good heart.'

I went into the theatre. I was not operating the switchboard until later in the week, Peter, the lighting director wanted to do it for the first few days, in order to 'tweak' it, before handing it over me.

I helped the other stagehands set up for the first act, then went and sat in the small room by the prompt. Sally, the stage manager, who also acted as the prompt, came in. She saw me sitting there. 'Are you all right Christopher? You look really upset.'

I managed a weak smile and said something like, 'Yes I'm alright, I just heard some bad news about a friend, I'm just thinking about it.'

She looked at me closely, but didn't ask me any questions. She patted my shoulder and said,

'Is there is anything I can do?

'I'll be OK in a minute.'

I tried to put on a more cheerful face, but inside I was seething about what Sylvia's father had told me. After I had dimmed the houselights and Sally had cued Ted to raise the curtains I went back to the pub and sat in the corner again with a drink. Now I had this knowledge, my feelings for Sylvia became deeper. I raged inside myself about what had happened to her, she was only a child then, but I would have felt the same if she was older. I was astonished at my extreme emotional response. I had not cried like that since I was a child, it was instant and overwhelming.

I was back on stage in time to raise the houselights as the curtain came down, then I helped the others setting up the second Act.

That evening, after the show had finished I made my way back to my flat in Clapham. I sat for a while, listening to a concert on the radio. I was not anxious to go to bed, I knew that I would have trouble going to sleep, my mind was too disturbed with what I had heard. When the concert finished it was after midnight. I washed myself standing at the kitchen sink, and cleaned my teeth, then went to bed.

As I thought, I constantly returned to what I had heard. I tried to imagine it. Sylvia screaming and trying to run away, being dragged into the woods, brutal hands on her body, the tearing of her clothes, her pleading cries, the hand clamped over her mouth, her eyes wide with terror. The physical shock of her being violated, not once, not twice, but three times! Then they left her, half naked, blood running between her legs, sobbing and terrified. Pathetically trying to drag her torn clothes around her, to stumble and limp through the woods and back to her aunt's house.

The images went round and round in my head, sometimes becoming part of a dream, a nightmare. I tried to protect her, I tried to fight the soldiers, they tied me up and made me watch, I struggled free, I managed to pick up one of their guns to mow them down, it was empty, there was no ammunition. They just laughed and went on with what they were doing, there was no end to it.

Eventually I woke, it was already light.

I was exhausted by my thoughts and dreams, but I knew it was hopeless just lying there, with them all festering inside me. I got up and washed my face in cold water. Looking in the mirror I saw my haggard and drawn look. I must pull myself together, I have so much to do.

I took my scooter and drove to the College. I had one more driving lesson, later in the day. Andy came in about 10 o'clock, we went soon after for tea in the V and A. He asked me how Sylvia was and I told him that I had seen her father the previous evening and apparently she was getting much better, but she would not be back before the end of term, which was the following week.

We talked about my trip and he then made me a very generous offer. We had both grown very interested in photography, he had told me that his parents had given him a camera for his birthday a couple of weeks before. He offered to loan it to me for my trip. It was a Pentax, with a 35 mm lense, and a 150 mm lense!

'Wow!' I said, 'that's great . . . are you sure?'

'Yeah, I think you'll need it, the 150 mm is quite a long lens, and the 35 mm is quite wide.'

I was overwhelmed with this generosity. I had been thinking of getting a longer lens for the Werra, but unfortunately the model I had only had a fixed lens, there was no provision for other lenses, and anyway I couldn't afford it, I was getting very low on cash.

'Well I am very grateful.'

'That's OK, maybe I can use your camera while you are away?'

'Of course.'

This was very good news, it widened the possibilities for photography, as well as the drawings.

That afternoon I took my last driving lesson, although I would be able to use the car for the test. The instructor was very pleased with me, he was confident that I would pass the test. He did offer me one piece of advice, 'If you make a mistake you can always ask if you can do it again, they will often let you.'

I called my parents and said I would come down early on Sunday morning. I also called Sylvia's number, got her father and asked if I could come and visit Sylvia again the following Monday. He went and asked her, although he knew the answer.

'She says, yes please!'

My pay packet that week was nice and fat, as expected after all the work the previous weekend, at least I could pay my rent for the next eight weeks.

Andy brought his Pentax in and I had a chance to try it. I tried out both the 35 mm lens and the 150 mm, they were great! I determined that when I got back from Palestine, I would make every effort to buy one similar. I thanked Andy profusely again.

On the Sunday I got up really early, 5am, and I was on the road with my scooter by 6am. In consequence I was at my parent's house by 8am, much to their surprise, my father came down to the front door in his dressing gown. I told him to go back to bed and I would bring them up tea. Something I had done every Sunday from a very young age. They loved this.

Later we had breakfast and they asked me how I was getting on at the College. I said I was doing quite well, in spite of the other things I was trying to do, and anyway I was probably going to do a lot of work while I was in Palestine.

My father went out to get a newspaper at the nearby shop. While he was out my mother produced an envelope, 'I want you to have this for your trip.'

'What is it?'

'It's some money I managed to save from the housekeeping.'

'I can't take this, you and Dad have been so good to me already, so generous.'

'Don't argue, I want to do it.' She said firmly.

'Thank you, you are kind, I was a little worried about money, what with one thing and another, but I will pay it back as soon as I can.'

'Don't tell your father!'

My father came back with two newspapers and during the morning we read them between us. Something we had done every Sunday when I was at home.

Sunday lunch was always a ritual, roast lamb, roast potatoes and sprouts. My contribution, apart from peeling the potatoes, was to make the mint sauce. While we were having lunch I told them a little about Sylvia and her family, how they were refugees from Latvia, her father was a doctor, her mother a teacher. I also told them that I was concerned about Sylvia, she seemed so frail and I was trying to look after her at College.

My mother listened carefully, she wanted to see if I was taking an interest in her, which was more than just friendship.

I knew my mother was anxious that I had a permanent girlfriend again, she couldn't wait for me to get married and 'settle down'. I tried to make it clear that this was only a matter of kindly concern. I knew I was not succeeding when my mother said, 'Oh, it would be nice to meet her next time we are in London, after you get back.'

After lunch Dad and I went for a walk. We lived on the very outskirts of the town, so quite quickly we were at the beginning of a country lane, which led up to the river, where there was an old watermill. It was a beautiful day, the sun shone, there was hardly a cloud in the sky. We stood on the weir gazing down at the gushing water. It was a place I had been to many times when I was a child. My father seemed to have a need to confide in me.

'You know we are very proud of you having achieved entry to the Royal College of Art, such opportunities didn't exist when I was young, very early I had to find a regular job. I did what I did and made the best of it, but it was not in any way creative, just a job. I was lucky to have it in the 30's when we were in the Great Depression, as it was known. I had dreams of other things but with a family there was little choice.'

He paused for a while as we watched a fish trying to swim up the gushing water, and giving up in the end.

'I think you should know that recently I went to the doctor, who showed some concern about my health. He sent me to the hospital to have some tests. He got them back on Friday. The prognosis is not good, unless I take care of myself.'

I did not say that I already knew that he had been to the doctor and had these tests. The news to me was the results of these tests.

'Did the doctor give you any medication?'

'Oh yes, for blood pressure and other stuff. He says that if I am careful, watch my diet, exercise regularly and generally look after myself, I should be around for years.'

'Maybe I shouldn't go to Palestine?'

'Of course you must! The best tonic in the world for me is to see you having these sorts of experiences, living the life I would like to have had. Life is an adventure, seize every opportunity.'

We started walking back.

'I have something for you.' He reached inside his jacket and pulled out an envelope.

'Here is some money to help you. I have always kept a small savings account, this is from that.

I started to protest, but he wouldn't hear of it. 'Listen, this gives me great pleasure . . . but don't tell your mother!'

I had to smile, here were both my parents being very generous to me, but insisting that I didn't tell the other one.

That evening I took the train back to London. I had decided to leave the scooter with my parents. I had made an arrangement with Jim, the student who had a similar scooter to mine, to borrow his for the scooter test I was having later in the week. Otherwise I could manage what I had to do before I left, using public transport in London. I didn't want to leave the scooter parked on the street in Clapham while I was away, even if it was parked outside the house I lived in. It was not safe. I also borrowed a medium sized suitcase from my parents.

My mother insisted on accompanying me to the station. When the train arrived she said, 'You will take care of yourself, won't you? I shall worry about you.'

'Yes mother, of course I will. It's an adventure, I am so looking forward to it, and anyway Simon will be there as well.'

She liked Simon and regarded him as a responsible friend. I didn't disillusion her. The train pulled out, she stood on the platform waving at me until we went into the road tunnel, just outside the station.

On the train I opened the two envelopes which my parents had given me. The one from my mother contained £25, the one from my father £50! £75 altogether! Wow! I had never had so much money in my life. This would take care of all my current financial problems and leave me with a surplus for when I came back. I called them when I got back to London and thanked them profusely, individually of course.

On the Monday I went to visit Sylvia again. When I arrived her father opened the front door for me as before and led me into their front room. Sylvia was sitting on the sofa, in her dressing gown, I could see the lacy top of her nightdress underneath, peeping out at the top. She looked even more like a child. I suppressed a surge of emotion as I looked at her, conscious of the terrible story her father had told me. She was looking much better and greeted me with a bright smile. Her father volunteered again to make us tea and disappeared, presumably to the kitchen. I sat on a chair facing her, but she patted the sofa next to her.

'I'm so glad you came.' She touched my hand, 'I'm much more cheerful this time, I'm sorry about all that crying last time.'

I noticed that she was barefoot, her feet were so small, I had a sudden desire to kiss her toes, with their little pink nails. I managed to suppress that urge, I felt that she would be totally shocked if I got down on my knees and kissed her feet. I decided to get the reason for my visit out of the way.

'Sylvia, I'm going to be away during the vacation, I have had an invitation to visit Palestine and Israel by an art society in Tel Aviv, to do a series of sketches and paintings around the country, to show how beautiful they are making it. It's like a travelling scholarship, they are going to pay all my expenses.'

She thought for a minute, 'Will you be away the whole summer?'

'Yes I'm afraid for the whole time.'

She looked a little disappointed, but then said, 'that's wonderful, I'm really pleased for you. When you come back will you show me some of your sketches?'

'Of course.'

Her father came in with the tea and a small plate of biscuits. After that he excused himself, saying that he had to do some studying for his upcoming final medical exam. I think he was just being tactful.

I talked to her about the trip, explaining that my friend Simon would be there. She had heard about Simon, but I hadn't given her much detail.

She listened to everything and seemed enthusiastic for me. I looked at my watch, it was getting late and I needed to go.

She saw that I was about to leave.

'Christopher, before you go I must tell you about another dream I had.'

I braced myself for a further ominous prediction.

'This was a happy dream, we were dancing together, we were at one of those College 'hops', we danced and danced, you were so good, we danced all night. Everyone stopped to watch us. We danced so long that everyone had gone when we had finished. We went out in the street and it was just getting light. You said you would walk with me all the way home. Then I woke up.'

Her eyes were bright, with what I thought was pleasure, and she seemed to be holding the image of us dancing in her mind. Then I saw that her eyes were bright with tears. She bowed her head and I saw the tears dropping on her neatly folded hands.

I put my arm round her thin shoulders. 'It's a lovely dream, we'll do it when the term starts again, at the first 'hop'. Don't be upset, I will look forward to it.'

She smiled at me through her tears. 'Yes . . . please come back safely, I shall worry about you.' She lifted her hand to wipe her tears away. I noticed that when she did that the sleeve of her dressing gown dropped down enough to reveal a bandage on her arm.

I kissed her cheek, tasting the salty tears, and hugged her tightly. 'Don't worry, I will be OK, it's an adventure. I will write to you.'

She held my hands briefly, before letting me go.

I went to find her father in the next room. 'I have to go now Dr. Haugas.'

He got up, 'Jorge,' he said firmly.

'Yes of course . . . George.' Why did I find it so difficult to call older men and women by their first names?

'I'll walk with you to the station, if I may.'

As we left the house I turned and saw Sylvia standing at the window, watching us. I waved and she raised her hand in reply, she did not smile though.

Her father and I set off down the street. 'She seemed much better. More cheerful I think.'

'Yes . . . she goes through these swings of mood though . . . when she is down its like a blackness descends on her, and she has a tendency to self harm. In my profession there is much research going on about this condition. It seems to be related to a chemical imbalance, rather than a psychological state. Although having said that, it is sometimes brought on by a trauma of some sort. People suffering from this condition are referred to as 'bipolar.'

Well she has certainly had the trauma, I thought. 'Is there any treatment for her?'

'Lithium carbonate is sometimes used, it's a by-product of lithium, which is an alkali metal.'

I was getting out of my depth. 'Is Sylvia being treated with this?'

'So far I have not encouraged it, I am not sure whether it has been tested enough yet, it may have unforeseen side effects. We'll see later.'

We walked on in silence for a while. Then he said, 'Did you know that she is something of a clairvoyant? She has dreams, which have, on some occasions, proved to have been correct.'

'But not always?'

'No, not always.'

I was relieved to hear this. I was determined to believe that her first catastrophic dream about me was incorrect.

'I told Sylvia that I would write to her.'

'She will be pleased about that.'

We reached the station. He turned to me and held out his hand, 'Good luck on your trip. When you're back, come and tell us of your experiences, you must meet my wife, she has heard a lot about you. We will care for Sylvia and hopefully she will be better when you return.'

On the underground train back I thought about what Dr. Haugas had told me. Poor Sylvia, it seemed that her condition was more serious than I had realised. Bipolar, Lithium, self harm, these terms kept returning in my thoughts. Self harm? I suddenly remembered the bandage I had glimpsed on Sylvia's arm. Was that the result of self harm?

I seemed to have suddenly accumulated people I worry about, my father, my mother, and now Sylvia. What happened to my carefree student days? At least I don't have to worry about Simon anymore . . . or do I?

The next day I had my scooter driving test. As agreed I borrowed Jim's scooter. I passed it OK. I hope I will do the same with the car test on the Thursday. Friday would be the last day of the summer term.

I went through my list of things to do. I was doing well, there was just the driving test, then if I passed, I would just need to upgrade my provisional licences to full. It would require going to one of the government departments in Westminster. All I needed to do then was carefully pack the things I would need, make a couple of last minute 'phone calls, to my parents and Sylvia, then

I would be on my way. Both Andy and my tutor were enthusiastic about my trip, I was then terrified part of the time, then excited another time.

Thursday came and I passed my test. The instructor's advice stood me in good stead. I did well in just about every thing, except my three point turn, which took me about five. I asked the person testing me if I could do it again. He said if we had time. I did it again perfectly and passed. Phew!

Friday came and I handed the switchboard operating over to Andy, promising the theatre that I would come in a couple of times before I left in the following week, to see if everything was OK.

I had a week exactly before I would set off the following Friday to Paris. I called my parents again, they were lovely and asked me again to take care of myself. I called Sylvia's number and got her father. When I asked if I could speak to Sylvia he said, 'I'm afraid she has sunk into a deep depression again. I hope she will recover soon and I will tell her you called.'

'I'll come again.'

'No Christopher, I think this may confuse her, she thinks you have already gone away.'

I didn't pursue it. Although I felt badly for her I still had many things to do. I started to make a list of materials to take with me, including film. I had a backpack and a shoulder bag, which as well as the suitcase I had borrowed from my parents, was going to be my entire luggage. The week passed quickly. I picked up my full driving licence. It had both the car and the scooter on it. I changed some money into francs, I didn't know what Israeli currency was. Simon would tell me when I got to Paris.

On the Friday I made my way out to Heathrow in time for the 7.30 flight. I managed to get a window seat again and soon we were hurtling down the runway. I was finally on my way.

Chapter 5

The flight was on time and I quickly went through immigration. I picked up my suitcase after waiting what seemed like an interminable amount of time for the luggage to arrive at the collection point. Customs just waved me through. I emerged on the concourse, to see Sayyid's smiling face already there to meet me. He greeted me in English. 'How are you?'

I was quite taken aback by this and responded also in English.

'Good, Simon says I must practice the English, good international language, almost as good as the French.'

I was not inclined to argue about this, but privately believed everyone in the world should speak English, it would make life so much easier.

We loaded my bags into the back of his battered Deux Chevaux. We set off for Paris. Sayyid drove with his usual murderous intent, muttering imprecations at every other driver, in what sounded like several languages.

I made very little conversation, I was too intent on clutching the sides of my seat. Although I couldn't see them I was sure that my knuckles were white. There's nothing like learning to drive to make one aware of how appalling other people's driving could be.

As we began to enter the inner city, the lights and sounds of Paris life again dazzled me. I soaked up the occasional patter of French as we stopped briefly at traffic lights, the small bursts of music from a well-lit café, as well as the occasional whiff of French cooking coming from the myriad small restaurants and cafés we passed.

Eventually we reached an area I recognised, St. Germaine. Soon we plunged into those small Left Bank streets which I had walked through with Claudine, four weeks before.

We finally arrived in a street with rows of small shops and art galleries, we drew up outside 7. Sayyid had mounted the narrow pavement on one side, with two wheels actually on the pavement, and two still in the road allowing just enough room for other cars to squeeze by. He got out and took my bags and put them down near the door.

'Je ne peux pas rester ici, et je te verrai plus tard. Passez par cette porte, demandez au concierge de l'appartement de Philippe Vatel, numéro 6, je pense.'

Great, I thought, just the time to lapse back into French.

He saw my confused look, as he began to get back into the car.

'Number 6, Philippe Vatel!' he yelled, and drove off at speed.

In the double doors of the 'Porte cochere' was a smaller door, which opened with a push. I dragged my bags inside.

It was similar in layout to the one Claudine lived in, but slightly larger. I turned to the concierge's door, and tapped on the half glass door. There was a light on inside and I could hear the sound of a radio. Soon I made out the silhouette of a figure shuffling towards the door. When it opened a rather elderly man with a grey beard peered out at me.

'Que voulez-vous?

'Philippe Vatel?'

He pointed across the courtyard to where there was the beginning of staircase.

'Au sixième étage numéro 6.' With that he turned, shut the door and presumably shuffled back to the radio programme I had interrupted.

I carried my bags to the foot of the stairs, there was a row of bell pushes, I pressed the one marked P. Vatel. After moment a voice said 'Qui est là?'

I mustered my French again 'Est ce que Simon la?'

There was a pause, then the sound of someone chuckling,

'Christopher your French is appalling. Come up.'

'Stop laughing and come and help me'.

I struggled up the stairs with my bags. When I got to the fourth floor I looked up the stairs and saw Simon lounging against the banister at the top. 'Come on,' he said. 'What's the matter, are you out of condition?'

'You might help!'

He just grinned at me. When I got to the landing he was on, I was totally out of breath.

'Fine friend you are!'

He grabbed the suitcase and started up the next staircase 'Only two more floors.'

We arrived at the top, there was a small landing and one door, which was partly open, we pushed our way in. It was a long room, with a skylight, which ran nearly the whole length, and a row of windows, which looked across the other rooftops towards the river. There were some paintings stacked against the wall, some drawings also on the wall. It was wonderful, it was like the best studio I had ever dreamed of.

'Wow! This is great!'

'Yeah well, it isn't mine, it belongs to Philippe. There are three others and Philippe. We rent rooms from him. I'll show you mine.'

He took me down a short corridor, running off the big room/studio we were in. He stopped at the first door, 'this one's mine.'

It was a much smaller room than the one we had been in, it had a similar view out of the window though. It had bookshelves running along one wall, filled with English, French publications, and I noted, a small number in Arabic. There were various journals scattered around the room, the bed was unmade. There was a half empty bottle of wine and a glass on a small table near the window. There was a drawing board propped up on the windowsill, with a half finished pen and ink drawing of the view.

'Bit of a shit heap I know, I clear it up every Sunday, which is tomorrow.'

The next room was on the other side of the corridor. 'This is Henri's, he's doing something with mathematics at the University. He's quite brilliant.'

This one was extremely tidy, the bed was perfectly made, and there was a much smaller bookshelf, with neatly lined books, quite a large table with two chairs. There were what looked like textbooks on the table and two notebooks, one of which was open, revealing neatly written sums and equations. Everything was clean and well ordered. The window had a far less interesting view, across the street. In the corner was something that looked like a small piano.

'What's that?'

'It's a harpsichord, Henri is an accomplished musician. He plays a lot of Bach, he says his music is like a series of beautiful equations. Bit anal is our Henri.'

We got to the last door on that side.

'This is Sayyid's, I won't take you in, he's a bit touchy about that.'

There were two more rooms at the end, one was a kitchen, the other was a bathroom with a loo.

It seemed that I was going to have Philippe's room. Compared to the other rooms it was positively luxurious, it even had an en suite bathroom, actually it was a shower and a sink, he had to share the communal loo down the corridor.

'Wow!' I said, 'This is luxury!'

'Philippe's parents are quite wealthy, they financed this.'

'Where is Philippe now ?'

'He's staying in his parent's house in Provence, it's in the Luberon area, near Bonnieux.'

I had no concept where this was in France.

'It's sort of Van Gogh country, not yet discovered by tourists.'

I took my bags into the room, Simon followed me.

'You must be hungry, let's go and eat.'

Before we left, Sayyid came in. Simon suggested he joined us, but Sayyid declined, he had other things to do.

He took me to one of the small café/restaurants round the corner. It was a 'cheap and cheerful place' rather like the one that Claudine had taken me to: long tables, communal eating.

'Where's Claudine?'

Simon didn't say anything for a few moments.

'We sort of split up.'

'Why?'

Simon looked round the crowded café, the table we were seated at already had four other people as well.

'Let's eat first, then we can take a walk down to the river.'

I was beginning to recognise this pattern. Whenever Simon had something to tell, which he didn't want other people to overhear, he would suggest we went for a walk.

While we ate, Simon asked me about my life in London. He was intrigued by my job in the theatre. He had heard about the revolution going on in English theatre. He knew about John Osborne and 'Look Back in Anger'. The New English Stage Company, based at the Royal Court Theatre and Kenneth Tynan, whose penetrating and sometimes acerbic comments and critiques were revolutionising the attitude to current theatre, changing the face of reviews.

I did mention Sylvia somewhere in my account of life at the College, but not in much detail. He immediately focused on this person in my life, I wished I hadn't mentioned her.

'So, are you getting involved with her?'

'No! Absolutely not! I'm just concerned for her, she seems a person who has been damaged in some way.'

He looked at me, there was a tinge of amusement in his expression.

'Oh Christopher, methinks you protest too much.'

I found myself getting defensive.

'All I said was that I was concerned for her, end of discussion!'

He laughed.

'Dear Christopher, you are the original Good Samaritan. You were even like that with me, anxious always to soothe my wounds.'

I felt quite angry at this misrepresentation of me.

'No I'm not! I just care about some people.'

'I rest my case!'

I must have glared at him.

'Christopher, it's alright, you are OK, there should be more like you.'

This did still not mollify me. How dare he cast me in this image, making me out to be some soppy 'do gooder'.

He saw that I was disgruntled still.

'Christopher, it's good that you are like this, it's one of the reasons I wanted you to do this with me, you have a natural empathy for people, you feel their pain, you will understand the pain of the Palestinian people, I love it in you.'

I was somewhat placated by this, although I hadn't thought of myself in this way.

'Come on, let's finish here, we'll go for a walk to the river, then I'll take you somewhere where you can really see a slice of Parisian night life.'

This intrigued me, and my mood lightened. We paid for our food then set off on our walk, it was not far to the river. When we got there we stood leaning against the embankment wall, gazing at the panorama of lights on the opposite bank. To our right were the bridges I had crossed with Claudine, and later had sat and drawn the view from one. It was where Simon, unrecognised by me in his Muslim attire, had praised my drawing. Further on I could see the mass of the Notre Dame. I shivered with delight at my growing familiarity with this city. I resolved that when my trip to Palestine was over and I had finished at College, I would find a way to come and live here.

'You were going to tell me about Claudine?'

Simon thought for a moment. 'The thing is I think she is working for the SDECE.'

My mind went back to the first night I was in Paris, walking back with Claudine to her apartment, after we had been to La Coupole. She had mentioned that Sayyid had warned her about being 'bugged' by the SDECE.

'She can't be! She thought she was being bugged by the SDECE.'

'Look Christopher, the intelligence agencies work in convoluted ways, it may be that she was trying to win your confidence, establish herself in your eyes as being one of the good guys.'

'But I knew nothing at that time, I was a total innocent, I knew about Cyprus and the Egypt stuff but nothing about what's going on in Palestine and Israel.'

'The point is she was sure that I had told you that stuff about Egypt and that you might have received material from me about that. Did she ask you?'

'Yes she did, I didn't tell her anything other than you had worked for Signals Intelligence in Cyprus, tracking Soviet military air movements, nothing more. After all, I didn't know her.'

Simon seemed pleased about this. 'Good for you!'

'I still don't understand why she needed to know about the Cyprus and Egypt stuff.'

'I think you were an unwitting victim of the SDECE's machinations. They thought if you revealed that you had been a willing recipient of covert information from me, they might encourage Claudine to develop a contact with you on the basis of you passing on any other information they might be interested in.'

I was flabbergasted by this conclusion. 'Simon! This is total paranoia on your part. At this rate you will end up mistrusting everyone!'

He went silent. I could see he was thinking about this, there were things going on inside him. I had seen this look before.

'That may be so, but this involves several countries, all of whom have things to hide. I have to be suspicious of everyone.

'Does that include me?'

'No of course not! You are the only one I can really trust.'

I was flattered by this, but still concerned about his changed attitude to Claudine.

'You know she is very much in love with you?

'Is that what she told you?'

'I saw it, there were tears in her eyes when she told me, she really loves you!'

I could see the turmoil going on in his mind, he wanted to believe me, but he was obviously torn by his suspicions.

'Tell you what, why don't you call her tomorrow, see if she wants to meet up, suggest lunch somewhere, I might join you.'

I was not quite sure why I should do this, but I was willing, because I really liked her, and maybe I could try and mediate in some way.

'OK. Now I'm going to take you somewhere very French, or at least very Parisian.'

There was a taxi rank nearby. We got in the first taxi and Simon gave the driver an address, also what sounded like some directions. We drove down countless streets, passing the Montparnasse area and La Coupole, way beyond where Claudine lived. Eventually we arrived in a street called Rue Jules Guesde. We stopped at the entrance to a building, which was set back from the road by a little garden, we entered through a gate and walked up the path to the building. As we got near the door I could hear the sound of music coming from inside. Simon pressed the bell push and a voice answered, asking 'Que voulez-vous?' Simon gave his name and the door was buzzed open.

We entered what seemed to be a large, low-lit room, there were pools of light here and there. The air was thick with cigarette smoke, countless Gauloise glowed in the dark. In a corner at a grand piano, lit by a spotlight, there was seated a dark bearded man, playing an unidentifiable melody, interspersed with singing, in a gravelly French voice, a recitative, it seemed larded with humorous French colloquialisms, and possibly salacious comments, which were being enthusiastically received, with regular laughter and applause, by a largely unseen audience at the further end of the room.

We edged our way down the side, gradually I was able to make out small tables with two or three people seated at each. As we passed, a couple of people called out greetings to Simon, and a rather beautiful young woman, with long dark hair, rose from one of the tables in the middle and hurried over to greet him, throwing her arms around him and kissing him fulsomely on the mouth. He didn't introduce me.

We reached the bar, which was presided over by a large man with an appropriately large moustache. He reached across the counter and shook Simon's hand, then he shook my hand.

Simon ordered two drinks. When they came I saw that they were of a watery white colour.

'What's this?

'Pernod.'

I sniffed it suspiciously, it had a faintly aniseed aroma. I took a sip, it was definitely aniseed.

'It's alright, it could be worse, like absinthe!'

I thought of Degas' 'The Absinthe Drinkers'.

We turned and surveyed the room, nearly all the tables were full, everyone was following the recitative by the piano player. There were bursts of laughter and the occasional response from one of the audience, which would produce more bursts of laughter.

I noticed that there were other instruments on the platform by the piano, a double bass, a drum kit, a clarinet and two guitars. I also noticed that there was a tiny dance floor space in front of the platform, hardly large enough for more than three couples.

'What is this place?'

'It's what the French call a 'Boîte de nuit', it literally means a 'night box', a cross between an informal nightclub, a jazz club, and a piano bar. Parisians love them.'

The pianist finished and there was an enthusiastic round of applause. The lights came up and I was able to see the audience more clearly. There was a cross section of ages, ranging I would guess, between early twenties through to late forties.

One of the tables became free, after ordering two more drinks we sat down. Simon looked very much at home, I had not seen him so relaxed for a long time.

'I love coming here, it has such a nice atmosphere.'

'How did you find it?'

'I first came here with a couple of the students I knew in the early days, when I was first in Paris. There are others, in fact there is one quite close to where Claudine lives, but I much prefer this one.'

'Your French is very good now.' I had noticed that Simon was laughing at some of the colloquial French terms in the recitative.

He shrugged, 'I guess I'm lucky; I pick up languages more quickly than some people. I'm actually trying to master some Arabic at the moment, with Sayyid's help . . . it's quite difficult.'

The lights went down, except on the little dance area and the platform. A group of men climbed on to the stage and took up the various instruments, the pianist resumed his seat behind the piano. After a short interval, while they tuned their instruments, they began a modern jazz piece.

I am not particularly enamoured with modern jazz, it's a little too formal and dry for me. Simon seemed to like it. I'm still stuck on the jazz revival period of the 50s, Bessie Smith, Mahalia Jackson, New Orleans music and Memphis.

After they finished this piece, the group struck up something much more lively and a couple got up and started dancing. As they did so, the young woman, who had embraced and kissed Simon, got up from her table, where she was seated with another couple, and came across to where we were, and grasping Simon's hand proceeded to drag him onto the dance floor.

Simon was very good and so was the girl, pretty soon the other couple left the floor to them and they became a sort of impromptu floorshow. When they finished there was a considerable round of applause.

The next piece was more languid and the girl draped herself round Simon, like a scarf, her arms were round his neck and shoulders and her body was glued to his, there was no escaping the eroticism of this. Two other couples got up and danced in a similar fashion.

After this they returned to the table, the girl appeared to be joining us.

'This is Jeanne.' He turned to her, 'Ceci est mon grand ami de l'Angleterre, il est un artiste aussi, trés formidable!'

She smiled at me and offered her hand, I gallantly kissed it and she giggled, turning to Simon and saying something in French which I didn't understand.

'Pauvre garçon, il croit que je suis une fille, devrions-nous lui dire?'

She had a surprisingly deep voice for a girl.

'Plus tard, permet de voir s'il devine.'

'Vous êtes mauvais!'

She kissed him on the cheek, smiled at me again, then got up and returned to her table.

I was rather put out by this exchange, although I didn't understand it, I felt that there was some joke here at my expense. I was being 'sent up' in some way, which I didn't understand.

'Well, what was that about?'

Simon shook with suppressed laughter

'You are obviously having an affair with this girl!'

Simon shook with even more laughter.

'Stop it! Tell me what it is about!' I could feel myself getting angry.

Finally, choking and spluttering with laughter, Simon said, 'She's not a girl, she's a chap, what is usually called a "transvestite". It's the same in French, his name is Jean, that's John in English.'

I sat back, completely thrown by this.

'But she . . . he looked so . . .' I ran out of words.

Simon looked at me with amusement.

'I've known him since I first came to Paris, he works in a bank during the day. I met him here first and we perfected that dance routine quite soon after that, it goes down well with this audience as you saw.'

'Well it certainly looked like more than a dance routine!'

He laughed, 'Christopher, are you being prurient here? Listen, Jean is happily married and has a small son, he just likes dressing up sometimes in women's clothing. Transvestites are not necessarily queer, many are heterosexuals who just like dressing up. If you moved in those sort of circles in London you would have come across them there.'

'What does his wife think?'

'She's fine about it, she first met him when he was dressed up as Jeanne . . . she's over there at the table with him.'

I felt rather silly and extremely naïve, I actually felt that I was beginning to blush.

Simon looked at me with that faintly amused expression, 'I know how you feel, I was totally shocked when I first found out, now I am rather blasé about it. Come on, let's have one more drink then we should go, its getting late and we need to have serious discussions tomorrow, about where you're going, and what I suggest you do. I have some more information to show you.'

We had two more Pernods, I was beginning to feel somewhat tipsy. When we left we passed by the table where Jean sat with his wife and friend, we said 'au revoir' and Jean blew me a kiss.

We had to walk some way before we found a taxi. It was by now, 1.30 in the morning. When we got back to the apartment it was nearly 2am, I panted my way up the stairs, while Simon positively bounded up. We didn't stay up talking, for which I was grateful, as I was suddenly feeling dog tired. I got myself a glass of water, cleaned my teeth in my 'en suite' bathroom, and after undressing I fell into bed and was almost immediately asleep.

In spite of the late hour we had gone to bed I was awake by 8am. I didn't feel too good, I had a headache, and my mouth was as dry as dust. I took some aspirin, which I had with me, drank copious amounts of water, then had a shower and shaved. By the time I started dressing I was beginning to feel slightly better.

I made the bed, and then headed down the corridor to the kitchen. I was surprised to find that I was not the only one awake. There in the kitchen, drinking coffee was a young man, about my age, with fair, close cut hair. He was neat and compact. Although he was sitting, I had the distinct impression that he was quite short. He had very pale blue eyes, almost grey. In every other way he was quite undistinguished.

He nodded at me as I came in and said in perfect English 'You must be Simon's friend Christopher, he has spoken much about you, I am Henri.'

I was both taken aback and pleased that he knew of me.

'You are Henri, the mathematician?'

He laughed at this. 'Yes, I play with numbers, I hear their music.'

'Simon says you are a brilliant mathematician.'

'Not really, at the moment I am only at the level of a sonata, one day though I hope I will reach the level of a symphony.'

I found this simile to music rather attractive. Having plodded my way though mathematics at school, the thought of thinking about those barely comprehensible sums and equations as music had never occurred to me.

Simon joined us. He was looking rather the worse for wear, his hair tousled and his eyes red. He greeted us with a grunted 'Bonjour,' and sat down clutching a mug of coffee.

'Big mistake, drinking wine and then Pernod.'

I felt rather smug as I had got rid of my headache and was basically feeling a lot better, certainly better than Simon was looking.

He looked at me, 'We need to talk, give me half an hour to clean up, then come along to my room, I've some things I want to show you, then we'll go out and get some breakfast.'

I stayed talking to Henri for a while. It seemed that he had gone to school in England for a couple of years, his father was in the diplomatic corps, or something, and had been posted to London. This explained why his English was almost flawless.

I made my way along to Simon's room and found him tidying up, he had made the bed and was putting his books and magazines in some sort of order. I sat on the chair in the window, where Simon's drawing was still propped against the windowsill. It was a beautifully detailed study, with almost every tile and window perfectly drawn. I was surprised, he had always drawn with much broader strokes when we were at art school, something I had envied, my drawings were more detailed, rather like this drawing, more anal, as Simon would say. I commented on this and Simon said, 'I was trying to do a Christopher drawing.'

'Why?'

'Oh, various reasons' he said vaguely.

When he had finished doing his tidying up he suggested we went out and got some breakfast and he would show me some material when we got back.

There was a café round the corner in a small square, it was Sunday morning and the café proprietor was still putting out the tables in the front. We sat down at one and after a while a young waitress came out and asked us what we would like. Simon asked for a brioche and a cup of chocolate, I also asked for a chocolate but with a croissant.

As there was no one sitting near us Simon felt free to talk about our visit to Palestine.

'When we get back to the apartment I'm going to show you a map of Palestine, showing all the towns and villages 'ethnically cleansed' by the Israelis. As well as that I have a list of all the names of the towns and villages and which province they were in. Also there are three maps showing how the Israelis have gradually usurped large areas of land that was designated as Palestinian.'

'So what are we trying to do there? We can hardly expect to make Israel disappear and no longer exist.'

'No of course not, but I want to expose to the world what the Zionists are doing, to bring to justice the principal people involved in these war crimes, and force the Israelis to withdraw to the original areas approved by the United Nations, and allow all the Palestinian refugees to return to their homes.'

'This is a very tall order!'

'I know, we may not achieve it all but at least we must try.'

I had a couple of questions I wanted to ask.

'These New Horizon people, why do they want to invite me, rather than other more established artists?'

'Well I gave you a big build up, promising young artist, at the most prestigious art school in Britain, highly regarded in artistic circles, award winner . . . that sort of thing. Also they liked your drawings, they are mainly abstract painters, what they wanted was someone more topographical in their approach, and you seemed to fit the bill.'

'What do you mean 'they liked my drawings', they've never seen them!'

'I gave them a couple of mine and said they were yours, the signature was a bit difficult, though as they have never seen it before it didn't matter.'

I thought I was going to explode, 'you forged a couple of drawings and said they were mine!'

'Well not exactly, I did the drawings and only forged your name.'

The blatant casuistry of this excuse actually made me laugh . . . 'Simon, you are a rogue!'

He smiled happily, 'Yes I know, but all's fair in love and war and it worked, its funny really. Anyway you know you are very good, and you can do it.'

There were a few more people arriving for their breakfast and the tables around us were beginning to fill up.

'Lets go back, I'll show you this stuff.'

When we got back to the apartment, Sayyid was in the kitchen drinking coffee and smoking. We said our 'Bonjours'. Henri seemed to have retired to his room, and was doubtless wrestling with his next 'sonata'. I went with Simon to his room. Shortly after, Sayyid joined us.

Simon then showed me a series of maps and documents, clearly demonstrating the massive scale of ethnic cleansing carried out by the Israelis between 1947 and 1949. Sayyid added his comments. I asked Simon if I could take these with me.

'No I don't think it's a good idea, the Israelis search everyone's luggage and carry-on before you even leave, then search it all over again when you get to Lod, the Tel Aviv airport, it would make them very suspicious of you. It's OK though, I can get you what you need when you are there.'

We talked some more about how I could go about recording as much as I could of the massive destruction carried out against the Palestinians. Going to areas where the Israelis had taken over the Palestinians' land and developed it, I would try and record what they were doing, but at the same time record the ruined villages, with drawings and photographs. It was a massive task to accomplish in the relatively short time I would be there. I was curious to know how Simon seemed to know his way round Palestine.

'I've been there twice in the last two years, the last time I was there for two months.'

I remembered Claudine saying that he had been away for two months whilst they were living in Greece. I asked Sayyid when he was last there.

'I cannot go there, I would be killed.'

I was shocked by this, I was about to ask him why he would think that, when Simon interrupted, 'Christopher, are you going to give Claudine a call?'

I had forgotten that I was going to call her. 'Yes, you're right, do you have a 'phone here?'

'No we don't have a 'phone here, it would probably be bugged if we did, the café we were in has one, we'll have to go back there.'

As we walked to the café I asked Simon why Sayyid thought he would be killed if he went back to Palestine.

'Have you heard of an organisation called The Arab League?'

'No.'

'It's a group of Arab States formed in 1945, primarily to promote Arab culture and trade, it includes Egypt, Jordan, Lebanon, Syria and Saudi Arabia, all surrounding the state of Israel. Understandably the Israelis are suspicious of them. Now, since their beginning another six nations have joined. They represent a threat to the state of Israel by their very existence.'

'So where does Sayyid come in?'

'Palestine is part of the League and there has been a strong movement towards forming a Palestine Liberation Organisation, it will primarily be to represent the concerns of the Palestinian people politically, but it will also have a paramilitary arm, called the PLA, the Palestine Liberation Army. Naturally the Israelis hate this idea and would regard it as a terrorist organisation, which is ironic when you consider that Israel was largely formed by what were considered at the time as terrorist groups. Sayyid is working with fellow displaced Palestinians towards establishing the PLA, and the Israelis are out to get him.'

I remembered that visit to the Bagdad café with Sayyid and all the people there who had greeted him warmly.

'What about you?'

Simon didn't say anything for a while, he seemed to be considering his reply. I was getting used to these thoughtful silences. We were beginning to be in sight of the café. Simon stopped, 'Look, I don't want to talk in the café, there is stuff which I can't risk being overheard. You make the call to Claudine then I will tell you more on the way back.'

'What do you want me to say to her?'

'If she's free, suggest you meet her for lunch in the Place des Vosges, she'll know where we usually eat there, it's in the Marais, tell her I may come along, sound her out, she may not want that.'

We got to the café and Simon ordered a couple more coffees and acquired some 'jetons'. They were sort of 'faux' coins and were only for use in these café 'call phones'. It was presumably to stop people smashing the machines to get money from them.

Simon gave me Claudine's number. She picked up immediately 'Allô?'

'Claudine, it's Christopher!'

There was a pause, she's just like Simon I thought, all these periods of silence.

Then 'Christopher! How nice, where are you?'

She seemed genuinely pleased.

'I'm in Paris for a couple of days, any chance you are free for lunch today? Simon says he will try and join us.'

Another pause, what's with these people!

'Alright, yes I can manage it, I just need to cancel something, but it can wait. Where?'

'Simon mentioned something about the Place des Vosges.'

'Yes, I know where he means, the Bagatelle. I'll see you there, say 1.30?'

I went back to Simon who was reading a French newspaper.

'Its OK, she said 1.30.'

When we finished our coffee we set off back to the apartment.

We walked along, the street was practically deserted, maybe they are all at church I thought.

'You wanted to hear about my involvement with the Palestine movement?'

I nodded.

'Well, I told you about the Arab League. They don't have a paramilitary side, their role is to try and mediate on the side of the Palestinians, using political processes. However,' Simon looked around, checking no doubt that there was no one near, 'they do have an intelligence organisation, which does its best to keep an eye on what the Israelis are up to militarily and any other information which they can use. Needless to say it is very covert and if the Israelis get to hear of it, they will react very badly, both politically and in other ways.' He paused again, seemingly searching for words, then, 'The fact is I am working for them, they pay me for information and support me here . . . in fact, although you will be financed by the Israelis, you will be working for them as well. Actually if you think about it, its quite funny really, I'm being paid by an Arab organisation, you are being paid by an Israeli organisation, but we are both working to indict Israeli leaders and the state of Israel.'

I didn't think it was funny at all. What initially had seemed like a jolly adventure, with a possible political result, now turned out to be an extremely dangerous venture, fraught with hazards, which could result in imprisonment at best, or the possibility of something even worse.

'Simon, this is really dangerous stuff.'

'Yeah I know, that's why I have been banging on about the various intelligence agencies who would be more than interested in what we are doing. You think I'm paranoid, well this is the reason for it.'

We were nearly back at the apartment, Simon stopped just before we went in.

'Do you want to pull out, now you realise how dangerous this might be?'

'Of course not! I'm just focusing up on the real hazards. Before I was thinking of it as an adventure, a rather romantic one but not really dangerous, now I realise that it's . . . really dangerous.'

When we got back to the apartment, both Sayyid and Henri were cooking up something together in the kitchen, they asked us if we wanted to eat with them. We thanked them and explained that we were going out to lunch. I looked at Sayyid with new respect.

It was getting near the time that I should set off to meet Claudine. Simon walked with me to the taxi rank, he told me that Claudine knew they were going to Palestine, but knew nothing of the political intent. He had also given her the impression that we had both been invited by New Horizons, so she was unaware that he was there with Palestine Aid.

'I'll join you later, I need to talk to Sayyid about some stuff.'

I sat in the taxi thinking about the conversation I had just had with Simon, as we made our way across one of the bridges and wound our way through various small streets on our way to the Place des Vosges. I was so distracted by my thoughts I scarcely noticed where we were going, until suddenly we were at the Place des Vosges. It was a very beautiful square with tall trees surrounding the square, and equally tall houses in the streets around it. The driver said, 'Où voulez-vous?'

Fortunately I remembered the name of the restaurant that Claudine had mentioned.

'La Bagatelle?

He muttered something in French I didn't catch, then drew up on a corner of the square. He pointed at the arcade along the side of the square,

'Promenade le long de là, c'est quelque part au milieu.'

I recognized the word 'promenade' so I paid him and started to walk along the arcade. I passed several small restaurants, then I spotted Claudine sitting at a table outside one of them. She rose when she saw me approaching and put her arms around me and kissed me warmly on both cheeks, she smelt so nice. I noticed that she glanced behind me.

'So nice to see you again!'

She seemed to genuinely mean it, I too responded saying how pleased I was to see her again.

'Is Simon coming?' 'Yes he said he would come a little later.'

She seemed satisfied with this and proceeded to ask me if I was looking forward to my trip to Palestine. I said that I was, but with some trepidation, reminding her that I had never been abroad until my first visit to Paris, now I was going much further, the Middle East! She smiled and patted my knee, 'We'll make a great traveller of you yet Christopher.'

She asked me about London and how I was getting on at the Royal College. I told her that I was doing my best in spite of spending time preparing for the trip, but I hoped that the work I would do while travelling around sketching and drawing, would be a valuable addition to my portfolio of work. I added that my tutor was all in favour of it. She asked me about my love life and I said that there was no one at the moment. I carefully avoided any mention of Sylvia, as I didn't want a repetition of the conversation I had with Simon. Although I suspect that, as a woman, she would be more understanding.

All the time we were talking I was aware that she was scanning the square, hoping to see Simon. When he did arrive it was from another direction, taking us both by surprise.

'Ca va?'

He immediately kissed Claudine on both cheeks and then fully on her mouth, I saw her flush with pleasure. Whatever had been the trouble between them seemed to dissipate. He sat down beside her.

'I hope Christopher has not been boring you with further tales of our dissolute youth?'

'On the contrary he has been entertaining me with his excitement about the trip you are both embarking on. How you are going round the country doing lots of drawing and painting.'

'Yes we are both excited, we're like young students all over again, setting off on an adventure together, longing to see how the Israelis have saved Palestine from itself!'

There was no ignoring the barbed manner he delivered this comment.

She looked at him affectionately.

'Simon, why do I feel that you have found another cause to support?'

It was Simon's turn to look defensive. 'It's not a cause! I just happen to care for people!'

I thought this was rich, when he had questioned my caring for Sylvia, making it look like some sentimental self indulgence.

'Tell me, what are you really doing there?'

'Just what Christopher said, we're going round the country drawing and painting, trying to make a record of how the country is changing.'

She looked at him doubtfully but plainly decided not to pursue it. She started to tell us what she was doing. Apparently a Paris journal with political leanings had asked her to do an article on how Algeria was developing after the French had left. She was still writing her book, which was about the effect of French influence on the North African States, and the Middle East, which would of course include Palestine, where the French had been great supporters for the establishment of the state of Israel.

'I need to go to Palestine at some point, but not for a while, I'll be interested in your comments about it when you get back.'

'Sure' said Simon, looking at me.

We talked and chattered together, enjoying the sunlight from our shady arcade, watching people with children playing in the square, commenting on them. We had something to eat and the inevitable bottle of wine. Simon seemed to have recovered from his hangover. He told Claudine that he had taken me to a 'Boite de Nuit' and introduced me to a transvestite, how I had been shocked and embarrassed. He told it in such an amusing way that we all started laughing, I could not be offended by him, although I was embarrassed all over again and felt myself blushing at first. At one point I noticed that they were holding hands under the table. I felt really pleased by this, I suppose I am a romantic at heart.

Claudine asked me what time my flight was on Tuesday, I told her that I needed to be there by 9.30 as my flight left at 11 am.

'I'll pick you up and take you to Orly if you like?'

I was really touched by this offer, I knew that neither Simon or Sayyid were going to take me there, and I was not looking forward to lugging my bags to the nearest taxi rank.

'Well that's really kind of you, are you sure you don't mind?'

'I wouldn't offer if I did. Anyway I need to check on some flight times myself, I'm going to Algeria next week.'

She asked Simon when he was flying to Tel Aviv.

'Not until next Sunday.'

'Good, if you are around during the week maybe we could . . .' she trailed off.

'Yes' said Simon, looking at her, 'We could . . . '

The implications of these two truncated statements were clear, I suddenly felt very happy for them. My God I thought, I'm a soppy sentimentalist at heart after all.

We stayed a while longer, looking out at that sunny beautiful square, not saying much, just a mellow silence. Eventually though we needed to depart, Simon and I back to the apartment, Claudine to some previously postponed appointment. Before she left she kissed us both on our cheeks and told me that she would pick me up on Tuesday at 8.45 in the morning outside the building where the apartment was.

After we got back to the apartment we had another long discussion about Palestine and our visit. Simon passed me the letter from 'New Horizons', it had a rather florid letter heading and was in what I assumed was Hebrew. He also gave me a translation into English, without the letter heading, which was a welcoming letter to their beautiful new country, and described my eligibility as an artist who hoped to record their magnificent achievements so far. Finally he gave me my El Al ticket to Tel Aviv.

Then Simon, Sayyid and I went for a meal at the restaurant round the corner. Here we talked about Palestine, Sayyid apparently came from Acre, a fishing port in northern Palestine. He still had a brother who lived there and who was a fisherman and also ran a small restaurant.

Simon was doing something the following day, with Sayyid. I didn't enquire what, but I was sure it was something to do with our covert trip to Israel, I knew he would tell me if it affected my side of the operation. He seemed to be wallowing in the details of this attempt at espionage. In fact he was a natural rebel.

I was quite pleased to have the day to myself. It gave me a chance to go to the Louvre again, without the feeling that I had to leave by a certain time. I also visited the Musee de L'Art Decorative and managed to get to Passy to see the Cartier-Bresson exhibition. I had bought some postcards at the Louvre, I sent one to my parents, and another to Sylvia. That evening Simon and I went to eat at the restaurant we had eaten at the first night I arrived. Henri joined us.

First thing in the morning I was up, washed, shaved and dressed by 8 o'clock, drinking coffee in the kitchen. Simon joined me about 8.15. At 8.30 we started to lug my bags down stairs.

Claudine was absolutely punctual, arriving dead on 8.45, parking as Sayyd had, with two wheels on the pavement. We loaded my bags and Simon grasped my hand and hugged me.

'See you there!'

Claudine drove through the early morning Paris traffic with skill and speed, managing without the stream of imprecations against other drivers which marked Sayyd's progress. When we were clear of the main incoming traffic, Claudine felt able to talk.

'Are you guys going to be alright over there?'

'What do you mean?'

She went silent while she overtook a slow moving camion, once we were clear she felt able to talk again.

'Listen, I know Simon very well, he has that glint in his eye, he's up to something, I don't want you to get into trouble there, either of you.'

I shrugged, 'It's really only a sketching trip, there is no agenda there.'

She sighed, 'Look, I know you are not going to say anything about what you are really doing there, but if it's anything to do with Simon its probably dangerous! He's a rebel, looking for a cause!'

I was amused by her reference to the James Dean film.

We reached the airport, Claudine pulled into the kerb by the departure door.

'I'll drop you here, then I'll find somewhere to park and come back. Don't check in until I get back.'

I unloaded my bags and made my way into the departure area. I looked for the El Al desk, it was right down the far end. I decided to wait near the entry door until Claudine returned.

There were many check-in desks, for both internal flights and international carriers. There was a constant change of information on the board behind the desks. Mainly Air France internal flights to such places as Toulouse, Nice, Cannes, Lyon, La Rochelle, Biarritz and Corsica. The international flights, which were further down, included flights to such far places as Damascus, Cairo, Morocco, Algeria and Tunisia. For the first time I felt exhilarated at the thought of all this foreign travel.

Claudine returned and we made our way down to the El Al check-in desk. There was a small line of people already there. Just before I joined it Claudine drew me to one side, put her arms around me and whispered in my ear.

'Please be careful there, and look after Simon, he feels things so passionately he will get himself and probably you into trouble'.

She kissed me, this time, gently on my mouth then pulled away. I felt a surge of affection for her.

I joined the queue and presented my ticket and passport. In answer to the question, 'Do you have any check-in luggage? I indicated my suitcase and rucksack. I retained my shoulder bag as it contained my sketchbooks, the camera and lenses as well as couple of dozen cassettes of film and the letter from New Horizons. I had a small English/Hebrew phrase book. I was given a boarding pass and a nod towards where the Departure entrance was.

Claudine walked with me as far as the entrance. As I went through I turned and looked back, she was still standing there before giving me a last wave and walking away.

I went through passport control where my passport and ticket were scrutinized and then stamped. The next stage was a baggage check. I was waved to a table for people on the El Al flight. Simon was right, they were extremely rigorous. A short, stocky dark haired young man patted me down, then emptied the contents of my shoulder bag on the table. He went through the sketchbooks page by page.

'Are these yours?' he asked, I nodded, 'Not bad,' he said. He then examined the camera 'Is there film in it' I shook my head. He then asked me to open it, which I did. Finally he read the letter from New Horizons, and for the first time he smiled, 'Good luck,' and waved me on.

I put everything back in the bag and moved into the departure area. There were already a number of people there. I sat down in a corner and looked around. Most of the men were wearing a sort of skullcap, but there were several who had a much more extreme attire. They wore what looked like thick black overcoats and black hats, they were all bearded, even the younger ones. They also had long black locks which hung down on either side of their face. Each one of them carried a book, which they bent over reading, their lips moving, they also seemed to be rocking back and forth. There was a middle-aged man sitting next to me, wearing a skullcap, he noticed that I was gazing at these men with some curiosity.

'They're Hasidic Jews, a rather extreme sect, they always dress like that whatever the weather. It's going to kill them when they get off the 'plane in Tel Aviv.' He had a distinct American accent. He seemed to take a kindly interest in me. He looked at my head, plainly to see if I was wearing a skullcap.

'I guess you're not Jewish?'

'I'm afraid not.'

He laughed 'That's OK, it's allowed'. He explained about the skullcaps. It shows Jewish humility before God, it separates the humble man from God above them. 'That's the story anyway, it's just a habit now amongst most Jews, although I think some men wear one to conceal their bald patch. I don't usually wear one except when I'm amongst this sort of company. In Yiddish they are called 'yamulke'. In Hebrew they are called a 'tippah'. He had just completed telling me all this when the flight was called. There was a sort of mad scramble to the door to get to the head of the line, so that they could get a seat of their choice by being the first on the 'plane.

My new friend from New York said, 'don't worry, we still have to get on a bus which will drive us out to the 'plane.'

He was right, after we passed through the door and had our tickets and passports checked again we went down a short flight of stairs and out on to the apron where two buses waited. We squeezed in the first one just before the doors shut. The bus moved off towards a line of 'planes, we were driven to the very end of the line where a sleek new 'plane with El Al markings on it awaited us. We were right by the door, so when it opened we were the first out, I followed the American up the steps onto the 'plane where we were greeted by smiling stewardesses who pointed us into the interior. We took seats in a row four back from the front, the American waved me in first, so that I was sitting by the window, he took the aisle seat leaving one empty between us. 'With any luck,' he said, 'the 'plane may not be full, so we will have a bit more room. By the way' he added 'my name is Jacob.' He held out his hand.

'Christopher,' I held out my hand in return and we shook.

The 'plane gradually filled up, but not completely, so we were able to retain the single seat between us. Jacob confessed that he was suffering from jet lag, having only arrived from Washington the day before, and might sleep during the flight.

'I'll probably snore.'

The door was shut, one of the stewardesses read out the safety instructions. There was a whining sound, which gradually increased in volume as the engines started up. The plane taxied to the end of the runway, it paused there for a few minutes, then with a mighty roar shot down the runway with increasing speed, faster and faster it went, then the bumping of the wheels on the runway suddenly ceased and we were airborne. At last I was on my way.

Jacob indeed did snore, he did more than that, he muttered in his sleep and occasionally his snores reached a crescendo. I did my best to ignore it, gazing out of the window as France unfolded like a map below me. We seemed to be hurtling along at a much higher altitude than my previous propeller driven flights, to and fro to Paris. I could just see the engines hung on pods below the wing. No propellers? How did they manage? sucking in air and blowing it out behind us.

Sometimes I would see a tiny aircraft, streaking along the other way, with a vapour trail behind it. I supposed we had a vapour trail too, although I couldn't see it.

France unfolding seemed green and lush at first, with tiny rivers and streams winking in the sunlight. We looked down on thread-like roads with little insect-like vehicles crawling along them. As we progressed south the landscape became more bleached and sparser, less forested, but with occasional strips of colour: lavender, yellow and red. To the east I could see a range of mountains, some of the more distant ones had snow on top, the Alps

I supposed. I glimpsed the sea in the distance, it must be the Mediterranean! Soon we swept over the coastline.

My thoughts were interrupted by a stewardess pushing a trolley of drinks. She asked me what I wanted, I settled for white wine. She poured the drink from a little bottle with a screw top, which she placed by the glass of wine already down on the little drop table shelf in front of me.

'We will be serving lunch shortly, do you prefer kosher food?'

I shook my head 'No thank you.' I had no idea what kosher food was like, but I didn't fancy it.

'I can give you a salad and cheese, also some fruit. Is that alright?'

'Yes that's fine.'

She contemplated the sleeping Jacob.

'I think he needs to sleep, he said he is suffering from jetlag, he flew in from Washington yesterday.'

She shrugged, 'If he wakes up and wants to eat, tell him to press this button up here.'

She pointed to a place underneath the lockers above.

She brought me some more wine and I returned to gazing out the window. We seemed to be passing over a large island, it must be Corsica. There were mountainous areas in the middle and a scattering of small towns along the coastlines. As we reached the end of the island I could see another one looming, which must be Sardinia. Corsica was French and Sardinia Italian. I remembered my school geography lessons.

Lunch arrived and I ordered another glass of wine. I picked at my salad, then, had some cheese with the bread roll that came with it. Jacob woke up and seeing that I was eating, reached up and pressed the buzzer for the stewardess. He asked her for some lunch then got up and went to one of the toilets. When he returned he looked much refreshed. He looked at me.

'Sorry about sleeping, it always takes me several days to get over jetlag when I fly this way.'

His lunch arrived and he too ordered some wine.

I continued to gaze out of the window, visualising my schoolboy atlas unravelling below me. We seemed to be travelling down the west coast of Italy.

Jacob finished his meal and sat back sipping a coffee.

'I guess this will be your first time in Israel?'

I nodded. 'Yes.'

'Why are you going there . . . a holiday?'

I explained briefly that New Horizons, who wanted me to record some of their new country as an artist, had invited me. I showed him the letter, which I kept with my passport in my shoulder bag. He seemed quite impressed.

'I do a lot business in Israel and have travelled around quite a lot. If you need any help let me know, I'll be based at the Dan H otel in Tel Aviv. Ask for Jacob Samuels, they know me quite well, I always stay there.'

I felt the 'plane swing to the left and glancing down I could see that we were passing through what must be the straits between the south coast of Italy and Sicily.

We continued eastward, and after a while I think I must have dozed off. When I opened my eyes the lunch tray was gone from in front of me, so was the glass, which I had my wine in. I looked down and could see that we were passing over another island. This one was really big. There were mountains in the centre and a thin line of mountains along the north coast. The pilot came on the speakers.

'Those on the left can see Cyprus below them'.

I was excited by this, it was where Simon had done his military service. As we reached the eastern end of the island, I saw what looked like a large port. I decided it was Famagusta. Simon's camp had been near there.

A few minutes later the pilot spoke again. 'In about twenty minutes we should be able to see the coastline of Israel, I will inform you when it comes in sight.'

There was a general stirring, every one sat up. Those near windows began to peer out, straining to see the slightest hint of the coastline.

I too found myself looking out, with a mixture of excitement and trepidation. This is where our adventure truly begins.

The pilot came on again, 'Now we see it, those on the left hand side will see it first.'

Half the passengers rose to their feet and began peering across the seats, leaning over to see out the little windows.

Suddenly someone began singing and immediately all the others joined in. I looked at Jacob, who smiled at me, 'It's the Israeli National Anthem . . . Hotkiva.'

He did not get up, but I could see that he was mouthing the words. When it was over he said, 'They always do this on El Al flights.'

Shortly afterwards the pilot came on again, 'Please resume your seats and fasten your seatbelts, we are beginning our descent.'

Chapter 6

After we landed and taxied towards the terminal, the 'plane stopped on the apron. Looking out the window I could see a large set of steps being wheeled up to the front of the 'plane. There was a series of thumps and bumps, the front door was opened and two young men came aboard. They were tough looking with short, cropped hair, one dark, the other fair. They moved down the 'plane as we all stood up and groped for our carry-on luggage in the lockers above. They were sharp eyed and looked at every passenger closely as they passed. I realised that they were some sort of security. They made there way to the back of the 'plane and I turned and saw them talking to two of the stewardesses. We began to shuffle towards the front door, I could feel the heat already. A steward and a stewardess stood smiling on either side of the door, bidding us farewell and welcoming us to Israel. I stepped outside on to the top of the steps. The heat hit me like a gong, I almost staggered as I made my way down the steps to a waiting bus. I had never felt heat like this before. How did people manage to survive in it? There was a curious smell in the air, a mixture of hi-octane fuel and hot dust.

We boarded the bus, I stood near the door as the others pushed past me to the seats. Although all the windows were open, they simply seemed to let the heat in. The doors were shut and the bus slowly moved towards the terminal, which was only a short distance away. When we reached there we waited a few minutes while a second bus caught up with us, the doors opened and we made our way into the terminal. As soon as we stepped inside the temperature dropped significantly, there was air-conditioning!

Jacob caught up with me.

'I'll be going through the Israeli passport control, as an American Jew I hold both passports. You will be going through the visitor's control. Don't forget where you can find me . . . the Dan Hotel. Nice to have met you.' He shook my hand and moved away to join another queue of people.

I joined the line of people who were queuing up for the desks marked, in both Hebrew and English, 'Foreigners'. I felt rather alone and nervous as we shuffled forward one by one. I presented my passport to the somewhat grim, unsmiling woman official behind the desk. She examined my passport carefully, glancing from it to my face and back again several times. I had checked with the Israeli consulate in London and had been told that as a temporary visitor I didn't need a visa.

'How long will you be in Israel?'

'About six to eight weeks.'

'What will you be doing here?'

I explained to her about New Horizons and showed her the letter. She read it carefully, then smiled and said, 'Welcome to Israel!'

She stamped my passport and indicated the luggage claim area.

When my suitcase and rucksack appeared I grabbed them and made my way to the customs area.

The customs were very thorough, as Simon had predicted. They went through everything, examining my sketchbooks, making me open the camera again, taking everything out of the suitcase, then repacking it untidily. Finally, marking my suitcase and rucksack with a chalk mark, they waved me through.

I emerged onto the main concourse. There seemed to be a sea of faces waiting to greet people. There were many signs, both handwritten and printed, held by people either aloft, or held modestly in front of them, some in Hebrew, quite a few in English, one or two in French, and several in Arabic.

I searched for my name, scanning the signs until I finally found one with CRISTOFER printed on it. It was held by a short, stocky man of about fifty, with black crinkled hair going a little grey at the edges. I started towards him and he spotted me, he approached with a broad smile, holding out his free hand.

'Christopher!'

I nodded and put my suitcase down in order to shake his hand. He grasped it warmly in a strong grip and shook it vigorously.

'I'm Yurem.'

He bent down and picked up my suitcase and led me towards the exit door.

'How was your journey?'

'Good.' I said. He was walking quite fast and I had difficulty keeping up with him, weaving our way between the crowds of people greeting and embracing other arrivals.

We got outside and again the heat hit.

'My car's over there,' pointing towards an area the other side of the road. We made our way across, dodging cars which had no intention of slowing down to miss us.

We reached a rather battered American Ford, parked at the end of a line of other cars. He opened the boot and slung my suitcase inside, then took my rucksack and threw that in. I hung on to my shoulder bag. I climbed into the passenger seat in front as he slid in behind the wheel.

'I know this looks a bit old and battered, but it has air-conditioning.'

He switched the engine on and a blast of cold air came out of the vent in front of me, to prove it.

'I'll take you to where you will be staying, I'll leave you for a couple of hours so you can freshen up and unpack. I have some things I need to do but then I'll come back and we'll go to eat. Tomorrow you can come to our gallery and headquarters. I hope to have someone who will be your interpreter and guide while you are here.'

We drove into Tel Aviv, it was a bit like driving in Paris. Yurem had the same lethal approach to driving as Sayyid, he also muttered imprecations at other drivers. Maybe it was a characteristic of people from this part of the world.

As we drove I was fascinated by the cosmopolitan nature of the town. There were Hebrew signs, Arabic signs and English signs. There were people in Arabic dress as well as Hasidic dress, all in amongst people with ordinary European attire. There were also many young Israeli soldiers, both male and female in uniform on the streets. They all carried guns.

Yurem explained, in amongst his more or less continuous abuse of other drivers, that military service was obligatory for both sexes, three years for males and two years for women.

'We are always in a state of preparedness for war, we are threatened by all our Muslim neighbours.' I'm not surprised I thought, remembering Ben Gurion's last quotation.

Eventually we stopped in a street close to the sea, in fact I could see it between some low building on the west side of the street.

Yurem got out and opened the boot, pulling my suitcase and rucksack out and depositing them on the pavement, I too got out and picked up my rucksack and slung it over my shoulder while he locked the car. He then picked up the suitcase and started across the road towards a rather shabby, three-story white building. I looked up at it.

'This is a modernist building,' I exclaimed with admiration. I had done my homework before leaving London, the College had an excellent library, and the librarian who was very good would get in anything that they did not have. I knew that Tel Aviv had been founded in 1909, in the sand dunes just outside the ancient port of Jaffa. It was intended to be a 'garden city'. Patrick Geddes, a British town-planner, was commissioned by one of the first mayors, Meir Dizengoff, to draw up a master plan for the new city. He began work in 1925 on the plan, which was accepted in 1929. Geddes didn't prescribe an architectural style for the city, but by 1933 a number of Jewish architects from the Bauhaus school in Germany, which was closed down by the Nazis, emigrated to Israel and the residential and public buildings were designed by many of them, in the Bauhaus style.

Yurem paused outside the building and looked at me with some interest.

'It's good to see someone who knows about this, and who appreciates them. They don't care about them here, they think they are old-fashioned and want them pulled down. Many of them are condemned. They don't maintain them. They want what they call modern, like that crap down there.' He pointed down the road to some rather tawdry glass and steel buildings.

'Still, what can one expect, they were all peasants ten years ago.'

I supposed he was referring to the latest wave of immigrants from Eastern Europe and Russia.

He led me into the building and we climbed up three floors to the top. He unlocked the door and we went in. There was a musty smell and there was very little light, only that which was leaking through and around the blinds which were pulled down.

He put the suitcase down and went and pulled the blind up in one of the rooms. There was a flood of light and with it the heat.

'The people who were here moved out, they heard that it was going to be pulled down. It was empty but we have put in a bed in one room and a small wardrobe. Over there,' he indicated another room,' its a sort of living room, we put in a table and four chairs. The bathroom is OK, it's got a shower, a washbasin and a toilet. The shower's a bit dodgy, it depends on the water pressure. There's some stuff to cook with in the kitchen and another small table and a couple of chairs. There is no air-conditioning I'm afraid, but there are the ceiling fans.' He pointed at the ceiling, where I could see a big 'punkah' fan.

'Its great, better than my flat in London.'

'OK, I'm going to leave you for a couple of hours, then I'll come back and collect you and we'll go and eat. If you need any stuff there is a store below us on Frischman, which has most of the general things. He speaks some English. Here's some Israeli money.'

He handed me several notes, and the key for the flat, a well as the entry key to the building. 'If anyone comes to visit and pushes your bell by the entry door, it will ring up here, check who it is then buzz them in by pressing this.' He indicated a button underneath the entry 'phone. 'OK, I'm going, see you later.'

After he left I wandered round the rest of the apartment. There were five rooms altogether. It was quite barren, apart from the pieces of furniture he had mentioned. The blinds, which were made up of wooden slats, could be wound up by a sort of hand crank, were closed in all the rooms, except the one he had opened, doubtless to keep out the heat at that time in the day. The bedroom had a small, simple bed with a side table, a lamp, and hanging over the bed, what I supposed was a mosquito net. There was a pillow and two folded sheets and a blanket. In the corner was a small chest of drawers and against the wall facing the bed, a wardrobe. They were all cheap pieces, obviously bought for my temporary use here, but more than adequate as far as I was concerned. I discovered one of the rooms had French doors leading out to a roof terrace, which had a rather shabby and tattered blind extended over about half of it. The walls were all painted white, with marks where pictures and other objects had hung. Everything looked a bit neglected. I supposed because it was probably going to be demolished, little had been done to it for some time. Still, I was very happy here.

I unpacked my few belongings. I had allowed for possible occasions when I may have to look reasonably tidy, so there was a proper shirt, a pair of trousers, clean shoes and a jacket, which I guessed would be far too hot unless the temperature dropped considerably in the evenings. Otherwise I had two pairs of shorts and several short-sleeved shirts. For footwear I had brought a pair of sandals and a pair of tennis shoes, plus, some white socks. I had also brought a sun hat, though I wasn't sure how I could keep it on my head while I was barreling along on a scooter.

By the time I finished unpacking and had a shower, it was getting on to early evening. Dusk was surprisingly brief. It seemed as if one moment it was light and the next it was dark. I was later to realise that as one got further south, dusk became more and more brief. I also realised that it was much later than it would be in England, we were probably three hours ahead here.

As I didn't know what sort of restaurant Yurem was taking me to I thought I should try and look rather tidy. It was still very hot, so I came up with a sort of compromise, I put on a short sleeved shirt, my reasonably tidy trousers and the pair of shoes.

When Yurem arrived we went downstairs to his waiting car. When we got in I asked him the time and reset my watch. It was 7.30 pm, three hours later than London.

It was a blessed relief to have the blast of air-conditioning again, although it caused the windows to mist up inside. Yurem explained that in the evening the air became much more humid because of its proximity to the sea.

We drove for about ten minutes, and then drew up outside a building which had an entrance with a canopy and a large neon sign, which proclaimed that it was 'OTTO'S PIANO BAR'. We went inside and down some stairs where we entered the restaurant and were greeted by a man of about Yurem's age. Yurem introduced him as Isaac, the manager. Isaac led us to a table, large enough to take four people. Yurem told Isaac that we were waiting for another person.

'I have someone who will act as your guide and interpreter, Tammy will be joining us here.'

Tammy, I thought, sounded like an Israeli version of Tommy. I rather hoped he would be a younger person, more my age.

In the corner a man was playing a piano, the music sounded familiar, I tried to think of where I had heard it before. I was just about to ask Yurem what the music was when he said, 'The reason this place is called 'Otto's Bar' is because, when Otto Preminger was here a couple of years ago making 'Exodus' he came here almost every night.'

That explained the piano music, it was the theme music to 'Exodus'.

I gazed around the room, it was very full, mostly quite young people, no one was very formally dressed, my choice of clothing was about right. Yurem explained that most of the people were involved in the creative arts, one way or another. Writers, painters, film makers, actors and directors. I had already noticed that many of the young women I had seen so far in Tel Aviv were dark haired, and often very attractive, this place was no exception. I was just thinking this when a young woman entered the restaurant and made her way through the seated diners. She stopped frequently at other tables, where she was greeted by various young men, who rose to kiss her on the cheeks. The women, I noticed, were a bit more reserved in their greetings.

She eventually arrived at our table, Yurem rose to his feet and after the customary kissing introduced her to me.

'Christopher, this is Tammy . . . she will be your assistant and interpreter.'

I was speechless for a moment, I had been expecting a burly young man at the very least, not an attractive young woman. I half rose to my feet but she said, 'Please don't get up.' She extended her hand and we shook, she sat down.

Yurem said something to her in Hebrew. She turned to me, 'Yurem tells me you are a very good artist?'

This embarrassed me, especially as all that had been seen of my work were actually forgeries done by Simon.

'No I'm not! I am just quite good at doing rather pedantic topographical drawings.'

'We could do with some of that here, everyone seems to want to be an abstract expressionist at New Horizons. Did you bring any of your work with you?'

'A couple of sketch books, one has some of my previous drawings.'

'Maybe I could see some?'

'I'll bring them when I come to New Horizons tomorrow.'

We talked for a while about where I should visit and decided to work out some sort of route when we met on the following day. I broached the idea of renting a scooter. They both seemed to like that idea. Tammy said she had a scooter but it was being repaired at the moment. She had lent it to a friend who had promptly had an accident on it. I asked Tammy how she spelt her name.

'T-A-M-I,' she replied.

While we were talking I saw Jacob enter the restaurant. He didn't see me, he walked to a table on the far side and joined a group of three men already there. Yurem noticed me looking.

'At least one of those guys is Mossad.'

I decided that I was not going to go over there after all. I pretended innocence, 'What's Mossad?'

'Israeli Intelligence, you don't want to mess with them, they're dangerous.'

I knew very well about Mossad, Simon had already warned me about them.

Our food arrived, I didn't remember our ordering anything. The manager came bustling up.

'Is everything alright?'

I asked what my first course was. It was something unidentifiable, rather like a mousse, but with some sort sauce or gravy over it.

'It's very good, our speciality.' He said something to Yurem in Hebrew. Yurem smiled.

I tasted it, there was a slightly grainy texture, rather like it was made with semolina, although it was definitely a savoury dish. The sauce or gravy gave it a sort of salty sharpness.

I nodded and said politely, 'It's very good.'

The manager looked pleased, and after a few more words with Yurem, bustled off. I noticed that Tami did not have the first course, just Yurem and I. When we had finished it I asked Yurem what it was exactly.

'Sheep's brains!'

I felt distinctly queasy for a while, but when the next course arrived it was a fish of some sort and I soon stopped dwelling on what the first course had been.

It appeared that Tami was also an artist and a junior member of the New Horizon's group. Although not an artist, but a doctor, her father had been a long term member. He had been in one of the first groups of Jewish emigrants who had come to Israel in the early 30s, before the British tried to curtail the number of Jewish immigrants allowed into what was then British Mandated Palestine. Her father had been twenty years old at the time. Tami had been born in 1940, when the Second World War was raging. They lived in Jaffa and as she was growing up many of her school friends were Muslims, so she had learned Arabic as easily as she had Hebrew.

I avoided asking her about what had happened in Jaffa at the time when the Israeli army was driving out as many Arabs as possible. With Yurem present I knew it could be a very inflammatory subject. I remembered what Simon had warned me about Yurem, that he was a good guy but also a passionate Zionist. I somehow sensed, though, that Tami would be more moderate in her views.

We were just finishing our meal when I noticed that the group which Jacob had joined got up to leave. As they passed our table Jacob saw me and came over.

'Christopher, good to see you again!'

He looked at Tami and Yurem.

'These are my friends at New Horizons.'

I introduced them and said I had met Jacob on the flight from London, and that I had explained to him about New Horizons.

'Well, good to see you are OK, I won't stay but I hope to see you around, don't forget I'm based at the Dan Hotel here.'

He left with his friends who had waited for him by the door.

'Seems a nice guy.' Yurem remarked. I nodded.

'He was very kind to me on the flight.'

We finished and Yurem picked up the bill. I made some feeble effort to pay my share, but he waved me away.

'You are a guest of New Horizons now.'

When we got to the car Yurem offered Tami a lift, but she shook her head, saying that she had her own transport. We agreed to meet at New Horizons about 10 am.

Yurem drove me back. On the way he made a slight diversion. We stopped outside a long, two-story building.

'This is where we are, New Horizons is at the back of this building, this is Dizengoff Street and the building next door is the Dizengoff Centre. As you may know, Dizengoff was one of the first mayors of Tel Aviv.' As a matter of fact I did.

He then drove me back to where I was staying, carefully explaining the route, which was quite simple.

So, in the morning you can walk round to New Horizons in about ten minutes.'

When we arrived at the apartment building I was in, he asked me if I had everything I needed. I said I had and thanked him for the evening, promising to see him at 10 o'clock the next morning.

I climbed up the stairs to what I could now consider my apartment and let myself in. The temperature had dropped to something much more bearable. It was still rather stuffy so I opened several windows to allow some circulation of air. The bedroom looked out towards the sea and there was a slight breeze, wafting in the smell of the ocean. I was aware of a constant sound, which I assumed were cicadas, Simon had described them to me from his time in Cyprus.

I went in to the bathroom, stripped off and washed myself all over. I realised that I needed to buy some more soap. The sliver I had brought with me was almost gone.

I was beginning to feel really tired, although it was three hours behind London time I felt as if it was later. I made the bed up with the two sheets and left the blanket folded at the bottom of the bed. I certainly didn't need it now, but later in the night it might get colder. I unfurled the mosquito net, which made a sort of fine net tent over the bed. Then I switched on the ceiling fan.

I went out on to the terrace and stood gazing down at the street below. It was still busy. The sky was clear and there were some brilliant stars above. Beyond the buildings across the road I could see the sea, there were a few vessels moving to and fro with their navigation lights on, reflecting in the water. I was still marveling at where I was. This morning I had been in Paris, now I was in the Middle East! I smelt the smell of a city built in a desert, a mixture of perfumes, the urban smells of traffic as well as more exotic ones, tropical flowers, spices, baked earth.

I could hear music from nearby cafés. It was Israeli music, which I'd heard from the early days of the foundation of Israel, played frequently on the radio for a time, a sort of celebratory dance music, the most frequently played at first was called Tzena . . . Tzena . . . Tzena!

As well as this there was also the plaintiff yearning sound of Arabic music, which provided a sort of counterpoint to the music of Israel.

So here I was, alone for now, contemplating what lay before me, a mixture of anxiety and enthusiasm. I looked forward to Simon's arrival.

Chapter 7

I slept restlessly, my mind turning over all the events of the day, culminating in my meeting with Yurem and later Tami. I was very pleased to have her as my assistant and interpreter. She spoke both Hebrew and Arabic, and her English was immaculate. The fact that she was also rather beautiful, with long dark hair, was more than a bonus.

I suppose I didn't get much more than four hours' sleep altogether, partly because we were three hours ahead of England, but also that it was light early. I was still dozing when I was brought fully awake by the distant sound of what seemed like wailing. I looked at my watch, which I had adjusted to Israeli time, it was 5.15am. I climbed out of bed. In spite of the early hour it was getting very warm, the sun was already touching the small ships sailing in the piece of the sea which I could observe from the bedroom window.

I went into the bathroom and switched on the shower, it coughed and spluttered a few times then produced some rather brownish water. I let it run for a couple of minutes and it gradually cleared. I remembered what Yurem had said about the shower. After I finished I shaved and put on the short-sleeved shirt that I had worn the night before, and a pair of shorts, another pair of white socks and the tennis shoes. I must get some soap for washing clothes as well, I thought.

I contemplated my white legs and arms and remembered that I'd brought some sun-block. After smearing a quantity on my arms, legs and face I had used up nearly half the tube, I added that to the list of things I must buy. I went round the apartment closing the shutters. Before I finished I went out on to the terrace, which was still in the shade, and looked out across the part of the city that I could see. The sun was already touching the rooftops. Even at this time there was traffic already on the street below me.

By now it was 6 o'clock, so I thought I might go out and walk around for a bit, try and begin to get the geography of this town, before it got too hot. The building was on the corner of Ben Yehuda Street and Frischmann, according to the street names on the plaque, which each street had conveniently displayed in both Hebrew and English. Remembering Yurem's directions I turned right on Frischmann and walked for about ten minutes down the road until I reached the junction with Dizengoff, where I turned right again and walked until I reached the building that contained New Horizon's offices and gallery. To the side of the door there was a list of four businesses, also in Hebrew and English, one of which was New Horizons. Having satisfied myself that I now could walk to it within 15 minutes, I walked past The Dizengoff Centre, which was quite a substantial building on the corner, then turned right on Bograshov and up the road until I reached Ben Yehuda street again. So in a way it was a journey round the block. Well that was easy I thought, as I made my way back to my apartment building.

It was still quite early, but the road was already busy. Frischmann continued the other side of Ben Yehuda. I crossed the road and walked down towards the docks.

After walking several blocks I arrived at a promenade called R. Herbert Samuel. From there I could see the docks quite clearly. There was a sort of marina immediately in front of me, with a number of sailing boats tied up there. Further along I could see what appeared to be some armed patrol boats. Further on still, in the distance, a warship of some sort, a destroyer or maybe a corvette.

I started to walk towards them, but at a certain point my way was barred by a tall, barbed-wire fence with a gate, inside which was a small building like a guardroom. Behind the gate were two armed marines keeping guard. There was a sign over the gate in Hebrew, which I presumed announced that this was a Naval Dockyard. I smiled at the guards, who didn't smile back. They were stocky and tough-looking and plainly not inclined to be friendly.

I retraced my steps. When I reached my apartment building I looked at my watch, it was 8am. I was feeling quite hungry and in need of a coffee, my Israeli money was up in my apartment. I started to climb the stairs and was about half way up when a young woman came down the stairs and passed me.

I didn't see her face as it was turned away from me, she seemed to be looking downstairs. I just noticed that her hair was black and she was quite slightly built. I started to say something but she continued downstairs quite fast and didn't seem to hear me. Up to now I had assumed I was the only person in the building, but I was obviously wrong.

When I reached the apartment I found that I had not locked the door, which was odd as I am usually meticulous about locking doors. I suppose I had thought that it was self-locking, as my flat door in London had been, I must remember to be more careful next time I went out.

I picked up the money and headed downstairs again. Yurem was right, there was a sort of general store just round the corner on Frischmann. I had noticed it when I went for my walk, it was shut then, but now it was open. There were shelves of things labeled in Hebrew, which were unidentifiable. I managed to find some instant coffee, but milk and sugar were more difficult to find, eventually I settled for what looked like condensed milk in a tin and decided I could do without sugar for a while. I asked the man behind the counter if he had any bread, he shook his head.

'There is bakery down road,' he pointed, 'find bread there.'

Yurem was right, his English was modest. I told him this was my first visit to Israel and that I might need some help identifying some of the products on his shelves. I would come back with a list later in the day. He nodded, but I was not sure that he fully understood what I was saying.

I made up my mind to leave shopping for now. I took my purchases back to the apartment and decided I would try and find a café before I went to New Horizons.

It had occurred to me that there might not be a refrigerator in the apartment, but there was one, it hadn't been switched on, I switched it on and was encouraged when it produced a sound which indicated that it was working.

It was now 9 o'clock in the morning, so I had time to find a café. I took my shoulder bag with one of my sketchbooks, as well as some drawing materials. I made sure the door was locked this time and headed downstairs. I found a café quite close to New Horizons.

I started to look through my phrase book to find something I could order to eat. The waiter, seeing me struggling, asked me in slightly halting English, what I wanted.

'Er . . . breakfast? Something with eggs?'

He nodded, 'Shakshouka?'

I had no idea what that was, but I had to learn something about the food here, so I said 'OK, that's good, and some coffee, please.'

He went off and returned shortly with a small cup of coffee and a glass of water. I looked at the coffee, I had never had such a small cup of coffee before, also there was no milk. Before I could ask he said, 'This is café Turk, very Israeli.' I tasted it, the taste was quite different from anything I had in England, sweeter somehow. When I reached the bottom of the cup it was thick with coffee grains.

As I waited for my 'Shakshouka' I looked round the café. There were several men reading newspapers and eating. In a corner a young woman sat with a coffee, reading a book. She had come in after me. She was not a girl, probably at least in her thirties, she had dark hair and was quite slender. Quite attractive, not beautiful but she had a fine face with strong black eyebrows, there was a mole like a beauty spot, just above the left hand corner of her mouth. She seemed deeply absorbed with what she was reading. I noticed the book was in English. If I had been a bit closer I would have used that to open a conversation with her.

My 'Shakshouka' arrived, it was a large dish of chopped tomatoes and onions, with eggs scrambled and mixed up with it. When I started to eat I found that it was heavily spiced, there was a plate of flat bread with it.

'Pita bread' said the waiter, pointing at it.

It was actually rather good. Although I was not used to spicy food, especially first thing in the morning, it went down very well. I asked for an orange juice. I'd noticed one of the customers drinking an orange juice, and it seemed a good idea after all that spicy food.

I sat for a while, thinking about what I was about to begin. I must ask Tami where I can get a road map of Israel, also one that showed the distribution of kibbutzim around the country. What I wanted to do was make an itinerary of those, but also co-ordinate it with the map I hoped Simon would be able to provide, showing where the destroyed villages and town were in relationship to the kibbutzim, to ascertain how much the kibbutzim were using land stolen from the Arabs. This way I could ostensibly appear to be recording the flourishing kibbutzim, as well as sketching and photographing the remains of the destroyed villages.

I asked the waiter for my bill. After I had paid I picked up my shoulder bag and set off for New Horizons. As I passed the table with the woman reading I glanced down to see if I could recognise the book, I couldn't, but it was definitely in English. She didn't look up as I passed.

I arrived at the building which housed New Horizons promptly, at 10 o'clock. The main door was open so I walked in and following directions which Yurem had given, walked down the corridor facing me, passing doors on either side which bore the names of the other companies. I reached a door facing me at the end of the corridor. Clearly marked on it was the name 'New Horizons'. I knocked, receiving no reply I pushed the door open and entered.

Chapter 8

I found myself in a long room, lit mainly by skylights, although there was a large window at either end. The skylights had blinds drawn across them. The room seemed to span the whole width of the building and must have been at least 40 feet long. Hung on the walls were paintings, in other words it was a gallery. Three large 'punkah' fans revolved on the ceiling. I quickly examined some of the paintings. They were all abstracts in a manner usually referred to as abstract expressionism.

There seemed to be no one else there. I looked around, there were two other doors in the wall facing me. I went to the door on the right, and after knocking opened it. No one was there but it was obviously a sort of eating room. A dozen small tables, each with four chairs arranged around them were scattered round the room. At the back there was a small bar. More paintings hung on the walls.

I went back to the main room and walked to the other door. Even before I got there I could hear the sound of voices. I tapped on the door, Yurem opened it.

'Christopher! We were just talking about you, Tami is here. We were discussing what would be good places for you to visit.'

He opened the door wide and I went in, it was obviously the main office for New Horizons. There was one large desk and a couple of small ones. There was also a fairly long table, with six chairs, three each side, suitable for meetings.

Tami was seated at the table, she rose when I came in and kissed me on both cheeks. After my time in Paris I had become familiar with this form of greeting. They had obviously been discussing a route for me. There was a road map of Israel laid out on the table.

We sat down, Tami and I on one side of the table, Yurem on the other. Tami asked me if I wanted a coffee, but I shook my head, explaining that I had just had a coffee with my breakfast.

I asked them if there was a map showing all the kibbutzim in Israel. Yurem thought for a minute, then said.

I'm sure there is, I'll find out today.'

I studied the map, it showed all the main roads in Israel. I traced a route going north from Tel Aviv, up to Haifa, then on to Acre, and up as far as the Lebanese border.

South from Tel Aviv the map went down past Gaza, which I knew was under Egyptian control at that time, then along the border with Egypt, across the Negev desert, south of which in Egypt was the Sinai Peninsula, largely desert, then a continuation of the Negev to Eilat, and the beginning of the Gulf of Aqaba-Lawrence of Arabia country. In the north of the Negev was Beersheba, in Israeli territory, east of this, towards the southern tip of the Dead Sea was Dimona, where, according to Simon there was a nuclear research facility, built with the help of the French in 1956, in order to be able to create a nuclear device, or bomb.

The eastern side of Israel was bounded in the north by Syria, who occupied the Golan Heights, which looked down on the Jordan Valley, which ran from the Sea of Galilee down to the Dead Sea. The whole of the eastern border of Israel was with Jordan. They were indeed surrounded.

I decided to put forward my suggestion about visiting a number of kibbutzim, without mentioning their proximity to ruined and destroyed Arab villages. 'Look, as I am only going to be here in Israel for eight weeks, I thought it would be a good idea to limit myself to visiting about twelve kibbutzim. If I could have a copy of this road map and also one of all the kibbutzim, I could map out a route I would like to take. Starting near Tel Aviv and going more or less clockwise around the country.'

Yurem nodded, 'That seems a good idea, I'll get hold of the maps today and we can discuss it over them.'

'Maybe today I could visit Jaffa, as that is very close by. Also find out about renting a scooter.'

Tami nodded, 'We can go to the scooter rental place after we leave here and see if we can organise that straight away. I can't stay with you all day today, I have to help Yurem with another exhibition we are having here. Tomorrow will be OK though, we can go to Jaffa together.'

Something I hadn't thought about properly before was the fact that Simon, who would be arriving in four days' time, was coming under the auspices of the Palestine Aid Organisation. How would Yurem, who obviously knew him, react to that?

As if reading my thoughts Yurem suddenly said, 'Your friend Simon is coming, isn't he?'

I nodded, not knowing quite how to respond.

'He told us that he was going to be working for the Palestine Aid Organisation.'

I hesitated, 'Yes, he thought it would be a good idea to work with them so he could report on what was going on.' I was improvising, so I was surprised at Yurem's next statement.

'Yes, that's what he told us . . . I think it's a good idea. I look forward to seeing him again, he is a good friend of Israel.'

I was relieved to hear this, I had expected a quite different response.

Tami and I set off, first of all to a scooter rental place, it was already swelteringly hot. They were mainly stocked with Vespas, I couldn't find one of my beloved Lambrettas. However the controls of a Vespa were just the same. I asked if I could have one fitted with panniers. The dealer said he would arrange that, if I could pick it up on Friday. I looked at Tami.

'That's OK we can go to Jaffa on the bus tomorrow.'

Actually that was good for me too, I could spend the rest of the day orienting myself around Tel Aviv and maybe getting myself some supplies. I agreed.

We walked back towards my apartment building, when we reached it Tami said, 'Sorry to have to leave you, will you be OK?'

'No its fine, it gives me a chance to walk around, see more of Tel Aviv and to get around on my own. I'm sure I'll spend quite a lot of time managing on my own, after all I can't expect you to be with me all the time.'

'Yes, but I'll make myself available as much as I can.'

As she left she called out. 'See you tomorrow at New Horizons, same time, OK?'

She set off, back to New Horizons. I went up to my apartment to make a list of things I may need. I took my shoulder bag with the camera and my sketchbook and went downstairs. I had intended to do a circuit of the immediate area I was in. There were some shops almost opposite, which I decided to investigate.

As I crossed the road I noticed a young woman looking in the window of one of the shops, as I approached she turned and walked swiftly away. There was something vaguely familiar about her. I couldn't think where I might have seen her before. It was only after she had turned a corner and was out of sight I realised where I had seen her, she was the woman who had been sitting reading a book in the café I had breakfast in.

One of the shops appeared to be a newsagent. There were postcards in a rack outside. They were mainly of Tel Aviv, the seaside nearby, a few of what looked like smiling workers in the fields of what I assumed was a kibbutz, then some postcards of Jaffa from previous times. I studied these carefully. They were all in black and white and stood out in contrast to the more contemporary views, which were all in colour. The ones of Jaffa were fascinating, they showed many views of the town, the people, the old port and views of Jaffa from the sea. I examined them all with great interest. Most of them were from the late 20s through to the late 30s. In other words they were all pre-war. Some in fact were pre-WWI. I decided to purchase six of them and I looked forward to the next day when I could go with Tami to Jaffa and see how much it had changed. I also bought two more contemporary ones to send to my parents and Sylvia, and I found and purchased a street map of Tel Aviv.

It was now midday and almost unbearably hot. I started to walk north up Ben Yehuda Street. Because the sun was now almost directly overhead I soon felt the need to be somewhere where there was some cool shade. When I reached Ben Gurion Avenue I turned left and made my way down to the sea. There was some sort of construction going on, which looked liked the beginning of another marina. I turned right and walked a little north, where I found a pleasant beach area, with a number of cafés and restaurants. I chose one, which had a large awning at the front, there were a number of tables already set for lunch. A few were occupied, but I found one completely in the shade and sat down. A man came out carrying a menu card. I asked him if he spoke English, he laughed and said with a strong Cockney accent, 'Yes mate . . . I should do, I come from Whitechapel!'

I was completely taken by surprise. I looked at him, he was short and stocky with dark hair, rather crinkly. I judged him to be in his early 30s. He had a smiling, friendly face. 'How long have you been here?'

'I came with my parents when I was sixteen, in 1952. The state of Israel seemed firmly established at that time and my parents were refugees from Poland, who came to Britain in 1938. They wanted very much to come to the homeland of the Jewish people, so we moved here. My father opened this place in 1956. After doing my military service here I became part of the business. Do you want something to eat?' I nodded.

'I'll get a menu.' He disappeared inside, returning shortly after with a menu. 'If you need any help choosing, let me know, my name is Joseph.'

'I'm Christopher.'

The menu was written in English with Hebrew underneath. I had no idea what to ask for. When he came back I did ask him to help.

'I could do you fish and chips if you like?'

I was tempted by this, not that I was an avid fish and chip eater, but it seemed an easy decision to make. Then I thought, this is ridiculous, here I am in the Middle East and contemplating eating fish and chips!

'I don't want anything big, I had a Shakshouka for breakfast.'

He nodded. 'That sounds good.' He studied the menu, 'OK, so something light.'

He ran his finger down the menu, 'How about 'Hummus bi Tahina' with some tomato salad?'

'What is it exactly?'

'It's a chickpea and sesame dip, with pita bread.'

'OK, and can I have an orange juice please?'

He scurried off, returning shortly with an orange juice and a glass of water.

While I waited for the food I decided to study the postcards I had bought. I got them out and spread them on the table. It was plain that Jaffa had been a thriving port and city, with many beautiful buildings. The orange industry had been a mainstay of its economy, I remembered when, after the war and we were able to get oranges once again, the first ones I saw all came from Jaffa. I must ask Tami tomorrow about Jaffa's history.

Joseph returned with the hummus and salad, while I continued to study the postcards.

I was just finishing eating, having enjoyed my hummus, and resolving to make a note of it as an ideal light repast, when a voice said, 'Hi, we meet again.' It was Jacob, clad in shorts and what I took to be an Hawaiian shirt. His legs were as white as mine, but much hairier.

Without asking he pulled out one of the other chairs at the table and sat down. 'Hot enough for you?' He wiped his brow with a coloured handkerchief. I nodded in agreement

'You'll get used to it after a few days, it just hits you at first. What's up? Are they helping you at New Horizons?'

I explained to him that Tami was going to be my guide and assistant, but she was busy today, although she had found time to organise a scooter for me, so I was using my time on my own, to orientate myself.

'That girl with the dark hair? Beautiful isn't she . . . lucky you. What's your plan?'

'I asked them if they could get me a map of the country and also one with all the kibbutzim on. Then I was going to choose about twelve so that I could do a circuit of the whole country, as well as draw and photograph them.'

'Sounds ambitious, but it's a good plan. How long do you think you'll be here?'

'Well, I hope about eight weeks.'

'So when do you think you will set off on this epic trip?'

'Probably about Wednesday next week, I want to see stuff in the immediate area first.' I also didn't mention that I was waiting for Simon to turn up, so that I could discuss this plan with him.

He thought for a while, then, 'When you finish this trip what will you do with the material?

'What I intend to do is accumulate enough drawings and photographs to present to New Horizons a record of my impressions of the new Israel. I will want to take some of the sketches back to London, so I can work them up into paintings and then see if New Horizons would like to set up an exhibition of them, as well as the sketches and possibly photographs.'

He nodded. 'I reckon they'll love that.' He looked at his watch, 'I've got to go, I have a meeting at 2pm.'

He stood up and held out his hand. 'Good to see you again, I'm sure we will run into each other often, in the end this is a very small country. I come here to eat nearly every day.'

I shook his hand and with a final. 'Take care of yourself,' he left.

I took out the map of Tel Aviv, which I had purchased when I bought the postcards. I identified where I was, more or less, then I looked around the map until I saw The Tel Aviv Museum of Art, which was on Siderot Rothschild, off Allenby Street. I decided to make my way there, at least it should have air-conditioning. When Joseph came by I asked for the lunch bill, which he brought promptly. It was quite a small amount, I paid with some of the money Yurem had given me. I asked him if he could direct me to the museum.

'Sure,' he said. 'Go back up to Ben Yehuda Street, then go south on that until you reach a fork with Allenby Street on the left, walk down Allenby past Shenkin Street, then to Siderot Rothschild, turn right on Rothschild walk a couple of blocks and you'll see the museum. It's a long walk though, you'd be better off getting a bus on Ben Yehuda Street.'

I thanked him. As I was leaving he said, 'I see you know Jacob, he's a regular customer here.'

I made my way up to Ben Yehuda Street, there was no shade, the sun seemed directly overhead and the heat was getting to me. I found a bus stop and quite soon a bus came, the route on the front was in Hebrew, so when it stopped I asked the driver for The Museum of Art, he nodded and I climbed aboard. I gave him the smallest denomination note I had and he handed me a ticket and a handful of change. I sat near the door, anxious not to miss the Rothschild turning. I needn't to have worried, the bus stopped right by it.

I leapt off and following Joseph's directions soon saw the Museum. It was a large, imposing modernist building.

The first thing I observed when I entered was a plaque saying that this had originally been the home of Meir Dizengoff, the first mayor of Tel Aviv. He had donated it to Tel Aviv in 1932. It was also the building where the State of Israel was first confirmed.

To my relief it was air-conditioned, not surprising I suppose, considering all the works of art here. Even in London the National Gallery was air-conditioned in the galleries that contained precious Renaissance paintings.

I began to wander through the various rooms, some very large, others more modest in size, as well as a considerable collection of contemporary Israeli artists, I was also pleased, surprised and astonished to see that there was a comprehensive collection of late nineteenth- and twentieth-century European art, ranging from Fauvism through German expressionism, cubism, futurism, Russian constructivism, surrealism, French impressionism, with works by Picasso, Chaim Soutine, Joan Miro and many others.

I spent the rest of the afternoon wandering from room to room, savouring the delights of this wealth of paintings, so unexpected here in the Middle East. By 5.30, when the museum announced that it was closing, I was culturally exhausted.

I left the building, going reluctantly into the heat again. Actually it was beginning to diminish, as it was now late in the afternoon. I decided to take a bus back to my apartment, the journey to the museum had been much longer than I'd realised.

There was a bus stop nearly opposite my apartment building. I remembered that I hadn't really got any proper supplies in. I had already eaten out twice today and I really didn't want to go out again. I made my way to the store near the building. The man I had spoken to in the morning was still there. By dint of searching through the shelves I managed to find eggs, a packet of pita bread, a pot of hummus, olive oil, a bottle of vinegar, as well as some mustard. In the back of the shop was an area devoted to fruit and vegetables, where I found some tomatoes and a lettuce, also oranges and apples. I paid for my purchases and left the store. As I made my way to the apartment I saw two people standing outside, looking up at the building. The man was dark haired, wearing a short-sleeved khaki shirt and a pair of light coloured trousers. He was about my age, quite muscular judging by his arms, and about the same height as me. There was something rather military about his bearing. The girl he was with had blonde hair down to her shoulders and a white shirtdress and sandals. As I approached they turned and began to walk rapidly away. I was beginning to think that I was already under some sort of surveillance.

As I entered I thought I heard a door being shut somewhere in the building. I waited to hear the sound of feet descending the staircase, but there was no further sound. This may be also part of checking on me. When I was in the apartment I put the bag of supplies in the kitchen, and before I did anything else stripped off and ran the shower. Although I had intended it to be a cold shower the water came out lukewarm at first, cool enough though to start with and as I ran it the water became gradually colder. I stayed under it for about five minutes, and emerged feeling quite refreshed. I then just put on my shorts and went into the kitchen. I put the eggs and the vegetables in the 'fridge, which I was pleased to see was working very well. I looked in the various cupboards and found a frying pan and a couple of saucepans. I decided that they needed a good wash before I used them, then I remembered that I hadn't got any washing up liquid, or for that matter, any soap. I must start a list. I took my notebook and went out on to the terrace. It was much cooler now, the sun was still just touching the sailing boats out in the bay, but the terrace was completely in the shade now. I began to make a list of some of the things I would need if I was going to continue to use the apartment as a base. I wondered if Tami would help me with the shopping the next day, when we got back from Jaffa.

When I had completed the list I went back into the kitchen and contemplated the few supplies I had purchased. I realised that I didn't want to have eggs again as I had them with Shakshouka in the morning. In the end I decided to simply make a salad with the lettuce and tomatoes, a dressing with the oil, vinegar and mustard, then open the pot of hummus and the packet of pita bread. I first washed the lettuce under the tap in the kitchen, and then dried it using a small towel from the bathroom. I did the same with the tomatoes and the apples. I found a large bowl at the back of one of the cupboards, shredded the lettuce into it, sliced the tomatoes and added them. After which I made a dressing, using the oil, vinegar and mustard, poured it onto the lettuce and tomatoes and tossed it. I then carried it all out to the terrace, after first dragging the small kitchen table and a couple of chairs out there as well.

By now it was nearly dark although there was some ambient light from the surrounding city. The sky was clear and the stars were very evident as well as a half moon. I ate slowly, enjoying the now warm air, filled with the scents from the city. When I was finished I took the dishes back into the kitchen and washed them up as best I could. Then, taking my notebook, I went out again onto the terrace. I found the light switch for the terrace lights and turned them on. I'd decided to keep a regular diary of each day, where I had been, what I had seen, and whom I had met.

Earlier I had thought that I had wasted a day but on reflection I realised that considering that this was my first full day here, I had managed to achieve quite a lot. My earlier morning walk had given me my knowledge of the proximity to New Horizons offices and headquarters, as well as a side trip down to the dock area. My later meeting with Yurem and Tami had given them the outline of how I hoped to usefully spend my time here. Then Tami and my visit to the scooter rental place had been productive in that I was able to designate what I wanted and arrange to pick it up at the end of the week.

After Tami left me to go back and help Yurem, I had managed to purchase a street map of Tel Aviv and Jaffa, as well as some wonderful postcards of Jaffa in earlier times. I'd found a nice place to have lunch, and made friends with Joseph, I'd also met up again with Jacob. The indulgence of spending the rest of the afternoon at the museum seemed justified by my earlier activities.

I wrote all this up in my journal, trying to remember as many details as I could. When it was finished I put the terrace lights off and sat looking at the stars and hearing again the ambient sounds of the city. As the evening before I savoured again the mixture of smells and perfumes arising from this city. Again there was the mixture of music, Arabic, Hebrew, and contemporary Western sounds. It seemed extraordinary that yesterday morning I was still in Paris. I felt as if I had already been here a long time.

Chapter 9

The next morning I again woke early. After I had showered and dressed in the only clean clothes I had left, I picked up my bag, which still had my sketchbook, camera and film in it, and set off to the café where I had breakfast the day before.

The same man came over to ask me what I wanted, 'Shakshouka?' he said helpfully.

I shook my head, 'Maybe something else?'

He thought for a moment, then said, 'Kedgeree?'

I had kedgeree once when I was in London. Each year Andy and I had helped one of our tutors do some large murals on paper for a charity ball which was held in the common room during the summer vacation period, when most of the students were away, either back to their homes or on holiday. As a reward for our efforts we were given a couple of tickets each for the ball. The affair lasted all night with lavish quantities of free champagne, culminating with breakfast about 5am, with kedgeree the principal dish. I liked it.

'Good, I'll have it, and a coffee and orange juice please.'

He brought them quite quickly, but I had to wait for the kedgeree. I looked around the café, it seemed to have the same clients as the day before. There was no sign though of the young woman reading a book.

I arrived punctually at New Horizons. Tami was already there, making a list of paintings which were going into the next exhibition. There was no sign of Yurem. Tami asked me how I had got on the day before. I told her what I had done and how I had eventually gone to the Museum of Art and how impressed I was by their permanent collection. She seemed pleased at this.

'You know I have nothing to compare it with, as I have never been anywhere else.'

I assured her that it was as good a collection of late-nineteenth and early-twentieth century art as the Tate Gallery in London.

She finished her list and was ready to leave. We then took a bus to Jaffa. It was not far, and it really was now a suburb of Tel Aviv. 'Where would you like to go?' Tami asked.

'Well is there an area known as old Jaffa?'

'al-Ajami is the remains of the older part.'

What happened to the rest of Jaffa?'

Tami looked out of the window of the bus. After a pause she said, 'A lot of it was bulldozed or blown up.'

'Why?'

She shrugged, 'It was the policy after the 1948 war.'

'What happened to the inhabitants?'

She bent her head, she seemed to be debating something.

'Let's not talk about that now, maybe later.'

I'd better watch it, I thought, I'm probing her too far. I still was not quite sure how she felt about the events of 1947 to 1948. I had to be careful to maintain my role as a sympathetic supporter of the State of Israel, I didn't want to blow it asking awkward questions.

We arrived in what I supposed was central Jaffa. It was filled with recently built structures, shops, business premises and residential buildings. We disembarked. There was a tall clocktower there which was plainly a remnant of the past.

'Let's walk from here, there are no bus services into the al-Ajami district. It's not far, about a ten minute walk.'

We set off through the busy streets, everywhere there was building work going on, here and there were empty sites, covered in rubble, doubtless the remains of the old city. I was really feeling the heat now, my shirt was already sticking to my back. Tami on the other hand was looking wonderfully cool. She was wearing shorts and had a sleeveless top, which I later learned was called a 'tank top'. She also had shoulder bag, which she carried on her left shoulder.

She was wearing sandals. It was impossible to ignore her breasts, which were made very evident in the skimpy top garment. I tried not to keep glancing at them.

'When we get to the al-Ajami district we'll find a café and have a tea.'

I was pleased to hear this, I was parched, although I wasn't sure that hot tea was the answer.

We set off walking, until we reached a checkpoint. There were two soldiers there, who asked to see our IDs. Fortunately I had my passport with me and Tami had her identity card. After they were inspected we were waved on.

'Why was that?'

'This is a restricted area still.' She didn't elaborate.

We worked our way through narrower and narrower streets, almost alleyways, until we eventually arrived at an open square. There were several cafés with awnings outside. Tami opened a muslin scarf that she had carried in her shoulder bag, I saw that it made a sort of shawl or wrap, which she draped around her shoulders, leaving enough of it to cover her breasts. We sat down at one of the cafés and I welcomed the shade from the awning, somehow the sun seemed almost vertical at this time of day. I realised that it was past noon, nearly 1 o'clock. The Arab owner came bustling out. Tami ordered something in Arabic.

'I put this on when I am in an Arabic café or restaurant, there is no point in offending Arab people unnecessarily.' She indicated the shawl. 'After all we have offended them enough already, by being here.'

The owner reappeared, carrying a tray with two tall glasses, each with a long spoon. On the top of the tea inside were green leaves floating.

'Mint tea.' Tami remarked.

I stirred mine with the long spoon and sipped, it was still very hot, there was a distinct taste of the mint and it was very sweet, but somehow rather refreshing.

'This is a very Arabic drink, but we have also adopted it. In the desert the nomadic tribes drink it in the heat, it makes you sweat then cools you off, it's far more refreshing than ice cold drinks, and far more effective.'

We sat and sipped our tea and gazed around. The buildings here were very old. It was difficult to see when they had been built. Certainly they had been here since the Britiish mandate began in 1923. Possibly when the Turks were here before.

'Tell me about Jaffa, is it very old?'

Tami thought for a moment. 'It's a very ancient city, there are archaeological remains which indicate that it was inhabited in 7500BC. It's a natural harbour and has been in use since the Bronze Age. It was under Egyptian rule until about 800 years BC. Later it was occupied by the Romans, then the Crusaders for a relatively short time. After that the Turks, then an Arab majority. There were lots of other invaders, Babylonians, Phoenicians, Persians . . . Now it's ours, or should I say, Zionist Israel's.'

'Why was it then blown up, bulldozed and largely erased?'

'Everyone did this, it has been demolished and rebuilt many times in the course of history. The British in 1937 blew up and destroyed large parts of the city. Now it was our turn.'

'What about the inhabitants?'

She looked away, then 'The population was forced out.'

This shocked me, and it must have shown on my face.' Where did they go?'

Again she looked away, 'Let's get something to eat, and then, when it is past the hottest time we'll walk around.' She waved at the owner, who came forward with a menu. It was in Arabic and Hebrew.

'Are you very hungry?'

'Not very.'

'Good, neither am I, let's order something light.' She spoke to the proprietor, who nodded and disappeared inside.

We sat quietly for a while. She had not answered my question. She seemed to be evading it. Tami could see that I was troubled by what I had heard. After a few moments she said, 'We are surrounded by Arab countries that want nothing less than our extermination, so we had to appear strong. If we were to survive as a country we had to do these things. I know it is terrible to think about it now, but we wouldn't be sitting here, if we hadn't.'

I was still troubled, but I knew that I had to try and be sympathetic to what she had just said. Indeed part of me was.

I nodded, 'Yes, yes, I understand.'

She looked at me, 'I don't suppose you do, but then, why should you. If you were Jewish, and more still, a survivor of the Holocaust, it would mean much more to you.'

While she was talking another couple arrived and sat at a nearby table. The man was probably in his late twenties, he had red hair, unusual I thought in this country where everyone had dark hair. The woman who came with him was about the same age, maybe slightly older. Initially she sat with her back to us, but at one point she turned her head to look at something the other side of the square. I noticed that she had a mole above the left hand corner of her mouth.

The proprietor came out with a salad each, some pita bread and a bowl of hummus. Hummus again! Oh well I thought, at least I like it, I would have plenty of time to experiment with other dishes during my stay in Palestine.

I was anxious to change the subject from the destruction and mass eviction of the Palestinian population to something more in content.

I groped in my shoulder bag and produced my sketchbook.

'Here, you said you were interested in my work, these are all sketches, but I have produced a number of paintings based on some of these.'

She took the book and began to look through it. She was plainly impressed and spent sometime looking closely at several of them.

'These are very good, I wish I could draw half as well.'

I asked her about her work and she said that if anything she was a figurative artist and was not at all supportive of the prevailing mode of abstract expressionism.

I was sympathetic to her stance, as I had to put up with action painting and so-called 'tachism' as well as Jackson Pollack, which was alo prevailing in the Royal College Painting School at that time. I saw no merit in riding bicycles over wet paint and squeezing paint out of tubes in a random way, claiming that it was creative. I was more on the side of someone like Peter Blake, who had been at the College a couple of years before me. His work was figurative and very original, in a rather graphic way.

We finished our modest lunch, and then began to explore the remains of the old city. I saw several things I wanted to draw and resolved to come back here the following day and possibly the day after. I mentioned this to Tami.

'I can come with you tomorrow in the morning, but I do need to get back home later in the afternoon, it's the eve of 'Shabbat', our Sabbath day, and it begins in the evening of Friday and continues until Saturday evening. I must be with my family, they expect it of me.

'OK, I understand, maybe if you come tomorrow you can ask the soldiers if it's alright if I can come on my own on Saturday?'

She nodded. 'I'm sure it will be alright, just make sure you bring your passport and maybe the letter from New Horizons.'

We continued to walk through al-Ajami. There were many old buildings and in places, many ruined houses. I remarked on them.

'These are casualties of the 1948 war, nothing has been done with them.'

'That was 15 years ago!'

'I think that the attitude of our government is that it is more important to spend money on developing Israeli settlements than wasting money on a bunch of Arabs!'

There was definitely a note of disaffection in her voice. I began to wonder if she might become an ally in what Simon and I were trying to do. I needed to talk to Simon about this, he would be arriving on Sunday. He told me that he would find me, as I didn't know where he was going to be staying. Now I knew that Yurem was aware of Simon's work with Palestine Aid, I assumed that Simon would be in touch with him to find out where I was.

I reckoned that I could spend a couple of days drawing and photographing parts of al-Ajami, I would come here the next day, as well as Saturday and maybe Sunday. I was quite excited about what I was seeing and anxious to begin.

We continued walking around for about an hour before leaving the area and making our way down to the old port.

It was very moving to stand on the quayside and look out to the Mediterranean beyond, to think that there had been a port here for nearly 10,000 years. What a history of traders and invaders; all had looked out from this point, seeing the same vista. Near the shore the sea was dirty and grey, further out it gradually became the azure blue so familiar from the many photographs I had seen of the Mediterranean. Tami was standing beside me, I wondered what she was thinking.

My comment though was, 'You know I came here to record this new country which Israel has made of Palestine, and now I am looking at thousands of years of history. It's very moving.'

We walked back through the streets and alleyways until we reached the checkpoint we had come in by. We showed our identification and were waved on.

I was curious about the idea that we had to show identification before going in and out of the old part of Jaffa. I asked Tami why this was so.

'When we had driven the majority of the population out, there were a relatively small number of Arab people left. They are confined to al-Ajami and have to get special permission to leave.'

'Can't they leave by another way?'

'There are two access points, the one which we have just left by and another on the southern end, all the other roads are blocked off.'

'So, they are virtually in an open air prison?'

'You could look at it like that.'

This is just like the Berlin Wall I thought, which had been built two years before in 1961. I refrained from making that comment.

On the bus going back to Tel Aviv, Tami asked if she could come and see where I was staying.

'Of course, but I need to shop for supplies before we go there, the store is very close to where I am staying, maybe you could help me?'

She squeezed my arm, 'I'd love to.'

We got back to Ben Yehuda Street, near the apartment building and went to the general supplies store I had been to in the morning. The owner was not there, a younger man was serving. It was just as well that I had Tami with me, as the young man didn't speak any English. I had told Tami what I had purchased so far, but I still needed sugar, tea, coffee, bread, and some sort of cereal, and some cheese. I also wanted some soap and washing up liquid.

There were containers of various fruit juices in a glass fronted chilling compartment, where the milk was. She asked me what sort of milk I wanted, cow's milk, goat's milk, sheep's milk. I settled for the more familiar cow's milk. She added a few other things and a couple of bottles of wine.

I paid for the purchases with the Israeli money Yurem had given me and we carried the bags up to the apartment. As we were climbing up Tami remarked on how quiet it was.

'It's nice in a way that you have the whole building to yourself.'

'Well I thought I did, but yesterday morning, after I had been out for a walk quite early, I came back and was going upstairs when a young woman came down the stairs and passed me. In the evening, when I had just let myself into the building, I thought I heard a door shutting somewhere.'

Tami looked puzzled. 'I'm surprised at that, Yurem assured me that it was a completely empty building. It's up for demolition soon, Yurem had to make a special request to have you staying here until they are ready to pull it down.'

We got to the top and I took my key out and let us in. We took the bags into the kitchen. The fridge was working still and was now quite chilled. We packed most of the stuff we had bought into it. Tami opened the cupboard doors and looked inside each of them. She examined the couple of saucepans that were there and wrinkled her nose at them.

'These are a bit dodgy, I'll get you some more. Do you cook?'

Having lived on my own in my flat in London I had acquired a few small culinary skills but I felt that none of them were appropriate here in this climate.

'A bit, but I am quite interested in improving.'

She contemplated me for a few minutes, then, 'I tell you what, I'll get some stuff and teach you some Arabic dishes. I'll get you a cookbook too.'

'That would be great, are you sure you don't mind?'

'I'd love to, cooking is my secret passion.'

We walked round the apartment together. She was very taken with the terrace. 'We could have a party here!'

We! I thought.

She laughed, 'It's alright, I was just kidding.'

She went on looking round the apartment, she thought it was good that I'd been given a mosquito net.

'Well I envy you this, I'm still living with my parents. Which reminds me, I have to get home, my mother gets upset if I am late for supper. Will you be OK? There is quite a nice place near New Horizons to eat, it's not expensive and does mostly Arabic food. I think it's called *Al-Jeddah*.'

'I'm OK, I have some eggs, some pita, cheese and wine, that's perfect for me. Tomorrow I'll get some other things.'

She looked at me doubtfully, 'Doesn't seem much.'

I grinned at her, 'Are you trying to mother me?'

She grinned back, 'Well I am Jewish!'

She left after that. We agreed to meet at 9.30am the following morning at New Horizons. She would contact Yurem and tell him.

After she was gone I went into the bathroom and stripped off and had another shower. It was going to become a pattern, a shower in the morning and another one in the evening. The heat during the day was so oppressive it seemed absolutely necessary to do this.

I wandered round the flat after that with just a towel wrapped round me. The sun was going down, the terrace was already in the shade. I carried the two chairs and the small kitchen table out there. I got out one of my sketchbooks and began to do a drawing looking across the rooftops as the sun slowly sank below the horizon. Soon I could hear the whining of mosquitoes and hastily went indoors and put a shirt on. I realised that I had still not got any mosquito repellent or more sun-block. I had enough of the latter for one more day, but I really needed the mosquito repellent now. I decided to put my trousers and shoes back on and go down and see if there was anything in the store we had just been to.

As I was coming out of the building I saw a man standing in the porch of a shop across the road. In the fading light I was sure that he had red hair; he turned and looked in the window of the shop. Odd, I thought, two red haired people in the same day.

I found what I wanted in the general store, at least I think I did. The assistant who spoke no English was still there, so I had to guess at the products by the pictures on their labels. One showed what looked like a mosquito, the other had a bright sun on it and what looked like a girl in a bikini. I also went again to the section where they had vegetables and fruit. I bought some more tomatoes as well as oranges, apples, figs and another lettuce.

When I went back to the apartment building there was no sign of the red haired man.

I made my way up to the apartment and after making sure the door was locked, set about making myself a modest meal. First of all I carefully washed the frying pan and saucepans. Tami had been right, they were a bit dodgy. My meal consisted of an omelette with a chopped tomato added, and a small salad made with the lettuce and some more of the tomatoes. I made a dressing up with the oil and vinegar and a little mustard. Finally I had an orange. All this was accompanied by at least two glasses of a rather nice dry white wine.

Feeling pleasantly replete I smeared myself with the anti-mosquito oil and taking a notebook went out to the terrace. I sat for a while, thinking about Tami and her reticence when questioned about certain things. She seemed as if she was ashamed of what happened to the Palestinian people of Jaffa, after the fighting had stopped. Why too had they never returned in any numbers? It was not hard to see that Jaffa was now primarily Jewish. Although she was reticent about these matters I felt a warmth in her, a generosity of spirit. She had not hesitated to help me find a scooter to rent and later to willingly help me get my supplies, then offer to teach me some cooking ideas, finally to seem concerned that I had enough to eat. The Jewish mother instinct, she more or less professed as much. We had only just met but I already felt a genuine rapport with her.

I opened the notebook and made a record of what I had done this day, where I had been. The visit to Jaffa, Tami's reticence about certain things, what my plans were for the next couple of days. It seemed important to keep a written record about my time in Israel and the remains of Palestine, as well as the drawings and photographs.

After washing up my plates and dishes I dug out a couple of books I had brought with me from the suitcase and climbed into bed. There was a small lamp on the bedside table, which I switched on. Then after releasing the mosquito net around the bed I settled down to read a small book on the history of Palestine and the Middle East. I had found it in a second hand bookshop in London, it was quite old and battered and the history stopped short at the time of the First World War. However, it was remarkably cheap, and enough to give me a good background to this area prior to the arrival of the Israelis. I read for about an hour, then, feeling myself falling asleep, I put the book down, switched off the table light and was soon dreaming.

Chapter 10

I woke about 5am, it was just getting light. Something had woken me. There again was that distant wailing sound which I had heard the day before. I realised what it was, it was the Muslim call to prayer from some distant mosque, probably as far away as Jaffa.

I used up the last of the sun-block I had brought with me. In spite of my liberal use of it the day before, I was already rather red. My fair skin was always prone to sunburn, until it finally turned brown.

I washed the shirt, underwear and socks I had worn the previous day and hung them up on the terrace to dry. I then had a small breakfast of the cereal, which was in fact museli, something I had in London and rather liked, and a glass of orange juice. I made a note to find some instant coffee. It was too early to go to New Horizons, so I sat on the terrace and did some more to my drawing. It was a panoramic and would be something I could add to over the next few weeks, whenever I was back in Tel Aviv.

At 9 o'clock I put the other sketchbook in my shoulder bag and the camera with half a dozen films and set off for New Horizons, after locking up the apartment.

When I arrived there I found Tami with an older man, she was helping him hang a couple more paintings on the walls of the main exhibition room. I could also hear the sound of other voices coming from the room with bar.

Tami greeted me with 'Shalom', then she turned to the older man and said to him, in English, 'Father, this is Christopher.'

He was a tall, slim, spare man, about fifty years old. He extended his hand, 'I'm very pleased to meet you, my daughter speaks highly of your work.'

I shook his hand and made modest self-deprecating noises.

'Tami is very kind to say that, but I'm a mere topographer.'

He ignored this remark and turned to Tami, 'Why don't you take Christopher in there and get him a coffee, I'll finish up here and join you.'

Tami took me into the room with the tables and chairs and we sat down at one of the tables. There were half a dozen other people there, five men and one other woman. They looked round as we came into the room and Tami, who was obviously well known there, said 'This is Christopher, he is an artist from England.'

There was a general murmuring of greeting. They were all, apart from Tami, in their 40s and 50s and looked as if they had been members of New Horizons since its inception in 1948.

Tami got up and went to the bar and ordered two coffees. While I waited for her to come back, a couple of the men, who were sitting near me, asked me how long I was going to be in Israel. I explained about the invitation from New Horizons. One of them nodded and said he knew about this and explained it to his companion.

While we were drinking our coffee several other people came in and greeted Tami, who was obviously popular. Tami did her best to introduce me to them and I tried to remember most of the names. A rather big man with a mass of wavy grey hair, seemed to be regarded with respect by all of them, his name was Avigdor Stematsky. Tami explained to me that he was a prominent founder member of New Horizons, along with Yossef Zaritsky, Marcel Janco, Yochanan Simon, and Aharon Giladi.

Tami's father came in and after getting himself a coffee, joined us.

'So Christopher, how are you finding Israel now you are here?'

'Hot!' was my first comment. Then feeling that this was an inadequate response I added, 'At the moment I have only been here three days, so I have been able to see this part of Tel Aviv and some of old Jaffa, so far, but I will be doing as much travelling round Israel as I can in the few weeks I will be here.'

He obviously knew about my invitation from New Horizons, and the fact that Tami was going to be my guide.

I asked him about his involvement with the art group, he told me that although he was a doctor he knew most of the older members, as they had been soldiers together in 1947 and 1948 at the birth of the State of Israel. He was friends with Yurem and voluntarily acted in an administrative capacity for the group. 'Also it seems I have become their resident doctor. Its amazing how many in-growing toenails, hernias, urinary infections, slipped discs, boils and other minor complaints I have been asked to diagnose.' he remarked ruefully, 'Usually at lunchtime!'

I liked this touch of humour, I warmed to him. I admitted that I hadn't had time to examine the paintings hanging on the walls in the main gallery but I would do so next time I came in.

'Yes do, let me know when you are next in and I will try and come and identify some of them for you.'

Tami looked at her watch, 'We must be on our way if we are going to rent the scooter and get down into Jaffa again.'

I stood up and grabbed my shoulder bag. I shook hands with Tami's father and said that I looked forward to seeing him again. We started towards the door. Then her father called her back, I waited by the door while he spoke to her in Hebrew.

When she came back we set off to the scooter rental place. It was about a ten-minute walk. I said how nice her father was and I would look forward to meeting him again.

'My father has invited you this evening to our place for the beginning of Shabbat. That is if you want to come.'

I thought about this for a minute, then, 'Does he know that I am not Jewish?'

'Yes, but we have a tradition of hospitality in our house, and as a stranger on your own here, he was pleased to invite you.'

I felt very unsettled about this invitation. Here I was on a mission to expose the iniquities of the Israeli people in their attempt to ethnically cleanse the Palestinians from their own land,. On the other hand it was a thoughtful and generous offer from Tami's father and it would be rude of me to reject it.

'That's very kind of him. I would like very much to come. Will your mother mind?'

She laughed, 'If you think my father is generous you should meet my mother, she will envelope you as if you were an abandoned child.'

So there it was. I began immediately to feel good about it. For some inexplicable reason I took Tami's hand and kissed it, 'Thank you.'

She blushed and looked away. Why did I do that!

We arrived at the scooter rental place. There on the forecourt was the Vespa, the two panniers had been added to it, also a longer saddle. It would do very well. I showed my driving licence to the dealer, he hardly glanced at it. Tami took care of the deposit and the rental for an initial six weeks.

'Its OK, it's down to New Horizons. Yurem gave me the money to cover it.'

I realised I hadn't seen Yurem this morning. I asked Tami where he was.

'He had to go to Haifa, his mother lives there and she has not been very well, he is worried about her. By the way, something I meant to tell you. You know the man you met on the 'plane?'

'Jacob.'

'That's right. Well he came by yesterday afternoon to talk with Yurem, I didn't know he knew him. I don't know what they were talking about. They went into the office and shut the door.'

That's strange I thought, he must have gone there after he met me at that beach café. I shrugged, 'Maybe he's interested in Israeli art.'

I climbed on the Vespa and started it up. Tami took her place on the pillion seat and put her arms round my waist.

'We are in good time now, the Palestinians will have had their morning prayers. It's their Sabbath today, although we will find many things open now, they usually have their café's and restaurants functioning.'

We set off. I prepared myself to drive on the right but at first I had to concentrate hard to get used to this. Tami gave me directions as we went. When we reached the checkpoint at the entrance to the al-Ajami district we showed our identity documents and Tami asked the soldier there if it would be OK for me to come on my own. He looked at my passport and nodded.

We wove our way down the narrow alleyways until we came out into the main square. Tami directed me to a place I could park the scooter. Once we were parked she got off and we locked the scooter with a locking device provided by the dealer. I retrieved my shoulder bag from one of the panniers and we set off across the square towards the old port. I had already seen a place where I wanted to take some photographs and start a sketch. When we got to where I wanted to sit and draw, Tami said she would leave me there and come back in a couple of hours to see how I was getting on.

I settled down to draw the ruined buildings by the port, which I'd noticed the day before. They'd obviously been attacked by the Israeli military, the Haganah as far as I knew, they were pitted with bullet holes and shell damage, a sad sight as they were probably beautiful old buildings.

As usual I was the object of much curiosity with people, mostly Arabic, peering over my shoulder, then moving on without comment. One young man though seemed anxious to talk to me. He asked me in English what I was doing. I explained that I was an artist from England and that I was interested in recording as much as I could about what had happened to Palestine since the arrival of the Israelis. He told me that his name was Hamid. He was about 25 years old. His English was very good. He was distracting me a bit, but I did my best to talk to him, as I was hoping to find out anything I could on the Palestinian reaction to what the Israelis had done to them.

At first he didn't seem to want to talk about it, he preferred to ask me questions about what art school I had been to. He said that he wanted to be an artist, he was self taught and had been drawing and painting since he was very young, he would have liked to have gone to an art school but there was none in Jaffa that he could attend.

I told him that I was there under the auspices of New Horizons, which he had heard of. I suggested that he came back in about an hour and a half, when I hoped that Tami would have come back, and that she might be able to help him. I suggested he brought some evidence of his work. He was pleased by this and promised to return in time.

I went on drawing, uninterrupted, enjoying the challenge of recording what I was seeing. I intended later to take a quantity of photographs as back up, so that if I didn't finish in time I would have a record on film to help me complete the drawings later.

It was getting increasingly hot and I realised I hadn't brought any protection for my head. Largely because the sunhat I had in my suitcase made me look rather silly. A moment of vanity I could regret if I didn't try and find something else. Perhaps Tami would help me.

I went on drawing until it was nearly time for Tami's and Hamid's return. I decided to take some photographs while keeping an eye out for both of them. I eventually saw Tami approaching across the square and waved to her. We went and sat on the low wall where I had been seated. She asked if she could see what I had done. I passed her my sketchbook and explained that when I returned the following day I would complete it. While she was looking at it I saw Hamid returning. I hastily explained about him and that he was going to show us his work.

When he arrived I introduced them. Hamid was a little reserved with her at first, but then Tami spoke to him in Arabic, his face cleared and he responded to her, also in Arabic.

Tami extended her hand for his book of drawings. Hamid looked at me nervously, then passed it to her. Tami moved closer to me, so that we could both look at it together. Hamid sat down next to me.

His first drawings, which he explained to us, had been done when he was very young, were still somewhat childish, but the subject matter was clear and graphic. They were scenes of great violence, some showed explosions and people running, there were drawings of people with their mouths open, seemingly screaming and raising their arms, pointing at some advancing horror, there were buildings in flames, some with holes in them as if they had been shelled, on the roads in front of them lay what looked like bodies. He had drawn these in black and white, but used a red colour to show blood running from them. The later ones showed the sea in the harbour, with bodies floating. There was a drawing of what was supposed to be a passenger ship, so crowded that some of the people were falling off the ship into the sea.

Later in the book, as his drawing improved, there were heads of people, men, women and children, all carefully observed, portraits in fact, and they all registered fear. There were a lot of drawings of ruined buildings, huddled groups of people. More recent drawings were of domestic scenes, people sitting cross-legged on cushions, men sitting in cafés smoking what looked like 'hubble-bubble' pipes. There were some animals, three camel drawings, dogs, and one cat. There were also three drawings of Israeli soldiers, with their guns, radios and other equipment. He had drawn a jeep with armed soldiers in it, and one tank, firing its gun.

It was a clear account of terrible events, like a diary of images rather than words, although there were notes written in Arabic on some of the drawings. I sat back, shocked. Tami was silent.

He was plainly waiting for some comment.

'I think your work is very good, do you have paintings as well?'

'Yes, but they are all at home, too big to carry around.'

I looked at Tami, she was deep in thought.

'He should have an exhibition?'

She nodded, 'But where?'

'Maybe New Horizons would like it there?'

She shook her head, vehemently.

I turned back to Hamid, 'I'm going to be here again tomorrow, maybe I could come and see your paintings?'

Hamid looked pleased and agreed to meet me here again the following afternoon, after prayers, and take me to his house. He then left us.

I packed my camera and sketchbook back into my bag and we made our way to a café where we had some coffee before ordering some hummus and salad again with pita bread. We sat and talked about what we had seen of Hamid's work. I think she was as shocked by it as much as I was.

'I did know that there was a lot of fighting but I had never seen it so graphically shown.'

'But you don't think it would be shown at 'New Horizon's gallery?'

She looked at me, 'Christopher, many of our members were Israeli soldiers at that time, they may well have been involved in the fighting in Jaffa, they want to forget what they did. There is a sort of collective amnesia about what really happened. To have it thrust into their faces would cause many to want to leave New Horizons.'

After we had finished our meal we sat for a while talking some more about Hamid's work. We also discussed my visit to Tami's home that evening for Shabbat. Tami explained that although they were not a particularly Orthodox household they did have certain basic ceremonies that they continued, more out of respect for her mother than anything else. She told me that she would explain what they were about when we next met up.

I needed to change into something a bit more sober, so I drove to my apartment. Tami came up with me and while I showered she sat on the terrace and looked through my sketchbook again. When I finished I put on another shirt and my trousers and my proper shoes. I paraded in front of Tami and she told me I looked fine. She also suggested that she took me shopping for some more clothes once Shabbat was over. I felt I was being 'mothered' again.

I locked up and we went down to the scooter, which I'd parked out in front. With Tami behind me. and her arms around my waist, I was beginning to become much more conscious of her body and breasts pressed against my back. I didn't want to become involved with her, but she was extremely attractive.

Tami directed me to where her parents lived. I made a point of remembering the way, as I knew that I would be returning to my apartment on my own later. It was fairly simple, we went north up Ben Yehuda Street for about 10 minutes then a right on Jabotinsky to Hamedina Square, then a left towards Pinkas and then right and we were there.

Tami's family lived in a low-rise apartment block, not more than four stories high. They were on the first floor. It had four bedrooms, a large living-dining room, a substantial kitchen, a bathroom with a toilet, as well as a separate toilet. It had a long balcony at the back, which looked out onto a pleasant garden, with semi-tropical plants and a small swimming pool. The building had obviously been built since the 1948 war, and was of no particular architectural merit, although pleasant enough.

I was introduced to Tami's family, her father I had already met, he stood when we came in and we shook hands, I thanked him profusely for the invitation to be here for the beginning of Shabbat. I was also introduced to Tami's brother, Benjamin, who was sixteen years old, then her younger sister Sharon, a very pretty twelve year old.

Tami's mother came bustling out of the kitchen and as Tami had predicted, enveloped me like a long lost son. She insisted that I called her by her first name, Miriam. She was busy preparing for Shabbat, but didn't cease a non-stop dialogue with me. Her opening remark, after her effusive greeting, was, 'This is the first time we've had a goy with us for Shabbat.'

This brought an immediate protest from Tami, 'Mama that is not a nice way to describe Christopher.'

For a moment Miriam was flustered, 'I'm so sorry Christopher, 'goy' is a Hebrew expression, it's a sort of slang way of saying a non-Jewish person, forgive me, I didn't mean it as an insult.'

This was accompanied by another large hug.

She then proceeded to explain the whole ceremony of the beginning of Shabbat.

'Shabbat begins with the lighting of two candles, the woman of the house always lights the candles because she is the one who has authority in the house.' She turned to the rest of the family, 'Isn't that so?' 'Yes Mama,' replied the two younger children obediently.

Tami rolled her eyes, and her father had the beginnings of smile at the corners of his mouth.

Then,' said Miriam, ignoring them, 'I recite the blessing, which will be in Hebrew. Tami will translate it for you later, won't you Tami?'

'Yes Mama.'

'We usually have the blessing of the children, but their getting quite grown-up now, so we sometimes do without it, although they know we love them.'

'After that we usually have Kiddush, which is a ceremony which can either be in the synagogue, or at home, between the blessing and our evening meal. I always insisted that we went to the synagogue, but lately the children have been very lax about this.' She turned her gaze on the children again, who looked sheepish.

'This evening we won't do Kiddush at the synagogue, as we have a guest who is not Jewish. Instead your father will recite Kiddush here.

She turned to me again, 'The lighting of the candles traditionally takes place not less than 18 minutes before sunset, so we have another hour before that. I need to go back to the kitchen and continue preparing the 'cholent' for the evening meal. Sharon you must come and help me.'

She looked at Tami, who was still wearing her shorts and a tank top, 'Tami, go and put some proper clothes on, what must our guest think of you dressed like that!'

Privately I thought she looked gorgeous, but I tried to look non-committal.

'Yes Mama.'

She turned to her husband, 'Ariel, you and Benjamin entertain Christopher.

So then I was left with Tami's father, Ariel, and Benjamin. I suddenly realised that I didn't know the family name. We sat down, I was on the sofa next to Benjamin.

I was trying to think of how to address Tami's father, so I started, 'Dr . . . ', He interrupted me, 'Please call me Ariel, Dr. Dayan seems so formal!'

So I had learned his first name and his family name in a very short space of time. I was still faced with my old problem of finding it difficult to address an older person by their first name.

'Er . . . Ariel, I understand from Tami that you were a soldier?'

He became serious, 'We were all soldiers at that time, I belonged to the Haganah, I was in the Alexandroni Brigade but there were also people who fought with the Irgun Zwai Leumi or the Stern Gang.' He said the last name with some distaste.

'When was that?'

'I joined in 1945.'

'What was it like then?'

He thought for a moment, 'Have you heard of the Notrim?'

I shook my head, 'I know very little other than the British had the Mandate here, which ceased in 1947.'

'The Notrim was a Jewish police force set up by the British in 1936. It was intended to be a police force to protect the Jewish settlements. It was trained and armed by the British and by 1945 was the core basis for the Haganah, which was the main faction of what became the IDF. I joined it in 1945.'

Benjamin, who had not said anything so far, pointed at a framed photograph on a bookshelf, 'That's Papa when he was a soldier.'

I got up and looked at the photograph. Ariel was standing with three other men, they were in a sort of uniform. There was no mistaking him, apart from his grey hair he looked much the same, even slimmer than he was now.

I noticed that next to it was another photograph of one person, also in uniform, much more up to date. When I looked at it I was shocked to see that it was Tami. I hadn't thought of her having done military service, but of course they all had to do military service here, the men three years, the women two. She seemed so young. Slung over her shoulder was a weapon, it looked like an Uzi. She was smiling broadly at the camera. Somehow I was shocked by seeing her as a soldier, even though I should have known. Somehow I felt that there was a loss of innocence.

'I'm going to be a soldier soon.' said Benjamin proudly.

'Well not for two years.' His father said.

'I have done my military service, in England. It was for two years.'

'Did you shoot people?' Benjamin was bright eyed with curiosity.

'No, as I said, I did my two years in England.'

'Don't you have Arabs there?'

His father interrupted. 'This is not a conversation we should be having now, on the eve of Shabbat.'

At that moment Tami re-appeared. She was wearing a simple, modest, pale green dress in cotton. It had a shirt top, buttoned up, but leaving one open at the top, so I could see her throat, but otherwise it was very demure. Her long black hair was tied back in a ponytail; I was struck by how lovely she was.

Miriam came bustling back in again, she eyed Tami, 'That's better.' She turned to me, 'See Christopher, she can look quite nice when she wants too.'

'I think she looks beautiful at all times.' I replied gallantly.

Tami blushed again.

'Now,' said Miriam briskly, 'I want you children to lay the table, it's getting close to the time I light the candles.' She went back into the kitchen.

Tami and the younger children set about laying the table. I sat down again with Ariel.

'What are your plans for the rest of your time here?'

I explained my intention to visit about twelve kibbutzim around the country as well as visiting not only Jaffa but also Haifa, Jerusalem and possibly Beersheba.

'That's a very ambitious plan, I doubt if you will manage to do more than half of that.'

'Yes it is,' I admitted, 'But if I don't give myself a programme and an objective I will just be wandering around aimlessly.'

'I suppose Tami will be travelling with you?'

'If she can give me the time I would of course like that, but I understand if she can't, and I'll manage somehow.'

'Before you start your travels come to New Horizons and I will tell you about some of the artists whose paintings are on the walls.'

'I would very much like that.'

We talked some more about my proposed trip, he mentioned several kibbutzim which I might find interesting. I listened politely but in my mind my own agenda was clear.

The table was laid and we were ready for the lighting of the candles. Ariel turned to me and said, 'It is normal for the men to wear a 'kippah', I have one here for you.' He produced one of the skull caps I had noticed the men wearing on the 'plane, and passed it to me. I was considerably embarrassed by this but tried to put it on, Tami came forward and producing a hair pin helped me fix it on the back of my head. Once it was secured I soon forgot I had it on.

Miriam brought in two wrapped loaves and placed them on the table. A glass of wine was poured and also placed on the table. There were already two candles there. We stood around the table and waited for Miriam. She'd taken off her apron, revealing a rather floral dress, the opposite of Tami's rather simple attire.

Miriam checked the clock and prepared to light the candles, we stood in silence round her. She struck a match and lit the candles, she then covered her eyes and intoned a prayer.

> 'Barukh atah adonai, eloheinu, melek ha'olam
> Asher kidish shanu b'mitz' votav v'tizivanu
> L'had'lik neir shel Shabbat. Amien.'

Miriam then uncovered her eyes. 'Now your father will recite Kiddush.' Ariel stood next to her, he picked up the glass of wine and held it in his hand, and after a moment's pause began. Tami, who was standing next to me, surreptitiously squeezed my hand.

> 'Vay'hi erev vay'hi voker yom hashishi
> Vay'khulu hashamayim v'ha' aretz v'khol tz'va'am
> Vay'khal elohim bayom hash'vi'I m'a'kh'to asah
> Vayish'bot bayom hash'vi'l mikol m'la'kh'to asher asah
> Vay'varekh Elohim et yom hash'vi'I vay'kadeish oto
> Ki vo shavat mikol m'la'kh'to asher bara Elohim la'asot
> Barak atah Adonai, Eloheinu, melekh ha-olam
> Borei p'ri hagafan. Amien.'

There was another pause. A bowl of warm water was on one of the side tables and we each in turn washed our hands, then there was a short blessing, and Miriam told us all to sit down. She insisted that I sat on her left-hand side and Benjamin sat on her right, Tami sat next to me.

Miriam unwrapped the two loaves of bread. She then broke them into pieces and distributed them to everyone at the table.

'This is what we call 'challah', they are made with eggs and other things, then braided and baked. Try some.' She broke off a piece and passed it to me. 'They are traditional for Shabbat and other holidays.'

I broke off a piece and tasted it, it was rather sweet for bread, and very 'eggy', which made them rather yellow to look at. I quite liked it, although it was too sweet for my taste. Nevertheless I made appreciative noises.

Miriam and Sharon went into the kitchen to bring the rest of the food. They returned with two bowls of what looked like a sort of stew.

Miriam sat down and proceeded to load a large portion onto my plate. I protested that it was too much.

'Nonsense, you need building up, you are far too thin.' She squeezed one of my arms, 'Look I can get my hand round it.'

Tami giggled next to me, 'I told you.' she whispered in my ear.

'This is a typical Shabbat meal.' Miriam continued, 'It's called 'cholen' and is cooked at least twelve hours before the start of Shabbat and will last until tomorrow evening. It's forbidden to do any cooking on Shabbat, amongst many other things.'

She kept up a non-stop conversation during the meal, asking me about my life in England, what were my parents like, where did they live, was I still living at home, how many brothers and sisters did I have. She was horrified to hear that I was an only child.

'You poor thing! No brothers or sisters!'

Personally I was quite happy to be an only child, but for Miriam it seemed very sad.

'You must have more to eat!' She proceeded to load more food on to my plate, in spite of my further protests. She obviously thought that more food would go some way towards making up for me being an only child. There was no doubt about her genuine warmth toward me and I was rather touched by this, but at the same time I felt guilty about how I was really in this country to find out about the terrible treatment of the Palestinian people, being carried out by the Israelis.

I didn't stay very late there, it was after all their Sabbath, so shortly after the meal was finished I expressed my thanks again for their hospitality and prepared to leave. Miriam hugged me again and insisted that I came on a weekday evening, where she promised me much more elaborate Israeli food. She also instructed Tami to look after me and to make sure that I had enough to eat. Tami escorted me to the door. She was plainly amused at her mother's attention to me and thanked me for being so polite.

'It was very kind of her and I enjoyed it very much, she made me feel very at home.'

'Tomorrow Sabbath ends at sunset, if you like we could meet up in the evening and you could tell me how you got on, as you will have been on your own down in Jaffa. Shall I come to the apartment?'

'Yes that's great, if you don't mind.'

'Stop saying that, I wouldn't suggest it if I didn't mean it.'

Just as I was about to leave she stopped me, 'Wait', she laughed, 'You are still wearing the kippah, they'll think you are a nice Jewish boy after all.' She unpinned it, 'There you are, a goy again.' She then covered her mouth as if she had said something rather rude, 'I'm sorry, I just told my mother off for saying that.' She giggled though and leant forward and kissed me on the cheek.

She waved to me as I drove off on the scooter. I made my way back without getting lost. When I arrived at the apartment building I decided to park the scooter at the back, rather than on the main road. There was an alleyway down the side of the building and a small yard at the back. I noticed that there was a van parked in the yard, I assumed it was someone from the next building, as I was sure that there were no other inhabitants in my building. Apart from that young woman who came down the stairs on my first morning, and the sound of a door shutting when I entered at the end of the afternoon, I had neither seen nor heard anyone else. The windows of the van were dark and it was impossible to see inside, neither were there any markings on the sides.

I made my way up to my apartment. I had decided again to write in my journal on the terrace, first I made myself some strong coffee, there had been none offered at Tami's.

I covered myself again with anti-mosquito oil before carrying my notebook and the coffee out onto the terrace. The temperature had dropped and it was now very pleasantly warm. I gazed across the buildings opposite at the sea with its little ships with their navigation lights on, moving about, I listened to the sound of the cicadas, the muted sound of traffic and the occasional bursts of Arabic music, I breathed in the scent of flowers and hot earth and thought myself very lucky to be here. Whatever the reason I was here for, it was a marvelous experience for me.

I also reflected on the evening at Tami's, her family and mother's warmth and generosity towards me. In spite of the fact that, like Simon, I was a committed agnostic and seriously against all forms of ritual, I had felt a curious sympathy for what I had just witnessed, it made me understand how binding their tradition and faith was, and how it had helped them survive the worst excesses of non-Jews, with their attempts to exterminate them.

I wrote about this experience in my journal in as detailed a way as I could, as well as the encounter with Hamid and my progress with drawing and photographing the remains of the ruined city.

It took me about an hour and a half and at one time I fortified myself with a couple of glasses of wine.

When I finally went to bed it was after midnight and I felt too tired to read, so I put the light out and lay there thinking. At first I was running through in my mind what I would be doing the following day, then my thoughts turned to Sylvia. I wondered if she had emerged again from her depression and I resolved the next day to send a postcard to her. I must also send one to my parents.

Chapter 11

I slept very soundly that night, when I woke I was surprised to see that it was already 7 o'clock, I had not been woken by the distant 'call to prayer' as I had the previous days.

I got up and went into the bathroom. After cleaning my teeth, shaving and having a shower, I dressed again in shorts and a short sleeved shirt and put everything else in the shower sink and filled it with warm water. I realised that I didn't have any washing powder, so I poured in some dish washing liquid.

I had muesli and fruit for breakfast. When I thought the clothes had soaked enough, I emptied the now soapy water and running the cold I rinsed each piece until all the soap was gone. When I had finished I squeezed the water out of them as best I could, then took them out onto the terrace and arranged them around in the sun. I made up my mind to try and find a clothesline, which I could string from various points on the terrace, and also some clothes pegs. I was normally quite tidy in my London flat but with the help of a nearby Laundromat I had never had to use a clothesline. I was really becoming quite domesticated.

I re-read my journal from the evening before. I made a few corrections, but by and large it was quite accurate. I hoped that I would see Tami in the evening, I wanted to tell her how I had been quite moved by the ceremony. I wondered what Simon's reaction would be when he finally arrived and heard about my Shabbat experience.

Another thing crossed my mind, the day was also the equivalent of the Muslim Sabbath? Was it today, would I find everything shut everywhere? I needed to set off and find out. My shoulder bag still had my sketchbooks and drawing materials in it. I had taken out my camera though and removed the used film and replaced it with a new one. I wondered whether to leave the used film in the apartment, but decided to keep it with me.

I went out on the terrace and discovered that my washing was already dry. I folded it as neatly as I could and arranged it in a couple of drawers in the wardrobe they had provided.

Locking the apartment I went downstairs and tried to find a door in the building which would take me out to the yard behind, where I had left my scooter. I eventually found a door which had a window in it that looked out into the yard, but it was locked and I couldn't find a key, so I was forced to go out the front door and round the building to the back.

The van was still parked there, as I went by I tried again to peer in the windows, but they were of tinted glass and it was impossible to see anything. I thought I detected a faint hum from inside, I pressed my ear against the side and heard it quite distinctly. I tried one of the doors, but it was firmly locked.

I put my shoulder bag in one of the panniers and started up the scooter and rode out onto Ben Yehuda street.

Turning left I headed towards Jaffa. It was not hard to find my way. About two streets down a sign, conveniently in Hebrew and English, directed me to Jaffa, down Hakoveshim, until it reached a junction with a street with the unlikely name of Professor Kaufman and finally to the clock tower, which seemed to be at the centre of New Jaffa.

I reached the checkpoint. Fortunately the same soldier who had been on duty the day before, when I was with Tami, was there and after a cursory glance at my passport, he waved me on.

I found my way to the main square, where Tami and I had lunch. The café we had been at was open, as were the others in the square. I thought of having a mint tea, but then decided to do it later, after I had done some drawing. I should have brought some water with me, I must get myself a water container of some sort.

I made my way back to where I had started my drawing yesterday. I parked the scooter nearby and locked it after taking my shoulder bag from the pannier. I had brought my silly sunhat with me and put it on, at least Tami was not here to see me looking so ridiculous. I must try and find something else.

My thoughts turned to what I was doing. Finally spending a day on my own I could allow myself some space to think about my situation. Why was I doing this? I had come here with a clear agenda. ~The Palestinians were good, but abused. The Israelis were bad and war criminals. Simple really, why was I getting confused? One Shabbat dinner and my certainty was already wavering. Once again I didn't know what Simon was going to say.

I settled down to my drawing. It was very hot but I was gradually getting used to it. I drew for about an hour and a half, I then looked at my watch, it was after one o'clock. I went on drawing for another 15 minutes, then packed my sketchbook back into my shoulder bag. I made my way to the cafe we were at yesterday and sat down at one of the tables under the awning. The man came bustling out and greeted me with, 'Salaam'.

I asked him if he spoke English, 'Yes, yes . . . I learn at school.'

'Some mint tea please, also some hummus and salad.' I must expand my diet, this would be the third time I had hummus and salad.

He brought the tea first and as soon as it was cool enough I drank it and when he came back with the hummus and salad I ordered another tea and an orange juice.

I resolved to learn some useful phrases in Arabic. It was going to be difficult as I found the writing impossible to understand, I would just have to write down useful phrases phonetically, in my notebook which I had brought with me.

I was just finishing my meal when I saw Hamid walking by, across the other side of the square. I called out to him, he came over smiling, and shook my hand.

'I was on my way to see if you were drawing, where you were yesterday.'

I told him to sit down. When the man came out I asked Hamid if he would like anything. He shook his head. I asked for my bill and when it came I paid it.

'You wanted to see some of my paintings?'

I nodded.

'You shouldn't leave your scooter where you can't see it, it's not safe.'

We set off back to the place I had left, it was still there. I put my shoulder bag back in one of the panniers.

'We should drive to my home, it's not far.'

I got on the scooter and started it up. Hamid got on the back. He did not put his arms around me, but held on to the sides of the saddle.

'Go straight ahead then turn first right.'

He directed me down several narrow alleys until we came to an area near the port. It opened onto a wider street, where he asked me to stop outside what seemed to be a ruined house. One side of it was just a heap of rubble, some stone steps on the front led to the next floor. The front of the house was pockmarked with bullet holes, and what must have been shell holes. Looking along the street I noted that nearly all the buildings were damaged in a similar way, some completely destroyed. There was rubble and stones scattered along the whole length. Some children were playing amongst the rubble, there was washing drying on a line across the road.

After I had locked the scooter Hamid led me up the steps of the house we had stopped in front of. We entered what I found was a small apartment. There were three rooms altogether. In the first room we entered there were two women and a young, bright eyed girl, about eight years old. Hamid introduced me to the older woman, 'Mama, this is Christopher.'

She nodded, half covering her face with her head scarf.

'My mother doesn't speak any English.'

I half bowed and said 'Salaam'.

He turned to the younger woman, 'This is my elder sister Jasmin.' She did not attempt to cover her face, but smiled and said 'How do you do?' in perfect English.

The little girl was bouncing up and down, plainly wanting to be introduced.

'This is Saba my neice.'

'Hello,' She said immediately, 'are you American? Do you know Frank Sinatra? Have you met Walt Disney?'

I was astonished at this burst of English.

'She's learning English at school . . . very fast it seems.'

'Yes, yes, I can recite 'Humpty Dumpty sat on the wall . . . .'

Hamid picked her up and kissed her on the cheek, 'Not now Saba, Christopher is a famous artist and he has come to inspect my paintings . . . maybe later.'

She wriggled out of his arms and sat down, 'Will you paint me?'

I looked at her, she was bubbling with vitality. 'If I have time I will do a nice drawing of you, not today though.'

Her bright eyes followed me as Hamid lead me into the next room. She called out something in Arabic. Hamid replied, also in the same language.

He laughed, 'She wants to come with us, I told her no.'

This room was a simple kitchen and eating room, there was a cupboard and a table with four chairs. There was a stove, with a large saucepan bubbling with something, and very little else.

The next room contained three beds and again little else.

There was another door off to the left, Hamid led me through. It was on the side of the building, which had looked badly damaged from the outside. There was a tarpaulin hung down one wall. Although there was a small window the light was not very good. This was Hamid's studio.

There were paintings stacked along one wall, and a makeshift easel in the centre of the room, on which there was a painting, which he had just begun.

'When I need more light I take this down.' Hamid pulled the tarpaulin down, revealing a huge hole, where a shell had landed and demolished nearly half the wall.

He began to take out some of the paintings stacked against the wall. He took the painting that he had just started down from the easel and replaced it with one of the ones he had just pulled out.

It was a dramatic, densely packed painting, filled with images of terrified people, their expressions of fear made clear by their eyes and open, perhaps screaming, mouths. Much of it was black and white, so that colour, mostly red, when it appeared, made a dramatic statement. It was a figurative 'Guernica'.

He then showed me a number of paintings on the same theme, as well as small groups and dramatic portraits. They were all very graphic scenes and plainly illustrating what happened during the expulsion of Palestinians from their towns and villages.

I spent some time looking at these images, the quality of the paintings varied, some were cruder than others, but there was no escaping the drama of the images or the meaning of them.

He showed me also some of his black and white drawings, they all conveyed the same message. They were reminiscent of Goya.

I asked him if I could take photographs of some of them. He was quite happy for me to do this. He displayed the ones I wanted on the makeshift easel, turning it towards the light from the hole in the wall.

When I had done enough he replaced the tarpaulin.

'Come,' he said, 'my mother will make us tea.'

We went back to the first room, where Saba was eagerly awaiting our return. Hamid's mother and sister went into the kitchen room and I could hear them making tea and perhaps more.

Saba sat down next to me and produced what looked like a school exercise book. 'Look,' she said, opening the book, it was full of her drawings. 'I did all these.' They were a childish version of Hamid's work, with stick like people, tanks and guns, some people lying down with red splashed all over them. She was obviously trying to imitate her uncle's work. In their simple way they were just as powerful as Hamid's.

'When I'm grown up I'm going to kill Israelis.'

I was shocked at hearing these words from an eight-year-old little girl.

I was about to protest when Hamid said, 'Saba, don't talk like that! We don't kill people!'

Turning to me he said, 'She doesn't mean it, she's very young. It's the sort of thing they hear at school, from other children. She doesn't understand yet.'

Saba didn't say anything, but she looked anything but contrite.

I reflected on what Tami's brother had said, when I told him that I did my military service in England and he asked me if I had shot anyone, and I had said no, I was in England, he then said, 'Don't you have any Arabs there?' The implication was obvious. With these attitudes amongst the children, it did not bode well for the future.

Hamid's mother came in with mint tea and some pieces of a sweet pastry. It contained pistachio nuts amongst others and was sweetened with honey. It was delicious but very sweet.

Hamid's mother said something to Saba in Arabic. Saba protested at what her grandmother said, but then got up and left the room, carrying her sketchbook with her, she was pouting.

I asked Hamid where his father was.

'He's dead.'

'Oh I'm sorry, when did he die?'

Hamid thought for a minute, then, 'We come originally from a medium-sized village, called Bayt Dajan, it was about nine kilometres east of Jaffa. In 1948 the Israelis came and after much fighting drove us out, my father was taken away with most of the other men in the village. We never saw him again, some months later we were told that he had died while he was in Israeli hands, we believe he was shot, along with a number of others.

'That's terrible! What did he do?'

'He was a doctor, the only one in Bayt Dajan. He looked after everyone, Arab people, Jews, Christians. He was greatly loved, especially by the poor people, he would take care of them, often for nothing. There was much killing at that time, we were driven out of the town, over 3,500 Arab people. I was ten when we left. We came here to Jaffa, thinking it was safe, it was still supposed to be part of Palestine, but the Israelis came and there was some terrible fighting, eventually nearly the whole Arab population was driven out, many fled by sea, others escaped by land, many are now refugees in Jordan and Egypt. The ones who went by sea ended up either in the Lebanon, or in Egypt.'

I was staggered by what he told me, three and a half thousand people!

'How did you survive?'

'More by luck really, we were hiding out with my mother's sister and we just stayed, not going out for at least a week. When things became quieter and there was no longer the sound of shooting we ventured out. It was terrible at first, all the buildings were damaged and the shops were shut, there was no market anymore. Then gradually a few traders appeared. The Israelis rounded us up and made the Arab people live in al-Ajami, where they could keep an eye on us. They took all the houses in the other parts and moved into them, bringing Jewish survivors of the Holocaust from Eastern Europe, giving them Arab houses, looting the ruined shops, everywhere there was looting. Somehow we managed to survive, but the beautiful city of Jaffa has been ruined.'

'Have any of the refugees tried to return?'

'They can't, there is no right of return, according to the Israelis. They have stolen our land, and they have stolen our country.'

'Can you go back to your village?'

'It doesn't exist anymore, just a few ruined and crumbling buildings, the better houses which were undamaged were taken by the Israelis who moved in refugees, many from the Holocaust. And there was more looting of course. The rest of what was the town the Israelis have filled with their own buildings, it and the land around has become a Jewish enclave. What was our land has been stolen.'

'Where is Jasmin's husband?'

'Mohammed? About six months ago he was arrested. He was with a group of people protesting about being confined to al-Ajami. They were all arrested by the Israeli army, they are in prison somewhere. We are not allowed to visit him, he is alive though, Jasmin had a message from him.'

No wonder Saba said what she did, I would probably have felt the same.

'How do you manage now for money?'

'I have a job in the docks, I have a special pass which allows me to go and work. There are quite a few of us who are allowed out to work for Israeli companies, we are not very well paid, but we have to survive somehow. It is very closely watched and we have to be back in al-Ajami before it is dark. Jasmin's husband went out to work, before he was imprisoned. Now we just manage on what I can earn.'

Its monstrous, I thought, these poor people, their homes stolen or destroyed, their town ruined or occupied, the survivors living in what was virtually an open air prison, only allowed out under strict controls. What were the United Nations doing about this?

I asked Hamid. He shrugged and replied that they were useless as far as the Palestinians were concerned. Every time they passed a resolution condemning Israel for these crimes, the Israelis just ignored it, and the rest of the world said nothing.

I looked at my watch, it was getting late in the afternoon, I needed to be back before sundown as Tami was hoping to meet up with me.

I bid Hamid goodbye and thanked him for letting me see his work and promised to return again soon. I put my head round the door of the kitchen and thanked his mother and Jasmine for their hospitality. His mother did not understand, but Jasmin translated for her, and she smiled and nodded. Saba rushed over to me,

'Look, I've done a drawing of you.'

She showed me her drawing, in her sketchbook, it was a long face with a mass of what looked like curly hair on top. The mouth was open, smiling with jagged teeth, the eyes were very blue. It was hardly flattering, she was only eight years old, but it had all her energy in the way it was drawn. I duly admired it and thanked her.

'Don't forget, you are going to draw me!'

'No Saba, I won't forget, I will come again very soon. She smiled and bounced up and down.

They all insisted on coming outside and waving me off. I was very touched by their kindness, as I had been with Tami's family.

I arrived back at my apartment at about 6 o'clock. I took my scooter round the back, the van had gone. I was about to walk round to the front of the building when I noticed that the door that I had tried to open from the inside was now slightly ajar. I entered, shutting the door behind me I noticed that there was still no key.

When I reached the apartment I smelt the faint trace of cigarette smoke. As I don't smoke my sense of smell is quite acute. I looked through all the rooms; everything was as I had left it. In spite of this I had the distinct impression that someone had been in here. Nothing was missing and nothing seemed to be disturbed, but I couldn't rid myself of the feeling that someone had been in the apartment.

After I had a shower and changed into clean clothes, I went out onto the terrace. It was still very warm, but with the sun sinking the heat was diminishing. I pulled out the sketchbook from my bag and continued the panoramic drawing, which I had begun when I first arrived. When I got up to go inside I noticed a cigarette stub on the floor of the terrace, I picked it up, there was enough left for me to just make out the name, it was something like 'Noblesse'. I must ask Tami about that name.

About 8 o'clock, the door bell rang. It was Tami, I buzzed her in.

She arrived at the door, slightly out of breath, she was carrying several large bags.

'Sorry I'm late but I stopped off and bought you some things.' She started unloading the bags on the kitchen table.

There were a couple of saucepans and a frying pan, what looked like a cookbook, a quantity of vegetables, several jars of spices, and a large plastic container with what looked like a soup.

'Wow!' I said, 'You shouldn't have gone to all that trouble.'

'Don't worry, most of it is donated by my mother. The saucepans and frying pans are from her collection of cooking implements, she has enough saucepans to stock a small store. I bought the vegetables on the way, the spices are also from my mother, as well as this borscht,' She indicated the container. 'She's afraid you may be suffering from malnutrition.' She laughed.

I was overwhelmed by this generosity of both Tami and her mother.

Tami busied herself putting things in the fridge and finding room in the cupboards for the frying pan and saucepans. She also found somewhere for the spices.

'Are you hungry? I could heat up the borscht and we could have it now.'

'Yes please.'

While she was doing this I got out some spoons and forks and put them on the table. I also got out a couple of glasses and the white wine from the fridge. When Tami had finished heating up the soup she served it up in a couple of soup bowls I had found in the cupboards. We sat down and I poured the wine. Tami lifted her glass and touched mine with it, saying 'Shalom', I too muttered 'Shalom'.

She laughed, 'You are supposed to look into my eyes when you say that.' I repeated it and gazed into her eyes, noticing for the first time that there were flecks of green in the brown, framed with long dark eyelashes. Not for the first time I realised that she was very beautiful.

The soup was very good, it was thick with ingredients and a meal in its self. I asked Tami what was in it. She told me that it was primarily beets with other things added. 'It's a peasant dish from Poland, where my mother comes from.'

After we had finished eating we went out onto the terrace, with our glasses of wine. I showed her the cigarette end, which I had found there.

'Noblesse . . . that's a popular brand . . . manufactured here.'

'I'm sure it wasn't here before, I don't smoke, so where did it come from?

When I got back from Jaffa I smelt cigarette smoke as soon as I came in. Do you think someone came in here while I was out?'

She looked puzzled, 'I don't know who would want to do that . . . I'll ask Yurem tomorrow, he would know.'

We had some more wine and sat quietly for a while, looking out across the rooftops to the sea, listening to the sounds of music and the endless susurrus of the cicadas.

I thought how extraordinary it was that after only four days I had visited Jaffa three times, attended a Shabbat, made friends with a Palestinian artist and his family, started my drawings, rented a scooter, and was now sitting sipping wine with a beautiful Israeli girl on a terrace looking across Tel Aviv. Simon would be jealous.

Which reminded me: Simon was arriving tomorrow. Should I meet him at the airport, or should I wait for him to contact me? I had rather wanted to make a trip to Bayt Dajan. I was very curious to see what was left after 1948 when Hamid and his family had been driven out, and his father had disappeared.

Almost in answer to my thoughts, Tami suddenly said, 'What do you want to do tomorrow?'

I made up my mind, 'I'd rather like to go to Bayt Dajan.'

She was interested by this, 'Why there?'

I told her that I had met up with Hamid and been to see his paintings, which very much impressed me. He had also told me that his family is from Bayt Dajan and that he had never been able to go back there. He also asked me if I could go there, so that when we next met I could tell him what it was like now. I didn't tell her about how his father had been taken away by the Israelis and had never been seen by them again.

'OK' she said, 'but I can tell you that it is now almost a suburb of Tel Aviv and there is not much left of the old village. I'll come with you.'

She looked at her watch, 'Wow, it's getting late, I'd better go or my mother will think I'm up to no good.' She looked at me and grinned, 'That wouldn't do, would it?'

Was she flirting with me?

We went back into the kitchen and she started to clear the table.

'I'll do that, it's the least I can do after you brought all that food.'

I walked down the stairs with her. I asked her if she would like me to drive her back home on the scooter, but she refused, pointing to the bus stop across the road, 'There is a bus that takes me to the end of my road, I'll be fine. I'll come in the morning, about 10.30?'

She crossed the road and I saw a bus coming, she waved to me and got on it when it arrived.

I went back into the building, but before I climbed the staircase I went to the back door to see if it was still unlocked, it was. I searched for the key but couldn't find it anywhere. This made me feel very insecure, I resolved to ask Yurem about it the next time I see him.

I returned to the apartment, and after I had washed up and cleared away the remains of the meal, washed the container from Tami's mother in order to return it, I went out onto the terrace and wrote up my journal. There was much to write about after my visit to Hamid's house. I reflected on what he had told me about their history. As I did so I was once again convinced that the Palestinian people had suffered a great wrong, and that their country had been stolen, as admitted by Ben Gurion. I resolved to go again after I met up with Simon.

It was quite late when I finished and the noises of traffic had diminished. The sound of the cicadas seemed louder than usual. I wondered when Simon would contact me. I didn't regret my decision not to meet him at the airport, he would expect me to have become more self sufficient here, and I would have much to report to him when we finally met up.

I also thought about finding the cigarette end. I was beginning to think that I was under some sort of surveillance, remembering the parked van, the young woman who had passed me on the stairs, finding the apartment door unlocked, the sound of a door shutting when I had entered the day before, the open back door, now the smell of someone smoking when I entered the apartment, later finding the cigarette stub on the terrace. It was all beginning to add up to something more disturbing, or was I becoming paranoid? I would tell Simon about all this when we met up.

I went to bed and fell asleep almost immediately, and dreamt of Sylvia running away from me, I chased her, calling her to stop. When I caught up with her I saw that she had changed into Tami.

Chapter 12

The next day I was up early, I had showered and dressed by 7am. I had also had my muesli and orange juice. I read through my notes on the visit to Jaffa and Hamid's house and his paintings. I also had the photographs of his paintings. I debated on whether I should ask Tami if there was somewhere I could get them processed. I decided against it, I would take all my negatives back to London and get them processed there. There was still time before Tami came, so I took my sketchbook out on to the terrace and continued with my panoramic drawing.

She was slightly late, and as she came through the door she began apologising, 'I was called by New Horizons, Yurem said he wanted to talk to me about something.'

I sat her down and offered her coffee, she shook her head and said that she had already had several cups with Yurem.

'Did you get a chance to mention the possible intruder in the apartment to Yurem.'

'Oh I'm sorry, I was distracted by what he was saying. I'll do it tomorrow.'

'That's OK, don't worry. Would you like some orange juice?'

'Oh yes, that would be good.'

I squeezed some fresh orange juice while she sat out on the terrace looking at my drawing. I brought it out for her there.

'Oh, I wish I could draw like this, could you teach me how to do it?'

'We all draw differently, it's like our handwriting . . . what you need is patience. Why don't you bring me some of your drawings tomorrow and I will see if I can guide you.'

'Thank you.'

As we sat sipping our juice, she gazed out across the city. She seemed distracted,

'Are you OK?'

'Yes, yes, I'm fine . . . just something that Yurem said, I'm still trying to puzzle it out.'

'Do you want to tell me?'

She shook her head, 'Not now . . . shouldn't we go?'

I nodded and gathered up my bag and sketchbook, I looked at my sun hat, then shook my head.

'Oh, I nearly forgot . . . I brought you this.'

She produced a cap from her bag. It was dark blue and had a large peak at the front, there was some sort insignia above the peak.

'Its an American baseball cap, the peak will keep the sun out of your eyes . . . or if the sun is behind you, turn it round and it will protect your neck and the back of your head. Try it on. I put it on and looked in a mirror. I thought I looked rather good in it.

'What do you think?'

'Its great . . . I must pay you for it.'

She shook her head, 'It's mine . . . so you can borrow it.'

'What about you?'

'I've got another one.' She produced a similar cap, but this was in a sandy khaki colour, the insignia on the front was in Hebrew. 'I got this when I was in the Army.'

'What does this say?' pointing at the insignia, 'יעידומה ליח'.

'It's the regiment I was in.'

She didn't elaborate. I was hoping she would, I was very curious about the idea that she had been a soldier, somehow it didn't fit with the image I had of her now.

I locked up and we set off down the stairs. When we reached the ground floor we headed to the back door, which led out to the backyard where my scooter was parked. The door was still unlocked.

'I can't find the key to this door so it is now permanently unlocked. It was locked when I first came here, I think it's rather insecure, anyone can come into the building.

She looked puzzled, 'I'll ask Yurem, he can get on to the people who still own it. They should know where the key is.'

We set off on the scooter, going south down Ben Yehuda. Tami had her hands round my waist, she seemed to be holding me more tightly than before. We passed the turn off to Jaffa. Gradually the buildings gave way to open country, dotted with many orange groves. After about half an hour we found ourselves approaching a small town. Tami leant forward and rested her chin on my shoulder. 'This is Bayt Dajan.'

We entered the outskirts of the town. There were a number of deserted houses and buildings. We stopped in the centre. I parked the scooter and we began to walk through the main road. There were a few people about. Tami stopped a woman with a young child walking along, carrying a shopping bag. Tami spoke to her in Hebrew. She was obviously asking her questions, the woman shrugged her shoulders in answer to one question.

Tami turned to me, 'I asked her where were the Arab people who lived here, she didn't know. She said that there were only Israelis living here, all the Arab people had left a long time ago. The woman pointed up the road and said something.

Tami said, 'There is a Israeli settlement which is about two kilometres up the road which is called Beyt Dagan, and another just to the east, called Ganot. They are exclusively Hebrew settlements. It seems that they were established on Palestinian lands, after the Arab people left.'

'Ask her why they left.'

The woman shrugged her shoulders again, and said something.

'What did she say?'

'She said she didn't know, it happened before she came here, but anyway who cares, they don't matter, it's our land.'

As she had been answering Tami, I noticed that she kept glancing at the cap which Tami was wearing.

We walked through the village. There were many contemporary buildings, scattered amongst them though were derelict houses and shops, some boarded up, some gradually falling down, there were also older buildings which now flourished as Israeli stores. There was also what had obviously been a small mosque, which now seemed to be used as a storehouse. Some of the older houses were now occupied.

A man came walking down the road, pushing a handcart with some sacks on it. Tami stopped him and began to ask him questions. It appeared that he had been one of the early settlers who came in 1949, when the fighting was over. Tami pointed to some of the derelict buildings and houses. She was obviously asking him who had lived there. She continued to ask him questions, he replied, occasionally pointing at buildings. At one time he glanced at me, she shook her head and said something rapidly. Eventually she appeared to be thanking him, we then walked on. She seemed pensive as we walked, at one point she took my arm and leant slightly against me.

'The last man I spoke to was one of the earlier settlers, he came from eastern Europe, he and his family arrived here in late 1947.'

She paused for a while, then, 'He told me that when they first arrived, the Palestinians had fled only a few days before, the shops and stores still had goods in them, the Israeli soldiers encouraged the new arrivals to loot them, as well as the abandoned houses. Everyone joined in the looting, the soldiers did too, there are many photographs of that time with the refugees carrying as much as they could, some using barrows and carts, all smiling and laughing. Many families also moved into the abandoned Palestinian houses, which had been looted as well, those which were not too badly damaged.'

'Let's find somewhere we can get some coffee.'

I looked up and down the street, there was what appeared to be a café about a hundred yards further on. We headed towards it.

When we were seated and had ordered the coffee, I told her that I wanted to take some photographs before we left Bayt Dajan. She nodded. I could see that there was something on her mind still, as there had been since she arrived this morning.

When the coffee arrived, with the customary glasses of water, we were left alone. I reached across the table and took one of her hands.

'Tami, you're worrying about something . . . tell me. Is it to do with your family?'

She shook her head.

I pressed on, 'Is it to do with Yurem? Am I taking up too much of your time?'

I could see by her face that I was near the mark, 'Listen I can find my way around. I have maps, I know more or less where I want to go, I'll be OK.'

Again she shook her head, then, she seemed to make up her mind.

'Its not that Yurem thinks you are taking up too much of my time, quite the contrary, he wants me to be with you a much as possible. As I do.'

She hesitated again, then, 'I must tell you why Yurem wanted to talk to me.' She paused again. I could see that she was having difficulty saying whatever it was.'

'When I went to see Yurem this morning, as he asked me to, he told me something.

I waited expectantly.

'He told me that someone had been to see him, a guy from the Intelligence Service . . . Mossad!

Shit, I thought, here it comes, I'm going to be expelled . . . and I've only just arrived!

'He told me that they wanted me to keep an eye on you, to see where you go, what you draw, what you photograph, what you are thinking, and if possible, what you are writing. Yurem doesn't want to go along with this, he likes you, he thinks you are here as a genuine artist. He doesn't have much choice though, Mossad is very powerful.'

She took her cap off and sat for a few moments with it in her hands, looking at it.

'You know, when I was doing my military service I was in the Intelligence section, it was more of a clerk's job, I collated information about the towns and villages which we had occupied and cleared of many, if not all of their inhabitants. In the process I learned things about our behaviour which were little short of inhumane, it has stayed with me ever since . . . which is the reason I ask all these questions when I visit these towns and villages.

I was surprised at this confession. Although I had suspected that she might be sympathetic to what Simon and I were hoping to do, I did not expect such a clear confession of her concerns.

I didn't know how to reply to this. She seemed so sincere in what she said, but I needed to be cautious in my response. I was infected by Simon's paranoia about who might know of what we were doing. I remembered his suspicion of Claudine . . . was she leading me on?

She continued, 'I shouldn't have worn this cap, the insignia shows that I was in military intelligence. People do not always tell the truth when they are first questioned by the intelligence services, they tend to tell you what they think you want to know. It doesn't mean that they necessarily mean it.'

I put my hand on her arm, 'I understand.'

She turned and looked at me, 'Do you? I wonder . . . you came here convinced of our wonderful new country, you don't know what suffering it caused to the Palestinian people.'

I was concerned, I couldn't tell her my true mission, even though she seemed so sympathetic to what Simon and I were trying to do. If she knew then her safety might also be at stake.

We left the café. I said that after I had taken some photographs I wanted to visit some other villages in that area.

After I had taken a number of photographs we set off again. I just took any road out of Bayt Dajan. Tami clung tightly to me, I felt her rest her head against my back. We passed through more olive groves, as well as oranges. It was all very well cultivated. We drove for about 10km until we reached a village called Biyar' Adas. We only knew this because there was a faded sign at the side of the road, there were more recent signs in Hebrew. I pulled to the side of the road and turned to Tami. She turned her face away from me and I realised that she had been crying, I could feel the damp patch on my shirt where she had been resting her head. I pretended not to notice, instead I asked what the signs said. Her voice was muffled, 'They are signs for the Israeli colonies, they are built on what was formerly Palestinian land, they are called Adanim and Elishama.'

We drove into what remained of Biyar'Adas.

'I know about this place, I've been here before . . . when I was in the army . . . we were investigating the activities of the Stern Gang.'

I pretended innocence, 'What was the Stern Gang?'

'It was one of the so-called terrorist gangs, which later became a part if what is now called the IDF, Israeli Defence Force, our regular army. They were guilty of various atrocities in Palestinian villages . . . including here.'

'What did they do?'

'You really don't need to know.'

'Please tell me.'

She sighed, 'I wish you didn't want to know these things . . . and I wish I didn't know them.'

She paused again, 'They came into this village with units of the Haganah . . . they massacred fifteen villagers, men, women and children.'

'Why?'

'They wanted to frighten the rest of the villagers into leaving . . . and they succeeded.'

She was still seated behind me, she turned and buried her face against my back again.

Then, her voice barely audible, 'Can we go back now please?'

On the way back to Tel Aviv, just as we were approaching the outskirts, Tami said in my ear, 'Let's stop somewhere on the way in, maybe a bar so we can have a drink, and talk a little.'

As we got closer in, she suddenly said, 'Take the turn to Jaffa. There is a bar I know near the clock tower.'

We stopped eventually at the bar, with a Hebrew sign, תומש ספר.

I asked what it meant in English.

'Exodus.'

We took a table outside, under the awning.

'What shall we drink?'

'I'm happy with white wine.'

We sat quietly while we were waiting for our drinks to appear looking at the old clock tower, sitting on its elongated island in the middle of the thoroughfare.

Tami reached across the table and took my hand.

'Christopher, I'm sorry to have been so emotional this afternoon. Believe me I am proud of being an Israeli, proud of this country we are building, proud of what we have achieved. It's just that when I see what it has done to the Palestinians, who have lived here for more than 2,000 years, how dreadfully they have been treated, how we seem to be trying to slowly eliminate them from history, I am torn between my passionate nationalism and my deep sympathy for the Palestinians.

Now that you have come here, wanting to record our magnificent achievements, only to come across . . . as you will . . . the suffering of the people we have dispossessed, I feel so guilty about what has happened, and I fear that you will see me as part of this.'

Her eyes began to fill with tears again.

Not as guilty as I feel, I thought. I was at a loss for words.

'Tami, I'm not here to judge anyone, I'm here as an artist who hopes to record as dispassionately as possible what I will see.'

She nodded slowly, 'I suppose that's what I am afraid of, you will see and hear things which will eventually turn you against us . . . or more particularly me.'

I suddenly felt a surge of warmth for her.

'Tami, I will not judge you, how could I? I know that you have a good heart, and I will try my best to see things through your eyes as we travel around.'

She suddenly leant across the table and kissed me, not on the cheeks but on my mouth, she started to say something then she stopped and turned her head away.

I suddenly remembered that Simon must have arrived, I wondered if he had been trying to contact me.

'I need to get back, Simon will have arrived, he may be trying to contact me, I'll run you home.'

'It's OK, I can get a bus.'

'No, I want to do it.'

'Thank you.'

I found my way to Ben Yehuda Street, with Tami clinging tightly to me. We made our way up to the area where her family lived.

Just before we got there, she said, 'Let me off at the end of the road . . . if my mother sees you she will insist you come in and then she will feed you and generally smother you, and you'll find it difficult to get away. She asks every day if you are eating enough.'

I stopped off on the corner. Tami clambered off and stood beside me for a moment, with her arm round my shoulders.

'Don't tell anyone about what I told you. There are people at New Horizons who I'm sure hold the same views, but there also people there who are passionate Zionists and will not hear one word of criticism about what we have done. Incidentally, my father is one of those. Will I see you tomorrow?'

'Yes, let's meet at New Horizons about ten.'

She hesitated, then kissed me full on the mouth again and fled up the road.

I drove back slowly. As I drove, I thought about the afternoon, going to those villages, hearing what Tami said, her own confession of sympathy and concern for the Palestinians, then her tears and obvious distress about what she knew. And going round and round in my head were those kisses. This was getting complicated, there was no doubt that we both were very physically aware of one another, but if we did get involved it was fraught with all sorts of dangers, for her as well as for me. For one thing, it could cloud my judgement, my claim to impartiality, for another, she would inevitably become involved with what I was trying to do, which could well get her into trouble after I left, especially if we did succeed in getting our findings published. But I was increasingly attracted to her, as she seemed to be towards me. I didn't know what Simon was going to say. Perhaps I wouldn't tell him.

I arrived back at the apartment block and parked my scooter round the back. I tried to go in the back way, but found to my surprise that it was locked again. I let myself in at the front and climbed the stairs to my apartment. I had hoped to find a message on the door from Simon, but there was nothing there. I let myself in and went into the kitchen to see what food I had, as I was now feeling quite hungry. I went to the bedroom and put my bags down. It was just getting dusk so I went out to the terrace, and there was Simon, looking at my drawing!

Chapter 13

He looked at me. 'Well there you are. Yurem said you were off with some girl, having a good time!'

I protested, 'Tami is my interpreter, she's not just some girl!'

Simon got to his feet and came over to me, he was laughing, 'Don't be so serious, I was just teasing you.'

He gave me a hug, 'I'm pleased to see you. I hear that Tami is very good, she speaks, English, Arabic and Hebrew, she sounds ideal . . . I can't wait to meet her. Come, let's go for a walk, you can tell me everything you've been doing.'

The familiar routine, a walk meant a private talk, away from prying ears. I looked at him properly. He had shaved off his beard, which curiously made him look older. I realised that I had not seen him without a beard since he had left England nearly three years ago. The naked exposure of his face showed it to be more careworn, there were more finely etched lines around his eyes and mouth.

'I'll just have a quick shower, then we can go.'

While I was showering he came into the bathroom and sat on the toilet seat.

'How's Claudine?' I managed to splutter through the shower.

'Good, she sends you her love.'

'So everything's OK between you now.'

'Yes, yes, we made up, largely due to you.'

I felt good about that, my protestations had worked, and I was glad they were together again. She seemed ideal for him.

I got out of the shower and began to dry myself.

'You are getting quite brown I see.'

It was true, aided by the cream I had been putting on, the initial redness had begun to turn to brown. It was mainly my face, shoulders, arms and lower legs. Riding on the scooter had increased my exposure.

'Looks good, the girls are going to love you when you get back.'

'What girls?'

'Well your little friend Sylvia for a start.'

I had a pang of conscience . . . I must send that postcard off, also one to my parents, who must be wondering how I am.

I locked up and we went down the stairs. I told him about the back door being open and not being able to find the key, now mysteriously it was locked again.

'Yes I know, Yurem brought me here and found the key.'

'How did you get into the apartment?'

'Yurem had a second set of keys.'

We cut across Ben Yehuda Street and took one of the turnings towards the sea. The night air was very mellow and the smell of flowers pervasive. When we approached the beach the air became more suffused with the smell of the sea.

'So, tell me what you have been doing.'

I told him about Tami and how good she was, avoiding any mention of my concerns about our developing attraction for one another. I told him how she had organised the renting of a scooter, how she had gone with me to Jaffa, first of all by bus, then on the Friday with the scooter. Then I talked of the meeting with Hamid, seeing his work and promising to go the next day to see his paintings, that I had been invited by Tami's father to go to the family apartment for Shabbat.

At this Simon looked incredulous, but I explained that I was curious to see people from both sides. He continued to look doubtful about this, but I told him it was a valuable contact, as I wanted to hear about her father's military involvement during the 1947/1948 war. Then my return to Jaffa by myself on the Saturday, meeting Hamid and going with him to his home to see his paintings, and how I was impressed by them and had taken photographs. How he had told me about his family and what had happened to his father, as well as his brother-in-law. Finally my trip with Tami to Bayt Dajan that day, and the reason I wanted to go. Tami's revelations of her time in the military intelligence section and how she was desperately moved by the plight of the Palestinians.

He walked in silence for a few minutes, then, 'You've done really well in such a short time.'

Praise indeed, I thought.

I then told him about my suspicions about being under surveillance. The woman who ran down the stairs that first morning, the red headed man and his girlfriend, the woman with the mole at the corner of her mouth, the sound of a door being shut somewhere in the building, the van parked out the back, which had now gone, finally, finding that cigarette end on the terrace. I added that I might be being paranoid about this, and that they were only odd, unconnected incidents, but that he himself had encouraged me to think like this. He listened attentively to everything I said.

'No, these all sound suspicious to me.'

I had neglected to tell him about what Yurem had said to Tami, that she should keep an eye on me and generally report on what I was doing. I don't know why I didn't tell him. I suppose I didn't want him to become suspicious of her.

We had been walking up the seashore as we talked and I saw that we had arrived near the café-restaurant which Joseph's father owned. I was pleased to see that it was open in the evenings.

'Are you hungry? I am . . . we could eat here.'

We sat down at one of the outside tables. It was still very warm, a breeze came in from the sea, laden with that salty smell. Out in the bay small lights twinkled on the fishing boats. Even here we could still hear the cicadas.

Joseph appeared, with a menu. 'Hello again, nice to see you.'

I introduced him to Simon, describing him as an artist friend, also from England. We ordered something to eat and a bottle of Israeli white wine.

Simon looked around, there was no one seated near us. He leant towards me. 'I'm not staying with you, I already have a place I can stay in Jaffa, in the Al Ajami area. I must figure out a way for us to communicate with one another.'

I told him of my plans to select about twelve kibbutzim around the country, ones that had been built on Palestinian land, photographing and drawing them and the Palestinian village remains.

'Good,' he said, 'I will give you a list of significant places to go. I can't help feeling though that you are going to be hard put to do as many as that. I will give you some key ones, any others you can fit in if you have the time.'

As we were finishing our meal I saw Jacob approaching us.

'Hey there, nice to see you again.' As before he sat down at our table, without waiting for an invitation. He looked at Simon with interest, I introduced him as a friend from England. I did not specify what he did.

Turning to Simon I explained that I had met Jacob on the 'plane coming over. 'He was very kind to me, he guided me through the intricacies of embarking and disembarking.'

Jacob asked me how I was getting on, I explained about my trips to Jaffa, and my being invited to Tami's house for Shabbat.

'He has the most gorgeous assistant.' He said to Simon.

Simon looked at me speculatively. 'He told me about Tami, he didn't mention that she was gorgeous.'

'I expect he wants to keep her to himself.'

I needed to change the subject, 'I gather that you paid a visit to New Horizons, and talked to Yurem?'

For a moment he seemed flustered, 'How did you . . . of course . . . Tami must have told you. Yes, New Horizons sounded interesting, I just thought I would drop in and see what it was like.'

Simon listened to this carefully. 'So what do you do?'

'Oh, sort of import/export, I'm based near Washington DC, but I come here a lot, and as Christopher knows, I'm also an Israeli citizen.'

I didn't want to continue this conversation, I wanted to talk with Simon, without a third person.

You caught us just as we were finishing up here. Having arrived this evening, Simon is feeling quite tired, so we'll be going . . . sorry, but I'm sure we'll see you here again.'

I managed to catch Joseph's eye and he brought the bill and I paid it. We left, but not before Jacob had started to question Simon about why he was here.

To my surprise, Simon answered truthfully, saying that he was here under the auspicious of Palestine Aid, as an observer.

We left and started to walk back the way we had come.

'Sorry about that, but I was beginning to get a bad feeling about him, he prys too much.'

'Don't worry, I was suspicious of him as soon as he started talking. That guy is CIA, I swear it! Import/export! . . . I'm based near Washington DC! You know what's near Washington? Langley, where the CIA headquarters are.'

'I was surprised when you told him that you were working for Palestine Aid, I thought you'd say you were just here as a friend.'

'Listen, he'd been to New Horizons and talked to Yurem, he would know already what I'm doing here, if I'd said anything else it would have confirmed any suspicions he had.

When we got near my apartment, Simon said, 'I'm not going to stay at your place, apart from the fact that you only have one bed, and a pretty virginal one at that, I need to establish myself in Jaffa. I'll let you know where I am in a couple of days and we'll meet up next time in Jaffa.

'How will you let me know?'

'I'll post a letter through the front door of the building. It will just suggest a place we might meet to have a coffee, nothing more. I'm afraid that you are under surveillance, so I don't want to leave any thing suspicious.'

'How will you get back to Jaffa now?'

'It's OK, I'll take the bus.'

I waited at the bus stop with him, as he got on the bus he said, 'I'll see you soon, have fun with your gorgeous assistant!'

As I climbed the stairs to my apartment I reflected on what he had said about my being under surveillance. It confirmed my own suspicions. I made myself some coffee and took it with my notebook out to the terrace.

I started to put down the day's events, there was much to record. How Tami was reluctant to tell me about her conversation with Yurem, the visit to Bayt Dajan with Tami admitting that she was in the Intelligence section when she was in the army, and the things she had learned while serving there. Then there was the visit to Biyar Adas, Tami's emotional response, asking if we could go back to Tel Aviv, her tears. Then her firm commitment to the State of Israel, as well as her strong reservations about what was being done to achieve it. Then I included our increasing attraction to one another. I hesitated when I wrote this last part, it had nothing to do with my mission here, but somehow I needed to record it. Finally I noted the arrival of Simon; our talk together, then the arrival of Jacob and our mutual suspicion of him, Simon confirming my own feelings of being under surveillance.

All this took over two hours, requiring several more cups of coffee. When I finally got to bed my mind was buzzing and I found it difficult to get to sleep. When finally did I embarked on a series of dreams, mostly of me running, with the knowledge that unseen people were pursuing me. Often I would be running towards a figure, which I thought was Tami, but when I got closer she turned into Sylvia.

Chapter 14

When I did wake, it was broad daylight and judging by the sounds of traffic, quite late. I looked at my watch and found that it was nearly 9 o'clock. I suddenly remembered that I was meeting Tami at 10.00 at New Horizons.

I hastily got up, showered and shaved, got dressed, took my bag, ran down the stairs, out and round the back to my scooter. I was rather shocked to find that it was sitting in a pool of oil. Something had caused the oil to leak from the bottom. I bent over it and saw that it was coming from under what I suppose was the gearbox. It was obviously unusable at the moment. I needed to get down to New Horizons as I was supposed to be meeting Tami.

I hurried down Bograshov, almost running as I did. I hate being late. I got to New Horizons in about ten minutes, all prepared to apologise profusely, only to find Tami completely relaxed, talking to an older man, laughing and joking and completely unconcerned that I should have been there ten minutes earlier.

'Don't worry, I was happy to be talking to Jakob, he seldom comes in nowadays.'

She introduced me. 'This is my friend Jakob Steinhardt, a wonderful figurative painter, he doesn't come here very often now as he is opposed to the views of people like Avigdor Stematsky and Yossef Zaritsky, who are referred to as 'lyrical abstractionists'. Jakob is concerned with more realistic images which denote our development as a country.' Jakob smiled politely. I liked his look, he had kindly eyes, seemingly not requiring glasses. He was very tanned with strong lines around his eyes. I shook hands with him, then turned to Tami, 'Sorry I'm late, I was going to come on the scooter but it seems to have sprung an oil leak. I have left it there, I wonder if we should contact the rental place?'

She responded immediately, 'I'll ask Yurem if I can use the 'phone, and call them, you stay and talk to Jakob, he is really interested in what you are doing.'

I sat down with Jakob, who said, 'I understand you are here to record the development of our beautiful new country?' His voice was deep with a very strong accent. I was struck by his appearance. I realised that he was quite old, although from the way he spoke, he seemed an energetic man with his faculties still acute.

'Yes, I suppose that is the brief, though at the moment I haven't strayed far from Tel Aviv and Jaffa.'

'So how long have you been here?'

'Well, I arrived last Wednesday afternoon, so I have been here just over five days.'

'That's no time at all, I'm sure . . . especially with Tami's help . . . you will soon see a lot more. Do you have any of your work with you?'

So far I only had the drawing I had been doing in al-Ajamil. I got out my sketchbook and showed it to him. He looked at it carefully,

'A nice drawing, Tami's right, you are a very good artist.'

'Not really, I consider myself just a topographer.'

'So, you don't regard Canaletto as a true artist?'

'Well, if I could aspire to his heights, I might then regard myself as a true artist.'

He laughed, 'You are well on the way.'

At that moment Tami returned.

'I fixed it, they are sending a mechanic to your place in half an hour; we'd better set off soon to be there in time.'

I turned to Jakob Steinhardt, 'I'd very much like to talk with you some more, will you be here later?'

'Yes, yes, I'll be here all day.'

Tami and I set off, back to my apartment. As we walked Tami described some of Jakob's paintings.

'He's a figurative painter, still steeped in the style of the French post-impressionists of the 20s and 30s. The thing that makes his work interesting is that he is transposing it into the recent history of the birth of the Israeli State in Palestine. He uses images which refer to the Arab past and the effect of the Israeli destruction of this past which is taking place. This is not popular with many of the members of New Horizons, particularly Avigdor Stematsky and his admirers. However there is a significant group of people in New Horizons who support him and his attitudes. We are heading for a schism I'm afraid.'

That's interesting I thought, I shall look forward to a further conversation with him.

We went up to the apartment to wait for the mechanic to arrive. Tami went into the kitchen and looked in the 'fridge and the cupboards.

'This evening I thought you could have your first cooking lesson, I'm going to show you a couple of simple dishes to start with. I told my mother that I was going to help you, she is totally in favour of anything which ensures you eat properly.'

My God, I thought, how many Jewish mothers am I going to have?

At that moment the buzzer sounded, I buzzed the door open, then went out onto the landing.

'Don't come up, I'm coming down.' I yelled down the stairs.

'OK mate, I'll wait here.' It was definitely an English voice, also it sounded a bit cockney, was the whole of the East End of London here?

We locked the door of the apartment and went down together, although if this was really an English bloke I didn't really need Tami's help translating.

The man at the bottom of the stairs was probably only a couple of years older than me.

'Hello mate, you having a spot of trouble with the scooter?'

It was extraordinary to hear this strong east London accent, here in Tel Aviv. He was stocky and sturdy with crinkly black hair, he could have been a brother of Joseph at the restaurant. He had an open friendly face and I warmed to him immediately.

He held out his hand, 'Andy . . . my name is really Andrej, but most people call me Andy.'

Well, another Andy, I thought. I shook his hand, 'Christopher.'

He eyed Tami, who had come down the stairs after me. I introduced them, 'Tami is my interpreter.'

He laughed, 'I know cockney's difficult . . . but an interpreter?'

'No, she's Israeli, speaks English and Arabic.'

'Pleased to meet you.' He shook her hand then said something to her in Hebrew.

She smiled at him, and replied in Hebrew nodding towards me.

He laughed, then turned to me, 'Where's the scooter?'

'Round the back, I'll show you.'

We made our way to the back of the building, as we did so I asked him where he was from.

'Stepney' he replied.

We reached where the scooter was still sitting in its pool of oil.

'I see.' He bent over the scooter, trying to peer underneath it. He then laid it on its side to get a better look.

'Yes, there should be a nut underneath here, which you undo when the oil in the gearbox needs changing, to drain the old oil.'

He looked around where the scooter had been. 'Can't see any sign of it, it may have just dropped off when you were riding it. I need to take it back to the shop, check it out, and put some oil in. I've got a pickup outside . . . maybe if I wheel it round you could give me a hand lifting it up?'

'Yes of course.'

We went round to the front where his pickup was parked. I helped him lift it up, it was surprisingly heavy. Tami had gone back up to the apartment.

'Give us a call later, I'll let you know when it's done and you can come and pick it up, bring your girlfriend.'

'She's not my girlfriend,'

He grinned, 'That's not what she told me.'

I was flabbergasted by this, but tried not to show it.

'Do you know Joseph?' I described the restaurant by the seashore.

'Oh yeah, Joseph . . . our families, came out here at the same time, in 1949, both were refugees from Poland, who came to London before the war. We're Arsenal supporters. We meet up here quite often . . . tell him we met when you next see him.'

He gave me a wave as he drove off. I made my way up to the apartment. When I got there I found Tami in the kitchen, she was sitting at the table, making a list.

'What are you doing?'

'I need to make a list of things we need to buy for the meal we're making this evening.'

'Did you tell Andy that you were my girlfriend?'

She blushed, 'He was trying to chat me up, so I said I was your girlfriend as well as your interpreter.'

She saw the look on my face. 'It's alright . . . it was just a device to put him off, I didn't mean it.'

She went back to her list. I noticed that her face was still flushed.

'I've made a menu for this evening's meal, how does this sound? We'll start with baba ghanouj, which is a sort of eggplant dip. I'll get some pita bread. Then we'll have babini, a tomato salad, followed by the main course, swordfish shish kebab. Finally lemon granita, which is a sorbet. I need to make that early as it needs to go in the 'fridge and get really chilled. What do you think?'

'It sounds wonderful, what's a sorbet?'

'It's a sort of water-ice.'

I watched her face, it was obvious that she was trying to distract me from the conversation about why she had told Andrej that she was my girlfriend. I wanted to reach out and touch her. This was getting serious. I managed to control myself. She looked suddenly vulnerable. How could a tough Israeli girl, who had done two years in the army, be vulnerable?

'Anyway.' She said, 'While you are back at New Horizons talking to Jakob, I'll do some shopping for some of the ingredients we don't have.'

'Let me give you some money.'

'Its alright, there is nothing very expensive we need, apart from the swordfish.'

'Please Tami, I insist, you don't need to support me, I have money from New Horizons, as well as some money I brought with me.'

'We'll sort it out later.'

She was quite firm, but later I was going to insist on giving her the money for whatever she had purchased.

We went down the stairs together, when we got outside she said, 'Let me have your keys, when I've done the shopping I'll drop it off here, then meet you at New Horizons.'

I made my way down to the club. Jakob was still there, sitting in a corner of the bar talking to another man. He waved to me as I came in, I went across.

'May I join you?'

'Of course, of course . . . come sit down.'

He introduced me to the other man, 'This is my friend Josef Zaritsky, one of the founder members of New Horizons.'

'This young man is Christopher, a promising young artist from England. He calls himself just a topographer, but he is more than that, we will see much of his work I think. He is here at the invitation of New Horizons to travel around doing drawings and paintings to show how we have made our country both beautiful and productive.'

'Well', said Zaritsky, 'That's a tall order, how long will you be here?' He had a thick accent, Russian I thought.

'I'm afraid I only have eight weeks maximum, I'm still studying.'

'Where are you studying?'

'The Royal College of Art, in London.'

'That's very prestigious I hear.'

'It is a very good school, the best, we think.'

'Who is your tutor?'

'Leonard Rosoman.'

'Oh, I know his work, he was a war artist?'

'Yes.'

It gave me some pleasure to know that my tutor was known here, so far from England, my view of life was still very parochial.

Jakob asked me if I planned to go to Jerusalem.

'Of course, I intend to see as much of . . . Israel as I can in the time, and Jerusalem is a must.'

'Well when you do go there you must come and see me. I live there now, I was Director of The Bezalell School of Art and Design there until 1958. I'll take you to see it, we also think it's the best.'

After a while we were joined by a younger man called Uri, I didn't hear his other name. Once again I was introduced, and my reasons for being there explained.

'How will you go about this?' he asked.

I explained my intention of working my way round the country, in the process of which I would visit several kibbutzim and try and record their activities.

'I also hope to visit several Palestinian villages, so I can compare them with the kibbutzim.'

'You'll be lucky to find any.'

'Why is that?'

'It's the policy of our Zionist government to destroy any evidence of the Palestinian people, you'll just find heaps of rubble . . . old abandoned houses . . . and the occasional house, looted by, and lived in by, Israelis. Soon all the evidence that there were a Palestinian people will cease to exist.'

Both Jakob and Josef raised their eyes to heaven.

'Oh Uri, don't start ranting again, what's Christopher going to think, if you go on like that!'

Josef turned to me, 'Uri is our equivalent of "an angry young man", you have those in England don't you?'

I nodded, though I privately wanted to hear more.

'You know it's true! Why do you deny it!' Uri glared at the two older men.

'I refuse to get into this . . . we've been through it all before, be happy we now have a country. I'm going to get a drink, anyone else want one?' Josef rose to his feet.

'Yes . . . I'll have a Goldstar,' said Jakob.'

'Christopher?'

'What's a Goldstar?'

'It's a nice beer, well regarded here.'

'I'll have one of those, please.'

'Uri?'

'I'll have a Nesser.'

Josef went off to the bar, I turned to Uri, 'What sort of painter are you, abstract or figurative?'

'I'm not a painter, I'm a sculptor.'

He still sounded a bit grumpy, I was anxious to hear more from him about what he had said, but it was plain that it was not a suitable line of questioning in front of the other two. I decided to leave it until sometime we were alone.

'What sort of sculpture do you do?'

'I work in metal, I weld objects together.'

'I'd really like to see some of your work. Do you have a studio?'

'Yes I have . . . ten of us from here rented an old warehouse which we divided up into ten spaces, so with the rent divided that way we don't have to pay a crippling amount.'

'Are you all sculptors?'

'No we are a mix of painters, sculptors, at least one potter and two illustrators, it's a good mix.'

'Where about is it?'

'South of Tel Aviv, not far from Jaffa. It's in an area called Qiryat Shalom. It's on an old industrial site. There's a good football club near there.'

'Can I come and visit?'

'Sure, I'm there most days, except Shabbat. Ask for me.'

Josef arrived back with the drinks. Goldstar was quite a dark beer, in a way surprising, I'd expected something more like a lager. It was nice though. I had got out of the habit of drinking beer since I had been introduced to wine.

I wanted to talk to him, but I was not quite sure where to begin. I decided to ask him if there were any of his works hanging in the main room.

'No, no, I'm not an abstract impressionist, or whatever they call themselves, I'm a figurative painter, I try to capture the essence of a landscape and the people in it. I work mostly in water-colours.'

'Where did you study?'

'In Kiev, the capital of the Ukraine, as it then was.'

Jakob interrupted. 'Josef is an old rebel, he rebelled against the communists in Russia, when it was Russia, not the USSR, and came here in 1926. He is a very respected artist here, he has won many prizes, including the Dizengoff Prize.'

'Prizes, prizes, who cares,' muttered Josef, 'They are only bits of paper or silly cups, they are not real life, they have no soul.'

'I tried to get him to join me at the Bezalell School of Arts and Design but he wasn't having any.'

Yurem came in. He saw me and immediately came over.

Christopher, 'How nice to see you! You are with the best company I see, these two characters are amongst our greatest artists, be careful though, they will drink you under the table. Where is Tami?'

'She had some shopping to do, she said she would join us later.'

'She is looking after you though?'

'Very much so, I now have two Jewish mothers, Tami and her mother. They are both afraid I may die of malnutrition.'

'Yes, that's the hazard of having a Jewish mother, having two, doubles the hazard. See you later.' He bustled off, stopping to talk to two other people.

Uri finished his beer and said he would be off, back to his studio.

'I'll try and come and see you in the next two days.'

'Great, just ask for me.'

I stayed talking to the two older artists. Their lives were so interesting. Jakob who was born in 1887, at a place called Zerkow, a small town in the district of Posen, at that time in Germany, now Poland, then studied in Berlin. After which he went to Paris for one year, where he met many of the impressionists and post-impressionist masters. He then returned to Berlin where with Ludwig Meidner he founded the expressionist group, Die Pathetiker (The Suffering Ones), which focused mainly on the graphic arts. His career was then interrupted by the First World War, and induction into the German military. After the war was over he returned to his art and began working in woodcuts using Jewish themes, something which he continued to do. Then the Nazis came to power, he was briefly arrested, then fled Germany and migrated to Israel, where he had been living ever since. His work has been exhibited in the US, Brazil and Holland.

I was fascinated by all this, the fact that he fought in the German army in the First World War, only to be arrested by the Nazis during their rise to power, presumably in the 30s. The fact that he had spent that year in Paris, meeting with impressionists and post-impressionists, sounded wonderful to me, I was longing in my turn to do something similar, once I had finished at the Royal College.

Josef was just as interesting. During the First World War he had fought with the Russians! He also had spent time in Paris in the late 20s. He had emigrated to Palestine in 1923, and was a founder member of New Horizons. Later, in the 50s, he spent time again in Paris, as well as Amsterdam and Brussels, before returning to live in a kibbutz, in what was now Israel.

I was in awe of these men, their history, their cosmopolitan lives, their success as artists. I felt pathetically inexperienced, what did I know of life like this, from my small provincial background in England, my military experience taking me no further than Aldershot, only 70 miles from my home. Yes I had been twice to Paris now, both visits for a few days only.

I got up and replenished our drinks. I had not eaten all day, I had been in too much of a hurry to have breakfast and was beginning to feel the effects of the three beers I had now consumed. I could see that the other two were inclined to go on into the evening, I didn't think I was up to it. Fortunately at that moment Tami appeared.

'I'm sorry, after I brought the shopping back to the apartment I decided to make the lemon granita and put it in the 'fridge, so it would be nice and chilled later.'

'I wonder if Andrej has managed to fix the scooter.'

'I'll go and use the 'phone and call them.' She hurried off to Yurem's office.

'She's a lovely girl, everyone loves her here.' Jakob remarked, 'She is always willing to help people, Yurem finds her invaluable. I wonder when she gets time to do any painting.'

Yes, I thought, I have been too wrapped up in my needs to express any desire to see her work, I would make amends for that this evening.

Tami returned, 'Yes, everything is OK, he suggests you come by early in the morning to collect it.'

We stayed a little longer talking to Jakob and Josef. I asked Tami if she would like a drink, she shook her head emphatically.

'We have some wine at the apartment, I'll wait until then.'

Josef heard this and was plainly curious. 'Are you two sharing an apartment?'

Tami laughed, 'No, absolutely not. I'm just going to give Christopher his first cooking lesson. If he is going to be here for several weeks he needs to learn to cook some of our sort of food.'

'I see.' said Josef, plainly not believing this.

'It's alright, my mother approves of this . . . she positively encouraged it. In fact she wanted to come as well, but I felt that one Jewish mother was enough for Christopher to contend with at a time.'

We talked for a while, then I got up to leave. I thanked the two men for telling me their stories and said I would love to see their work. Tami and I left.

As we walked up Bograshov, I enthused about Jakob and Josef. I also mentioned meeting with Uri. Tami frowned, 'I know Uri . . . he has a studio in the same building where I have mine . . . did he sound off about the Zionists?'

'Yes.'

'I bet that went down badly with Josef and Jakob.'

'Not really, they just raised their eyes to heaven as if they had heard it all before.'

'You know he's a member of the Jewish Communist Party?'

'No I didn't know.'

'They have a radical opposition view to the Zionists, whose main policy seems to be to occupy all of what was Palestine and drive the Arabs out. Uri's lot wants a democratic solution where the country is shared between the Israelis and the Palestinians. I must say, although I don't agree with all his views, I do agree with that.'

So there it was, a clear statement of her views, which in a sense, were parallel to what Simon and I had been thinking. The difference was that she was a Jew and more importantly, an Israeli. Where, Simon and I could be accused of anti-Semitism, she could not. I must tell Simon this and see if he thinks we can trust her.

'So, you have a studio there? I've been meaning to ask you when I might see some of your work. I'm planning to visit Uri, maybe tomorrow, its down in Qiryat Shalom isn't it? Maybe while I'm there I could come and see your studio?'

She was quiet for a minute, then, 'I would love you to see it . . . but I'm afraid you will see what a poor artist I am.'

I don't believe that, please let me see your work . . . after all you have seen a little of mine.'

'OK, tomorrow, though I have to do something with my mother in the morning, if you go to see Uri, can you make it in the afternoon?'

'That's perfect, I want to go to Jaffa again in the morning.'

'We can meet at the studios.'

'How will you get there?'

'I didn't tell you, I got my scooter back, it's repaired.'

'When did you get it?'

'Last weekend.'

'Why didn't you tell me? We could have gone in convoy.'

Again she was quiet as we walked, then, 'I rather liked riding with my arms round you . . . it makes me happy.'

We reached the apartment building and went inside. I shut the door and turned to her. 'I'm glad . . . I like it too.'

She smiled at me, and I was tempted to kiss her, but I still held back.

Before we started upstairs I noticed an envelope lying on the floor, I picked it up, it just said 'Christopher' on the envelope, I knew it was from Simon.

I waited until we got to the apartment before I opened it, there was just one line 'Meet tomorrow morning in al-Ajami, at the "Akbar" in the main square at 10am'. It didn't say anything else . . . typical Simon.

I could hear Tami in the kitchen, opening cupboards, taking out saucepans, chopping things.

I went into the kitchen, where she was putting out tomatoes, an aubergine, garlic, olive oil and various spices, on the kitchen table. She was wearing an apron, and looked really businesslike. She indicated another apron, which she had also put on the table.

'That's for you.'

I held it up. 'I'll feel rather silly in this.'

'If you splash olive oil, tomato juice and other things over you shirt and shorts, you'll feel even sillier!'

'Yes miss,' I said meekly, and put it on.

She grinned at me, 'In the kitchen I'm in charge, so you have to do as I say.'

'Yes miss.'

She then laid out on the table an eggplant, some parsley, a red pepper, a lemon, some olive oil, and a sort of paste in a bowl.

'What's that?'

'Its tahini, made from crushed sesame seeds.'

She then guided me through the intricacies of first making baba ghanouj, then the babini, and finally the main course.

'I changed the fish dish, to fish baked in sesame sauce. Swordfish shish kebab was too much of a fuss.'

My role in fact was more of a kitchen maid. I peeled things, ground garlic, washed things, chopped things, added oil to things and generally did the menial tasks. Tami was both confident and competent. She knew exactly what she was doing. How long something should be in the oven, how long it should be chilled, how to time each course so we could eat sequentially.

Finally when everything was prepared and on its way, I cleared the table of the cooking things and laid two places for us to eat, got out a bottle of wine from the 'fridge, as well as two wine glasses from the cupboard.

'Oh, I got some candles, they are in that box over there, with two cheap candle holders, light two and put them on the table. We are going to have a romantic dinner . . . take your apron off.'

'Yes miss.'

'Stop that!' She came round the table and kissed me on the mouth, gently.

We sat down opposite one another, I opened the wine and poured it, we each took our glasses and touched them across the table, gazing into one another's eyes, as instructed earlier. This was our own private dinner party 'Shalom,' said Tami.

'Cheers,' I said.

We drank. Tami reached across the table and took my hand, 'I have things to tell you, but after we have eaten.'

We ate our meal, which was indeed delicious, I thanked Tami for doing it.

I didn't . . . we did it! It was a group activity.'

After we cleared up we went out on to the terrace. I waited for her to speak.

'So, you've things to tell me?'

Tami looked out over the city. I could see that she was thinking about what she had to say. She became serious.

'Christopher, I can trust you can't I?'

'Of course!'

'This is difficult for me. You have come here in good faith to record our achievements, what I am going to say may well disillusion you.'

'Tell me.'

'Over the last two years I have become increasingly critical of what our Zionist government is doing to the Palestinians. This really began when I was in the Intelligence section during my military service, as you saw, when we went on Sunday to Bayt Dajan and Biyar Adas, when I became very upset. Since I left the army, I have become more convinced that what we are doing to the Palestinians is dreadful. I have joined a group of anti-Zionists, who think as I do. Needless to say we are very unpopular, although our numbers are increasing.'

'How do you conceal this from the people at New Horizons?'

'With difficulty . . . although there are a number of younger members who also think as I do. We tend to keep a low profile when we are there . . . except for Uri, as you witnessed. Let me be clear though, most of us are not communists.'

'What about your father?'

'He will hear nothing of this . . . he is a committed Zionist, and will not accept any criticism of them. He becomes very angry if I try and make my views heard.'

I went quiet for a while, Tami watched me anxiously, she was obviously wondering if this had upset my view of Israel, and had turned me away from her.

What I was actually thinking was . . . is this the right time to reveal what Simon and I were actually here for? I wanted to blurt it out and tell her all . . . but the caution which Simon had instilled in me made me hesitate. I decided to appear more surprised and concerned at what she was telling me, but at the same time, seem sympathetic to her dilemma, without necessarily agreeing with her.

'Well,' I said, 'I didn't know about all this, we only hear about how heroic the Israelis are, and how those wicked Arabs are trying to destroy you. We are all very conscious about the Holocaust, and all are encouraged to feel only sympathy for the Israelis.'

'Well it's true we are threatened and somehow we have to survive, but it should not be at the cost of innocent Palestinians.'

'Do you not think that it will all resolve itself in the end, that in time you will all be able to live peaceably together?'

'Not the way the Zionists are going, the Arabs will never forgive us . . . this is the Middle East remember . . . an 'eye for an eye' and all that.' We lived together for over 2000 years . . . Arabs, Jews, Christians, in relative peace . . . until we arrived . . . the Ashkenazis . . . led by the Zionists.'

'Ashkenazis?'

'There are two main Jewish sects . . . the Ashkenazis and the Sephardics. The Ashkenazis are descendants of Jews from France, Germany, Eastern Europe, and more recently the US.

The Sephardics are Jews from Spain, Portugal, North Africa and the Middle East. There is another sect called Mizrachi, close to the Sephardics, they are also from North Africa and the Middle East. Many believe that the Sephardics and the Mizrachis were the true Jews, the Ashkenazis are only converts from eastern Europe.

'Are there differences between them?'

Tami thought for a moment, 'You know after I finished high school I had to wait a couple of years before doing my military service, so I decided to do a course at Tel Aviv University on the ethnicity and history of the Jewish people. I found many things we should be proud of . . . but also many things we should be ashamed of.'

'What sort of things?'

'Our treatment of the Sephardics, for a start.'

'What happened?'

'In the 50s, after the war of Independence, a flood of Jewish people came from all over Europe, the Middle East, North Africa, as well as from the US. Initially it was impossible to house them all, so a series of tented encampments were set up, called 'maabarahs'. They were minimalist, with very basic sanitary conditions and water supplies. As more houses were built the first people to be housed were the Ashkenazis. The Sephardics and the Mizrachi, and others from the Yemen, Ethiopia and North Africa were sent to the worst 'maabarahs', where facilities were bad, or non-existent, and would be amongst the last to receive housing.'

'Are there any 'maabarahs' still in existence?'

'Not many, they hope to close the last ones this year.'

'Are there any near here? I'd love to go and see one.'

She thought for a minute, 'There was one about 20km east of here, on the road to Jerusalem. I'll ask Yurem if it still exists.'

'Maybe we could go there tomorrow afternoon, after I have visited Uri's and your studios?'

'Yes I'll call Yurem and see if it still exists, and where it is.'

She then went on to tell me how there was a definite policy of segregation at the schools, the Sephardics had to wear different uniforms, and how in some schools they had different entrances, which they were obliged to go through. They also received a lower standard of education. She knew this because her brother and young sister had observed it at their schools. I found this appalling, it sounded exactly like what was going on in South Africa with 'apartheid'.

We sat in silence for a few minutes, then I said, 'I'm very interested in what you've been telling me, maybe as we travel around you can show me things which I might not find or see on my own. Hopefully we'll be spending a lot of time together?'

She reached out and took my hand again, 'If that's what you want, it will make me very happy.'

We had another glass of wine and sat looking out across the buildings towards the sea. It was plain I think to both of us that we were becoming deeply attracted to one another. I didn't know how to deal with this, what would happen if we had a relationship, then I went away and returned to England?

As if reading my thoughts, she suddenly said,

'It's all right Christopher. I'm not going to cling to you . . . its obvious we are very attracted to one another . . . you are only going to be here a few weeks . . . we might as well enjoy it . . . then you'll go away, and I'll survive it.'

I was astonished at this directness, in my limited experience it was the man who made tentative advances, always fearful of rejection, this was new to me.

She was watching me, smiling.

'Someone had to make the first move . . . and you were hesitating.'

She moved her chair closer to me and put her arm round my shoulders,

'You do like me . . . don't you?'

In response I put my arms around and kissed her, she responded in the most passionate way. I wanted to go further but she gently pulled away from me.

'Christopher I really wanted to stay tonight, I had planned to tell my mother that I was staying with a friend who lives near here, but she asked me to come back not too late, as she wanted me to help her sort out some documents she needed for tomorrow morning. I'm really sorry, I feel as if I have led you on. Forgive me.'

'I understand.'

I did understand, though part of me felt really frustrated. I knew she was being quite honest and I took consolation in the fact that she had confirmed what I already thought.

She looked at her watch, 'It's getting late, I must go.'

'I'll walk down with you.'

I waited with her at the bus stop. As the bus arrived she kissed me on the cheek and said 'I'll see you tomorrow, at the studios.' She waved as the bus drove off.

I returned to the apartment. As I cleared the table, washed the dishes and pots and pans, my feelings were euphoric. It seemed incredible to me that a week ago I was just leaving Paris, knowing nothing of what was in store for me, and now, not only was I considerably more informed, but, I was becoming more involved emotionally with Tami. I thought of Simon and what his response was going to be, and decided that I was not going to reveal the full extent of my relationship with her, but I would tell him about her anti-Zionism, and how she could be such a help to us.

When I had finished clearing up I took the table out on to the terrace, got out my notebook and started to write up the day's events.

The incident with the oil leak and the arrival of Andrej. Meeting the two older artists, and their stories. The encounter with Uri, and his vehement anti-Zionism. The fact that Tami had a studio in the same building that he did. I skated over the meal and all the preparation, just noting the information that Tami gave me about the Ashkenazi and Sephardic Jewish sects, as well as the Mizrachi and other minor groups. The discrimination by the Ashkenazis towards these groups. Finally the 'maabarahs', to which these groups were confined. It was all valuable information, which I would relay to Simon. I made no mention of Tami's bold confirmation of our feelings towards one another.

When it was finished I sat for a while, savouring one more time the smells and sounds of this new city, before having a shower and retiring to bed. Where I dreamed of Tami and then Sylvia. I just had to see how things progressed.

Chapter 15

I woke early the next day, there was the distant sound of the call to prayer. I got up quickly and went to the bathroom. After I had washed and shaved, I prepared my usual breakfast of muesli and orange juice, taking it out on to the terrace, where it was still cool. I tried not to spend too much time thinking about Tami and the pleasures which may lie ahead. I concentrated on the things I was trying to do, this day. First I must go to the scooter place and pick up my scooter. Tami had ascertained that Andrej started work at 8am. It was about a 15 minute walk from the apartment, I wanted to get there about 8.15. I was meeting Simon in al-Ajami at 10am. I wanted to be in good time as I didn't know exactly where the Akbar was.

I left the apartment at 8am exactly, and walking briskly I was at the scooter rental company by 8.15. The proprietor was there and he directed me down the back to where Andrej was working. The scooter was ready, sitting up on its stand.

'I checked it and everything is OK, I put more oil in, after I had replaced that nut. I took it out round the block, it was fine. You'll need some more petrol soon.'

'What do I owe?'

'It's on the house, don't worry about it.'

'Thanks a lot.'

'Where's your girlfriend?'

Without thinking I said, 'She had to do something with her mother.'

He grinned, 'So you don't deny it anymore?'

I changed the subject, 'How long have you been here?'

'Nearly four years. When I came here I was eighteen, I thought it would get me out of National Service, how wrong I was, I had to do three years in the IDF almost as soon as I arrived. Talk about 'out of the frying pan . . . '

'Do you like it here?'

He looked around, to see if anyone else was nearby, 'I hate it here, they're racist and arrogant, and brutal, I'm going back to England as soon as I have enough for my airfare.'

'Strong stuff.'

'Wait 'till you've been here a few weeks, see what they're doing to the Palestinians, it's outrageous.'

This sounded promising.

'Maybe we could meet for a drink one evening?'

'Sure, give me a call, here's my number and we'll meet.' He handed me a card. 'You can bring me up to date about what's going on in London.'

I drove off, down to Jaffa. I knew it was still early for my meeting with Simon, but I had more drawing I wanted to do.

I decided to work in the clock tower area, near the café that Tami and I had been to a couple of days before. It was more of a concession for people like Yurem, to show that I was interested in the contrast of the new developments as well as in the ruins of old Jaffa. While I was making up my mind where to sit I noticed a post office that was open, I hurried inside with my postcards and waved them at the man behind the counter, pointing to where the stamps should be. He laughed, 'You want stamps?' in perfect English.

Even though it was still not 9am, the area was teeming with people. I realised that many people started very early in these hot climates, later in the afternoon they would have a 'siesta', after which they would continue working well into the evening. Sensible, I thought.

It was already getting very warm, I had adjusted to the heat, but I still used sun-block, and carried the baseball cap, which Tami had loaned me, in case I was in the direct sun.

As I began my drawing, I reflected on Tami's revelation about her feelings towards me, it was not really a revelation, more of a recognition. It was true, I had hesitated, but for reasons to do with why I was here. She had made it acceptable, I was going to be here a short time, why not enjoy our time together? Also, by her confessions of being an anti-Zionist, and her distress at what they were doing to the Palestinians, it made it easier for me, I felt that we were close together on this and I was not deceiving her. Although I did still need to talk to Simon about her views on the Zionists and their treatment of the Palestinians. I didn't intend to tell him about Tami's declaration of . . . what? Her feelings about us? I think that Simon would immediately feel that it might bias my thoughts about what we came here to do.

I only had time to begin the drawing, but I knew I would come back later and continue with it.

I drove my scooter to the checkpoint, one of the soldiers I had seen before was on duty there, he just waved me on.

I worked my way through the narrow alleyways until I reached the square, where Tami and I had our first lunch that time in one of the cafés. I parked my scooter outside and asked the man if he knew where the 'Akbar' was. In his halting English he gave me some directions. It was not far, I got there about 9.45. It was a small café with an awning outside and I found a table there. I sat down and ordered a coffee. At exactly 10.00 Simon arrived.

He greeted me warmly and after ordering a coffee for himself, he asked me how I was doing. I looked around, there was no one else apart from us sitting outside.

I gave Simon a detailed account of the previous day, starting with the incident with the scooter, and how I met up with Andrej. I explained how disaffected he was and why, also how he intended to go back to London as soon as he had saved the fare. I talked about the two older artists, who I had spent time with at New Horizons, and how interesting their histories were. Then I mentioned Uri and his angry railing against the Zionists, and how I was going to his studio this afternoon.

I then told him about what Tami had said in the evening, without describing our intimate meal. However I did tell him about her observations on how the Ashkenazis treated the Sephardics, and how the latter were confined initially to the worst 'maabarahs', and received housing and other benefits long after the others. I described the segregation at schools, reminiscent of 'apartheid' in South Africa. Also how she revealed her anti-Zionist feelings.

Simon listened carefully to all this, then, 'That all sounds great, you're doing really well, are you writing all this down somewhere?'

I told him about my journal, and how I wrote in it every evening, describing what had happened to me each day.

'Where do you keep it?'

'I take it with me wherever I go, it's in my shoulder bag now.'

I indicated my bag, which was under the table. Simon had also brought a bag, which he had put under his chair when he arrived. He bent down and retrieved it. Groping inside it he produced a folder, which he passed to me.

'Here is a list of villages destroyed, and in some places massacres were committed. The land was often taken by the Israelis and then farmed by them. No compensation for the Palestinians were even considered, it was straight theft. These are drawn from comprehensive records kept by the Palestinians. There is a rough map indicating where they are. Keep it safe . . . put it away now and study it later.'

I put it in my bag.

'Simon, I'm wondering if I could now reveal to Tami what we are doing here. She seems very much in sympathy and is vehemently anti-Zionist.'

He thought for a minute, 'I think it's too early to reveal that much . . . I think you should go along with her and in the process glean as much information as you can from her. After all, if, as you say, she worked for military intelligence when she was in the army, then she may know things which we would find very difficult to discover. You mustn't forget though that she is an Israeli, and ultimately she is probably proud of that, even though she may be critical of what the Zionist government is doing. Just string her along . . . pretending to be surprised at what she is revealing.'

This was more or less what I had been thinking, although I didn't like the term 'String her along . . . ', but I let it pass for now.

'So what will you be doing?'

'I've been meeting up with the Palestine Aid lot. As an observer I can only listen to what they are doing and what their plans are. There is some likelihood that I may be going down to Gaza, there's a lot going on there.'

'I had thought of going there, but as it's still under the control of Egypt, it seemed more important to spend my time in the Israeli part of the country.'

'I'm still wondering how to pass messages to you if I find myself based in Gaza. Your place is insecure, especially now I know that Yurem has a set of keys, I can't send letters there, who knows who might pick them up.

'What are you doing later today?'

'I'll be here, in al-Ajami . . . why?'

'Well I'm going to see this guy Uri's studio in Qiryat Shalom, this afternoon. I could meet you back here later, say 5 o'clock? Maybe we could go to Hamid's place and you can see some of his paintings. I'd like you to meet him, unless you want to come with me to Uri's?'

'I've got some things to do in Jaffa, so I won't go with you to Uri's, but we can meet up here later . . . say at 6pm?'

'OK, sounds good.'

It was still quite early, not yet 11am, we stayed and talked for while longer and Simon discussed some of his dealings with the Palestinian Aid group. I told him that I was going to stick around in the Jaffa area until the weekend, then the following week head off on the first part of my 'grand tour' of the rest of the country. He reminded me to read the material that he had passed to me, saying that I should base my trip on that. We parted, agreeing that we would meet up at 6pm. and go to Hamid's place. I went back to the clock tower area and continued my drawing for a couple of hours, then had a brief snack before setting off to Qiryat Shalom to find where Uri's and Tami's studios were. It was not hard to find and took me only 15 minutes, in spite of getting lost once and overshooting it. I found it in what must have been a rather industrial area, which was being rapidly redeveloped. Most of the older buildings had been demolished, leaving one old warehouse, set back on its own. I figured that this would be it, and I was right.

The main door was open, so I walked in. There was a narrow white corridor with doors at intervals on either side. Some of them were open, others shut. I went to the first one that was open, inside there was a young woman with a pottery wheel. She was in the middle of 'throwing' what looked like a rather elegant vase. I tapped on the door and she went on with what she was doing and said something in Hebrew, which I assumed was an invitation to come in. I said in English 'I'm looking for Uri's studio?'

She looked at me for a moment, then, 'Are you American?'

'No I'm English.'

'Which Uri do you want?'

That threw me, I had no idea of his surname.

'The one who does metal sculpture?'

'Oh that Uri . . . the rabble rouser . . . what do you want with him?'

'Well, I came to see his sculptures. Why is he a rabble rouser?'

She answered my question with a question of her own, 'You're from England . . . yes?'

'Yes I am . . . from London.'

'So what are you doing here?'

I told her I was here under the auspices of New Horizons and what I was going to be doing during the time I would be here.

She seemed to like that, and decided to give me directions to Uri's studio. I found it quite quickly. Although his door was open I tapped on it anyway. He was welding something and had the visor down, and seemed not to hear me, I waited until he had finished, then tapped again.

He turned and pushed the visor up, 'So you found us.'

'Yes it wasn't difficult.'

He turned and looked at what he'd been doing. It was a tall structure like an irregular obelisk. When I looked at it closely I could see that it was made with pieces of weapons, gun barrels of various sizes, sections with trigger guards still attached, wheels of some sort of gun carriages, pieces of tank tracks, what I assumed were breech-blocks, all the metal parts, building up a sort of collage of weaponry. He turned back to me, 'What do you think?'

'It's great, what are you going to do with it?'

'I think I'll put it in to the next exhibition at New Horizons.'

'What will you call it?'

He thought for a moment, 'Maybe I'll call it "A homage to the Palestinians, who fought for their homes and villages". It's made with scrapped Palestinian weapons, captured during the 1947/1948 war.'

I was silent at this.

'What do you think?'

'I think it will alienate a lot of people.'

'Good.' he said, 'I hope so.'

Inside I was delighted at his iconoclastic attitude, another rebel . . . wait until Simon hears about this!

Although I hadn't seen much metal sculpture like this, I did genuinely like it.

There was other work in his studio; I wandered around looking at it. There were more metal sculptures, mostly small pieces. What really interested me was the more conventional stuff, modeled heads, some small nude figures, reminiscent of those maquettes which Degas had done of dancers. Mostly cast in plaster, there was one, which was still in progress, it was on a pedestal which had a base which could be revolved, it was wrapped in damp clothes.

'May I look at this?'

'Sure, go ahead.'

I carefully unwrapped the piece . . . laying the damp cloths to one side. It revealed a head I was beginning to know very well. It showed the form of the face with great clarity, the cheekbones, the nose, the ears, the eyes, the shape of the head, the sweep of the hair, all familiar to me. It was Tami.

'This is great!'

'Yes, she has a great head.'

'I didn't know you knew her.'

He was thoughtful for a moment, 'We were in the army together, same outfit.'

'Intelligence?'

He looked at me, 'Yes, how did you know?'

I tried to look non-committal.

'Oh, I get it . . . you're getting involved with her?'

'Maybe.'

He laughed, 'Let me tell you . . . I was involved with her . . . she's one tough cookie . . . don't be fooled by her nice manner, she knows what she's doing.'

I was rather shocked to hear that Tami had been 'involved' with him. Indeed I suppose I would have been rather shocked at anyone else she might have been involved with. I knew that this was an extremely immature response on my part. Although I had spent my time at art school, where we liked to think we had liberal views, and 'free love' was the order of the day. Somehow this only applied to the boys, it didn't seem to apply to the girls. If one was involved with a girl, it was outrageous that she had previous experience. This attitude was completely hypocritical, it demonstrated double standards. I knew that logically this didn't make sense, but somehow I found it difficult to accept. Why should I feel like this about someone I had only just met, what right did I have to feel like this anyway?

All these conflicting thoughts went through my head and must have shown on my face, because Uri looked at me derisively.

'Huh . . . you've really got it badly . . . don't worry, she's a really lousy screw!'

I had an urgent desire to hit him, but considering his size and obvious fitness, I knew I would come out of it badly.

'I wouldn't know.'

'I see . . . you haven't made it yet . . . don't bother.'

I felt I had to get out of there, otherwise I would really hit him and bear the consequences.

'I have to go!'

I left him still grinning, and made my way quickly down the corridor getting as far away from him as I could.

I past a studio, which had its door open, there was a man bending over a drawing board, I tapped on the door and he looked up. 'Do you know which studio Tami Dayan is in?'

He was quite startled and at first didn't understand my question, then he said,

'Ah, you're English?'

His accent was very strong, he probably came from one of the eastern European countries, which one I had no idea.

'Yes.'

'I think she is in number 20.'

I looked at the number on his door, it was 15.

I walked further down the corridor, past 16, 17and 18, then reached a sort of T-Junction. I wasn't sure whether to turn right or left. I decided to go to the left and had just turned when a familiar voice called out, 'Christopher!' I turned back and there was Tami standing outside an open studio door, a little way down to the right.

'I was waiting for you.' She came towards me, when she reached me she put her arms round me, and pressed her face against my neck. I stiffened. She pulled back.

'I'm so glad you came, I thought you might have changed your mind. I've been coming in and out of my studio, looking out for you.'

She looked at my face, 'What's the matter, you look upset?'

'Nothing.'

'Something has upset you, tell me.'

I wasn't going to say anything, but then I realised that having this stewing inside me was not good, I would just get twisted and bitter, for no real reason. Tami was showing me real affection and I didn't want to spoil it. Again I thought, 'This is nonsense, just hypocrisy.'

'I just went to see Uri . . . he said something which made me angry.'

'Tell me?'

'Not now, maybe later.'

She looked at me, she obviously wanted to hear more.'

I hesitated, part of me knew I shouldn't blurt it out now, I was too upset, but maybe, just for that reason, I should get it off my chest.

'OK . . . he told me you and he had a relationship.'

She sighed, 'Why did he tell you that?'

'I think he thought you and I were having a relationship and he wanted to stake his claim.' I certainly was not going to tell her about the comment he made about her sexual ardour.

'He's such a shit!'

'Anyway I came to see your studio.'

'Well here it is . . . it's a mess I'm afraid.'

I looked around, there were a number of paintings stacked, with their faces against one wall. On another wall there were stuck a number of drawings and sketches, mostly in charcoal.

I walked over to look at the drawings. There were a mixture of subjects, some nudes from, I would guess, a life drawing class, mainly in charcoal and pencil, nicely done with strong chiaroscuro, I liked them. Some quick sketch portraits, catching people's expressions.

'These are very good.'

She looked pleased, although her response was quite self deprecating.

'You're just saying that to please me! I know I am an amateur compared to you.'

'I wouldn't say that if I didn't mean it.'

I went over to some of the paintings stacked against the wall. The style and quality of these paintings were very different from the drawings. There were many styles, some influenced by the impressionists, others rather cubist, a few small abstracts, some works with a distinct influence of Picasso, with faces shown full face, with profiles as well.

I knew what she was trying to do, she was trying to find a way to make her work more significant. She was looking for, what one of my earlier tutors described as, 'significant form', in her work.

I had struggled with this myself, only recently I'd realised that trying to force it was wrong, it had to grow out of what one could already do. In my case I was a good draughtsman, it was how to transpose this into actual paintings that was difficult, although recently I was beginning to have some success. I was totally sympathetic to what she was trying to do, but I wasn't sure that I could help her.

She had been watching my face, 'You don't like them!'

'I didn't say that.'

'No, but I can see you don't.'

I thought for a moment. She wanted my approbation, as artists we are all seeking approbation, although we pretend not to care.

'I see what you are doing here, you are seeking a 'voice', something which makes your work significant. It's something all artists are trying to do. We want our art to be significant. You are not alone in this, I've struggled to find my 'voice' . . . still do. I think the only way to go is find what one is best at, work at that and maybe . . . maybe, something may come out of that.'

I could see she was not satisfied with this. So I continued searching through her paintings until I found two that really attracted my attention. They were like painted collages, a mixture of buildings and people, capturing the look and feeling of a place with a collection of seemingly jumbled images. One had been painted in Tel Aviv and Jaffa, mixing the old and sometimes ruined buildings of Jaffa with the newer ones of Tel Aviv. Interspersed between the buildings were street sand alleyways, crowded with figures in western costume, mixing with Hassidic Jews and people in Arabic attire. The figures in the streets stood about in a way reminiscent of the work of the Lancastrian painter, Lowry. The whole feeling of the painting seemed to capture the town or city without being too specific in its detail.

The other painting captured what I assumed was the essence of Jerusalem, although I had not yet been there. There was a wonderful naivety these works. It was clear now why her sketches were a collection of people and fragments of buildings, all material for these painted collages.

'These are really good! I love them. The enthusiasm I felt for them must have been quite clear in my face.

Tami looked surprised, she laughed, 'They were just an idea I had, I didn't think anyone would like them, which is why I buried them amongst the others.'

'I really like them, this is the way you should go!'

She flushed with pleasure, as she studied the two paintings. 'Do you really like them?'

'I really . . . really . . . love them.'

She began to examine them, as if seeing them for the first time. I could see my enthusiasm had managed to encourage her.

She turned to me, 'Thank you . . . you've made me feel much better. It's lonely you know, trying to believe in what you are doing, with no one other than oneself to judge.'

'I know exactly what you mean, I go through this all the time, it's our lot I'm afraid, it must be the same with writers and most creative people, we are always on our own.'

I looked at my watch. It was getting late in the afternoon.

'Listen, I know I suggested we went to visit the 'maabarah' this afternoon, can we put it off until tomorrow? I want to go back to Jaffa and meet up with Simon again, he's going to Gaza and may be there for the rest of the time on this trip.'

She thought for a moment, then, 'Let me have the keys to the apartment, I'll get some supplies in and cook you supper when you get back, OK?'

I hesitated. in truth I was not sure I wanted anyone to have the keys to the apartment when I was not there.

She saw my hesitation, 'It's alright Christopher, I won't go through your underwear, I respect your privacy, I just want to cook for you.'

She came over and kissed me lightly on the cheek. This time I didn't pull back, I gave her the keys.

I made my way back to Jaffa in record time, where I found Simon already seated at one of the café tables outside.

'Hi, how was his work?'

'It's interesting, he's good.'

'What sort of stuff does he do?'

'Metal sculpture.'

'Describe it.'

'Well, it's a sort obelisk shape, made with pieces of old weapons, welded together in a kind of metal collage.'

'How big?'

I thought for a moment, 'I'd guess about 8ft tall.'

'So, what's he going to do with it?'

'He's talking of putting it in the next exhibition at New Horizons, entitled 'A homage to the Palestinians, who fought for their homes and villages' Pretty good, eh?'

Simon roared with laughter, I hadn't seen him laugh like this for a long time. Finally when he had finished, he said, 'I bet that would go down like a lead balloon. He sounds like one of us, you should cultivate him.'

'Yeah . . . well . . . he's a bit of a shit!'

Simon laughed again, 'Most of us are.'

'I'm not!'

'Not yet Christopher . . . but you'll get there. Anyway, why do you think he is?'

'Oh, just something he said.'

'What?'

'Nothing to do with what we are doing, or trying to do, it was sort of personal.'

Simon looked at me, he started to ask again, but seeing the look on my face, decided to leave it alone, and changed the subject.

'I don't suppose you've had time to look through that list I gave you?'

'No, I haven't, but I'll get to it this evening.'

Simon looked around, there was still no one sitting near us.'What you should concentrate on are the ones where massacres took place, like Deir Yasin, and Al-Dawayima. Deir Yasin is well known, and documented, even the Israelis admit to it, but Al-Dawayima is much less clear. See if you can find out more, there is a well known Israeli writer and journalist called Amos Keinan, who was apparently there at the time of the massacre, see if you can track him down, I think he lives in Jerusalem. He's a notoriously difficult man to approach, but a very courageous journalist, not well liked by the Zionists because of his open criticism of their methods.

I made a note of his name.

'Maybe your interpreter girl . . . what's her name?'

'Tami.'

'She may know how to track him down.'

I made another note.

'What happened at Deir Yasin?'

'It was a dreadful event, there are various reports, obviously Arabic ones, almost all oral which of course the Israelis deny. One of these witnesses, Saleh Abdel, claims that there were at least 455 dead, 170 of which were women and children. The UN and not surprisingly the IDF, disagree with that figure. Ben Gurion noted in his diary, 'rumours' that the army had slaughtered 70-80 persons. An Israeli soldier-witness is quoted as saying that the initial attack had resulted in as many as 80-100 Arabs, men women and children being slaughtered. They killed the children by breaking their heads with clubs.'

I made a involuntary sound at this, I couldn't control it, I had never heard of anything so disgusting.

'There was according to him, "not a house without dead". He apparently arrived with the second wave of Israeli soldiers. He reported that the remaining Arab men, women and children were then closed up in their houses without food or water. The Israeli sappers then blew up the houses, with the people in them. There were other reports of rape and random killings. One soldier boasted that he had raped a woman then shot her. Another young woman with a newborn baby was employed to clean the courtyard where the soldiers ate. She did this for several days then they shot her and the baby.'

Again I made this involuntary noise. I listened to what he was recounting, with horror and disbelief. The Holocaust was still fresh in our minds, it had fueled our guilt ridden enthusiasm for a State of Israel. Within three years of its end, the Israelis, who we had supported, had perpetrated these crimes on a people who had nothing to do with it, who had simply tried to defend their homes and villages against what they saw as an 'occupying force.'

'Where does all this information come from?'

'A variety of sources, some Israeli, from their own records, some Palestinian, from sworn statements, some from reports by the UN and other agencies, as well as various journalists and private individuals. I also got a lot of information from Sayyd, but there are other sources here. There's a man called Walid Khalidi, who is collating all the evidence he can about the Nakba.'

'Where does he live?'

'Last I heard he was based in Beirut. He's a historian, he got his degree at Oxford. Since then he has devoted most of his time to researching and documenting Nakba. He was born in Jerusalem, but for obvious reasons bases himself outside the country. The Zionists hate him and try to deny everything he says.'

'I hardly think New Horizons will finance me making a trip to Beirut.'

Simon laughed, 'No you're right, it would not be popular.'

I made a note of this name, then turned to Simon again,

'Any other names?'

Simon thought some more, 'Yes, there is another man called Schlomin Tzabar, he is an artist and writer. Although he is passionate about the founding of Israel, and fought in the 1947-48 War, as well as Suez in 1956, he is outspoken in his anti-Zionist views and abhors their policy of ethnic cleansing. I think he lives in the Haifa area. You could try and get to him.'

I noted his name as well.

Why is this sort of thing not publicised?'

'It is, but you have to search for it, it's never on the front page, if it's seen at all in most newspapers it's lost somewhere in the later pages. Every editor is afraid of being accused of anti-Semitism. Anything that can be seen as critical of Israel is largely suppressed.'

'So what hope do we have with our findings?'

'There are a few publications, like the Manchester Guardian in England, Le Monde in Paris, Der Stern in Germany, which will publish controversial subjects, but they will do it on the basis of well-researched material. That is why what you and I are doing is so important. All the notes you are making, plus your photographs and drawings are very good material for these publications. Incidentally, don't get your photographs processed here, wait until you get back to England.'

We sat talking for a while longer, then Simon said, 'what you should also know is that there were massacres by the Arabs.'

'When?'

'Well the first one I know of was in the 30s, but there were others in the 1947-48 war. The main massacres and attacks against Jewish civilians were usually instigated by some previous incident perpetrated by the Israelis. They were relatively few though. The difference between the actions of the two sides was that the Israelis were systematic and intended to intimidate the Palestinians with fear, so that they fled from their homes and villages, and became refugees in other countries, with no hope of returning. As a result of this over one million Palestinians were dispossessed of not only their homes but their country. Remember the quote from Ben Gurion? "We have stolen their country!".'

I was silent for a while, thinking about what Simon had just told me, there was so much that I had still to learn.

Simon stirred. 'OK, let's go and see your artist friend.'

'Hamid?'

'That's the one.'

I persuaded Simon to get on the back of the scooter, where he clung to the saddle as I drove. I headed through the narrow alleyways until we reached the ruined area where Hamid lived with his family, in that damaged house.

Simon surveyed the rubble strewn street, I could guess what he was thinking.

'This has remained the same since 1948?'

'That's what Tami tells me, she says that the Israeli government's policy is that it's a waste of money to rebuild something for Arabic people, if they don't like it they can leave.'

'They will do something about it in the end, they'll bulldoze it, or blow it up, then build new houses for only Jewish people. That's their modus.'

We climbed the steps to the door of the house that Hamid and his family lived in. The door was partly open. I tapped on the door and called, 'Hamid'. After a few moments he came to the door. He looked surprised and pleased to see me, he eyed Simon with curiosity.

'Hamid, this is my friend Simon from England.'

Simon held out his hand and said, 'Salaam aleicum.'

I was surprised at his use of Arabic, Hamid also responded in Arabic and shook Simon's hand.

'Salaam aleicum.'

'Hamid, I brought Simon to see your paintings, he is also an artist.'

Simon said something in Arabic, and Hamid looked pleased.

I was beginning to feel rather secondary in this exchange. What was it about Simon that he always managed to command people's attention? I felt very inadequate.

'I told Simon that you were a very good artist and painter.'

'Yes, Simon just told me that.'

Well, I thought, that puts me in my place.

Hamid invited us in. We went into their living-room,

Hamid's mother and sister were there, as well as Saba, who squealed with delight on seeing me. She immediately bounced up and down and said, 'Are you going to draw me now?'

Hamid reproved her saying, 'Saba! It's rude to start asking that, when they have only just arrived, sit still and be quiet!'

She sat down, and was quiet, although her eyes were bright with mischief.'

Hamid introduced Simon, who greeted them in Arabic. I could see that they were pleased that he spoke some Arabic to them. I noticed that Saba greeted him in English though, 'Hello, are you an artist too?'

'Well yes . . . but not as good as Christopher.'

She seemed satisfied with this, although I noticed she watched him carefully, her eyes flickering between us. I wondered what was going on in her inquisitive little mind.

Hamid turned to Simon and I, 'Would you like to see my paintings now?'

Simon nodded.

I shook my head, 'I'll stay here and talk to Saba, there is not much room in your studio and I have already seen them, show them to Simon.'

Hamid's mother and sister went to the kitchen to make tea.

Saba looked at me, 'Are you going to draw me now?'

'Yes Saba . . . but you must try and sit still.' She immediately started to bounce up and down. I got out my sketch book and a thick soft pencil.

'I don't like that man.'

'What man?'

The man who came with you . . . the one who said he's not as good an artist as you, he doesn't speak very good Arabic.'

'Saba, he's my best friend! At least he knows some Arabic . . . I don't know any.'

'You're nicer . . . I'll teach you Arabic.'

I sighed, 'I'd love you to teach me Arabic, but I have to go travelling . . . I won't have any time . . . maybe when I come back.'

'Where are you going?'

'I'm going to travel round the country

'Why.'

'I want to see it.'

She thought about this, 'Can I come with you? I could speak Arabic for you, I can be your assistant.'

I nearly burst out laughing, the idea of me travelling round the country with an eight-year-old assistant interpreting for me was both touching and ludicrous.

'Saba, I don't think your mother would let you go, apart from it not being proper for you to be travelling alone with a man, also Saba . . . you're only eight years old!'

'I'm nearly nine!'

This was indeed a ludicrous conversation, I had to distract her.

'I'm going to start drawing you now, I want you to sit still and stop talking.'

For a moment she sat still, I could see that she was bursting to talk again, her eyes were sparkling with inner thoughts. I began to draw before she could start again. She was quiet for a few moments, then, 'How will you manage without someone to speak Arabic for you?'

'I have someone who will travel with me and interpret for me.'

She thought about this, 'What if you meet an Israeli who doesn't speak English?'

'This person speaks Hebrew as well . . . now stop talking!'

She made a face, then held her lips together with her fingers, making murmuring noises behind them. I couldn't help it I burst out laughing.

'You are incorrigible!

'What's incorry . . . incor . . .' She was having trouble with this word,

'She tried again 'Incorrible . . . does that mean you think I'm horrible?'

'No Saba, it means . . . you won't stop talking!'

She giggled, then made her face look serious, the corners of her mouth turned down and deep frown lines appeared between her eyebrows. I sighed, 'if you don't stop talking and making funny faces, I won't draw you.' I laid down my pencil and pushed my sketchbook to one side. That worked, she sat up straight and made her face normal.

I managed to do a quick drawing, which I think was a quite good likeness, her eyes came out well, I had captured her mischievous look, with it's bright intelligence, and the humour around her mouth. She's going to be beautiful when she grows up, I thought.

I showed it to Saba, who took it from me and studied it carefully, I could tell she was very pleased with it. 'Am I really like this?'

'Yes Saba.'

'I've never seen me before . . . except in a mirror.'

Hamid and Simon returned. Simon nodded to me with a look of approval. 'I saw Hamid's work, he's really good, very talented.'

Hamid looked pleased at this.

'Did you photograph them?' Simon asked me

'Yes, all of them.'

Saba was bouncing up and down, 'Look . . . look, Christopher drew me!' she held up the drawing.

Both Hamid and Simon looked at it, 'That's beautiful Saba, it's really like you.'

'Can I take it to school to show my friends?'

'I don't think it's a good idea Saba, you know that there are people there who will think it's against the faith.'

She made a wailing noise.

He turned to me. 'In our faith one is not supposed to create images of people, it's against our religion. Almost all of us do it, but there are some people who are very strict in observing this. I don't want her to get into trouble with them.'

'Can't I just show it to my friends?'

'Ask them round here to see it.'

That seemed to satisfy her, she went back to studying the drawing. Hamid's mother and sister came in with tea and some backlava, they then went back to the kitchen, Saba went with them, complaining that she wanted to stay with us.

Simon said again how much he liked Hamid's paintings and drawings. We discussed how we might find some way for him to have an exhibition. He agreed that probably New Horizons was out of the question, but wondered whether there might be somewhere else in Jaffa where it could be done. Hamid said he knew a space he might be able to use in al-Ajami. We talked some more, in English, which I was relieved to hear. Finally we decided to leave. Simon said a few words to Hamid in Arabic. As we were about to drive off Saba came rushing out, still holding the drawing, 'When you come back from your travels please come and see us.'

Hamid took her hand and lead her back indoors, she was still waving as we drove off.

Simon asked me to drop him off near the café where we had met. When we got there he got off and said, 'I'm not leaving until noon tomorrow, can we meet up here at 8.30, for one last chat?'

'OK I'll be here.' I drove off.

When I got back to the apartment building I went and parked round the back. There was still a large pool of oil where I had been before, so I parked further away. I had noticed a small heap of sand in the corner, left over from some previous building work. I looked round for a shovel I could use, but there was nothing, so using my hands I took several handfuls over to the pool of oil and gradually succeeded in covering it. As I was taking the last handful over I felt some sort of lump in the sand, it was quite small so I picked it out, I brushed the sand off it and there in the palm of my hand was a nut. I went back to the scooter and kneeling down I could see the one, which Andrej had put in, it was identical.

Well, I thought, someone had taken the nut from the scooter, letting the oil drain away, and buried it in the heap of sand. I was shocked by this realisation, was someone trying to cause me an accident? If so all they had to do were to unscrew it enough and the oil would have drained away slowly without my noticing it, until the gearbox seized up, probably when I was driving fast . . . or was it just a rather heavy-handed warning? I made my way round to the front door of the building and was fumbling in my pocket for the key, when I remembered that Tami had them. I pressed the buzzer. After a few moments Tami's voice came on.

'Hello?'

'It's me . . . Christopher.'

She paused for a moment. 'Stay there, I'm coming down.'

I was about to protest but she had hung up. I waited, then heard her steps running down the stairs. She opened the door and came out quickly, shutting it behind her. Before I could say anything she said, 'I need to talk to you, let's go for a walk.' She grasped my arm and almost marched me across the road, I started to protest.

'Just hold on Christopher, let's go somewhere quieter.' She glanced around as she said this, Ben Yehuda Street was crowded with people going home, or going out. We turned down Frischmann, towards the sea, almost immediately it was quieter, we walked about a block then stopped. Tami waited while a couple walked by. When they were gone the street was almost empty, there was no one near us.

'There is something I must tell you . . . that apartment you are in is bugged.'

'What! Where?

'I was in the kitchen doing some stuff for dinner, I dropped something on the floor, I couldn't see where it had gone, so I knelt down and found it, as I was getting up I saw the bug under the lip of the kitchen unit.'

'How did you know what it was?'

She looked at me, 'Christopher . . . I was in the Intelligence section doing my military service . . . as part of my training we were taught about bugging devices. I was never involved with bugging anyone, but I knew how it was done.'

'Were there any others?'

She sighed, 'Yes . . . there was one under your bedside table . . . so if you make love to anyone, it will provide entertainment for whoever's bugging you.'

It was my turn to sigh, 'So if we . . .' I trailed off, unable to finish the sentence.

'I know.' She said.

'Were there any others?'

'I looked in all the rooms and apart from the bathroom there was one in all of them.'

'What about the terrace?'

'That seems to be clear, I guess they thought that there was too much ambient noise out there, you know, street sounds, traffic, the sound of music etc.'

'What should I do? Pull them out?' Who is doing it anyway?'

'No, no . . . they would think you had something to hide. My guess it's Mossad, as you know they want me to keep an eye on you.'

'But I haven't done anything!' Not yet I thought, but I will.

She put her arm round me, 'Poor Christopher, what must you think of our country, when it treats you like this.'

I was beginning to feel uncomfortable with my subterfuge about why I was here in Israel, in the face of her sympathy and concern. I was lying to her and she didn't deserve it. What should I do? I could reveal all and risk betraying Simon, as well as put myself at risk. She was after all an Israeli citizen, who believed in her country and its survival, despite rejecting the actions of the Zionists. It would be her duty to report what we were doing here. I was not an innocent and impartial artist . . . I was a spy!

She was watching me, and could see the turmoil which was going on in my mind, without knowing what it was about.

'Christopher . . . it's alright, you're not doing anything wrong. Let's go back to the apartment.'

We set off back there. I suddenly noticed that I was still clutching the nut, which I had found in the sand. I showed it to Tami, and told her that I was concerned that it had been removed deliberately.

'Maybe it was an accident, and it just fell off in the yard and rolled there.'

I pretended to agree with her, it was getting too close for me having to make a confession about what I was doing here, and I didn't want to make her any more suspicious of what my motives really were, but I knew that eventually I was going to have to tell her, if there were any more incidents like these. I could do it without involving Simon, I could say that his reasons for being here were entirely altruistic.

I suddenly remembered that I had left my shoulder bag in one of the panniers of the scooter. When we got to the building I told Tami to wait for me, while I went round the back to retrieve it. When I got there, in the fading light, I saw a man bending over my scooter.

'Hey!' I yelled, 'What are you doing?'

I went towards him. I'd seen him before, he was the dark haired rather muscular young man, who had been standing outside my apartment building, with a blonde girl in a white dress. They had moved off as I approached them.

At that moment I saw that he had my bag over his shoulder.

'That's mine, give it back to me!'

As I reached for the bag, he suddenly took a swing at me, I ducked and avoided it, before he could try again I brought the edge of my right hand hard down on the muscle which runs from his neck to his shoulder, this temporarily paralyzed his right arm, I then swung the edge of my hand hard across the bridge of his nose, there was a distinct crack and blood stared pouring from his nostrils. He yelped with pain and dropped the bag in order to use his left hand to try and stop the bleeding, he then ran up the alleyway, leaving a trail of blood, just as Tami appeared at the end, he pushed past her and turning right, ran off.

I sat down on the step of the back door, I was shaking, I had hurt my hand when I hit him with the edge of it, and now it was throbbing. I hate violence of any sort, I'm really a total wimp. It was because of this that I had become interested in Jujitsu when I was at my first at art school. It was an extra-curricular activity, run by one of the staff who had acquired some expertise. I was interested in it as a defensive skill.

When I was in the Army, doing my National Service, to alleviate some of the boredom I felt, I found out that one of the PTI's (Physical Training Instructors) specialised in the martial arts, which he had learned when he served in Japan as part of the occupying force, after the end of the war. He was not only skilful in Judo but also in more aggressive forms of the arts such as Karate and Aikido. Through him I had learned a degree of self defense and some more aggressive techniques. This was the first time though that I had employed them in real conflict, and I was rather shaken by the experience. I was by nature a pacifist, so aggression was alien to me. Curiously I felt rather guilty at having used such force. Also I was seriously out of practice and had not had the opportunity to exercise these skills for sometime, hence my aching and damaged hand.

At that moment Tami arrived breathless.

'Christopher! What happened?' She sat on the step next to me and put her arm around my shoulders, she could feel me shaking.

I tried to pull myself together, I almost felt like crying but it was absurd for me, a grown man, to behave in this childish way. After all I had been trying to defend myself!

'He was stealing my shoulder bag, with all my sketches and the camera, I had to stop him. He tried to hit me . . . now I feel bad, I shouldn't have hurt him so much.'

'Well it certainly looked like you did him some damage, but don't feel bad . . . he obviously deserved it.'

She hugged me and kissed my cheek, 'I must say I didn't think you had it in you. Where did you learn how to do that?'

'I just lost my temper when I saw he had my bag, I hate thieves. I shouldn't have hurt him though, I feel bad about that.'

'Wow Christopher, you're a hero!'

'No I'm not, I'm a coward really.'

She kissed me again, 'Come on, let's go up to the apartment, I need to show you those things, then I'll feed you.'

As we walked back to the front door she said 'Remember, don't exclaim when you see them, and let's not talk about anything we don't want them to hear. Obviously we should talk about what just happened, that man who tried to rob you. We should discuss it as if it was an ordinary attempt to rob you. Maybe it was.'

We climbed the stairs, she opened the door of the apartment and lead me inside. After I had dumped my bag in the bedroom she showed me the first 'bug', it was under the lip of the bedside table. It was tiny, not much bigger than a button. Then she took me into the kitchen and showed me another one under the lip of the kitchen fitment. Finally in the other two rooms, which I never used anyway, but there was a 'bug' in each of them.

Tami started to prepare the meal. I offered to help, but she waved me away, saying that it was a simple meal, which she had already more or less prepared. She poured me a glass of wine and I went with it out on to the terrace, partly to see if I could find any bugs, and partly to be on my own for a while.

I couldn't find any bugs, so I sat down and sipped my wine and reflected on what had happened. It was increasingly clear that I was not only under surveillance, but there was now a possibility of violence being inflicted on me.

It seemed that although I had not done anything overtly wrong, or what could be seen as anti-Israeli, indeed, quite the reverse, I had maintained my apparent enthusiasm for the new country of Israel, and my desire to record it as best I could. Simon and I had been very careful where we had our conversations, making sure there was no one nearby. The only thing which might have roused their suspicions was my interest and friendship with Hamid, who I had now visited twice, the second time taking Simon with me. Somehow though our reasons for being here had been suspected before I had even arrived, and I had found myself under surveillance almost immediately.

I was trying to think about my next course of action when Tami called me in to eat.

Tami's 'simple meal' consisted of something called 'samak bil tahini' as a main course, preceded by a 'chickpea and olive appetizer'—both quite delicious. I realised that I was never going to be a cook of anything but the most simple dishes. Her expertise put me to shame.

After we finished I cleared the dishes away and we went out on to the terrace. Although I had checked, and so had she, that there weren't any bugs out there, nevertheless we moved over to the wall where we could look down on the busy street below us, with all its sounds of music, traffic and people.

'Why do you think this is happening?'

'No idea.' I lied.

She put her arm round me. I think you do . . . but you're not telling me. Please tell me, whatever it is . . . I don't mind.'

I was getting so close to telling her, but I knew that once I had taken that step there would be no turning back. I needed to distract her, change the conversation somehow, lead her away from this subject.

'I think that man was just a common thief, I don't think he had any other motive. At least I managed to stop him and get the bag back.'

'You certainly managed that OK, he didn't look too good when he passed me. Where did you learn to do that?'

I explained how and why I had learned the martial arts. She seemed impressed by this. 'Well we did some basic self defence when I was in the IDF, but nothing as advanced as that.'

'I've never used it in real combat before, it made me feel sick inside. I'm not like that really, I'm a pacifist and all violence between people disgusts me. Now I've done it, and I'm now disgusted with myself.'

I turned towards the apartment, 'I need a shower . . . wait for me, I won't be long.'

I went to the bathroom and ran a shower. As I stood, letting the lukewarm water course over me, washing away the violence which I had just experienced. I thought that man, whoever he was, would be careful if he ever returned. I still felt sick though at my own behaviour. Why had I damaged him so badly? That burst of blind violence was alien to me.

When I was finished I dried myself and wrapped the towel round me and went back to the terrace, Tami was not there. I went into the kitchen, she was not there either. I called out, 'Hey, where are you?'

'In here.'

She was in the bedroom. I went in, the bedside table was not there, the lamp was on the floor beside the bed. In the bed was Tami, with the sheet drawn up to her chin, the invitation was obvious. As I went towards her she bent over and switched the lamp off.

So we became lovers. I don't write about these things, privacy is important to me. The only comment I will make is that Uri's description of her degree of passion bore no resemblance to mine. Also, it was plain that I should get a larger bed!

Later Tami got up and went to the bathroom, I heard her run a shower. She had already told me that regretfully she could not stay, she hadn't prepared an excuse for her mother. It seemed that Jewish mothers still held a strong influence over their children even when they were quite grown up. Maybe it was just the girls who suffered this.

When she came out of the shower she was still drying her hair with one towel, the other towel was wrapped round her. She sat down on the bed.

'I'm sorry Christopher, I would have loved to stay but I must go back home. It's not just my mother, my father is getting suspicious about the amount of time I spend with you. He likes you well enough, but you're not Jewish and he would be very unhappy if he thought I was falling . . . having a relationship with a gentile. Soon we will be travelling round the country together and there's nothing he can do about that.'

She finished drying her hair and standing up she took the other towel off and stood for a moment naked, before she started putting her clothes on. I was struck once again by her beauty. I had spend a great deal of time at the art schools drawing and painting naked women, and very occasionally men, indeed at the Royal College there was a plethora of models, some in almost every studio. They came in all shapes and sizes, some fat, some thin, all ages. Tami though had the most beautiful body I had ever seen. She saw I was watching her.

'What are you thinking?'

'That you are absolutely beautiful!'

She laughed, 'I don't think so . . . my legs are quite short . . . my breasts are too small . . . my hips are too narrow. My mother says, that's not good for child bearing . . . '

She would have gone on, but I kissed her . . . that stopped her.

I walked down the stairs with her and across the road to the bus stop. Before we parted she said, 'Tomorrow is the eve of Shabbat, my mother wondered if you would come again, but I made some excuse for you . . . that you were going to meet up with your friend. You didn't want to come again, did you?'

'No, you're right, thank her very much though. Maybe I could come for a meal when we get back from our first trip?'

'She'd love that! So tomorrow we are going to the maabarah, what time shall we meet?'

'I'll come here about 10.30, OK?'

We agreed. That would give time for me to get back from my meeting with Simon.

I went back to the apartment where I remade the bed, which looked like a disaster area. Carried the bedside table back from one of the other rooms, went to the kitchen and washed the dishes as well as the cooking utensils. Tami was a wonderful cook, but she seemed to use every pot, pan, bowl, dish and implement that I had, reducing the working surfaces and sink to a major mess. After doing all that it was getting quite late. I still took my notebook out onto the terrace, and did my best to record the events of the day. My first early morning meeting with Simon, my visit to the studios, the meeting and conversation with Uri, glossing over his comments about Tami. The meeting with Tami in her studio, then my return to Jaffa to meet again with Simon, and hear his account of the massacres at Deir Yasin and Al-Dawayima. Then our visit to Hamid's, and my drawing of Saba.

After that my return to the apartment building, then Tami coming down to march me off down a side street, so that she could tell me that the apartment was 'bugged'. Then our return to the apartment building, the violent encounter with the robber and my resorting to the martial arts.

Going up to the apartment and seeing the bugs. Then the meal which Tami had prepared. I made no mention of what happened later.

All this took me until well after midnight. I undressed and climbed into bed, it smelt deliciously of Tami. I lay and reflected on what had happened. It was done now and there was no going back, we'll play it out and just see what happens. I put the light off. My last thoughts were that I must brush up my martial arts skills. I resolved to start exercising every morning, going through all the movements that I knew. I was very aware that I could find myself in situations where I would need to defend myself, and possibly against more than one opponent.

Chapter 16

I woke with a start. I had been dreaming of Sylvia, I could see her, although she could not see me. She was dancing alone in a forest. She was happy, her eyes were shining, she had flowers in her hair, as she twirled, with her thin arms above her head, she laughed. I came out from where I was and started towards her, she didn't see me until I was so close that I could reach out to touch her. Then she suddenly saw me, her eyes widened with fear, she started to scream soundlessly, I put my arms round her and she struggled and tried to pull away, she was so thin and light, like a small bird. 'I'm back, I'm back . . .' I kept saying. She continued to struggle but gradually seemed to calm down. Finally she turned to me and suddenly kissed me passionately, I could feel her thin body trembling. Then she turned away and ran into the forest, and soon vanished in the trees. I started to follow her when I suddenly heard her screaming and screaming, I ran into the woods, she was in a clearing, being held down by the three soldiers, they were tearing at her clothes, I shouted and ran towards them, one of them turned, his gun was raised, he took aim at me and fired . . . I woke up with a start.

I lay for a while thinking about this dream as it gradually faded. I looked at my watch, it was just after 6am. I got up and made my way to the bathroom. After I had shaved and cleaned my teeth I went out onto the terrace. The sun was just coming up, it was still cool enough though, and I began a series of exercises to strengthen my hands and improve my reactions. I was right, I was seriously out of practice with my martial arts skills. I worked hard for nearly an hour, then went and had a shower. After I had got dressed it was nearly 7.40, I had no time to eat. I ran downstairs and round the back. I checked the scooter, as far as I could see, it was OK. I started it up and headed down to Jaffa.

Simon was already there, sitting outside, under the awning.

There were quite a lot of other people sitting nearby. It was going to be difficult to have a secure conversation.

'Hi!' I said, 'Let's have a coffee, then maybe go for a walk?'

'OK.' He looked around, 'A lot of people stop here on their way to work though, it may soon clear.'

We ordered coffee, and I asked for pita bread with scrambled eggs, for some reason I was starving.

'I thought your friend Hamid was a very interesting artist, he should be encouraged.'

'I know, I thought you'd think that, the question is . . . how?'

'You did photograph all of them?'

'Yes.'

Simon thought for a few minutes, 'Maybe after we get back I could show some prints to Sayyid, he may have contacts with galleries who might be interested, in Paris. There's a lot more sympathy for the Palestinians there.'

By now the early morning customers had gone, looking round there was no one near us. I then recounted everything that had happened after I had left him the previous evening, except what had happened between Tami and me, he didn't need to know that.

Finding the bugs seemed not to surprise him, but my martial arts activity did. He knew I had started to take an interest in them when we were first at art school but I think he thought it was just a passing phase on my part. I hadn't told him that I became much more advanced during my two years at Aldershot, it didn't seem relevant to our lives after we met up again.

'Wow Christopher! That's amazing, I never thought it of you . . . great!'

I felt embarrassed. 'I hated it, I'm not a violent person as you know, I've only used it in competitions, never in a real situation, I'm really out of practice.' I showed him my bruised hand. He admired it.

'I guess you're right, you need to get up to speed again . . . practice, practice, practice! I'm proud of you, I never thought you had it in you.'

'I don't!'

'Christopher! You're a warrior at heart!'

'Oh shut-up!'

'OK.' He was laughing though.

I needed to change the conversation. 'You remember I'm going today with Tami to see a 'maabarah'? That's where the Sephardic Jews are still waiting to be housed.'

'Ah yes, Tami, your beautiful assistant, when am I going to meet her?'

'I don't know . . . probably never.'

There must have been something about the way I said that, because Simon suddenly looked closely at me. He started to say something, I hastily cut across him with a question, 'How are we going to keep contact, when you are in Gaza and I'm traveling around the country?'

'I've been thinking about that. The thing is I'm going to try and make frequent trips back here. What I'll do is try and contact you directly, I'll come to your apartment building and buzz you, if you're there I'll come up and talk to you. If you're not in, I won't leave a written message, I'll leave it with Hamid. He and I talked about this. He's a good guy.'

'OK, that sounds good, but how do I get hold of you?'

'You won't be able to, you'll just have to wait until I make contact with you, you're on your own I'm afraid. I was worried about this initially, but now I'm not, you're plainly able to look after yourself.'

'You think so?'

'Absolutely, you've grown Christopher, in every way, I'm proud of you, you know now very much what we're trying to do, and you found out things that even I didn't know about.'

I must have blushed, although I thought it was rather patronising, it was good to hear this praise from Simon. I had always looked up to him as somehow my superior, now I realised we were equal in every way.

I looked at my watch, it was nearly 9.30.

'I've got to go.' I stood up, so did Simon.

'Look after yourself Christopher.'

'And you . . . you look after yourself.'

Surprisingly, we hugged. I got on the scooter and as I drove away I waved, just before I turned the corner I looked back, he was still standing by the table, he waved again and as I turned the corner.

On the way back to the apartment I stopped at a filling station and topped the scooter up. It was just as well, it was nearly empty.

I got back to my apartment building in good time. Before I went upstairs I went across the road to the shop with postcards and bought two of old Jaffa, one for my parents and one for Sylvia.

I went out on to the terrace to write them, it was already getting quite warm. I sat down to think of what I should write. My parents would be happy with a simple message saying I was having a lovely time, and how everyone was nice to me. How I had a very nice girl assistant. This would please and intrigue my mother. Sylvia was another matter. After some thought I realised I needed to write her a letter, with descriptions of where I had been and what I had seen. I felt I could be more explicit in a letter about the treatment of the Palestinians, certainly not something I wanted to put on a postcard. I felt she would understand this and be sympathetic to my need to come here and witness what was going on.

Tami was due any minute, I didn't have time to go and buy a writing pad, I would leave it until later in the afternoon. I looked around the terrace. If I was going to continue doing my Judo exercises I needed to set up a 'makiwara', which would enable me to strengthen my hands, especially the edges, if I was going to use them with any force. I really needed a stout post, it's base buried in the ground. There was no way that I could dig a hole in the terrace but I noticed that the canopy had two thick vertical metal rods supporting it, I went over and looked at them, one on either side of the French windows, which opened out onto the terrace from the rest of the apartment. They stood away from the wall by about three inches. That was good. I gave them a good yank and they seemed pretty sturdy, well fastened to the floor. The gap from the wall would give me the opportunity to wind several layers of a thick rope round it at about chest level, making it into a sort of pad. This could be perfect for the toughening of my hands. If I made another pad lower down, this would serve to help with my kicking exercises, I would have a dual purpose makiwara. I must ask Tami if there was anything like a ship's chandler, where I could buy some thick rope.

At that moment the buzzer sounded. It was Tami. She came up the stairs two at a time. She arrived breathless and virtually threw herself into my arms.

'I was so worried about you after yesterday, I could hardly sleep. I had these terrible dreams about you being attacked and I was helpless, not knowing how to defend you!'

I was quite overwhelmed by this concern for my welfare. I suppose I just hadn't reckoned on her caring so much, but then I thought about what eventually occurred last evening and realised that her feelings for me were really genuine. We moved out onto the terrace.

'It's alright, I'm fine, and nothing happened after you left, and in fact . . . I was extremely happy.' I then went on to describe my early morning exercises and how I was determined to bring myself back to the level I had reached when I was in the army, being coached by that PTI, who was a martial arts expert. I told her about my intention to create a 'makiwara', what that was, and what it was for. She seemed rather impressed by this.

'We are going away quite a lot though.'

'Yes I thought of that, I'd have to practice on you!'

She laughed at that, 'That won't toughen you up . . . quite the opposite, you'll get soft.' She kissed me. I could get used to this. She had changed from her customary shorts and tank top to something more elegant (to my eyes), a skirt of some pale blue material, rather full, and a white shirt blouse with short sleeves, unbuttoned at the front, sufficient to show the fullness of her breasts and the beginning of a cleavage. She was wearing open white sandals, which revealed her red painted toenails. Once again I found her strikingly beautiful, and told her so. She blushed and thanked me.

We had a coffee out on the terrace, by now the sky was becoming quite cloudy. I asked her if there was any chance that it might rain.

'It might do, we sometimes have sudden rainstorms at this time of year. Then it clears and seems to become even hotter. Maybe we should get going, it's about an hour of driving, we don't want to get caught.'

I grabbed my bag and after locking up I followed her downstairs. We set off down Ben Yehuda, travelling south, Tami was giving me directions until we reached Hal Hashiryon, where we turned onto the main road to Jerusalem. By now we were clearing the outskirts of Tel Aviv. The countryside opened up before us.

Tami had told me that it was about 30 kilometres to the maabarah, I reckoned that was about 20 miles. This was the second time I had traveled outside Tel Aviv and Jaffa, the first time was our trip to Bayt Dajan and Biyar Adas, now I was going even further.

We soon passed Bayt Dajan and were heading for another village called As Safirya. Everywhere there was evidence of cultivation. It was clear that the Israelis were intent on making the land flourish, doubtless on land stolen from the Palestinians. As we sped along the road I couldn't help noticing all the dead dogs on either the side of the road, it seemed that they liked to kill as many dogs as they could. I also noticed at intervals the rusting carcasses of tanks and other military vehicles, left over no doubt from the 1947-48 War, lying in the undergrowth, either side of the road.

I was aware that Tami was holding me tightly with her arms round my waist, and I could also tell that she was resting her head against my back. I wondered what she was thinking.

We sped on past more dead dogs and rusting wrecked tanks, as well as miles of well-developed orchards, orange groves and vineyards. There was no doubt the land was being transformed by the Israelis, but what had happened to the Arab people who had lived here for thousands of years? Did anyone care?

Tami stirred, 'When we get to a place called Gezer turn right. It's about two kilometres further on from there.'

'What if it's in Hebrew?'

'Don't worry, I'll keep an eye out for it. We still have about three kilometres before we get to it.' She was now sitting upright and peering over my shoulder. She still had her arms around my waist. She saw the sign first, it was in Hebrew, but also conveniently in smaller letters, in English. There were two other names with it, under an arrow which pointed further on. The other names were Kefer-bin-Nun, and Mishmar Ayyalon.

'What are those?'

'They and Gezer are now exclusive Hebrew settlements. It was originally a Palestinian village called al Qubab, but it was wiped out in 1948 by us, the inhabitants were driven into refugee camps, then we stole their land and now call it ours.

I was astonished at the degree of bitterness I was hearing from her. I decided to wait until we stopped before I asked her why she was being like this today.

I took the right turn and drove down what was a secondary road, which as we progressed turned gradually into an unmade road and finally just a track, until it virtually ended in what was the camp, or 'maabarah'.

We dismounted and I set the scooter on its stand. Even as we stopped a crowd of children surrounded us, laughing and calling out to others to join them. They were chattering and plainly asking questions. Tami started talking to them and trying to answer. They crowded round her, trying to touch her. Gazing at her with astonishment, as she seemed to be talking to them in two languages, one Hebrew the other I supposed was Arabic. She made them laugh, she smiled and laughed with them.

We started to make our way into the camp, I followed, hardly noticed by the children who were plainly entranced by Tami. She seemed to have a natural affinity towards them.

The maabarah was indeed just a camp. It consisted of some 50 tents, arranged in lines. There was a broad avenue in the middle, a sort of main street, whereas the lines behind this were quite narrowly separated. Strung across the main area were washing lines attached to tents on either side. Each one carried washing flapping in the breeze. Everywhere there were children playing, some of whom stopped their games and joined the crowd around Tami. The ground the tents and the 'main street' were on was just earth. There had obviously been a shower before we arrived, so it was now muddy.

A few women had come out from the tents, Tami went over to where they were, followed by a small gaggle of children. She stayed talking with them, while I wandered round looking for positions I could do some rough sketches from. I also got out my camera and started taking shots. Some of the children saw what I was doing and started to follow me. Whenever I looked like I was going to take a photograph they gathered themselves in front of me and smiled and giggled at the camera and jumped up and down, in the end I resigned myself to taking group photographs of them. Like all children they either looked serious or giggled and laughed, some making awful faces. I also managed to separate a few of them and took some individual portraits.

Eventually I caught up with Tami.

'Is this it?'

She nodded, 'This is it, they have one tap for the whole camp and two latrines. There was no electricity for the first five years, now they have it intermittently. The drainage is poor and when the weather is bad their tents get flooded. There are a few aid agencies that come and do their best to help them. There is no resident doctor. If someone is ill or has an accident they have to go to one of the exclusive Israeli settlements up the road and try and get a doctor to come here, sometimes they get one but more often than not they are told to bring the patient to the settlement. There is no transport for them, so they have to walk.'

'Where are they from?'

'Mostly Sephardics from north Africa, Morocco, and Algeria, some though are Mizrachi from Yemen, Angola and Somalia.'

'What languages were you speaking?'

'Mostly Hebrew, some Arabic and some Ladino.'

'Ladino?'

'Ladino is a form of Hebrew, spoken by Sephardics who were mostly from Spain, until they were driven out, then they lived in one of the North African countries. Although some lived as far away as Bulgaria.'

'How long have they been here?'

'Some have been here for ten years, others more recently.'

'Ten years!'

'I know, it's outrageous, but the social housing system is handled mainly by the Ashkenazis, who look down on the Sephardics and the Mizrachi. I told you that before.' She really was in a bad mood today.

'I don't see any men.'

'The men are all out working.'

'Where?'

'They get work as cheap labour with local farmers.'

'Well that's something.'

'Is it? Many of them were doctors, lawyers, engineers and professional people, they can't work in these occupations because the Ashkenazis look down on their abilities. Just because they are forced to live in a place like this doesn't mean they are less intelligent or less able. It just means they are discriminated against.'

I could see that she was really upset about all this.

I noticed she had taken her white sandals off and was walking barefoot in the mud, carrying her sandals in her hand. I offered to put them in my shoulder bag, which she accepted. I also noticed how pretty her toes were with their brightly painted toenails, even though they were now muddy.

We stayed a couple of hours, which gave me time to make some rough sketches, which I could work up later, I also took a great many more photographs. After a while the children got bored with watching me and went back to playing their various games. I asked Tami why they were not at school. She explained that they were still on their summer holiday but would be going back to school the following week.

'There isn't a school here, is there?'

'No, they go to one of the settlements which we passed, Mishmar Allyon I think. She turned to one of the women who were nearby and asked her something in Hebrew. The woman replied at some length, she appeared quite angry about something.

Eventually Tami turned back to me, 'Some go to Mishmar, others go to the one at Gezer.'

'What was she so upset about?'

'It appears that they are discriminated against at these schools, the Sephardic and Mizrachi children are made to wear different uniforms from the Ashkenazis and enter the school by a different door. They are also given a sub-standard education, even though they are Jews

'That's outrageous!'

She nodded, 'I know, and this is something that I and my anti-Zionist friends are very vociferous about . . . amongst many other things of course.'

Surely I thought, she's one of us? I went back to my sketching and photographing. After a while a man emerged from one of the tents. He saw me and walked over to me, he was limping quite badly. He spoke to me in Hebrew, I shrugged and said 'I'm sorry I don't speak I'm English . . . English.' I pointed at myself.

'Ah, English . . . I speak little English, very bad though.'

He thought for a moment then, 'What you do here?'

I showed him my sketches, He looked at all of them with interest, he pointed at me, 'artist?' I nodded vigorously. He looked puzzled, he turned and looked at the camp, raising his arms with his palms turned upwards,

'Why here? . . . ugly, bad!'

I tried to explain that I was here to record the new Israel, I even got out the now rather worn letter from New Horizons. It was of course in English and I could see he didn't really understand it. Eventually I realised I was out of my depth and called out to Tami, and she came over.

I asked her to explain what I was doing, how I was here to do drawings and later paintings all over Israel.

She turned to him and explained in Hebrew what I was trying to do. At one point he again turned to look at the camp and raise his arms in the way he had done for me and said something to her. She replied at some length, and he asked another question.

I asked her what he said.

'He wanted to know why you wanted to draw and paint such an ugly place. I told him that you were an artist and you felt it was important to show every aspect of the new Israel. He said it was a good idea to show the world how they treated some of their people.'

'Ask him where he is from and what he does.'

She asked him and he replied in English.

'I am engineer . . . I from Ethiopia.'

'What sort of engineer?'

'I make bridges.' He made a curve with his hands.

'Wow,' I said. 'What's he doing now?'

'He works on one of the local farms. He had an accident and damaged his leg, he is recovering, then he will go back there. He says the farmer is good to him, and is paying him while he is off. He looks after the farm machinery.'

'Why did he leave Ethiopia?'

'I already asked him, he said that there was a lot of discrimination against Jewish people there, especially since the Israeli state was formed. Also he wanted to come to Israel as he thought that he could contribute, that they would need people like him to build the new Israel. He and his family have been here five years and the only work he can get is on a farm. So he is rather bitter, not surprisingly.'

She touched my hand. 'How are you doing here? Have you done enough for now? I don't want to rush you, but I want to show you another place on the way back to Tel Aviv. We can always come here again.'

'Yes I'm OK, I've done enough for now.'

We said our goodbyes, or rather Tami did, I just nodded and smiled in the background. The children heard we were leaving and came to wave us off. We left many smiling faces.

'Some of the women wanted to feed us, they were all so generous, even though they live in all that squalor.'

We headed back towards the settlements. When we got past the dirt track part of the road Tami leaned forward and said in my ear,

'Can I have my sandals back?'

I skidded to a halt. I had completely forgotten that she was still barefoot. I got the sandals out of my bag, Tami was trying to brush the mud off her feet.

'Here', I said, 'let me do it.' I took out my handkerchief and while she balanced on one foot I wiped as much as I could the mud off her foot, then replaced the sandal. I repeated this performance with her other foot. Just before I replaced the other sandal I couldn't resist kissing her toes.

She giggled and nearly lost her balance. 'You're mad!' she said.

We set off again heading back towards Tel Aviv. After about six kilometres Tami told me to take a left turn, we travelled down this road. At one point we saw a faded sign which said Abu Shushar. Almost immediately there was a newer sign, which said Ameilim and Pedaya.

We reached the abandoned village of Abu Shushar first. It was a sad sight, the few buildings that were left were badly damaged, presumably by gunfire and explosives. They were all becoming overgrown by plants and weeds, they were beginning to disappear back into the earth. In a few years there would be little remaining, just overgrown rubble.

We stopped and I parked the scooter. Tami got off and began to wander into what must have been the main square of the village; She appeared to be looking for something. She stopped in front of the remains of a large house. It was badly damaged, all the windows had gone as well as the doors. The walls that were remaining were full of bullet holes and marks of heavier weapons. Tami walked to where the front door must have been and peered inside. She stayed there for a few minutes and made her way back to me. Her face was heavy with sadness.

'Come on,' she said, 'Let's go.'

I was going to protest, after all we had only just got here, but I could see that she just wanted to get away. 'Let me just take some photographs, I'll be quick.'

She nodded and went and sat on the scooter. Her head was bowed and her long dark hair concealed her hands, which were holding her face, I could see by the way her shoulders shook that she was crying. I didn't go to her, I could see that it was some private grief.

I made my way quickly round the village taking photographs. It was indeed a very sad sight, nearly all the buildings and houses were badly damaged, some were just piles of rubble. I tried to photograph as much as I could, and as fast as I could. Then I hurried back to Tami. She had finished crying and was wiping her face with her hands. As I approached she turned her face away to hide her red eyes and flushed cheeks.

'OK, let's go.'

She settled herself behind me and as I drove off she put her arms round me and rested her head against my back.

We set off for Tel Aviv. As we approached the outskirts she said, 'Do you mind if we go back to your apartment, I need to wash my feet and generally tidy myself up before I go home?'

'Yes of course.'

When we got back to the apartment I went and made some coffee, while Tami went to the bathroom. I thought she was just going to wash her feet, but I soon heard the shower going. After about ten minutes she emerged, wrapped in a towel and drying her hair with another one.

'Sorry about that, I suddenly felt the need for a shower. I feel much better now.'

We moved out on to the terrace, I took the coffees with us. We sat under the awning. The sky had cleared and the heat had come back, but there was some shelter from the sun here, also there was a breeze from the sea.

We drank our coffee while Tami dried her hair. She still looked very sad. I didn't question her about what had upset her at Abu Shushar, I felt that she would tell me when she wanted to.

When she had finished her coffee she sat for a few moments, looking out over the buildings to the sea.

'I'm sorry Christopher, I should have told you why I wanted to go to Abu Shushar. When I was at school in 1946, there were many different ethnic and religious pupils there. There were Christians, Muslims, Copts, and others in our classes. We all mixed together happily, there was no discrimination. One of my closest friends was a Muslim girl called Jasmin. We spent a lot of time together. We were very young at that time, seven or eight years old. She came from Abu Shushar. One summer she asked me if I would like to come to her village and stay with them for a week. I pleaded with my parents to let me go, my mother thought it was fine, she liked Jasmin, who had come to our house several times. My father was not very enthusiastic, but he was away a lot, doing his military training. My mother simply overruled him

So I went to Abu Shushar with Jasmin on the bus. When she was at school during term time she stayed with an aunt in Jaffa. During the holidays she went home by herself on the bus, it was normal.

Jasmin's mother was lovely with me. She had three sisters and a brother; they also were very nice to me. The brother Arif was twenty, the next was Dalia, who was eighteen, and was about to go to the University in Jerusalem. Then another sister called Aliya, she was fifteen. I think there had been another boy, but he died quite young. Jasmin was the fourth child. The last was a baby girl called Sabriya.

Their father was a doctor, rather like Hakim's father. He was highly respected by all the people. They were nearly all Arabic people in the village, but other people came from all around when they needed medical help, Jews from nearby settlements, Christians, Coptic people, all sorts. He was highly regarded and often gave his services free to people who were poor and unable to pay.'

She paused for a while, I could see that she was going to tell me what happened and why she was so upset when we went there.

'Jasmin and I remained very good friends, and in 1947 I was invited again, this time my father forbade it. There was increasing fighting between the Jews and the Palestinians in various parts of the country, and he thought that it was too dangerous for me to go there. He was probably right, but I didn't understand it at the time and sulked for the rest of the holiday. In 1948 full scale war broke out and I didn't see Jasmin again. By this time I was eight going on nine, I was confused about the whole war, I was still very young. I knew my father was away fighting and we were all worried about him. When the war was over, Jasmin never came back, I missed her very much. It wasn't until several years later when I was studying in Jerusalem that I found out what really happened to Abu Shushar.

In 1948 it was attacked by the Israelis and the inhabitants were driven away and presumably became refugees, but where? Jordan, the Lebanon, Egypt?

But it was worse. Aryeh Yitzhaki, an Israeli historian, a lecturer in Bar Ilan University in the Faculty of Eretz Studies, had been doing research for a book he was writing about the history of the 1947-48 War. He said that there was a massacre at Abu Shushar. A soldier of the Kheil Mishmar Guards Unit claimed that a soldier in the Kiryati Brigade captured 10 men and 2 women. All were killed, except a young woman who was raped and then disposed of. On May 14 units of the Giv'ati Brigade assaulted the village and fleeing villagers were shot on sight. Others were killed in the streets or axed to death. Some were lined up against a wall and executed, no men were left and the surviving women had to bury the dead. A later report claimed that between 60 and70 people were massacred, men women and children.'

She stopped and wiped her eyes. I realised that tears had been streaming down her face as she recounted all this, I went over and put my arm around her shoulders, she was shaking. She rested her head against me, burying her face in my neck, she murmured something I didn't catch.

'What did you say?'

She raised her face and whispered in my ear. 'Please make love to me before I go home.'

Later, when we had made gentle love and laid there, pressed against one another, she said, 'I wish it was not Shabbat, I so much wanted to stay with you tonight.'

I kissed her, 'I wish that too.'

We lay there for awhile, then she looked at her watch. 'I need to go, my mother will have a fit if I'm late for the beginning of Shabbat.'

'I'll run you back?'

'Would you? That would be great. Just to the end of the road though, if my mother catches sight of you she will insist that you come in.

'She went quickly into the bathroom.

When she came out we went downstairs. She got onto the scooter, and wrapped her arms around my waist again. I set off up Ben Yehuda Street, it was already very quiet, many people were either at home or in the synagogues, for the start of Shabbat.

I dropped her off at the end of her road, and after a quick kiss she fled up the road to her family's apartment.

I drove back slowly, reflecting on the afternoon. Tami had been so desperately upset by the visit to Abu Shushar, about the memory of her friend, whom she would probably never see again, the terrible story of what happened there. I was becoming hardened to all these dreadful stories I was hearing, each one worse than the one before. Was there no end to it? How could there be any peace between the Palestinians and the Israelis after these dreadful events.

When I got back and parked the scooter round the back, I wondered if it was safe there anymore, although what choice did I have? I supposed I could put it inside the building, in the entrance hallway. It was a thought, but I couldn't be bothered to do it, I was tired after this long day and the trauma of what I had heard. I realised also that I had not eaten since the breakfast I had with Simon. Before I did anything else I went across the road to the shop where I had bought the postcards, to see if they had writing paper and envelopes. Fortunately it was still open and I managed to purchase both, as well as some stamps. I asked the man there who spoke passable English how many I would need to post a letter to England, he indicated how many.

I went back to the apartment and had a shower. I then remade the bed and carried the side table back in from the other room, where we had put it to avoid any salacious eavesdropping by whoever had 'bugged' us. Interesting how we had come to accept it as a constant presence.

I then went into the kitchen and looked in the 'fridge, there was nothing there to make a meal. I wondered if the restaurant by the sea might be open, the one which Joseph ran with his father, if not I would probably have to go as far as Jaffa, where there were restaurants which would be open, though I had enough of driving.

I put the writing pad in my shoulder bag and walked down to the sea, then along to the area where the restaurants were. When I reached it I was delighted to see that it was open. I hoped that Joseph would be there. Instead another young man came out with the menu card. I asked him where Joseph was.

'It's their Shabbat so I run the restaurant until it's over. I'm Palestinian. Tomorrow evening they will be back to open it.'

I was rather impressed by this, it seemed to mean that there was the possibility of a trusting relationship between these two people.

He could see what I was thinking and laughed, 'I know it seems odd, a restaurant owned by Jewish people having one of their managers a Palestinian. It's not unusual, there are friendships and working relationships all over, some of us believe in a peaceful co-existence. We have to accept that the Israelis are here to stay, we just have to learn to get along.'

Again I was impressed by this, and said so.

'We have no choice.'

I ordered something to eat, and a glass of wine. While I was waiting for the food to arrive I got out the writing pad and began my letter to Sylvia. I began by telling her of my arrival here and the meeting at New Horizons. I included my visits to Jaffa and finding out about its history. I explained how I was getting about on a scooter and my visit to various locations and my drawings. I also said that I had a nice assistant and interpreter. I didn't mention that she was a young woman. Why didn't I? I don't know. Maybe I felt she might be jealous, though why should she be? We were not having a relationship. Somehow though I felt that it might upset her, she was so fragile. I hesitated to tell her of my feelings about the way the Israelis had treated the Palestinians. Maybe later.

My food arrived. I was ravenous, so I began to eat straight away. While I was eating I reflected on my growing relationship with Tami. What had started in theory as a purely physical enjoyment was beginning to turn into something deeper and more serious. Our shared concern for the plight of the Palestinians, our deep criticism of the Zionist government and its actions against minorities like the Sephardics and Mizrachis, were drawing us closer together on other levels. But more than that I was beginning to feel that Tami was falling in love with me and that I was feeling the same way towards her.

My musings were interrupted by a familiar voice, Jacob. As usual he plumped himself uninvited at my table. His first remark was,

'I see you've found one of the few places to eat at the beginning of Shabbat. At that moment the young Palestinian man arrived with a menu for Jacob, 'Malouf here ensures that it is open for people like us.'

I'm not sure that I wanted to be like him. These were only thoughts, I didn't voice them.

'I just ate . . . I was thinking of going.'

'Oh stick around for a bit, I'd like to hear how you are getting on. Where's your friend?'

'He's not here, he went off down to Gaza.'

'That's a shame, I thought you guys would be traveling around together. Have a glass of wine with me.'

I don't know why but I accepted his offer, and against my better judgement, I stayed.

'So what have you been up to?'

I thought carefully about what I had actually been up to. What could I safely tell him? Jaffa yes, Hamid no, al-Ajami . . . I guess so, Bayt Dajan . . . why? Biyar' Adas . . . No! The maabarah? No! Abu Shushar? . . . No, No, NO!

This rather narrowed the field. I didn't want to appear as if I had been idle. On the other hand I didn't want to make him suspicious of my motives for being here.

I decided to obfuscate.

'Quite a lot, first I went into Jaffa, both in the old part al-Ajami and the new developing part. I did a number of drawings and took a few photographs. Then I went to Bayt Dajan . . . '

Jacob interrupted me, 'Why did you go there?'

'Well we didn't particularly go there, we were more interested in the two Jewish settlements up the road, Beyt Dagan and Ganet.'

He seemed satisfied by this, 'What did you think about them?'

'Very impressive to see how well they have been developing the land, I took a number of photographs.' I was of course lying through my teeth, we didn't go anywhere near them. 'I hope to visit them again and do some drawings.' More lying.

'So what else have you been doing?'

I racked my brains for something to tell him.

'One day I had some problems with my scooter, I had to have it picked up by the outfit I was renting it from. They took it back for their mechanic to work on it. So I spent most of that day at New Horizons talking to two wonderful old artists.'

'Oh, who were they?'

'One was Jakob Steinhart and the other was Josef Zaritsky.'

'You did well, they're both quite famous here. I have met Zaritsky, he was principal of the Bezalell School of Art, in Jerusalem.'

'Yes I know, he asked me to visit him, if I go to Jerusalem. He said he would show me over the school.'

'That's very good! You must do it.'

I remembered something else.

'Last week, Tami's father invited me to come for the beginning of Shabbat.'

'Good God! You're not Jewish! Did you go?'

'Yes.'

'You're better than me, I would've made every excuse I could think of, and I'm Jewish!'

'Tami's mother was wonderful to me, I was smothered and overfed. She obviously thought I was suffering from malnutrition.'

'Yes, beware of Jewish mothers, they'll kill you off with food. By the way, how is your beautiful assistant?'

'Tami? She's very good, she is very patient with me. She's at home now for the beginning of Shabbat. Apparently her mother asked me again, Tami made some excuse for me.'

'Good girl! You've done well, considering you've been here less than ten days.'

I felt relieved, I had managed to convince him that I was making good use of my time. I wouldn't have cared what he thought if I hadn't realised that he was working with one of the intelligence agencies, almost certainly the CIA. Also he was passing information to Yurem.

'Well I must be going, I have already stayed longer than I meant to.'

'So where do you think you might go next?'

I was almost tempted to say 'Mind your own business!' But I didn't, it would not have been a sensible thing to do.

'I was thinking of heading up to the Haifa area.'

'That's a good idea.'

I left him to walk back to the apartment. I was fuming about all those questions.

When I got back to the apartment I took the table and writing pad out onto the terrace. It was quiet out there, apart from the endless sound of the cicadas, and the distant sound of Arab music. There were hardly any traffic sounds.

I finished the letter to Sylvia by telling her about the two artists, Jakob Steinhart and Josef Zaritsky and how interesting they were. I described my visit to the studios, where Uri and Tami were. I also described the visit to the 'maabarah'. I ended it . . . With Love, Christopher xxx

I sealed it up with the address on and what I hoped were the correct stamps, and printed 'AIR MAIL' on both sides. I would post it tomorrow; I had noticed a postbox on Bograshov.

I sat for a while looking at the stars, smelling the evening perfumes of tropical flowers and baked earth, and pondered my feelings about Tami. Was this love? It was certainly a stronger emotion than anything I had felt before. What would become of it?

I went and got my notebook and began the task of recording the events of the day. The visit to the maabarah. The blatant discrimination by the Ashkenazis. The man who was an engineer, who was condemned to working on a farm, mending farm machinery. The general squalor of the camp. The generosity of the people in spite of this. The visit to Abu Shushar and Tami's obvious distress and the terrible story she told. This all took me some time and again it was quite late when I finished.

When I went to bed I was very conscious of Tami's fragrance, which pervaded the bedclothes, it made me very much want her to be there. This is madness I thought, as I drifted off to sleep.

Chapter 17

I woke early in the morning. It was very quiet outside, which surprised me as the traffic usually built up from about 5.30 onwards. Then I remembered it was still Shabbat. I got up and made myself some coffee and went with it to the terrace. The temperature was perfect. After I finished my coffee I began a series of strengthening exercises, trying to bring myself back to the level of fitness I had before I stopped regularly practicing Karate. As I didn't have a 'makiwara' I supplemented it by wrapping a towel round one of the upright posts, supporting the canopy. It was not perfect but it was all I had. The edge of my hand still hurt, so I started very gently at first. I knew from experience that it would take several weeks before my hands were really up to scratch.

Tami had not said that she would see me this evening, in fact we hadn't made any arrangement when we should next meet up. I decided to devote the day to working up my sketches. They were mainly pencil sketches. I had brought pens and inks, as well as watercolours and pads of watercolour paper. I had hardly any food in, just fruit, mainly oranges, and coffee. I wondered if the shop downstairs might be open. I resolved to go down there later.

I went out on to the terrace, the table was still there. I pulled it well under the awning, then carried my sketch books and materials out and began to work. Although it was now hot I had become used to it. I became totally absorbed with what I was doing. Time passed quickly, when I finally looked at my watch I was surprised to find that it was after midday. It was time for me to go in search of food.

I brought the table in, with my sketchbooks and materials and left them in the kitchen. I took my shoulder bag, which had my notebook, and headed off down the stairs. I needed to think of somewhere that I could hide the notebook, it was ridiculous that I had to carry it around with me, but where? Given that some persons had penetrated my apartment in order to set up those 'bugs', it meant that there was no secure place anywhere in the apartment.

When I got outside the heat hit me, it was after all, noon, the hottest time. I put my baseball cap on and went to the shop, it was definitely closed. I decided to drive down to Jaffa. I walked round the apartment building to the yard at the back. The scooter was gone! I was completely shocked. I must have stood there with my mouth open, searching the small yard as if I would find it, but it was gone!

I know I had locked it. What to do? I couldn't call Tami, I didn't have her number and anyway it was Shabbat.

I stood there trying to think of my next move. I racked my brains for whom I knew. Then I had a brainwave, Andrej! I got out my notebook, I had tucked his card in there. I found it. His name was on it, Andrej Kowalski, General Mechanic, Scooters a speciality, followed by a 'phone number.

I had seen a 'phone point on the road opposite which led down to the sea. I made my way down there. I found some coins and dialed the number. The 'phone rang for sometime, I had almost given up when it was picked up.

A voice which sounded like an older woman answered 'Dziendobry?'

I hesitated, 'Is Andrej there?'

There was a pause and an exchange between two people in a foreign language, then, 'Kto To?'

'I tried again, 'Andrej? It's Christopher.'

There was a pause, then 'Oh hi, what's up?'

I quickly explained to him what had happened.

'Oh shit!' He thought for a minute, 'Where are you?'

I told him that I was in a pay box.

'OK, I'll call the police, what's your address?'

I gave it to him.

'Right, call me back in about 10 minutes.'

I hung up and went for a walk round the block.

When I called back he picked up instantly,

'Right, go back to your apartment and wait, the police should be with you in about half an hour. Call me later in the evening and let me know what they said.'

I thanked him profusely. I went back to the apartment and waited. Sure enough after about half a hour the buzzer sounded.

I picked up the internal 'phone, 'Hello?'

'Police.'

'Hold on . . . I'll come down.'

Two uniformed police were there, one male and one female. They wore dark blue uniforms with short-sleeved shirts or tunics. They also wore peaked caps with a prominent badge in the middle. They both carried side arms and batons.

The man said in English, with a strong Israeli accent, 'We understand you've had a robbery?'

'Yes, my scooter seems to have been stolen . . . from the yard at the back of the building.

'Show us.'

I led them round the back of the building to the yard. They walked around, the woman police officer examined the sandy patch in the corner.

'What's this?'

I explained the oil leak. I didn't elaborate on it, and didn't say that I thought it had been done deliberately. I did tell them though about the man I caught trying to steal my shoulder bag.

'What happened?'

I told them that I had surprised the man and he had dropped the bag and run off. I didn't feel it necessary to recount the fact that I had probably broken his nose.

'Why didn't you report it?'

'I didn't think that it was necessary as I had retrieved the bag and the man had run off.'

'It's important to report any incident like this, we try to keep track of any potential criminal activities.'

They asked for particulars of the scooter, make, colour, registration number, also whether it was mine or rented.

'It's rented.'

They then asked about what I was doing here and where I was from. Then they also asked to see my passport.

'It's in the apartment.'

We trooped upstairs. They were curious about what I was doing in this building.

'We understood this building was empty, why are you living here?

We had reached the apartment, I explained that I was here under the auspices of New Horizons. I got out the letter one more time and they examined it with curiosity.

'So you are an artist?'

'Yes.'

'May we see some of your work?'

'I got out my main sketchbook and showed them what I had been doing, especially the ones I had been working on this morning.

They seemed very impressed. The young woman policeman spent some time examining each one carefully.

'These are very good. You know I wanted to be an artist, but my father wouldn't let me go to art school. I had applied to the Bezalell School of Art in Jerusalem and was accepted, but my father wouldn't let me go. Maybe I will go one day.' She added wistfully.

I started to tell her how I had met Jakob Steinhart when the buzzer sounded. It was Tami.

When Tami reached the apartment she was carrying a bag. She was astonished to see me there with two police officers. Her initial reaction was that I had been arrested. She started to expostulate in Hebrew.

The police officers replied in a placatory manner. She soon calmed down and turned to me. 'What happened?'

I explained that I had gone down thinking that I might go to Jaffa, looking for somewhere to eat. I had then discovered that the scooter was missing.

'I didn't have your 'phone number, and anyway it was Shabbat and I didn't want to disturb you and your family. So I phoned Andrej and disturbed his Shabbat instead. He called the police.'

The two police officers showed signs of wanting to leave. The man said, 'We'll get in touch with you if we find out anything.

'He looked around, 'You don't have a 'phone here?'

Tami interrupted, 'Call my number.' She gave it to them. She also gave them the number of the company it was rented from.

As they left the young woman turned to me, 'I think your work is wonderful, I look forward to seeing your exhibition.'

'Thank you.'

I had a twinge of conscience, as she went down the stairs.

As soon as the door closed Tami put her arms round me. 'Poor you.' she said. That's all you need.

'I didn't expect you so early.'

'Yes, I know, I'm early . . . I had a screaming row with my father.'

'What about?'

You . . . sort of.'

'What!'

I told him that I took you to the 'maabarah' . . . then I took you to Abu Shushar. He was furious. He said that I was giving you the wrong impression of Israel. We went on for some time, getting more furious with one another, until I more or less accused him of murdering Jasmin!'

'Oh my God!'

'He ordered me out of the house. So I said, fine, I was going to live with you!'

I was speechless.

'Did you really say that you were going to come and live here with me?'

She gently stroked my face, 'I only said that to make him even more angry. I didn't mean it. Or at least . . .' She paused and struggled for words, 'unless . . .' another pause . . . 'you wanted this.' She turned away, her face flushed. Then burst out laughing. 'Don't worry, I didn't mean it. Although I am going to stay here tonight!'

'What!'

'That's not the right reaction.' she kissed me.

'Anyway, the good news is, I brought my scooter, so at least we have transport.'

I was shocked by this dramatic turn of events. One part of me relished the idea of Tami being here, sharing my bed and all that was associated with it. On the other hand, it would make my relationship with New Horizons very difficult. It was inevitable that they would get to hear of this, her father was closely associated, not only with Yurem, but almost everyone else at the club. It would also affect Tami's standing there. How was I going to explain all these reservations to Tami, without offending her?

Tami was watching me, she could see the conflicting emotions which were going through my head, I have always found it difficult to conceal my thoughts.

'Come Christopher,' She led me out onto the terrace. 'Tell me what you really think about this.'

We leant over the wall of the terrace, looking down onto Ben Yehuda, where the traffic was already beginning to increase.

How was I going to begin?

I put my arm round her, 'Tami, I love the idea of having you here, I can't think of anything nicer . . . '

'But?' She interrupted.

'But I think it's fraught with all sorts of problems.'

I then ran through all my reservations and concerns. She listened carefully, without interrupting, until I finished.

She sighed, 'I know you're right, I just let my emotions run away with me. I was angry with my father, I was upset by yesterday, seeing the 'maabarah', then re-visiting Abu Shushar, with all those memories. When we made love I so wanted to stay with you, but I had to go back home because of Shabbat. All

I was thinking about when I was there was you. The row with my father was a result of all that.'

I folded her in my arms and kissed her all over her face and neck.

'Mmmm!' she said 'Careful, we may find ourselves in bed again. You must be starving, let's go out and find something to eat.

I looked at my watch, it was nearly 8pm. I suppose all that business with the scooter and the arrival of the police had gone on longer than I realised. Apart from my early morning coffee and orange juice I had not eaten all day, I could feel my stomach rumbling at the mere mention of food.

We went downstairs, Tami's scooter was parked at the curb in front of the building. Given what had happened to the scooter I had been using, I was concerned about hers. I suggested we put it inside.

'It will be alright there, I've locked it. This is a busy street, people would notice if anyone tried to break the lock on it. Believe it or not, there is a low level of crime here.'

The shop I had bought my supplies from was still firmly shut.

'Come on', Tami said, 'Let's go to that restaurant you like, the one by the sea. I'll treat you to supper.'

We set off down Frischman towards the sea. Tami took my hand. Well I thought, here we are, boyfriend and girlfriend walking down the road holding hands. There was something both charming and odd about this. I had been here only two weeks and now had an Israeli girlfriend, and she had an English boyfriend. Who would have thought it two weeks ago. I was glad that Simon was nowhere near to see this, he would have been shocked and probably disapproving.

She had surprisingly strong, square hands, as opposed to my rather small slender ones. She had a very strong grip too.

We made our way to the restaurant. It was not very crowded yet. We took a table outside. Joseph came bustling out with the menus.

'Hey, back again so soon, can't keep away eh? Malouf told me you were here last evening.'

He looked at Tami, 'I see you are making friends already.'

'This is Tami, she's my interpreter.'

'Right . . . I'm sure you need one of those in the evenings!'

Tami flushed, and said something sharply to him in Hebrew.

He said something else then backed away and walked off, smirking.

'What did you say to him?'

'I told him to mind his own business, we are having a planning meeting, to do with how best to spend your time here. He seemed to think that was funny.'

'Well I suppose it was.'

She looked at me and suddenly burst out laughing. She squeezed my hand hard under the table, 'Is it that obvious?'

'What?' I said, innocently.'

She squeezed my hand even more fiercely, 'If you don't stop that, I'll drag you back to the apartment and make passionate love to you . . . without any supper!'

'Yes miss!'

'And stop that too!'

All this rather adolescent banter cheered me up, I ceased to brood over the scooter being stolen. I stopped worrying about how to carry out our mission here. I was meeting people who I liked, both Jewish and Palestinian. I was finding out more about the virtues of people here as well as the iniquities. Now that Tami and I had become more open about our feelings for each other, more lighthearted if you like, I felt almost optimistic about the time I would be spending here. I refused to consider how it would all end.

We ordered our meal and some wine. While we were waiting for the food we began to talk about what should be the next place or places we should visit. Since Tami had shown me several villages, where tragic and brutal events had taken place, it seemed that she was as anxious to underline the plight of the Palestinians as I was. I still didn't want to reveal that my sole purpose for coming here was just that. I wanted it to appear that I had been gradually led into this, and I certainly didn't want to implicate Simon. I was not trying to deliberately deceive her, but I didn't want her to know that this was a deception against New Horizons, who had generously invited me here.

'I'm pleased about all the things you have told me, it has made more aware of what the Palestinians have been suffering. Now I want to find out more.'

I told her that I wanted to head up to Haifa next, maybe going en route to visit some areas which were being developed as well as those I had seen in the area we passed through on our way to the 'maabarah'.

'I'll make a list for you.'

'Maybe we can do some of those and return here in the evenings. Before we base ourselves in Haifa?'

She thought about this, then agreed. 'When we move up to Haifa I have a friend who will loan us her apartment. She's away at the moment, doing some course in Jerusalem. I'll get in touch with her, when we know we are going there.'

'That's good . . . you seem to have a lot of useful friends.'

'We were in the IDF together. You know Israel is a small country still, everyone knows everyone else.'

We talked some more about our pending trips, then I asked a question I had been meaning to ask for sometime.

'Tami, what do you do for money?'

She was a bit puzzled by my question, I don't think she understood it at first. Then her face cleared, 'Oh I see what you mean, how do I earn a living?'

'Yes.'

'Well, when I finished my military service, I joined up with a friend to open a gallery, we specialised in Israeli paintings and sculptures. We were quite successful. We had several exhibitions of contemporary Israeli artists. They sold well to visiting rich American Jewish visitors, who paid the high prices we set them at. As is usual with galleries we got 50 per cent, the artists got the other 50 per cent. They were happy and so were we. After a time, my partner got greedy and started asking for 75 per cent. The artists not surprisingly didn't like this, so they refused to show with us anymore. I sold my investment in the business to him and took the money so that I could do what I wanted to do, become an artist myself. I also earn a little money from New Horizons and occasionally act as an agent for some of the younger artists. I don't charge them much, but every little helps. I get by OK, but I'm still living with my parents, and trying to save up enough money for my own apartment.'

I was most impressed by this, I was beginning to realise how little we knew of one another. I suddenly wanted to know every detail of her life. She was virtually the same age as me, but she seemed to have done so much.

'What about you Christopher? Tell me about you.'

'Nothing to tell.'

'Oh come on Christopher, tell me about yourself, tell me about your parents, tell me about where you grew up, tell me about art school. You know a lot about me, you've met my family, you know what I did in the IDF, you now know about what I did when I had finished my military service.'

Put like that I suppose there were things to tell. Most of us think we have lived uninteresting lives, whereas others are much more interesting. I suppose we ourselves with our day-to-day existence can't help thinking that we are too ordinary to be of interest to anyone else. The fact is we are all different and this very difference makes us more interesting to other people.

So I told her about growing up during the war, the air raids, school with other pupils getting killed, the bombed houses, the rationing. Moving to where we lived now, early art school, military service, then the Royal College, and going to Paris before coming here.

She listened to this entranced, occasionally asking questions. She held my hand under the table as I talked, I could see her trying to conjure up images of what I was telling her.

When I finished, saying, 'That's all there is really.' She was silent for a while, then,

'Thank you, I feel as if I know you much better now, it makes me even closer to you, thank you. You see, you've led an interesting life. She kissed me on the cheek. After this she became more serious.

'I should call my mother, she was quite upset by the row I had with my father.'

At that moment Joseph came by, I asked if he knew where the nearest pay phone was. 'Use our 'phone . . . you're not calling the UK are you?'

'No it's local.'

'OK, it's in the back.' He indicated the interior of the restaurant.

'It's for me.' Tami said.

'That's fine.'

She went inside.

Joseph stayed. 'She's a lovely lady . . . are you . . . ?

No . . . I should be so lucky!'

Tami came back frowning. After Joseph moved off, she sat down

'I told her you rejected me and made me cry . . . '

'What!'

'Yes, I told her that you said I was a totally immoral person and you wanted nothing more to do with me.'

'You didn't!'

She burst out laughing, 'Of course I didn't, I said you were very polite, and thanked me for the offer, but you said it wouldn't be proper to take advantage of me.'

'What did she say?'

'She said she knew you were a very nice boy and would you come for supper very soon.'

We giggled about this, like children, for a few minutes. Then she grew more serious.

'She went on to say that my father was feeling bad about the row we had and wants me to come home so he can make it up.' She sighed, 'I told her that you had your scooter stolen and I was trying to help you report this to the police, and also call the company you rented it from, so I might be late.'

She looked at me, 'I'm sorry . . . but I must go back later, more for her sake than anyone else . . . but we still have time for you to take advantage of me! Let's go soon!'

I insisted that I shared the bill with her and we left. As soon as we were out of sight of the restaurant she put her arm round my waist and leant her head against my shoulder as we walked along.

Later we lay, temporarily replete from our increasingly passionate lovemaking, watching the lights and shadows of passing traffic, dancing across the ceiling, Tami sighed, 'I wish I could stay here, I don't want to go back, I don't want to make it up with my father, his opinions about the Palestinians are so fixed that we will never agree, we will always have these rows. There'll always be this between us and my mother suffers in consequence.'

She sighed again and turned, burying her face in my shoulder, murmuring something I could not hear.

'What did you say?'

'Nothing.'

We lay there quietly, I could feel her breath fluttering against my neck. After a while its rhythm changed, became softer, gentler, her body relaxed, and she was asleep. I felt a wonderful tenderness towards her, she seemed extraordinarily vulnerable at this moment. I wanted this feeling to go on forever.

After a time though, when I could feel myself also on the verge of sleep, I made myself stay awake and very gently tried to wake her. She began to stir and suddenly, with a cry, she sat up. She looked around, wild eyed, saw me and flung herself against me.

She began to sob, 'Oh Christopher! I had this terrible dream . . . you were . . . you were lying in the road somewhere, somewhere foreign, maybe your country, I couldn't tell. You were covered in blood and as I made my way towards you a truck . . . a truck came along and simply ran over you. It was horrible . . . horrible. She shook with sobs.

I put my arms round her, she pressed her face against my neck, I could feel her tears running down my cheek.

'It's alright Tami, it was only a dream, it doesn't mean anything.'

She gradually calmed down, drying her eyes on a corner of the sheet. I leant over and retrieved a handkerchief from my shorts, which were lying on the floor next to the bed. She snuffled into it and blew her nose.

'Thank you.'

'I thought I should wake you, otherwise we would both sleep all the night.'

'I know, I should go.'

While she was in the shower I tidied up the bed. She came out of the bathroom drying her hair.

'I'll come tomorrow early. Eight o'clock?'

'I meant to call Andrej, but it's too late now. I'll go and see him in the morning early, why don't you meet me there. I should be there about 8.30.

'OK, that's good.'

I walked her downstairs. Her scooter was still parked safely outside. She clung to me for a moment before getting on.

'See you tomorrow.' She waved and drove off.

I went back to the apartment. My watch said that it was 11.30. Although I had felt very tired earlier I seemed to have woken up. I moved the bedside table back from the other room and generally tidied up. Then carrying my notebook I went out on to the terrace and wrote up the events of the day. Early morning exercises, followed by several hours of working on my drawings. Then the stolen scooter, the contact with Andrej and him calling the police. The arrival of the police and not long afterwards, Tami's arrival. I mentioned having supper with her and her row with her father. I didn't mention in detail what happened later, but did say that Tami was a great help in every way.

The other thing I omitted was the incident of Tami's dream, should I be disturbed by this? It was very similar to Sylvia's dream. Then I remembered that it was only a dream, I knew that people's dreams had little obvious connection to real life, they were more likely to denote some inner concern about something quite different. Maybe she was anxious, as I was, about our developing relationship, and where it was going, perhaps that I would inevitably be leaving, and where would that leave her?

When I got to bed it was nearly 1 o'clock, with very little further reflection, I fell asleep.

Chapter 18

In spite of being so late to bed I was awake at 6am. I lay for a little while, thinking about Tami, and what was happening to us. This was not to do with our plan, but seemed to be inevitable.

The bed smelt pleasantly of Tami and sex, but I needed to do the laundry. I found the crumpled and rather grubby handkerchief which I had given her last night and added it to the sheets.

I got up and stripped the bed. Fortunately Yurem had provided a spare set of bedding. I made some coffee and went out on the terrace and did my exercises. After I finished I had a shower, made up the bed with the spare set of sheets. I then put the sheets I had stripped in the basin of the shower. After I had stoppered the drain, I added liquid soap from the kitchen, then filled it up and left them soaking. I headed for the rental company. Andrej was already there.

He greeted me with, 'Good news, the police have found the scooter, apart from the locks to the panniers it was undamaged.'

'Where was it?'

'In an area called Qiryat Shalom, behind an old warehouse there.'

'I know where that is.'

He looked at me curiously, 'How come?'

'There are some artists' studios in the warehouse. I visited an artist there, who I met through New Horizons.

'Who is that?'

'It was a guy called Uri.'

'Sculptor? Welds metal?'

'Yes, that's him.'

'Be careful with him, he's a nutter!'

That was an interesting comment.

'In what way?'

At that moment Tami arrived. 'Hi . . . any news?'

I told her what Andrej had said about the police finding the scooter in Qiryat Shalom.

'Sounds like it was near the studios. We'd better go and look at it.'

'Don't bother, the police are bringing it back here later this morning. Give me a call after lunch and I'll let you have a report.'

Tami had her scooter. I climbed on the back. 'I need some breakfast, can we stop on the way at a café?'

'My mother gave me some food for you, but let's stop somewhere anyway.'

We set off and I put my arms round her waist. It was very strange sitting behind her, her hair blew back in my face. It smelt of shampoo, which was lightly perfumed, I kissed the back of her neck,

'Stop that! Or I'll crash.'

I desisted. Soon she stopped outside a café. We went inside. While we were having breakfast I told Tami about Andrej's comment about Uri.

'What did he mean, "Uri's a nutter"?'

She thought for a moment, 'Well for a start he's seriously unstable. He's unable to relate to other people emotionally. He has fixations and occasionally very disturbing behaviour. On the other hand he is highly intelligent. I think he has a form of autism. You know what that is.

I nodded.

She paused again. I could tell that she was having difficulty in formulating something she wanted to tell me.

'Let me try and explain my brief, and I really mean brief, relationship with him. I was twenty years old, in the IDF, and a virgin. Most of the girls I knew had lost their virginity by the time they were eighteen. I was a freak as far as they were concerned. Uri and I were in the same unit, we spent a lot of time working together, travelling regularly around the country. We were down in Hebron, billeted in the same house. When he wants to he can be quite funny. I found him intelligent and amusing, nothing more. He on the other hand fixated on me, he wanted to know what I was doing, where I was going, who I was going with. He made it clear that he was really attracted to me and persistently asked me to go to bed with him. I resisted for a time, then in the end I thought "What the hell, it's got to happen sometime" and . . . and . . . I gave in. It only happened three times, to be quite honest I didn't enjoy any of them, I didn't enjoy the sex, I didn't like his body, and I didn't like him.'

'Do you think he is still fixated on you?'

'Yes, I think he may be. I stopped posing for him because he was constantly badgering me to have sex with him again.'

'Do you think he might have stolen the scooter out of spite?'

She was taken aback by that question.

'I hadn't thought of that . . . I suppose it's possible . . . but how would he have known where you are staying?'

'I don't know, but it's odd that it ended up behind the studios.'

'Well maybe, but that's not proof of anything, it could just be a coincidence.'

'Yes, you are right, let's leave it to the police.'

We finished our breakfast. Just as we were preparing to depart Tami said, 'I'm going to spend some time with Yurem today, he needs help with some stuff. He's been very good about loaning me to you, but I do actually work for him, so I owe him some time.'

'That's fine, I've got some things I need to do, some laundry for a start, I also want to go to a bank and change some money, we'll need it if we are going to stay in Haifa and travel around. Also I want to buy some boots, I can't go on tramping around on rough ground in tennis shoes!'

'Try a money changing place, they may give you a better rate of exchange than a bank. There are several further down Ben Yehuda. If you can hang on until this afternoon I'll take you to a place where you can buy some boots.'

'OK, I was planning to go to New Horizons anyway, to show Yurem what I have been doing so far.'

She dropped me off outside my apartment building and after giving me a kiss, drove off.

When I got back to the apartment, the soaking sheets were ready to rinse out. It was quite difficult doing it at the bottom of the shower. I stripped off, as I was going to get soaked, and with some effort I managed to rinse them and then squeezed them with my bare hands, trying to get as much of the water out as I could. I then carried them out to the terrace. I had purchased a washing line, and with difficulty I hung the sheets onto it, trying not to let them trail in the dust on the floor of the terrace.

I then put some clothes on and went into the kitchen and squeezed some orange juice. I noticed that I was low in supplies of oranges as well as everything else. After I had drunk the orange juice I put my sandals on and made my way down the stairs and then to the store round the corner. I bought some basic supplies, pita bread, butter, more oranges, milk, serial, coffee, some olive oil and vinegar. I got back to the apartment and made some coffee, then took my notebook and the map of Israel out on to the terrace. I needed to plan the trip north to Haifa. Before we left the area we were in I wanted to visit a couple of villages quite nearby that Simon had mentioned, which the Israelis had apparently occupied after driving out the inhabitants, then had taken the land, destroyed the village and developed it, establishing their own settlements. We had been to Bayt Dajan which now was known as Beyt Dagan, a Jewish settlement on village lands. We had also been to Al Qubab and Abu Shusha, where there were also Jewish settlements on village lands. I now wanted to check out two other villages, one was Al-Khayriyya and the other was Kaffr 'Ana, more or less in the same direction. There were others whose land had been quite simply absorbed by the Tel Aviv conurbation, Al Jammasin, Jarisha, and Al Abbasayyim, whose lands were now part of Lod airport. I had made a note of some which would, though close by, be on our route when we traveled north, like A-Harram and Ijlil-Al-Qibliyya.

It was quite difficult to trace all these, as a lot of them were recorded with only the Israeli settlement names, but sometimes the old Palestinian names were still there on the map.

After I had spent some time tracing just this few, I realised I was getting quite hungry. Glancing at my watch I saw that it was after noon, so I decided to pack my sketch books and my note pad in my shoulder bag and set off first of all to find the money changers that Tami suggested. As I went downstairs it occurred to me that I still hadn't found anywhere to hide my main notebook. When I reached the bottom of the stairs I walked down the passage which led to the backdoor. About halfway along I had noticed what looked like the door to a storage area, which might have been used for cleaning materials. It had a key in the door, but was not locked. I looked inside, sure enough there was an elderly broom, a bucket with a mop in it and various rags which had probably been used for dusters. There was also a shelf at the back which had a couple of cans with dried up paint and some equally dried up brushes, as well as some empty cardboard boxes. I decided to hide my notebook behind these boxes. When I put it in here it seemed completely hidden. I shut the door and locked it, putting the key in my pocket.

When I came out I set off south down Ben Yehuda, keeping as best I could in the narrow strip of shade. Although I had become accustomed to the general heat I tried to avoid walking in direct sunlight when possible, especially at this time of day, when it was at its hottest.

Tami had not told me how far down Ben Yehuda the money changers were, so I just kept on walking. I eventually reached the fork where Ben

Yehuda became Allenby on one side and Hakoveshim on the other. I took the Allenby side, which turned out to be correct. After a couple of blocks I saw three of them, one on the west side and two on the east side. They had their various rates on a board in the window. The information was mainly in Hebrew, but they helpfully displayed each country's rate next to a miniature of its flag. I compared their rates and went to the one I thought was the most favourable and changed £25. I was pleased that it gave me 75 Palestinian pounds in return.

I set off back up Ben Yehuda. Just before I reach Bograshov I spotted a shoe shop on the other side of the road and crossed over. There were some shoes in the window, mostly women's, but peering inside I could see shelves with men's shoes and boots. I tried the door, it was locked. There was a sign in Hebrew and English, 'CLOSED FOR LUNCH!' I'll come back here with Tami later, I thought.

I looked in the window again, as I did so I saw reflected across the street a familiar figure, it was the young man with red hair. He was also looking in the window of a shop, I wonder if he was watching me? At that moment another familiar figure joined him. It was the dark haired woman with a mole on the corner of her mouth.

I turned and prepared to cross the road. The young woman said something to him and they set off down Yehuda in the direction I had come. I watched them turn left at the next corner. Well I thought, looks like I'm still under surveillance. I don't know why, but I felt rather exhilarated by this. I walked on to Bograshov and turned down it, heading for New Horizons. I kept glancing over my shoulder, but saw no further sight of them.

When I arrived at New Horizons I didn't see Tami at first, so I supposed she was in the office with Yurem. I went into the bar area. There were a few people there. In the corner Josef Zaritsky was sitting with another man. He waved to me to come over.

'Christopher! Nice to see you again. He indicated the man next to him, 'This is my friend Johanan Simon, he's an old renegade from New Horizons. He and a few others left the group after a serious argument with Avigdor Stematsky, They all left at the same time.'

I was intrigued by this, 'I'd love to hear why you left . . . can I get you something from the bar?'

Josef asked for a beer, Johanan shook his head, 'Maybe later.'

When I returned to the table with a beer each for Josef and I, they had pulled another chair up to their table.

'Come, sit down. I've been telling Johanan about why you are here, and how good I think your work is.'

I made modest noises and changed the conversation. I turned to Johanan, 'Tell me why you decided to leave New Horizons?'

Johanan glanced at Josef, 'Let's just say it was a difference of opinion.'

'Joseph snorted, 'It was more like the outbreak of the Third World War! You could hear them as far as Ben Yehuda!'

'Tell me!''

Johanan thought for a moment, he obviously wanted to choose his words carefully.

'There were a group of us who disagreed with the idea that abstract art was the way to go, Stematsky was convinced it was. We thought that New Horizons was becoming egocentric and bourgeois. Avigdor was incensed by this, and suggested, rather forcibly, that we should leave. So we did! Incidentally, I no longer regard myself as a Social Realist either.'

At that moment Tami appeared. She saw me with Josef and came over. Before she could speak Josef said, 'Tami let me introduce you to my old friend Johanan Simon, he is an old reprobate who abandoned us for the Social Realists.' He turned to Yohanan, 'This is Tami . . . she is our favourite lady here, she is the main reason I stay with New Horizons.'

Tami laughed, 'Don't take any notice of him, I've heard him say that about every woman who comes here, last week, he said exactly the same thing about Rachel over there.' She nodded in the direction of another young woman sitting talking with two older men at another table.

She turned to me, 'I need to talk to you about the scooter.'

I excused myself from the two artists, promising I would come back, and followed her out into the main room.

'Sorry, I just wanted to speak to you on your own. I've got to spend about another half an hour helping Yurem, then I thought we could go and have some lunch on our own, at a café I go to sometimes, just down the road.'

'Any news on the scooter?'

'Yes, yes . . . sorry, I was just using that as an excuse to talk to you on your own. It's OK, I spoke to Andrej and he said that it was undamaged, apart from the locks on the panniers. He said that he would repair them and we could pick it up tomorrow.'

'Good, that suits me, I can get on with working up my other drawings. Should I come and say hello to Yurem?'

'Yes, but leave it for about half an hour, while he and I finish up what we're doing.'

She thought for a minute,

'I'm a bit worried about Yurem, he seems very thoughtful about something, but won't say what it is. I don't think it's anything to do with us though. Let's talk over lunch.'

'She went back to the office, and I made my way back to Josef and Johanan.

Josef immediately asked me if I would like another beer. I declined, saying that I had not had lunch yet, and that I was going somewhere with Tami to discuss our route round Israel.

Josef went off to the bar and I sat down with Jochanan. He asked if he could see some of my work.

I got out my main sketchbook and passed it to him. He was perusing it when Josef returned.

'You're right,' Johanan remarked to him, 'This young man has remarkable talent, above all he can draw! Which is more I suspect, than most of these abstractionists and so-called expressionists.' He made this last remark gazing round the room.

Josef sighed, 'Now you see why Johanan made himself thoroughly unpopular with Avigdor.'

Personally I agreed with Johanan, he echoed my own thoughts about abstract expressionism. But I was not about to join in with this contentious discussion.

Johanan handed my sketchbook back to me. 'Very good, I look forward to seeing your paintings. Come and see where I live in Herzeliya, it's not far from here, I'll show you some of my recent paintings.'

'I'd love to see your work, maybe next week?'

He gave me his address and 'phone number, 'Just call me, I'm usually there, in my studio.'

He asked me some more questions about my plans while I was in Israel, and I gave him my stock reply, which was to record, as an artist, this new country of Israel. I also made it clear that these sketches would be used as the basis of paintings, which I would do when I got back to the College.

'Well' he said, 'Judging by what you have done so far I'm sure it will be excellent.'

As always I felt rather dishonest, although as an artist I hoped he would understand.

I saw Tami hovering by the door.

'I'm sorry but I need to go now, I will call you next week and if it's alright I'll come and see you, I really want to see your work.'

'He looked pleased at this.

Josef also said he would like me to see his paintings when I came to Jerusalem. I shook hands with them both and went and joined Tami.

'Yurem would love to see you, I told him you were here.'

We went into the office. Yurem was sitting at the big table, looking rather harassed, writing what appeared to be a long list. When Tami and I came in he put down what he was doing and rose to his feet.

'Christopher! How nice to see you. I'm sorry, I feel as if I've been neglecting you, it's just I got so busy with the annual exhibition. I hope Tami has been looking after you.'

'She's been wonderful . . . in every way.'

Tami dug her elbow into my side, fortunately Yurem didn't notice.

'Good, good . . . I knew she would be the right person for you. I hear that your scooter was stolen, though Tami tells me that it's been found and you'll get it back tomorrow.'

'Yes fortunately the police found it and it was not seriously damaged.'

'Still, it's bad that it happened at all.'

'Well we'll get it back in time for us to start our serious travels, which we hope to begin this week.'

'Yes I'm going to give you some more money to help you with your travels.'

I was beginning to feel increasingly bad about taking advantage of Yurem's and New Horizons' generosity towards me. It was one thing before I came here, when I regarded them as representing the bad people. Now that I had experienced nothing but kindness and genuine interest from these people my feelings were very ambivalent. I wondered what Simon would think about this.

In spite of these reservations I thanked Yurem profusely. Tami and I then left and made our way to the café.

It wasn't far, and when we got there it was very quiet, hardly any other customers. Tami explained that it was usually busy between noon and 2pm, when all the office workers came there for lunch. It was now after 3pm.

We sat down and ordered our meal. Tami started to tell me about her morning with Yurem.

'It's the time of year when we start planning our annual exhibition. There's quite a lot of preparation to do, contacting all the members to find out if they want to exhibit, preparing a catalogue with suggested prices, if they want to sell, writing profiles of each exhibitor with photos if available, trying to get sizes of the works which are going to be exhibited so space can be allocated, settling on a date which they can all agree to. It's a lot of stuff, and poor Yurem tries to manage on his own, with help from me, and sometimes Rachel. I told him that we were going traveling soon and he said that was OK and Rachel is going to help him while I'm away. She's very capable and willing.'

'Did he mind that we were going away?'

'No, no, he was very happy, he wants you to see as much as you can. Yurem is a very kind man and very supportive of you.'

I had another twinge of conscience.

'No, there's something else that's bothering him and I don't know what it is. He kept saying we must make the best of this exhibition, who knows if we will still be doing it next year.'

We ate for a few moments in silence. Tami had managed to wrap her legs round mine, under the table, something which I found most comforting.

I told her about Johanan inviting me to visit him at his studio in Herzeliya.

That's good, it's not far. Can I come

'Of course, I want you with me all the time!'

She laughed, 'I'm sure you don't mean that, you'd soon get fed up with me.' But I felt her legs tighten round mine.

We stayed there for another half an hour, then Tami said she needed to get back to Yurem.

'Christopher I meant to tell you, I must be at home this evening, it's my brother's birthday and I must be there. Will you be alright?

'Yes Tami, I will try and survive without you.

"But you will miss me?'

I kissed her, 'Yes I will, of course.'

I headed back up to the apartment, checking frequently to see if either the red headed man, or the woman with the mole appeared. Not that I could do anything about it.

I worked away at my drawings while the light lasted. At about 7.30 I stopped. I laid the drawings out and examined them. The first ones I had done were of old Jaffa, they captured the sense of a city which although now in ruins in many places, was nevertheless a still beautiful and an enduring monument to its history. In contrast the area being developed by the Israelis was rather brash and insensitive to the architectural vernacular of the old city. However I had recorded it in some detail.

In spite of the rather brief time we had been in Bayt Dajan, I had enough material to work up into more detailed drawings. I was beginning to think that when I got back to London and the College I would try and produce a series of painted collages, showing both the development of Israel and the destructive ruin it was built on. I must admit this was partly inspired by some of the work that I had encountered in Tami's paintings, but also along some of the lines of Peter Blake's early work. I still had to work up a series of sketches I had done at the 'maabarah', I'm not sure what reaction I would get from New Horizons on these.

I had not had time to do any sketches at Abu Shushar, but I had taken a quantity of photographs, which I hoped would provide sufficient material for several paintings.

It was not a huge amount of work but I had still only been here for two and a half weeks.

I poured myself a glass of wine and sat out on the terrace. I was happy about what I had done so far . . . it gave me material for at least a dozen paintings. I couldn't wait to get on with them, but there was still a long way to go, I had only just begun.

I reflected on my conversations with the two artists at New Horizons and wondered if there were any Palestinian painters still functioning. How could I find out about them, assuming that any still existed. I can't believe that Hamid is the only young Palestinian artist, there must be more . . . who to ask? It was too late to go and see Hamid now, maybe tomorrow at the end of the day.

I wondered also about Simon. I knew nothing of Gaza, other than it was under Egyptian rule, and had now many refugees from the 1947-48 War.

I looked in the 'fridge, there was not much choice for supper, some eggs, a few tomatoes, the remains of a lettuce and some pita bread. I didn't want to go out and eat again, so I made myself an omelette and a small salad from the tomatoes and lettuce, with the pita it was sufficient to assuage my hunger, I then went out onto the terrace and began to write up my notes. I had retrieved my notebook from the cupboard in the hall.

I remembered my early morning meeting with Andrej, and my conversations with him about Uri, and him warning me about him. My later conversation with Tami about him, and her description of their brief relationship. My suggestion that he might have stolen my scooter. Tami didn't actually dismiss the idea, but neither was she convinced. My trip down Ben Yehuda, looking for the money changers, and then my encounter with the red headed man and the woman with the mole. My arrival at New Horizons and meeting with Josef Zaritsky again, as well as Johanan Simon and his invitation to visit him at his studio in Hertzilya.

Although I didn't write it down, I mused about my increasing ambivalence about the reason I was here. I seem to swing backwards and forwards, when I visited those destroyed villages, and witnessed Tami's distress, I felt nothing but anger for the Israelis. Then meeting people like Josef and Johanan with their genuine interest in what they thought I was doing, Yurem with his kindness and generosity, Joseph at the restaurant, Tami's warm hearted mother, even Andrej, in spite of his disaffection with the Israelis, was genuinely kind and helpful. I was confused. On the other hand I had hardly started my travels, there were more revelations to come. But it was simpler when everything seemed black and white, good or bad. I tried not to think too deeply about my rapidly developing relationship with Tami. I suddenly felt very far away from my home and my life in England, would I ever get back there?

Chapter 19

The next morning, after I had done my exercises and had coffee and pita with a little humus for breakfast, I went downstairs and put my notebook in the cupboard, before I started on my way to the scooter rental place. Andrej was there, so was the scooter, I could detect some scratch marks around where the locks were on the panniers, otherwise it looked OK.

When I asked how much I owed them for the repairs, Andrej said it was all covered by insurance. It was no problem, he also added, 'They were just relieved that it hadn't been wrecked. You might think of finding somewhere safer to park though, you haven't had much luck so far.'

I nodded, 'I was thinking about that too.'

I looked at my watch, it was only just 9am, too early for Tami to be at New Horizons. I debated on whether to go back to the apartment. But decided not, there was nothing to do there. Instead I went back to the café which Tami and I had lunch in the day before, as it was near to New Horizons.

I was shocked to see Tami seated at a table in the corner with Uri!

I sat down at a table where I could watch them.

They were having a heated discussion and at one point I saw him reach out and try and touch her. She angrily brushed his hand aside. Uri was obviously angry with her, I prepared to get up and go over there if it looked like he may get violent. Suddenly he got to his feet, leant over and said something in her ear and stormed out of the café.

Tami sat with bowed head, looking at her hands, she was obviously shaken by this encounter with Uri. I waited a few moments before getting up and going to her.

She was startled by my arrival.

'What are you doing here?'

'I'm sorry, I wanted to see you, but I thought you wouldn't be at New Horizons until 10 o'clock, so I came here to have a coffee while I waited.'

'So, did you witness what just happened with Uri?'

I nodded, 'I was getting ready to interfere if he became violent.'

She smiled briefly and touched my hand.

'My hero.'

'Tell me what it was about.'

She hesitated, 'Well it was about you really.'

I waited.

'He wanted to know why I was spending so much time with you.'

'What did you say?'

'I told him it was none of his business. As you saw, he became quite heated.'

'Then I told him it was what Yurem had asked me to do, act as your interpreter and assistant.'

'Did you tell him we were lovers?'

'No, as I told you it was none of his business. He thinks we are though, and more or less said so.'

She watched me for a moment, then reached over the table and took my hand, 'I love it that we are lovers, I'm on your side remember. I also think that you are a real artist, and . . . you have a natural empathy for people on both sides of the question.'

She looked around, fortunately there was no one near us to overhear. 'I have every intention of continuing to help you . . . but don't forget that in the final analysis I am an Israeli, and like it or not we are here to stay . . . what I want is that we can all live in peace and understanding, as we have done for thousands of years, before the Zionists came and fucked it up. I just hope we can try and redress some of the terrible things that have happened, one of the ways is to expose the people who were primarily responsible for these things.'

I was impressed by this rather lengthy speech. I was also very relieved.

As a result of this exchange I almost forgot the reason I had come to meet up with Tami, I was going to ask her who would know about recent Palestinian artists, if any.

'So why did you want to see me?'

'I always want to see you.'

She laughed, 'It's my body you want.'

'Well . . . '

'I need to go into New Horizons, Yurem will be there at 10.00 and he has some things he wants me to do. Did you pick up the scooter?'

Yes it's OK, just a few scratches.'

'Walk with me.'

On the way I asked her if she knew of anyone who would know about contemporary Palestinian artists.

'Yes, Yurem does, he's very interested in that subject. Why don't you come by at the end of the afternoon?'

When we got to the door of the building she put her arms round me and kissed me. 'My hero,' she said.

I walked back to the café, my scooter was still parked outside. I realised that I hadn't had any coffee, rather than go back in there again I decided to go to the beach café and see if Joseph was there. I could ask him about the two villages I wanted to see. I drove there and parked on the other side of the road from the café, where I could keep an eye on it. I was becoming paranoid about security now. I began to plan my day. I wanted to visit at least one of the villages which had been destroyed and its land taken by the Israelis.

I also needed to buy some boots. I had forgotten to ask Tami where she would suggest, I didn't want to go to an ordinary shoe shop, like the one I had looked at on Ben Yehuda. Maybe if I went to the café on the beach, I might see Joseph, he may have an idea. What I wanted was something sturdy and cheap.

When I reached the café Joseph was busily setting up the tables outside, under the awning. He greeted me warmly and asked me if I wanted anything to eat. 'Have you got any museli?'

'Sure.'

'I'll have some muesli, some yogurt and a glass of orange juice, also a coffee.'

'OK, let me just finish putting the tables out and I'll get it.'

After he finished, he emerged with the food and the coffee. He eyed the meal. 'Are you on a diet?'

I laughed, 'No I like this stuff, as you know it's not easy to find in England.'

He looked around, there were no other people there. 'Do you mind if I sit with you for a while?'

'Please do, I wanted to ask you some things anyway.'

'What did you want to know?'

'Well some directions for a start.'

I told him about the two villages close to Tel Aviv that I wanted to see.

'Well you can forget about Al-Khayriyya for a start, it's now the city rubbish dump.'

'Is there no trace it?'

'You might find the odd derelict building or house, but the majority of the village land is now used for the rubbish dump.'

'What about the other village?" Al-Mas' Udiyya?'

'That's now part of a suburb of Tel Aviv.'

I was shocked to hear about this. So much for my attempt to find these villages on my own, without the help of Tami.

'How do you know about all this?'

'Come on! I live here don't I? Actually I'm a bit of an amateur historian as well, it started when I was in the IDF, the unit I was in was part of a rapid response force, we were trained to move speedily around the country, always ready for aggressive defence wherever we went. In the process I began to have some knowledge of the towns and villages we occupied and destroyed.'

'Wow! Did you have a lot of fighting to do?'

'No, it was just a series of exercises, it was clear that the Palestinians, were cowed by what had happened with what they call the Nakba, those that remained seem to have given up any resistance, they were just happy to have survived. The majority were driven out of the country, never to be allowed to return. Anyway, as a result of this I became very interested in the history of these places.' He looked round, other people had arrived and were occupying some of the tables.

Joseph got up, 'Sorry, I must get on with my job, but if you're interested in all this, tomorrow is my day off, let's meet and I'll show you the book I'm writing.

'Great! I'd love to see it.'

I sat for a while, drinking my orange juice and thinking about what he had told me. I wondered whether I should go to where these villages had been, and see if there were any remnants of buildings or houses.

When Joseph came by I asked for my bill and paid it. We agreed to meet there on the following day, about noon, so that he could show me what he had written. My last question to him was where I could find some boots. '

'Try the old Jaffa market, you'll find everything there.'

I headed off down to Jaffa, I roughly knew it was on a road near to the café that Tami and I had stopped at. I still didn't find it, so I decided that I needed to ask for directions. The first two people I stopped to ask didn't understand English, so they had no idea what I was asking. A young woman came along with a pushchair with a small baby in it. Fortunately she did speak some English and gave me clear directions. It wasn't far and I found it quickly.

I also found somewhere to park and plunged into the alleyways of the 'souk'. It was another world, I finally felt that I was in the Middle East. I don't know how to convey the kaleidoscope of images I was suddenly encountering. Not only the sights but the sounds and smells as well. It was like plunging into an artist's palette. Every inch of the crowded alleyways seemed to offer a myriad of textures and colours. At first I found it difficult to focus on anything, there was so much. A small covered shop, hung with garments and lengths of brightly coloured satins as well as silks and cottons, jostled for space with another stall selling beaten copper pots, bowls and plates. It in turn was crowded against a stall hung with leather bags, camel saddles, dagger sheaths and boots with ornate designs, not what I was looking for, but fascinating in the richness of their designs and ornament. Further on there were shops with lamps and pendant perforated copper shades, another shop selling many coloured cushions. The stalls selling fruit and vegetables, green, yellow and red chilis, aubergines, avocados, okra, and courgettes, jostled with, mangoes, pomegranates, lemons, oranges, grapefruit, cherries, persimmons, apples, figs, peaches and nectarines, which in turn crowded with the spices, a whole palette of colours themselves, saffron, tumeric, chili, cayenne, mustard, and overall was the yearning Arabic music, colouring the very air with its sounds.

I was so overwhelmed by this visual feast that I lost my sense of the reason I was there. I wandered mesmerised through the twisting narrow alleyways. Everything I looked at was a potential work of art. I felt as if I did nothing else but record the images I saw at every turn here it would be time well spent, even if I did nothing else during the whole remaining time I would be here in Palestine.

I must have been there for the best part of an hour before I pulled myself together. After much searching I found a shop which seemed to deal in military surplus stuff. I was familiar with this sort of store, we had several like it in London, they were called 'army surplus.' I picked a pair of boots, which were khaki coloured, with strong rubber soles and canvas tops. They laced up and seemed to me to be tough and light desert boots, just what I wanted. I tried them on and they fitted. I haggled with the owner of the store, who turned out to be an Israeli, who spoke English. They were ideal and very cheap. He told me that they were army issue, as supplied to the IDF.

I made my way back through the souk to my scooter. I had managed to take quite a lot of photographs and I was determined to come again and do some drawings.

It was getting quite late in the afternoon so I headed back to New Horizons. Tami saw me when I came in and came over. 'Yurem and I are just finishing something. I told him you wanted to find out about Palestinian artists and he'd love to tell you about the ones whose work he knows. Give us half an hour and he will be free.'

I went into the bar and bought myself a beer and sat at a table in a corner. There were a few people there, some greeted me quite warmly. This is nice, I thought, I seem to have been accepted as a fellow artist. I started rummaging in my bag for my small sketchbook, I thought I might do a quick sketch of the room.

'Hello Christiopher, how are you doing?'

I looked up, it was Tami's father.

'I understand that you and Tami are off on a long trip soon, around the country?'

'Yes, I've been trying to work out a good route. I thought initially we should head towards Haifa, stopping on the way to visit one or two kibbutzim. I would very much like to see them and understand how they work.

That's a good idea. You'll find that most of them have progressed a lot since the 1947-48 War, at first they were only interested in subsistence farming, but now they're becoming more commercial enterprises, with lots of improved irrigation and much new modern farming equipment.'

'That's interesting, I supposed before I came here that they were entirely agricultural, that everyone lived communally.'

'As well as that, some are now into manufacturing products, such as plastics and engineering equipment. They are becoming profit-making enterprises.'

'Wow, so my romantic idea of self sufficient, non-profit agricultural kibbutzim is obsolete?'

'Well they are still self sufficient, but they have become more diverse.'

'And the Palestinians?' As soon as I said that I knew it was a mistake.

He turned to me, 'What about the Palestinians?"What are they doing? Where can they go. There is no place for them here.' He said this with vehemence.

I hesitated before my next question, I knew that I was moving into a dangerous area, but somehow I found I couldn't contain myself anymore.

'But surely this was their country before?'

'There never was such a country as Palestine!' He almost spat out these words, his eyes glaring at me.

I thought for a moment. If I went on like this I was going to really alienate him, so I didn't say, 'I wonder then why there are people called Palestinians?'

I said rather lamely, 'Oh, I see.' Though I plainly didn't.

He seemed to make an effort to calm himself down.

'Look,' he said, 'You mustn't take any notice of what Tami says, she is just pretending to be a rebel . . . she'll grow out of it, this is Israel now and we belong here, these so-called Palestinians should just go back into the desert where they belong . . . and take their camels with them!'

'Tami has never said anything about these things to me.' I was lying through my teeth of course.

'We've never discussed anything political, she is just trying to help me see as much as I can of your wonderful new country.'

He began to calm down. I was astonished at his anger, he had seemed such a moderate and balanced man.

'Look,' he said, 'Let me take you round the exhibition as far as it is at the moment, I will try and name some of the artists.' So we set off round the exhibition, which was still in the process of being hung, we had to pick our way through stepladders, kneeling artists cutting mounts for their drawings and prints, sweating sculptors trying to manoeuver their sculptures into the most propitious places, and artists who had successfully hung their work standing around chatting to other artists. He pointed out works by Zaritsky, Streichman and Stematsky, those favouring 'lyrical expressionism'. As well as artists favouring a more figurative statement, like Raffi Lavie, Moshe Kupferman, as well as Uri Lifshitz. There was a very odd piece of work entitled 'Panic over Trousers', by Igael Tumarkin. It consisted of a pair of trousers, which had been soaked in plaster, allowed to dry, then hung against a black background. They looked like a walking ghost. We continued round the room avoiding obstacles along the way. Eventually we arrived back in the bar area.

'Can I get you a drink?'

He thought for a moment, 'I'll just have a coffee.'

I went to the bar and ordered two coffees.

When I returned with them he seemed anxious to talk.

'What will you do with all the sketches and photographs you are taking while you are here?'

'I intend to do a series of paintings based on the material, then bring them back here and have an exhibition, if that's what everyone here would like.'

'How long will that take?'

'I would think at least a year before I had enough for a reasonable exhibition.'

He seemed disappointed at this.

'I had hoped it would only take about six months.'

'Paintings, especially the way I work, sometimes can take months to complete." Can't you do an exhibition of just your sketches for now?'

I began to realise that he was trying to find out what sort of thing I was doing, what direction I was going in, would it put Israel in a bad light? I shook my head, 'No, it doesn't work like that, some of my sketches are just like shorthand, something to remind me of the subject, when I have time I work them up to proper drawings later.'

He nodded, but I could see he was not satisfied.

Tami appeared in the bar area and came over to us.

'I won't be long, I'm just finishing up some stuff with Yurem, then you can come and talk to him about Palestinian artists.' She went back to the office.

Tami's father looked at me, 'Why are you interested in Palestinian artists?'

'Well it's part of the history of this country.'

'No it's not! This country is Israel, anything that went before is of no importance, or relevance!'

Oh dear, I thought, I'm in trouble here. I wish Tami would come back, how am I going to get out of this.

'Sorry,' I said, 'Yurem thought I would find it interesting, in contrast to the work that the Israeli artists are doing.' I felt despicable, by lying like this I might be getting Yurem into trouble.

'Well I'm going to talk to Yurem.'

Oh Lord, I thought, I've really messed up here.

At that moment Tami reappeared. 'Yurem is ready to talk you now.'

I hastily got to my feet. I turned to Tami's father 'Sorry I have to go.'

As we walked away I heard him say, 'Tami, I want to talk to you later.'

'What's that about?' Tami muttered.

'I'm afraid he was upset with me for wanting to find out about Palestinian artists, and I lied by telling him that Yurem thought it was a good idea.'

'Why did you tell him that?'

'I'll tell you later, right now I'm going to confess to Yurem, and hope he will understand.'

As always, Yurem was pleased to see me. 'I hear you want to know about Palestinian artists?'

'Yes, yes, but first I have a confession to make.'

I told him about my discussion with Tami's father and how I had lied to get out of it. To my surprise he burst out laughing.

'You did right, that's exactly what I would have said. Poor Ariel, he belongs to a group of rather extremist people. Sorry Tami, but you know what he's like. Unfortunately we have many like him here. We love him really, but we try and avoid any discussions about the Palestinian people. He tends to get rather angry.'

She nodded.

'I'm so sorry Yurem, it was quite childish of me,'

He put his arm around shoulders, 'Don't worry about it, you did right. Now let me tell you about some Palestinian artists you might try and look up.'

He seemed to know a surprising amount about this subject.

'Well, I was born in this country when it was called Palestine and from an early age I was determined to be an artist. I had a voracious appetite for all the examples of artists that I could find. Europe seemed far away, the likelihood of someone like me going to Paris, London, Madrid or any of the other major capital cities where the great galleries are, seemed very remote. So I had to make do with books, monographs of artists like Degas, Manet, Monet, Cezanne, Renoir and Seurat, or groups like the impressionists, post-impressionists, cubists, primitism, vorticists, abstractism. So many 'ism's', I can't remember them all.

I also began to realise that we had our own homegrown artists. In those days we seemed to live in a much more multicultural society, especially artists, who are naturally independent of both ethnicity, social mores and class. Yes we have political attitudes but it doesn't affect the aesthetics of what we do, the subject matter yes, but the quality of the work, no. Art is a great leveller, both parochially and internationally. Anyway I began to look into our own artists and craftsmen and found some outstanding examples. They came from Jewish, Christian and Arabic backgrounds, we were all Palestinians.

What I'll do is give you a list of artists I think you should look for. There are some prime ones though which you may be able to find here, though many have moved to Beirut or Cairo. One of the artists you should look for is Ismail Shammout. He has already done some powerful work, which illustrates the trauma we perpetrated on them when we began to win back what we now regard as our country. Their term for this period is called 'the Nakba'. There were many things we did during this period which we are not proud of. He has recorded some very emotional moments. He is living now in Beirut and continues to be a most prolific artist. He has a young wife, called Tamam, she is also an artist and is showing signs of being very talented as well.

Another really interesting Palestinian artist and craftsman is Jamal Badran. At the age of thirteen he travelled alone to Cairo, and studied at the School of Applied Arts and Crafts. After graduating in 1927 he started working on the restoration of the Al-Aqsa Mosque. In 1934 he got a scholarship to study at the Central School of Arts and Crafts in London. When he finished there he returned to Jerusalem to teach at the Arab College and the Rashidyeh School. Then in the late 30s he and his brothers opened Studio Badran for the Arts, in Jerusalem. They lost their studio in 1948 as a result of the war. He then taught in Syria and later as a UNESCO expert of ornamental arts and crafts in Libya. Last year he opened another studio in Ramallah. You should be able to visit him there.'

I was finding all this fascinating. I glanced at Tami, and it all seemed a revelation to her.

Yurem glanced at his watch, 'Look,' he said, 'This is a very interesting subject, I could talk at some length about it, but I don't really have time now. What I suggest is that I give you a list of artists to research, and when you and Tami come back from your travels I'll take you both to dinner at Otto's Bar, and give you much more information. In the meantime Tami maybe will type up the list I have already written and give it to you.'

I thanked him profusely, and begged his forgiveness again.

'Christopher, if that's the extent of your iniquities you are as pure as the driven snow, as far as most people are concerned. Remember when you come back we'll have that dinner. Go well.'

Tami and I went back into the main area. 'I must go and talk to my father, I wonder what that's about?'

'Well I'm afraid I got into a heated discussion with him, about the Palestinians, and he said that I mustn't be influenced by you and your opinions. I told him that you certainly didn't discuss anything political to do with the Palestinians, and that you were only interested in showing me your beautiful new country. I suggest you deny any accusations about that.'

She laughed, 'Poor Christopher, you haven't had a good morning here, have you? Anyway let me get this over with, then we'll go and have a drink, I do have to be back here afterwards though, as you see we are busy here right now. Maybe this evening we could go and eat at Joseph's.'

I waited for her in the main room, trying to keep out of the way of the artists who were trying to get their work placed. I could see into the bar where Tami was talking to her father. They seemed to be having a rather heated discussion, and at some point Tami got up and began to leave. Ariel's face looked like thunder and he called out something to her, she flushed and shouted some thing back to him, making a number of people sitting nearby turn their heads. She stormed out of the bar and came towards me her face still flushed and angry. 'Come on,' she said, 'let's get out of here.'

Wow, I thought, this is all my fault.

We made our way out onto the street, I could see that Tami was trembling with anger. She led the way up the road. I kept quiet, I knew she would tell me when she was ready. We passed the café where we had lunch, a little way beyond was what looked like a bar.

'Let's go in here.' She lead the way in and went to a small table in the corner.

As soon as we sat down she bowed her head, I could see she was crying, the tears were dropping on the table. I went to the bar, and came back with two glasses of wine. Tami had pulled herself together and was blowing her nose on a tiny handkerchief.

'Here,' I said, 'Drink this, and use my handkerchief.'

She accepted both gratefully, and blew her nose loudly.

'Oh dear, you seem to see me constantly in tears.'

'What happened?'

She sighed, 'I told him that I hadn't had any conversation with you about the Palestinians. I don't think he believed me. We argued a bit, then I got up to leave, as I was going he called out that I must be home early. So I said that I wouldn't be, that you and I had to discuss our route round the country. Then he tried to order me to come back. I lost my temper and said I was 24 years old and didn't need to be ordered about like a child. Then I shouted . . . I may stay the night!'

'Whoops! I bet that didn't go down well.

'That's when he shouted at me.'

'Yes, well, half the bar area heard it.'

'I don't care!'

I put my arm around her shoulders and kissed her on the cheek.

'Neither do I.'

She began to relax, she even giggled a bit.

We sat for a while. I pointed out my new boots.

'I've got a pair just like that, they're IDF issue, where did you get those?'

'In the souk.'

'Are they new?'

'Straight out of the original packaging.'

'Yeah, I bet it was pilfered from one of the military stores.'

'Shall I give myself up to the police? Tell them that I've been receiving stolen goods?'

'They won't care, most of them get their boots and other equipment in the souk.'

We finished our drink and Tami said she had to get back to New Horizons, 'Just for a couple of hours, I need to do some last things for Yurem, I'll type up that list for you as well. I'll see you back at the apartment.' She kissed me and left.

I made my way back to the apartment. When I got there I decided to put the scooter inside the entrance area. As I was the only person living in the building I didn't have to worry about inconveniencing anyone else.

I collected my journal from the cupboard in the hall, where I had been storing it every day. When I got to the apartment I took off my boots and went out onto the terrace and sat for a while thinking about the last couple of hours at New Horizons—my craven behaviour with Tami's father, culminating in my blaming poor Yurem. I was still feeling ashamed of doing this, in spite of Yurem's generous attitude towards me. I reflected on his genuine interest in my enquiry about Palestinian art and the information he was giving me. His own memory of growing up in what he referred to as Palestine, remarking how cosmopolitan it was at that time, as opposed to now. This seemed to confute Simon's opinion that he was a confirmed Zionist. As far as I was concerned he had been nothing else but considerate and helpful to me, unquestioning in what I wanted to do.

I also reflected on Tami's public row with her father, and her announcement that she may stay the night with me. This was certainly going to affect Ariel's attitude towards me. I was less concerned about this than what would Tami's mother's reaction be, how would she feel about this? I looked at my watch, Tami seemed to be taking a long time.

I was beginning to add my thoughts to my journal when the buzzer sounded, it was Tami.

'Hi, I'm going to bring my scooter inside as well.

'Do you want any help?'

'It's OK.'

She came panting up the stairs. 'I brought some more wine.'

She was carrying what looked like a heavy bag.

'Wow', I said, 'how many people are we expecting?'

'There are some other things as well.'

She emptied out some food containers as well as the wine and a small bag.

'What's this?'

'Oh, some underwear and T-shirts, a spare pair of shorts, toothbrush and toothpaste, and some cosmetics. I went home and told my mother about the row with my father. That was why I was so long.'

'What did she say?'

'She quite understood, and wondered why I hadn't done it before. She thinks you are lovely boy, and need looking after, hence the food.'

I was stunned, so much for me worrying about her mother's reaction.

'Umm . . . does that mean you are staying?'

She turnd to me, 'You do want me to . . . don't you?'

'Yes . . . yes, I love it!'

'Well we are going to be traveling together for the next two weeks, I thought we might as well begin now.'

In truth I was rather excited at the idea of us living together, even if it was for only a brief period. It was not something I had done with anyone else before. Other than in the army, and that was very different.

She became very brisk, 'OK, I'm going to put this stuff away, then we'll go out.' She busied herself in the kitchen putting away the foodstuff. 'We can eat this tomorrow, I want to eat out this evening.'

She also found an empty drawer to put her T-shirts and panties in, and hung up a small cotton dress she had also brought.

When she was finished she came back out to the terrace and stood next to me with her arm round my waist, gazing out at the fading sunset.

'This is nice . . . maybe we should stay here always.' Then, 'I know . . . I know, you are leaving eventually and this is being pulled down.' She leant her head against my shoulder.

'Nice dream though.' She turned and kissed me lingeringly.

'OK let's go.'

We walked down to the beach area, she had her arm round my waist and I had mine round her shoulders. She was not really short but I was quite tall.

Joseph was pleased to see us.

'Can't keep away, eh?'

On the way I had told Tami about Joseph being something of an amateur historian, and that he was going to show me what he had written so far. I was going to come here the following day to see it.

We ordered our meal and began planning our trip. I said that I wanted first to go to Herzaliya and visit Johanan Simon.

'That's not far, we could do that tomorrow and come back here at the end of the day and set off on our main journey on Wednesday.'

'Sounds good. Then we can head off for Haifa and stop at a kibbutz on the way?'

She thought for a moment, 'There's one I spent a month at one summer . . . 1960 it was, just before I did my military service. It's near Hadera, well on the way to Haifa. Its called 'Givat Haim', I remember the man who ran it . . . Chaim something . . . If he's still there he'll show us around. He was a nice guy.'

'OK let'sdo that.'

We talked more about Haifa and nearby settlements. I wanted to find a way of going to Acre, where Sayyid's brother lived. I didn't mention it as I really wanted to go there by myself, somehow I didn't think it was a good idea for Tami to be with me. However I may not be able to avoid it. I'll just have to find a way to talk to him on my own, even if she did come.

As it was now obvious to me we were both interested in finding out as much as we could about the stealing of land from the Palestinians, as well as evidence of the massacres and expulsion of the people, I no longer felt inhibited about suggesting that we collected as much information as we could, in order to indict those who were responsible for this.

One of the things I wanted to do when we got to Haifa was seek out an artist-journalist, Shimon Tzabar. Although he was passionate about Israel, he was outspoken in his criticism of the policy of discrimination against the Palestinians. Simon had suggested I tried to contact him. Maybe Tami could help track him down. Later, when we got to Jerusalem I also wanted to find a journalist called Amos Keinan, who had reported on the Deir Yasin massacre. He was reputed to be a very difficult man, not very forthcoming, if not downright rude and arrogant. In spite of this he was reckoned to be an outstanding poet. I wondered where I could get hold of a book of his poems. If they were in translation maybe I could read some of them and approach him from that direction. I asked Tami if she knew of any of his poems which had been translated into English.

She thought for a moment, 'As far as I know there are none. Why?'

I told her that I wanted to meet him when we got to Jerusalem, and I thought I might start by discussing his poetry.

'I think you'd be better off discussing one of his articles.'

'Where would I find those?'

'He writes a satirical column in the newspaper 'Haaretz', called Uzi & Co., I'll get you a couple of back numbers. They are in English.'

'That's great!'

I thought for a moment, 'The other person I'd like to meet is Shimon Tzabar, he's living in Haifa.

'Yes! He's a wonderful artist and writer, also, like Amos Kiernan, a satirist and deeply critical of the Zionists. This is great! I have always wanted to meet these two.' She squeezed my arm, 'I'm really looking forward to this trip.'

It seemed that we were on the same wavelength and there was no more need to try and conceal the reason that I was here. I still didn't want to mention Simon's involvement in this. Also I didn't want to reveal that I was taking money from New Horizons, especially in the light of Yurem's kindness and generosity, whilst looking to expose the iniquities of the Israelis under the Zionist movement.

We finished our meal and asked Joseph for the bill. Tami insisted on paying it. As we left I waved goodbye to Joseph, 'See you tomorrow.'

I thought we were going back to the apartment, but Tami tugged me the other way, 'Let's go for a walk by the sea, it's so beautiful now.'

It was indeed a lovely evening, with a two-thirds moon shining brightly and the stars speckling the sky. The temperature was just right. We walked what seemed a long way, the lights from the café were hardly visible, there seemed to be just the sandy beach stretching ahead of us, with a few lights in the far distance. We had taken our shoes off and were walking by the water's edge.

Tami stopped, 'Let's go for a swim.'

'I haven't got my costume with me.'

She laughed, 'Don't be silly, you don't need one.'

With that she stripped off, 'Come on, I'll race you into the water.'

I hastily took my clothes off.

Ready?'

We took off and raced into the water, Tami was surprisingly fast. We plunged in, the water was warm, so different from the sea where I grew up, where the water seemed icy all the year round. Tami started splashing water into my face, and I did the same in return, we became like children, giggling and splashing, I started towards her and she tried to run away, I managed to catch her, she was as slippery as an eel, I held her with difficulty, then she relaxed against me and raised her face to be kissed, I could feel her breasts pressing against me. We kissed for a long time, then she suddenly sank dragging me down under the water with her. We emerged, spluttering and laughing.

Later, when we were on the beach again, sitting waiting for the warm air to dry ourselves off, she put her arm round me and leant her head against my shoulder, she sighed, 'Why can't it always be like this?'

There was no answer to that.

Later when we lay in the bed, watching the lights dancing across the ceiling, with Tami's head resting on my shoulder, I found myself saying,

'What's going to happen to us?'

She thought for a moment.

'Maybe I'll run away with you back to England.'

This immediately threw me into a panic. The ramifications of it were too complex for me to contemplate at that moment. I remained silent.

She laughed suddenly, 'Hey, I didn't really mean it! So many people would be upset, my father would probably shoot me, or you. My mother would insist on coming with us, my brother and sister would never forgive me. Yurem would probably understand but wouldn't be able to show it. Your parents would be shocked, and the Royal College would probably throw you out.'

She rolled over with her back to me; I put my arm around her, and in spite of the narrowness of the bed we fitted perfectly together. I pressed my face against her hair and inhaled her perfume, I gently kissed her neck.

'Mmm' she said, 'I like that,' pressing back against me.

We lay like that for a while, and gradually her breathing slowed and deepened, and I realised she was asleep. I watched the lights some more, before also falling asleep.

Chapter 20

I woke early as usual. Somehow in the night we had rolled over and Tami was now behind me, with her arm around me. I laid there for a while savouring the sweetness of the moment, before gently easing myself out of bed, I turned and saw her fast asleep, with her arms around the pillow. She was certainly lovely; I felt a surge of sadness, as I knew this would all end when I went back to England.

I picked up my shorts and made my way to the kitchen, and drank two glasses of water. After a brief visit to the bathroom, where I cleaned my teeth, I made my way out to the terrace, and began my series of exercises. These usually took an hour. I had nearly finished when I heard Tami calling from the bedroom.

'I'm out here.'

She appeared in the doorway, wrapped in a sheet.

'My God! She said, 'Do you always get up this early?'

'What time is it?'

'It's not seven yet!'

'Well I usually get up at six.'

'You're mad!' She turned away, 'I'll make some coffee, come in when you've finished.'

I finished my exercises and went into the kitchen. Tami had made the coffee, she had also squeezed some orange juice and put the pita bread and museli out on the table. I was used to preparing my own breakfast and found this both nice and rather disconcerting.

While we were eating we discussed what we were going to do. Tami said, 'I need to go into New Horizons this morning, Yurem is getting some money for us, I also need to brief Rachel about what Yurem and I were doing, as she is going to take over while I'm away. Also I should call my mother, and hope my father doesn't pick up.'

'Maybe you could call Johannan Simon and ask if it's alright for us to come and visit this afternoon?'

'OK, I'll do that and also pick up the list of Palestinian artists that Yurem's going to do for you.'

'At 10.00 I'm meeting up with Joseph, he's going to give me a history lesson.'

'So let's meet up here at one o'clock, have something to eat . . . we can have that food my mother made me bring. Then after that go and see Johanan Simon at Herziliya . . . if that's OK with him?'

'OK that's good.'

She leant across the table, 'You know I love being here like this.' She kissed me, 'Now go and have a shower, while I clear this up.'

I resisted saying, 'Yes miss!'

While I was showering I thought about the fact that Tami and I would be virtually living together for the next two weeks. How was I going to keep my journal up to date? I decided that I would have to be 'up front' with her, and tell her that I was keeping a record of my time here as a background to my eventual exhibition. This was true up to a point, except I would probably never have an exhibition here. It also contained a lot of my plainly critical thoughts, as well as my feelings for Tami.

I finished showering and after Tami had gone in to have her shower, I went out to the terrace and started writing up yesterday's events, as I had not even thought about doing them the previous evening. I had done quite a lot before Tami emerged, her hair still wet. She sat in the sun, brushing it while it dried, I noticed that there were red highlights in her hair, I had thought it was completely black. She looked so lovely. I noticed that she was wearing a blue skirt, instead of her usual shorts. I finished writing my notes, she had not asked me what I was doing but I decided to tell her anyway.

'I usually write about what has happened during the day every evening before I go to bed, but I didn't last night. For obvious reasons . . . '

She grinned, 'I'm sorry, was I a distraction?'

'Yes . . . will you please distract me every night!'

She laughed, 'I'll do my best.'

My God I thought, we're behaving like a couple of adolescents, it's time to stop this.

'What time are you seeing Yurem?'

She looked at her watch, 'Oops! It's nearly nine o'clock, I promised Rachael I'd be there at nine.'

She went inside, I followed her in, she grabbed her bag and started towards the door, then came back and kissed me, 'I'll see you at one.' She shot off down the stairs. Well, if this is domestic bliss, I suppose I could get used to it.

It was still too early for me to go and see Joseph. I tidied up and made the bed. In spite of its narrowness we seemed to manage very well.

I was wondering what information Joseph may give me about the history of Israel that I did not already know.

I set off in good time, getting to the restaurant at three minutes to ten. Joseph was not there yet. An older man was serving, I assumed he was Joseph's father. I ordered a coffee, when he brought it he asked me if I was Christopher. When I said yes he told me he had a message for me from Joseph.

'He apologises, he had to go to Jerusalem, he's a reservist in the IDF and he gets called to go on impromptu emergency exercises.'

I thanked him for the information then sat there while I finished my coffee. It was too early for lunch, and anyway I would wait for that when Tami came back to the apartment.

I got out my sketchbook and began to do a drawing of the area around the café. It was not particularly inspiring, but it was another record of how the Israelis were developing the seafront. I did my best with it, but it was still a rather dull drawing.

I was just finishing it up when a familiar voice said, 'There you are, I might have guessed, when you weren't at your apartment.'

It was Simon. He sat down, 'Are you eating? I'm starving!'

I was taken aback by his sudden unheralded arrival.

'No . . . I've just had coffee, I ate earlier back at the apartment.'

'OK. I'll order something, I need to talk to you.' He looked around, most of the tables near us were full. 'Let's leave it until I've eaten, then we can go for a walk.'

Joseph's father came over to ask if Simon wanted anything. Simon gazed at the menu, then ordered.

I looked at him, he was still beardless, and his face was thinner but very brown.

What's been happening with you?'

'Quite a lot really, that's why I need to talk to you. What about you?'

I tried to remember when we had last spoken. It was at that time when I just had an encounter with the man who was trying to steal my bag.

'I had my scooter stolen.'

'What!'

'It's OK, I got it back.'

I told him the whole saga, including the visit of the police and how I suspected Uri.

'Why.'

I realised that I had inadvertently strayed into an area that would be difficult to conceal my involvement with Tami.

'I guess he's jealous.'

'What of . . . you?'

I hesitated, then I thought that he might as well have the whole story. So I told him about Tami being in the IDF with him, their brief relationship and his continuing to carry a torch for her. Joseph's father appeared with the food and put it down in front of Simon. When he had gone Simon resumed the conversation.

'So what's that got to do with you?'

I hesitated. He looked at me, then suddenly burst out laughing, 'I get it . . . you're screwing Tami.

I felt the colour rushing to my face.

'You are aren't you?'

'Well . . . I prefer to put it more delicately than that.'

He threw his head back and laughed even more.

'How ever you put it, that's what it's about, isn't it?'

'I guess so. She and I are heading up north tomorrow, to Haifa, we're going to at least one kibbutz on the way. After that I want to go to Acre and then on to visit as many other of the places you mentioned as I can.'

'I'd love to meet her.'

'How long are you here?'

'I'm getting a lift back to Gaza late this afternoon. I only came today to talk to you.'

'What about?'

'We'll go for a walk when I finish this.'

As soon as he was finished we set off walking up the beach, retracing the route that I had walked with Tami the night before, twelve hours ago.

'I've been getting a lot of information while I was in Gaza.'

'What sort of information?'

'Well the Israelis know that the Arab League are planning a big attack, involving Syria, Jordan and Egypt. They are preparing for it, the Israelis want the excuse, if it happens, to annex large parts of the West bank, drive the Egyptians out of Gaza, push the Jordanians back to the eastern side of the Jordan river and consolidate their hold on the Sinai. The other thing they want is to take the Golan Heights in the northern border with Syria.

'That's a pretty ambitious aim.'

'Yeah I know, but don't forget, they've got the Americans behind them.'

We walked on until we were nearly at the point where Tami and I had done our 'skinny-dipping'.

'In the meantime, the Palestinians are preparing to have an "intafada".'

What's that?'

'I suppose the best way to describe it is . . . it's an insurrection.'

'What wll that entail?'

'Everything, from peaceful demonstrations to violence.'

I thought about this, apart from Hamid and his family I hadn't really met any Palestinians. I tried to imagine Hamid involved in some sort of violence and somehow it didn't fit. Then I remembered Saba saying that when she grew up she would kill Israelis. Maybe it was her generation which would become involved with the possibility of violence. Tam brother seemed to assume that killing Arab people was only natural.

We continued walking. Simon asked me where we were going after Haifa and I gave him a brief outline of the circuit of Israel I was hoping to do.

'You'll never do all that, concentrate on five or six locations, definitely go to Acre, it's not far from Haifa and meet up with Sayyid's brother, Faisal, he has a café by the harbour, called Salome's. It's important that you meet him, in the event that we have to get out of here in a hurry and don't want to go via the airport he'll have a way to go by sea. It's only in an emergency though, as it is quite hazardous that way.'

'Do you think it's likely?'

'I'm not sure but I'm getting a lot of warnings, both from Paris and locally. Mossad are definitely on to us, though it's not clear to them whether we are a threat or just harmless students playing with politics. If they firm up on something they see as a threat, they'll fall on us like a ton of bricks . . . then you'll need to get out of here fast!'

In spite of the seriousness of what he was saying my mind was wandering to what Tami and I had been doing here, at this very spot, the night before, scarcely twelve hours ago. I could still see her naked figure, running into the sea. Somehow what Simon was saying seemed less real, less believable.

I brought my mind back to what he had been saying.

'Do you think I should go on with this trip?'

'Oh yes, the more you can see and record the more we can use to show what the Israelis are doing to subjugate the Palestinians, and steal their land. However I do think you should give yourself a shorter list, I can't help thinking that time is running out for us, one of the places you should try and get to is Dimona.'

I tried to remember what was so important about Dimona, Simon had mentioned so many places at the beginning of our talks I almost needed to consult my notes to remember what had taken place and where.

He could see that I was struggling.

'It's where they are researching the possibility of creating a nuclear device, with the help of the French and for some reason, the Canadians.'

'I imagine it's well guarded.'

'Yes you may have to get to it at night. Try and get a photograph of the building, it will probably be well lit up. Don't get spotted, you'll be in real trouble if you are.'

As we continued walking I began to think about shortening my list of places to see and record. I had begun to feel that time was running out after Simon's warnings. Haifa was still a definite, and in the light of what Simon had said I needed to go to Acre, although I couldn't imagine I would need Sayyid's brother's services to escape.

I suddenly remembered what Tami and I planned to do this afternoon.

'Do you know an Israeli artist called Johannan Simon?'

'Of course, he spent time in Mexico and South America, which wonderfully influenced his painting. Lovely man.'

'Well Tami and I are going to see him in Herzilya this afternoon, why don't you come.'

Simon looked at his watch, 'I can't do it, I'm getting a lift back to Gaza at 4pm. I'd love to have seen him again, I love his work.'

'OK then, come and have lunch with us, you can meet with Tami.'

'That sounds good, when you go off to Herzylya I'll try and do a quick visit to Hamid before I go back. I want to hear from him about this possibility of an intafada.'

I suddenly remembered something, 'Maybe it's not a good idea coming to the apartment, it's bugged. It's very inhibiting if we want to have any conversation. Let's go back to the café and I'll see if I can catch Tami before she leaves New Horizons and get her to meet us there.'

We hurried back. Joseph's father was still there. I asked if I could use his 'phone.

'Of coure, you know where it is.'

I got through to New Horizons, Tami answered the 'phone.

'Simon's here and he wants to meet you. When you finish come and meet us at the café.'

'OK, I'll be about half an hour.' She hung up.

'She's coming.' I said when I got back to the table.

It was beginning to get very hot, so we decided to have a beer each. We sat under the awning watching the people passing, some making their way down to the beach. Out at sea there were yachts sailing and further out a couple of cargo ships were passing, an Israeli patrol boat sped by.

'You know I shall miss all this when we leave, it's a great country . . . without the Zionists. Of course you realise we may never be able to come back here again if we publish our findings.'

I thought about Tami, what will happen to us?

Almost on cue she arrived, slightly out of breath, I stood up, so did Simon. A couple of well brought up English boys!

'Tami, this is Simon.'

Simon to my surprise, almost bowed.

'Very pleased to meet you,' and he shook her hand.

Tami was plainly flustered by all this formality and went rather pink.

'Please sit down, it's only me.'

We sat down, and almost immediately she said, 'Sorry, I must go to the bathroom, I just rushed out to be here in time . . . I'll have a beer too.' She hurried off.

We sat for a moment, then Simon said, 'My God she's gorgeous . . . you lucky sod!'

I tried not to feel smug, but I was rather pleased by his response.

When Tami returned we ordered her a beer. She turned to me, 'Yurem sent you his regards. He also gave us ample funds to cover our trip.'

She then turned to Simon, 'I understand from Christopher that you are working down in Gaza with the Palestine Aid Organisation?'

Simon nodded, 'Yes, I'm an observer.'

'What does that entail?'

Simon thought for a moment, 'Mainly making sure that the aid is fairly distributed.

'Is that a problem?'

'It can be in some areas, there is a certain amount of corruption amongst Egyptian officials, a lot of pilfering, both by them and some Palestinians who liaise with them. It's endemic I'm afraid. By and large though a lot gets through.'

'In general what is the mood of the Palestinians?'

Simon looked at her, 'What do you want to hear? That they're happy and contented?'

She shook her head, 'No, I want to hear how it really is.'

He appeared to be thinking carefully, then, 'They're very unhappy, they long to return to their homes, they are increasingly angry, a new generation is growing up who are intent on attacking your country, which was theirs, but you stole it. At the moment they are held in check by their elders, who believe in a moderate approach. The older people accept the inevitability of the division of their country, they want a dialogue with the Israelis, an agreement about what is their land and what is now Israeli, they also want compensation for what has been stolen or destroyed. Above all they want to be able to return to their land. What they see instead is a continuing occupation of their land, and a continuing oppression of their people.'

I was astonished at this outburst. I had thought that he would be more cautious in revealing what he thought.

I don't know what sort of response he expected from Tami, defensive, angry? What he got was a quiet nod from her and, 'I agree with them, there should be a proper dialogue and agreement, otherwise the younger people will have to resort to more aggressive methods. I'm afraid with the Zionists there will be no chance of a meaningful dialogue, they will continue to steal from the Palestinian people and in the end there will be violence.'

Simon looked at her speculatively. 'You're the first Israeli I have heard who has recognised the inevitability of this.'

'Oh there are many of us who think like that.'

'I'd like to meet some of them.'

'Well you won't find any in Gaza.'

'I realise that . . . maybe Christopher can.'

I felt the need to say something. 'I already have met some and Tami belongs to a group who think like this. Needless to say they are not popular with the Zionist government. Anyway when we get to Haifa we are going to try and get to see Shimon Tzabar, like you suggested.'

'That'll be good, let me know what he says.'

Tami joined in. 'When we get to Jerusalem we're also going to try and meet up with Amos Keinan and find out more about the Deir Yasin massacre.'

I was beginning to realise that unconsciously we had become a group of three, sharing the same views. There seemed no longer a need to confess to Tami what we were really doing here, it had become self evident. The only thing I still didn't feel like confessing was the subterfuge we had exercised on Yurem and New Horizons, I continued to feel guilty about that.

'Let's have lunch.' I was beginning to feel hungry.

Tami hesitated, 'I don't think I can, I've got things I need to do back at the apartment. Why don't you two have lunch here, I'm OK, there's stuff for me to eat back there.' She turned to me, 'Let me have the key, I'll see you there . . . don't forget we're going to Herziliya.'

She stood up and turned to Simon, 'Very pleased to meet you. Maybe we'll have more discussion next time.' She held her hand out, Simon had also risen to his feet and also had his hand out, they shook hands, then she turned and hurried off.

Simon and I sat in silence for a few moments, watching Tami's receding figure until she turned off left to head for the apartment.

'What do you think?' I wanted Simon's approval.

He thought a moment. 'She seems genuine enough. Did you convince her about the plight of the Palestinians?'

'On the contrary, she made all the running, I pretended to be ignorant of what the Israelis were doing. I told her how I was always convinced that it was right that the Israelis had their own state and that the wicked Palestinians were just trying to destroy them.'

I went on to say how she took me to places where massacres had taken place and people driven from their homes and villages, never to be allowed to return. I told him about our visit to Abu Shushar and Tami telling me about her friend Jasmin, and how the village was attacked and she never saw her friend again. How she had wept. How we had gone to the 'maabarah' and she had explained about the Ashkenazis and the Sephardics and their ill treatment.

I made sure I included how I always acted surprised at hearing all these bad things about the Zionists, that we had always been led to admire the Israelis and their struggle for a homeland. I told him how I had began to gradually let her appear to convince me of some of their iniquities. It was she who discovered that the apartment was 'bugged' Simon hesitated, then, 'Are you in love with her?'

I was taken aback by this question, Simon did not usually ask such personal questions.

I thought for a moment, I was not sure how to answer. 'I don't really know what love is . . . yes there is a powerful attraction . . . and all that entails, but is it love? I don't know. I do love her for everything, she is kind and concerned, especially about the plight of the Palestinians, we are very sympathetic on many levels. I don't know what I shall feel when I have to go, or for that matter how she will feel.'

'Well I guess you are not really in love. It's just sex in fact.'

I hated this diminishing of my relationship with Tami, I felt it deserved more.

'No! There's more than that!

'Like what?' '

You wouldn't understand.'

'Poor Christopher, you're such a gullible romantic.' He laughed. It's the only time I came close to hitting him.

He saw the anger on my face and immediately said, 'I'm sorry Christopher, that was a stupid remark, I was just teasing you, I shouldn't have said it.' He put his arm around my shoulders, 'Forgive me.'

I was instantly mollified, although I pretended not to be.

'She's a very special person, although she's an Israeli she is deeply concerned about the treatment of the Palestinians, she's just like us.'

'Look Christopher . . . I'm just concerned for you. I don't want you to get into an emotional situation here and suddenly have to leave.'

'No, I'm realistic about this, I know that it's an impossible situation, I am deeply involved with her, but at the same time I know there is no future in it.'

He thought for a while, 'I believe you, I think she is on our side . . . but, as I've said before, she is, in the final analysis an Israeli, and her loyalties lie here.'

I knew he was right, indeed had she not said this herself.

We sat in silence for a while, then Simon said, 'I don't really feel like more to eat, I'm going to go down to Jaffa and see if I can see Hamid, then I'm going back to Gaza.

'OK, I'll walk with you to the bus stop, then I'll go to the apartment and have something to eat with Tami.'

We walked back towards the apartment and the bus stop, which was nearby. When we got there Simon turned to me and said, 'I'm really concerned about what I'm hearing about the intafada. The Israelis will respond with brutal violence at any sign of insurrection. I'm OK down in Gaza, it's still under Egyptian control, but whenever I come back here where it's controlled by the Israelis I feel as if I'm under surveillance, you must be as well. It may be because you are with Tami they have not yet taken any action, but they will at the least sign of trouble. I think your days here are numbered. I think you have to move quickly if you are going to get any more information useful to us.' He put his arm round my shoulders, 'I don't want anything bad to happen to you, you're my responsibility.'

I laughed at this, 'Simon, I'm not a child, I elected to come here, I'm responsible for myself. I'm aware of the hazards of what we are trying to do, you made it plain to me from the beginning, nevertheless I decided to come, you didn't bully me into it, you showed me the facts and I agree with you. So don't come all that "I'm responsible stuff" please!'

He looked rather sheepish for a moment, then grinned, 'You're right, of course, you're right, you are quite grownup now.'

'Cheek!'

We both laughed then. I looked up Ben Yehuda and saw the bus coming.

'Give my regards to Hamid.'

'I will . . . I'll try and let you know what he says.'

'Oh, and give my love to Saba, tell her I'll come and see her when I get back.'

'Another of your women, you know you're practically engaged to her, it's traditional in the Middle East for young girls to be betrothed to much older men, what with Tami as well you're on the way to starting a harem.'

He stepped on to the bus. As it pulled away he waved, 'Take care, see you when you're back.'

I watched the bus as it went on down Yehuda, diminishing into the distance. I suddenly felt very cold and shivered. I looked around, there was brilliant sun on the other side of the street, this side was in the shade. That must be why I shivered.

I made my way back to the apartment and pressed the buzzer, Tami buzzed me in.

Tami was surprised to see me. 'I thought you were going to eat with Simon, I didn't expect to see you for at least another hour.'

'What did you think of him?'

She was heating up something her mother had provided, and while she thought about it she paused.

'I'm not sure.'

'What do you mean, you're not sure?' I must have sounded rather irritated for Tami was quick to react.

Don't misunderstand me, I can see that he is attractive and intelligent and doubtless has a great heart, but . . . what's he doing here? Why is he pretending to be supportive of the Palestinians . . . I think he has some deeper reason.'

'Like what?'

'Maybe the destruction of Israel.'

I was shocked to hear this. 'No! He is anti-Zionist it's true, but he's always said that Israel is an established fact, that it should work with the Palestinians so that they can be partners in this new country, not try to dominate it and suppress the Palestinians and steal their land. Surely that's what you believe too?

'Yes, well maybe you're right, it's just that I don't quite trust him.'

'Well believe me, that's what he's against.'

I could see that she was looking at me with concern, then she put down the ladle which she was about to serve her mother's borscht with and came towards me, she put her arms round me and kissed me, 'I love you, you're so loyal.'

I didn't know quite how to take this but I decided not to continue this argument, I really wanted to be close to her at this time. I already felt that our days together were numbered. I kissed her back and held her tightly.

We sat together and ate the food her mother had provided. We talked about our trip. She had been in touch with her friend in Haifa who was very happy that we stayed in her apartment. She had also managed to get in touch with Chaim, the man who headed the kibbutz that she had worked in. He was still there and was really pleased that we were going to visit, he wanted to show Tami how much the kibbutz had developed since she was there. We could stay the night if we wanted to.

We cleared up, and went down to set off for Herziliyya. Tami wanted us to take her scooter. I climbed on the back when she had started it up and settled myself behind her, with my arms round her waist. It was nice to hold on to her like this, her hair blew back in my face and I smelt the scent of her shampoo. I rested my head against her back, I could just hear her heartbeat. Once again I thought about what was going to happen to us in the end. Would it work if she decided to come back to England with me? How would we manage in my little flat? What would my parents think? I suddenly thought of Sylvia, I realised that I had only written to her once since I had been here. What would she think? I resolved to write to her when we got back from Herziliyya.

We sped up the coast and quite soon we were on the outskirts of the town, Johanan Simon had given us some directions. He lived apparently near a place called the 'Nili Garden', in a road called Etsel, off Ramat Yam. Tami said she knew exactly where that was. We found the house without much difficulty, at first it seemed quite small but after Johanan had greeted us and ushered us in, it became apparent that it extended a long way back, a large part of which was occupied by Johanan's studio. I don't know if he had a wife but I certainly didn't see her, although there was evidence of a woman's touch, with a small arrangement of flowers and a neatness in what I took to be the living-room. He led us through to his studio. I was immediately struck by the size of it and the wonderful light provided by large windows on what I assumed was the north side of the studio.

'This is wonderful!' I exclaimed.

He beamed at this.

'Yes I'm rather pleased with it. When we moved here last year I had this extension built. I'm just getting used to having all this space.' He laughed, 'I'll have to start doing larger paintings.'

I looked around, there was a large easel with a rather small painting on it. In front of it was a stool, Johanan plainly liked to sit when he was painting. There was a comfortable old armchair nearby. It had obviously been with him in whatever place he had worked in before, it sagged in the middle and there were various paint marks on the arms and the back, also surprisingly on the seat. It looked like he might have sat on a tube of paint at some time. There was also a long trestle table against one wall, with what looked like various sketches scattered about, and a small pile of sketchbooks at one end. On a shelf above it there was a collection of art books.

On the other walls were more drawings pinned, and on one a photograph of a young nude woman. There were also a couple of simple wooden chairs. It looked like, and was, an artist's studio. There were also paint marks on the wooden floor to prove it. Around the floor leaning against the walls were paintings, some facing the wall, a few were facing out. Tami was kneeling and looking at one, 'I love this.' she said, and held it up, I went across to look at it.

It was quite a small painting, it showed what looked like a group of agricultural workers resting under a tree, in the foreground there is the remains of a meal, laid out on a white cloth, rather like a tablecloth. There is a basket, a wine jug, a half a melon with pieces of it, looking as if they had been eaten and the skins had been left, a knife and what looked like a large salami sausage. In the background there are other people in a field, some just sitting on the ground resting. In the distance there was a small village and a building, which could be a church. And in the far distance a line of blue hills.

What struck me most was the use of strong colours, yellows and reds, with some green, giving an overall impression of heat. There was a naivety to the style of the painting, rather like a 'Douanier Rousseau'. My first thought though was that it owed something to the influence of Derain.

I echoed Tami when I said 'I love it too!'

He seemed very pleased by our spontaneous responses. We went on looking at other paintings stacked against the wall, there were many in the same idiom, although I did find some which he must have painted at an earlier period. They were less exciting with more muted colours, they lacked the blazing heat of his later work and were much more conventional. The later landscapes were more lyrical in their conception.

Johanan sat in his paint daubed armchair, smiling happily at our enthusiasms. Eventually he looked at his watch and said, 'I think it's time for a glass of wine. He went to a 'fridge in the corner of the room and took out an already opened bottle of white wine. On a shelf above the 'fridge was a row of glasses. He took three down and poured us a glass each, then went back with his to the armchair.

I realised that I didn't know anything of his history

'Tell me Johanan, have you always lived in Israel?'

'No, no, I was born in Berlin, before the First World War, actually in 1905, so I was too young to be in that horror.'

He studied for a time in the studio of Max Beckmann. He later went to Paris and joined a group of young painters round Derain. He also became interested in the work of Leger. I have always found these Fauvist artists quite sinister, especially Max Beckmann, but there is no doubt that Johanan owed his use of strong colour to all of them, particularly Derain. I was pleased to have noticed this connection when I saw the first painting.

He emigrated to Palestine in 1936 and was a member of a kibbutz until he later fought with the Haganah in the 1947-48 War. He settled in Tel Aviv in 1953 and in 1954-55, and again later. In 1961 he travelled in South America and the United States. He also spent time in Mexico where he became interested in the work of a Mexican artist called Diego Rivera who was married to another artist called Frida Kahlo.

I was unfamiliar with these two, but resolved to find out more about them when I returned to London.

Johanan had settled in Herziliyya in 1962, only the year before. He told us that he was very happy here, and intended to stay. 'My travelling days are done,' he remarked, 'this is where I want to be.'

'I think it's wonderful you have been to all these places, so far I've only been to Paris and here, I wish I could have all your experience.'

At that moment the door opened and a young woman came in. Johanan turned and said, 'Ah Sharon, come and meet my friends . . . this is Christopher from England, and this is Tami . . . she works at New Horizons, and is also an artist in her own right.'

Sharon came forward, she seemed rather shy, she held out her hand and said something in Hebrew to Tami, who responded in Hebrew.

Tami turned to me, 'She apologises and says that she's learning English, but is not very good yet.'

I took Sharon's hand and said, 'Shalom . . . and I'm afraid that's the full extent of my Hebrew.'

Tami translated this and Sharon smiled.

I realised looking at her that she was the young woman in the nude photograph on the wall.

As if reading my thoughts Johanan said, 'Sharon is kind enough to model for me.' He asked her if she would like a drink but she shook her head and said something in Hebrew to Johanan. Then she turned to us and held out her hand again, 'Sorry . . . I go,' she struggled for words . . . 'cook . . . supper.'

'She went out.

'Sweet girl, she is very kind to me.' Johanan said.

Tami looked at her watch. 'We must get going, we hope to start early tomorrow and I have lots of things to do before we leave.'

Johanan stood up, 'Thank you for coming, please come again when you get back.'

He came to the door, 'Take care on your trip, you know what these Israeli drivers are like.'

He was serious, I think.

As we set off, Tami said, 'Let's go down to the beach before we go back to Tel Aviv, I haven't been here for a couple of years.'

It was only a short distance. We parked the scooter and went for a walk along the beach and stopped at a small café. I ordered two coffees and we sat for a while, breathing in the sea air.

'What did you think about Johanan?'

She smiled, 'I think he's lovely, he seems to be very happy where he is. I loved his paintings, they aren't great art but they have a wonderful naivety and great colour, I'd love to have one.

And he also has that beautiful young girl to look after him!'

She laughed, 'Yes, well, that must make him happy too.'

When we finally set off back to Tel Aviv Tami asked me to drive so that she could sit behind me.

'When we start our travels tomorrow we'll be driving separately, I want to sit with my arms round you one more time, as it maybe the last time I'll get to do this . . . and I love it.'

There was something prophetic about this, as if she could already see the end of our relationship.

It was getting dark by the time we reached the apartment building. While Tami heated up the remains of her mother's food, I started to sort out what I wanted to take with me.

My main concern was what to do about my notebook. I had another one, which I intended to take with me. Should I also take the main one with me, or leave it in the cupboard down below? If I took it with me it would be vulnerable to theft or loss, if I left it behind and if someone was determined enough, they might find it eventually even in that broom cupboard by the back door. Also I needed to safeguard the undeveloped negatives which I had accumulated to take back to England. I felt that if I took them with me there was always the possibility that they might be lost or stolen. After much thought I decided to continue to use the broom cupboard downstairs, as a hiding place.

I needed to go there and hide these things away, without Tami knowing. I don't know why I still felt the need to conceal things from her, it was a hangover from Simon's paranoia about security I suppose.

I found a bag which some of the purchases from the general store had been put in. As well as that I put some of my underwear socks and sandals in another bag. I told Tami, who was still in the kitchen, that I was going downstairs to put some stuff in the paniers of the scooter.

'OK, but don't be long, everything is ready to eat.'

I put the bag with the clothing in the right hand panier of the scooter, then went back to the utility cupboard near the rear door. I put the bag with

the negatives in at the back of the shelf at the top, as well as my notebook. I then replaced the things in front, and added a couple of cans of dried up paint I found on the floor. All this concealed what was at the back completely. To find my notebook and the bag of negatives someone would have to empty out everything on the shelf. I locked it and took the key with me.

I went back upstairs. Tami had just put the food on the table. As we ate we talked some more about Johanan's paintings, then moved on to discussing our trip. Tami had already called Chaim at the kibbutz, and he was expecting us.

'When we get to Haifa I'll call my mother, just to put her mind at rest that we are OK.'

We cleared up and Tami went to have a shower. I sat out on the terrace and wrote a letter to Sylvia. I still had some envelopes and I put the letter in one, sealed it and addressed it, just as Tami emerged from the shower. 'Writing to one of your girlfriends?'

'Not exactly.' I gave her a brief description of Sylvia and my relationship with her.

'Poor girl, she sounds like a very damaged person. You're a really good Samaritan aren't you?'

I was getting very irritated by this portrayal of me, first Simon, now Tami.

'No I'm not! I'm just concerned about some people.'

She came over and put her arms round me. 'Listen, I love it that you seem to care about people, I want you to care about me in the same way.'

'You know I care about you.'

She sighed and looked at me, 'But you are going to leave me aren't you?' She shook her head, 'I know, I know, it's inevitable, there's nothing we can do, I'm sorry, I shouldn't go on like this, let's just enjoy the time we have.' She laughed, 'I'm turning into a pathetic wimp, aren't I? Forgive me, this is not what I intended it to be. It was supposed to be merely a physical affair, with no attachments. Let's go out and sit on the terrace.'

The truth was, I too was already feeling the inevitability of the end of our relationship, there seemed no solution. My feelings for her were stronger than I realised, but I couldn't stay here. Maybe she could come to London?

I went back to the kitchen and brought out some white wine and followed her out onto the terrace. I put the lights out and we sat there looking at the stars and sipping the wine. After a while she reached out and held my hand.

'I'm sorry about that outburst. I really thought it was simple, we'd make love while you were here . . . then you would go and I would get on with my life. Now . . .'

'Now?'

'Now I realise that it's not that easy.'

'Yes, I feel the same.'

The kibbutz we were heading for the next day was near Hadera, about 40 miles up the coast towards Haifa. We reckoned that it would take just over an hour and a half maximum, depending on the traffic.

That night both of us were restless. Usually, after we made love, we fell asleep easily, twined around one another. This night we were both sleepless, I laid very still, trying to give the impression I was sleeping, in the hope that Tami would drift off. I could tell though, by her slight movements, that she was wide awake, her mind buzzing with thoughts, as indeed mine were. In the end I got up and made us some hot tea, I had managed to purchase it from the general store. I was surprised to find it, I suppose it was a remnant of when the British had the Mandate here. This seemed to work, after we had sat up sipping the hot sweet drink Tami gradually slipped down beside me, and I soon realised she was asleep, with her arm around me. I carefully slid down beside her and quite soon felt myself drifting off.

Chapter 21

I woke early, she was still sleeping, so I carefully got up and after a visit to the bathroom went out onto the terrace and sat writing my notes for the previous day. The surprise arrival of Simon. His information about the growing restlessness amongst the Palestinian younger people and the possibility of an 'intafada'. His warning that we were becoming increasingly vulnerable. The arrival and introduction of Tami, followed by Simon's outburst about the repression they were feeling under the Israelis, her reaction, agreeing with him. Simon's suspicion of her and then his acceptance that she was on our side. Later, Tami's suspicion of him.

When I finished I went back inside. Looking in the bedroom I saw she was still asleep, so I went to the kitchen and made some coffee. I took one in for Tami and gently shook her. She woke with a start and grabbed her watch.

'Oh dear, I meant to get up earlier than this, why didn't you wake me?'

'I thought you needed the sleep, you had a rather restless night. Anyway we're in no rush.'

'I was rather hoping to get there by lunchtime, never mind, we can stay the night there if we want to.'

She stretched luxuriously. 'I had such a lovely dream, we were in a sailing dinghy, you were an expert with it. We sailed out to sea, and seemed to go a long way, I could see another coastline on the horizon. 'I said "Aren't we going back?" you said "No, I'm kidnapping you, you're coming with me", then you woke me up . . . we nearly made it.' She laughed and stretched out her hand to me. I kissed her on the mouth. She tried to push me away, 'I haven't brushed my teeth yet! I'm all yucky!'

She sat up and reached for the coffee. The sheet slipped and one delicious breast appeared, I wanted so much to climb back into bed with her, but I realised that if I did that, half the morning would be gone.

'OK, I'll go and have a quick shower, then it's all yours.'

When I came out of the shower Tami was packing things into her rucksack. Her scooter didn't have panniers, so she would ride with that on her back. I suggested that I might be able to put her stuff in my panniers, after all most of her stuff was cotton t-shirts, panties and her boots. If she wore the boots I was sure I could get the rest of it in.

'Yes if you can that would be great, I hate riding with that thing on my back.' She laughed, 'If you get caught speeding when I'm not around, and they search your panniers, they'll think you're a transvestite.'

This reminded me of Paris, and my embarrassment at the 'Boite de Nuit.'

While she went into the shower I took her stuff down and put it in the other pannier, there was still enough room to put my shoulder bag in, when we started off. I suddenly remembered that I had not posted the letter to Sylvia. I went back upstairs to collect it. When I went in I found Tami looking through my sketchbook, she had obviously taken it out of my shoulder bag. I was rather put out that she had been looking in my bag, fortunately I had already hidden my main notebook.

'Sorry' she said, 'I just wanted to look at them again.'

I also noticed that she had taken out my spare notebook, which I hadn't yet started.

OK' I said, rather shortly.

She could see that I was annoyed. 'I'm sorry, I should've asked you . . . please forgive me.'

She came over and put her arms around my neck, 'It's just that I love your drawings, I do wish I could draw as well as that.'

My ill humour vanished, I couldn't resist this praise, I kissed her.

We carried the rest of our stuff downstairs, after checking the apartment to see if there was anything we had missed, I locked it.

I still had the letter to Sylvia, which I had stamped with the last of the ones I had originally bought from the shop across the road. Tami told me that there was a post box a few blocks up Ben Yehuda in the direction we were going. We set off with Tami leading. When we reached the post box she pulled in to the side, while I posted it.

We started our journey north and it seemed very soon we were passing through Herziliyya.

I was keeping Tami's scooter in view all the time. Occasionally a car or truck would overtake me, and slot in between us, then it would overtake her and once again I was close behind her. The terrain we were travelling through varied from arid to signs of cultivation and the growth of building development. Small communities had extensive building going on and there was every sign of them becoming towns. Israel was firmly establishing itself in this land.

We passed Natanya, where there was a kibbutz I had thought of visiting before Tami had suggested the one near Hadera. We were making good time and it seemed likely that we would get there by lunchtime.

Not long after Natanya a large military looking truck passed and slotted itself in behind Tami, this was followed by a second similar truck, which drew alongside me, I felt distinctly crowded, I glanced across, it's cab was right next to me and I saw the passenger looking at me, he turned his head and said something to the driver, the next thing I knew, the truck began to force me off the road, I tried to slow down to let it pass, but it seemed to slow down as well, the last thing I remember was leaving the road and flying through the air.

'Christopher! . . . Christopher? I heard a voice calling me, I opened my eyes and there was Tami, her face anxious and concerned.

'Oh my God you're bleeding!'

I tried to sit up, my head hurt.

'No, no! Try and lie still! Let me see where you're bleeding.'

I felt her rummaging through my pocket for my handkerchief. There was something warm running down the left side of my head. Tami found my handkerchief. She put her arm around my shoulders and gently raised me to a sitting position, the blood was running down my neck and into my shirt.

Tami quickly made a pad of my handkerchief and pressed it against the left side of my head.

'Can you hold that pressed against your head?'

I lifted my left arm up and immediately had a shooting pain from my shoulder, I brought my right had across and managed to hold the handkerchief pressed against my head, although it was quite painful. I heard some voices and saw a man and woman clambering down from the road. They spoke to Tami in Hebrew, she answered them and then all three looked at me with concern.

'These two people were driving by and they saw there had been an accident, and want to help.'

The man said something else and came over, and knelt beside me and began to examine me.

'He's a doctor.' Tami explained.

He looked at the side of my head, he turned to the woman who had come down with him and said something to her, she got up and went up to the road.

'He's asked her to get his doctor's bag from the car.'

He looked at me, 'You are English?'

'Yes.'

'What happened?'

'All I remember is being driven off the road by some truck.'

He felt round my body and asked me if I felt any pain anywhere else. My left leg felt as if it was bruised. I suddenly felt ridiculous lying on the ground.

'I'm going to get up.'

'Let me help you.'

He and Tami helped me to my feet, I felt quite dizzy for a moment, then it passed. The woman reappeared with the doctor's bag. The first thing he did was to take out a large dressing, which he applied to the side of my head, to staunch the bleeding. It seemed to work. Then he took out a sort of light which he shone into each of my eyes. He held up his hand and asked me how many fingers I could see. I had a ridiculous desire to say 'seventeen!' but I curbed myself, 'five'.

'Take a few steps.'

I walked a few paces, other than a bruised leg, and the beginnings of a headache and my shoulder hurting, I felt OK. Though I still felt the side of my head was throbbing and painful. I turned to see where my scooter was. It had landed someway beyond where I had fallen, and hit my head against a small tree, at first sight it seemed undamaged, it had landed on a soft sandy patch.

The doctor turned to Tami,'Where were you two heading?' He spoke in English.

'We were heading for a kibbutz near Hadera, it's called Givat Haim.

'I know it, Chaim is a good friend of mine, sometimes I do time there as a temporary, when the usual doctor there is away. I think I should take him in my car.' He nodded at me. Then we can have him checked out properly.

I began to protest that I was OK.

Tami immediately said, 'I think the doctor's right, you had a nasty bang on your head.'

'What about my scooter?'

She walked over to it and pulled it upright, the handle-bars were twisted and there was some damage to the front mud guard.

'Well that looks as if it needs a good check over too.'

She thought for a moment, 'I'll ask Chaim if he could send out a couple of guys with a pickup, to bring it in.'

'Well I'll need my shoulder bag.'

She got it out of the panier and handed it to me. Because of my damaged shoulder I couldn't put it on properly. The doctor grabbed hold of it and slung it over his shoulder, 'I'll take it.'

'I'll follow you on my scooter.' Tami called out as we clambered up onto the road.

I clambered rather painfully into the back of the doctor's car, he had given me a wad of dressings to hold against the side of my head as I was still bleeding profusely. The woman sat in front with the doctor. He turned his head, 'My name's Aaron Fischer, this is Arella . . . appropriately named, as it means 'Angel', she is my nursing assistant. She turned and smiled at me, she was rather beautiful, 'He likes telling people that, but I'm far from being one.' Her English was surprisingly good.

'I'm Christopher.'

'What are you doing here Christopher?'

I told them my story about being an artist, and the invitation from New Horizons, and even managed to get out the now rather tattered letter from them. I think they were trying to distract me.

'Well it seems you are a very good artist.'

I made my usual collection of modest noises.

Arella said, 'I'm English actually, I came here with my parents ten years ago, after I had been trained as a nurse at UCH.' This I knew was the University College Hospital in London.

She said, 'I'd like to see some of your work.'

'Maybe when we are at the kibbutz.'

In spite of their efforts I was beginning to feel inexplicably tired. My skin was becoming clammy and cold, in spite of heat coming through the half open windows. I was also beginning to feel quite nauseous.

'I'm sorry, but I feel rather unwell.'

Aaron turned his head and glanced at me.

'We should be there in about ten minutes . . . do you think you can hang on?'

'Yes, yes, I'll be OK.' I wasn't so sure about that, but I couldn't just ask him to stop on this busy road. I closed my eyes and tried to calm down.

'Tami's keeping up.'

I turned my head, she was about a hundred yards behind. I wished she was here next to me, I could fall asleep on her shoulder.

Sure enough, after about ten minutes I could feel the car slowing down, then we swung off the road and after a brief pause at some gates, while Aaron identified himself, the gates opened and we entered what looked at first like a military camp.

Aaron seemed to know where he was going, he pulled up outside a new, long, low, white structure. Then he and Arella helped me out of the car and into the building. Once inside I could see it was some sort of medical centre. There was a small reception area, with a young nurse seated at a desk.

'Is Doctor Ephraim in?' Aaron asked.

'No, but he should be back in an hour. He went to Haifa to collect some supplies.'

Tami, who had just arrived, translated this for me later, as well as the following conversation.

Aaron continued, 'This man has just been involved in a road accident, I think he may be suffering from delayed shock, we need to get him into bed as soon as possible. The young nurse got up quickly, 'Follow me.'

She led us down a short corridor to a large room, which contained six beds. They were all empty, she quickly turned the bedclothes down on the first bed. I was undressed by Arella and Tami before being put in a hospital robe. My head was throbbing and I was shivering, although it was plainly very warm, even inside here. I was helped into bed, and the bedclothes were pulled up around me.

I heard Aaron asking something, which contained the word X-Ray.

The nurse said something back.

'Damn!' I heard him saying, in English.

Tami turned to me, 'He thinks you might have a fractured skull, and wants you to have an x-ray. Unfortunately the radiologist is off today.

Great, I thought, just what I need, a fractured skull.

She sat on the edge of the bed and stroked my forehead, her hand was wonderfully cool.

'You feel so hot.'

I was still shivering. It was difficult to imagine that I felt hot to her hand.

'Listen,' she said, 'I need to find Chaim and see if he can get a couple of guys and a pickup to go and get your scooter and bring it back here. I'll come back here straightaway. I hope I don't have to go with them, I measured the kilometres to here, so they should be OK. I want to stay with you.'

'I feel such a wimp.'

'Don't, you've just had a bad accident.' She went off to find Chaim. Arella came over, 'How are you feeling?'

'Like shit!'

She too put her hand on my forehead, 'You feel very hot.' She said something to Aaron, who felt my pulse. Then he turned to the nurse and asked her something in Hebrew. She shook her head.

I felt myself drifting off to sleep, I was drifting down, there was a sort of darkness which was gathering, my shivering was increasing as I drifted down towards the darkness, I saw a distant figure, I couldn't see who it was, then I realised as I came closer, that it was Sylvia. She held out her arms to me, she was calling me, and then I suddenly woke up. To my surprise it was already dark.

I seemed to be surrounded by people. There was Tami, Arella, the young nurse, and two other men, all gazing at me with concern. My shivering seemed to have stopped and I was no longer cold.

'What's up?'

'We were worried about you,' said Aaron, 'You seemed to be sinking, your blood pressure was very low.' He indicated the man standing next to him, 'This is Dr Ephraim, and over there is my good friend Chaim, who runs this kibbutz.'

I was slightly overwhelmed by all this attention.

'What time is it?

'10 o'clock.'

'Have I been asleep all that time?'

'More like unconscious, you were suffering from shock, I managed to clean up the side of your head and stitch the cut.'

'Stitches!'

'Yes I had to put nine in, you'll still have a scar, but it won't be as bad as it would have been if I hadn't.'

I felt the side of my head, there was now a bandage holding the dressing in place, it still felt very sore.

'Thank you very much, I'm beginning to feel much better now, I think I should get up.'

'Certainly not! You need to stay here tonight and we'll see how you are tomorrow.' He felt my pulse again, then he nodded his head, 'Yes it's improving.' He put his hand on my forehead, and nodded again, 'You should be OK by tomorrow . . . but no violent exercise. You lost a lot of blood you know.'

I looked across at Tami, she reached out her hand for mine.

I'll stay the night with him.'

I looked at the man he had called Chaim, 'I'm really sorry to cause all this trouble, I was very much looking forward to meeting you, Tami spoke so highly of you.' He looked pleased.

'Well you are welcome, you're the first to be treated in this facility, we have only just finished putting it all together, and you are our first customer.'

He turned to Tami, 'You remember our medical facilities were rather minimal, we would have had to take him to the Rambam hospital in Haifa before, but now we are much more self sufficient.' He beamed.

I noticed his English was very American.

'Yes, you had several doctors and nurses and one room at the end of one of the billets, and no other facilities.

He turned to me, 'We'll talk about all this tomorrow when you are feeling better.' He shook hands with Aaron and Ephraim and left.

Dr. Ephraim came over to me, 'Aaron thinks you should have an x-ray, and I agree with him. The radiologist will be here tomorrow and we'll do it in the morning.

I must have looked rather alarmed, so he assured me that it was quite painless, but he had agreed that it was necessary, just in case I had any evidence of a fracture. Then he left with the nurse, leaving Aaron, Arella and Tami.

'Well you're in good hands now,' said Aaron, 'I'll come in first thing in the morning, on my way back from Haifa, I'll leave Arella with you overnight, she'll call me if there is any cause for alarm, but I'm sure you're going to be OK.

'I'll stay here, I'll use one of the other beds,' said Arella.

Tami looked really put out, 'I intend to stay here, surely there's a place for nurses to stay?'

'It's because I'm a nurse I intend to stay here.'

I saw Tami's nostrils flare.

'I want to stay as close to him as I can!' She reached out and held my hand.

Arella was surprised by this outburst, as indeed I was. She was thoughtful for a moment, then, 'Very well, there is a room that a nurse on night duty can stay in, let me go and talk to the nurse who is on duty at the moment, she may have not expected to stay the night, so the room might be free.

When she had left the room to find the nurse I looked at Tami.

'Wow! That was a bit strong!'

Tami looked a bit sheepish, 'I know . . . it's just that I'm becoming very conscious of the fact that you will be leaving soon . . . and I want to be with you as much as I can.'

I was enormously touched by this and reached out and put my hand over hers. She sat on the edge of the bed.

'Do you think that truck driving you off the road was deliberate and not an accident?'

I told her how I had seen the passenger looking at me, then turning to the driver and saying something, after that the truck edged me off the road.

'Sounds deliberate, who could it have been?'

'Well they looked like IDF trucks to me.'

She thought for a moment, 'Yes I remember two trucks passing me, I wasn't really paying attention, then I suddenly noticed that you had gone. I pulled into the side and waited for you to catch up, when you didn't I came back looking for you.'

'Thank God for that!'

'Yes, I talked to the guys who went back and collected your scooter. They said you were lucky, if it had happened about half a kilometre further on the area was very rocky, with lots of large boulders and the scooter would have had much more damage and you might have been killed!'

At that moment Arella came back into the room.

'Well that's OK, she was dreading having to spend the night, she had planned to go out with her boyfriend, but with you turning up she had resigned herself to having to spend the night here. She was so relieved not to have to. She called D. Ephraim, who said it was OK as along as I was here.' She turned to Tami. 'What we'll do is four hours on and four hours off. It's 11.00 pm now.' She looked at her watch, 'More or less. Now, do you want to do the first four hours . . . which will take you to 3am, or shall I?'

Then what?'

'You'll go and sleep in the nurse's room.'

'What will you do?'

'I'll stay here.'

I could see that Tami didn't like that. She was about to protest.

I decided to interfere. 'Tami, you must have some sleep, we still have a long journey ahead of us. I shall probably be asleep very soon, so I won't be much fun . . . unless you like listening to me snore. Why don't you go and try and get some sleep now, I already feel much better. Arella will call you if anything changes.

I saw her begin to hesitate. 'Are you sure?'

'Yes I'm fine . . . never felt better.'

She kissed me, and rather reluctantly left, not before saying to Arella, 'If anything happens you will call me won't you?

Arella assured her that she would.

I lay awake for a while, conscious of Arella in the room. She didn't make much noise and after a time I felt myself drifting off and quite soon I must have fallen asleep. I had various dreams, none of which I could remember. Then I dreamed of being in the warm sea, with some girl I didn't know. We were both naked and playing about as Tami and I had. I chased her through the water and caught her, she was as slippery as an eel, but I managed to hold her. She struggled at first, then she turned her face up to me to be kissed, and suddenly I saw she was Sylvia, her small breasts and thin body were pressed against me, I kissed her passionately and she responded, then suddenly slipped down from my arms and disappeared under the water, I waited a while but she didn't re-appear. I waited longer, but she still didn't re-appear, I became worried and dived under water to find her, she was nowhere to be seen. I surfaced and started to call for help, no one responded . . . then I suddenly woke up. Arella was bent over me.

'Are you alright?' She felt my forehead. 'You're not hot anymore.'

'I was dreaming, I thought someone I knew had drowned.'

'Yes, you were calling out, I was worried.'

'I'm OK, it was just a bad dream.'

'Do you want anything?'

'Just some water please.' I was suddenly very thirsty.

There was an empty glass on a table by the bed, I must have drunk it before I fell asleep. She picked it up and took it to a sink in a corner of the room, she ran the tap and filled it up. When she came back she placed it on the table and sat down on the edge of the bed.

'Do you want to go back to sleep now?'

I shook my head, 'I'm wide awake.'

'Would you like to talk?'

I nodded, 'Yes.'

She went and got a chair from the table she had been sitting at. She had switched off most of the lights in the room and had just kept one on over the table, where she must have been reading. She pulled the chair over by the bed and sat down.

'Tell me about where you live in London and which college you are at?'

I explained about being at the Royal College and where I lived in Clapham.

'Were you born in London?'

'No, I grew up on the south coast.' I described to her where.

'That's a lovey part of the country. I envy you growing up near the sea.'

'Yes, when I was at art school there in the summer we would sometimes sneak off and go down to the beach. Weekends I spent the time with a friend walking in the Purbeck Hills. In retrospect it all seems idyllic.'

'I wish I'd grown up somewhere like that. I grew up in Edgware, that was very boring and suburban. When I go back to England I'm going to try and live near the sea. Maybe I can find work in a hospital there.'

'You want to go back?'

'Oh yes, I can't stay here.'

'Why not?'

She hesitated, 'I love the country, but I can't stand what they are doing to the Palestine people.'

'What does Aaron think?'

'He thinks as I do, but he was born here, he won't leave . . . he feels that he can alter it by opposing it politically. He's a good man, he goes to the

Palestine villages and gives his services free, the Zionists hate it and try and obstruct him.

'Do you go to these places with him?'

'Oh yes, that's how I know about the appalling treatment of the Palestinians.'

'Tami thinks as you do, she is also an Israeli, but was born when it was still Palestine, so many of her friends at school were Muslims, in consequence she speaks Arabic as well as Hebrew and of course English. Many of her Muslim friends disappeared in the 1947-48 War. She still mourns them.'

'When do you think you will go back?'

'Very soon, within the next few months, I'm already contacting friends in London who are willing to put me up.'

'I'll be back in London then, college starts in September.'

'Maybe we can meet up there? I'd like to see you again, you must let me have your address in London.'

At that moment Tami entered the room.

'I couldn't sleep . . . I was worried about you.'

Arella looked at her watch, 'Well it's nearly time for your shift anyway.' She turned to Tami, 'I've checked his pulse, it's normal, he's no longer hot, so I think his temperature is normal. I haven't checked his blood pressure, I could do it if you like, but as he seems normal in other respects I think it can wait until morning when Dr Ephraim comes in.'

Tami looked relieved. 'That's great . . . I'll stay here now, you can get your well earned rest.'

There was something rather barbed about the way she said this.

Arella seemed unconcerned by this as she began to gather up her things: the book she had been reading, a notebook she had been writing in and a rather efficient looking medical bag.

'OK I'll be off, I'll be just down the corridor in the nurse's room.'

She turned to Tami, 'Call me immediately at the slightest indication that there is something wrong.'

'Of course.'

Arella came over to me, 'We'll finish that conversation later.' After she left the room Tami said,

'What conversation?'

I started to explain about Arella's intention to go back to England, and her reasons for wanting to do that.

'I heard her say she wanted to meet up with you in London.'

'Yes she did.'

'Why?

'I don't know, maybe she's just being friendly . . . maybe she doesn't have any friends in London any more . . . I don't know.'

I could see that Tami was upset about something, my head was beginning to ache again, I didn't want to get into a discussion about what was troubling her just then. To be quite honest I wanted to go back to sleep again, but she had just come in and it was obvious that she wanted to have some conversation with me.

'Did you manage to sleep OK?'

'No, not really, I kept waking up and worrying about you . . . I also had a bad dream.'

'About me?'

'Sort of.'

'Tell me.'

She shook her head, 'Not now . . . anyway you're alright.'

She came over and bent down and kissed me. She eyed the bed, 'I suppose they'd take a dim view if I climbed into bed with you.'

'Well they did say no strenuous exercise . . . does that count?' She grinned,

'With us? . . . I'd say so!'

She seemed to be getting her good spirits back.

She went and sat on the next bed, 'Maybe I could lay out on this bed, next to you, and we can pretend we are patients in a mixed ward, having a flirtation.' She took her shoes off and stretched out on the bed. She lay on her side, looking at me. She said.

'Do you come here often?'

I couldn't resist that line from the John Osborne play 'Look Back in Anger', which I had been working on back in London.

'Only in the mating season!'

Tami's response was a great burst of laughter. She eventually spluttered to a stop with tears running down her face. 'Where did you get that from?'

I explained to her about the play.

She was fascinated, not only about the play, but also the fact that I worked in the theatre.

'How long have you been working there?'

'Just over two years.'

'Tell me about it.'

I started to explain to her about how, as a student with a very small grant, I needed a job in the evenings. When I first started working at this theatre I knew very little about it. It was not until I had been working there for about two months that I realised that it housed a very interesting new theatre group called The New English Stage Company, headed by a man called George

Devine. Their aim was to revolutionise theatre productions, with young writers like John Osborne, John Arden, N F Simpson, Nigel Dennis, and Ionesco.

I began to elaborate on the various productions I had worked on, and the actors involved. Tami listened attentively for a while but gradually drifted off to sleep. I only knew this after I had given her a vivid description of a play by Jean Paul Satre called 'Nekrassov', which was rewarded by a gentle snore from her.

I too must have also fallen asleep shortly after. The next thing I knew was being gently shaken by Arella.

"Time to wake up, it's 7.30.' She contemplated me, 'How are you feeling?'

'I feel fine, a bit bruised in places. I want to get up.'

'Hang on, I'll just wake up sleeping beauty here, then I'll help you.' She went over and shook Tami awake. Tami sat up yawning and rubbing her eyes. 'What happened?'

'I was telling you about my fascinating life in the theatre and you promptly fell asleep.'

She giggled, 'Sorry I was very tired . . . but tell me later.'

I started to get out of bed. Arella came back and offered her arm for me to hang onto. I waved her away.

'I'm OK, I'm not an invalid.'

When I stood I felt OK, but when I started to walk I realised that my left leg was badly bruised, it was quite painful and I couldn't help limping. Arella and Tami were watching me carefully.

'I'm fine, where's the bathroom?'

I'll show you, follow me.

'She led me down the corridor and indicated the door.

'If you're going to have a shower, try not to get your head wet. Do you want me to help you?'

'No thank you, I'll be OK.'

When she'd gone, I looked around. It was a very simple bathroom, there was another door in the corner. I opened it, there was a loo and a small sink. There was also a window, which was partly open. After using it I opened the window wider and returned to the bathroom, shutting the door behind me.

I stripped off the robe with difficulty and examined myself in the mirror over the sink. My left shoulder was badly bruised and going purple, and the top of the arm showed a long graze down to the elbow, with bruising around it. I couldn't see my legs in the mirror, but by bending sideways I could see more grazing and bruising all the way down to the ankle on the left hand side. I looked at my face in the mirror. My head was bandaged and the left eye was half closed and swollen, showing signs of going black. A long strip of plaster ran down the left side of my face, presumably where I had been stitched. Generally speaking I looked a mess.

I was just trying to get into the shower, when the door opened and Tami came in.

'I'm here to help you . . . whether you like it or not. Let me look at you first.'

She made stand there naked, in the middle of the floor, while she thoroughly examined me all over. She was very concerned about my head and the left hand side of my body.

'You're really damaged, do you still want to go on with this trip? Or should we go back to Tel Aviv, where I can look after you?'

'Absolutely not! I'll be OK in a couple of days, I may limp a bit but that's all, it's only bruising, I haven't broken anything.'

She looked doubtful.

'Tami it's alright, I'll be OK.'

'Well let's hear what Dr Ephraim says.'

'Stay with me while I shower, I've got to try and keep my head dry.'

She helped me wash myself, I had difficulty still trying to lift my left arm, so she held it up and washed that side, being careful where there were grazes, so they didn't bleed. When she finished she dried me carefully with the rather diminutive towel, which was hanging off a hook on the wall. She then lifted the hospital robe over my head.

'There, I didn't want you walking naked down the corridor, you might shock the nurse.'

I made my way carefully back down the corridor to the ward. Tami walked with me, being careful not to support me, but ready to help if I needed it.

When we got to the ward Dr Ephraim was there already, talking to Arella. He turned to me as I came in

'Arella tells me that you seem much better?'

'Yes I feel fine, apart from some bruising.'

'Good . . . what I'll do now is take your blood pressure, then we'll go to the radiography unit and have you x-rayed.'

He walked me to his office along the corridor, leaving Tami and Arella where they were. He seated me by his desk and after applying a tourniquet he took my blood pressure. 'Good,' he said. 'That's back to normal, nothing to worry about there.'

He then took me to another part of the building, where the radiographer was housed. We went into the room, there was a tall thin man with greying hair, wearing a short sleeved shirt seated at a desk in the corner. Dr Ephraim introduced me, 'This is Christopher, he's English, he had an accident, he went off the road and knocked himself out, I was concerned he might have fractured his skull, although he seems alright today, I still think we should x-ray him, just to make sure.' He turned to me, 'This is Dr Eichler, our radiologist.'

The doctor stood up, he was indeed very tall, in spite of the fact that he was very stooped. He held out his hand and smiled at me, I noticed he had several teeth missing, he was very thin and I thought he looked rather ill.

He gently turned my head with his hand, particularly examining the left hand side.

'It looks like the left hand side is where the main damage is.'

He spoke English clearly but with what sounded to me like a German accent.

'I will x-ray him thoroughly on all sides though. Any chance of that bandage being taken off?'

Dr Ephraim nodded, 'Shall I do it now?'

'Hold on while I get the equipment started.'

I sat down on a raised padded couch against the wall, and contemplated the rest of the room. Apart from the desk and chair there were two more chairs and a grey filing cabinet. A small framed photograph sat on the top of the cabinet. I got up and went to look at it. It was of what I assumed was a family group. An elderly couple occupied the centre of the photograph, ranged on either side of them were half a dozen younger couples, I noticed all the men wore black hats. Seated on the ground in front of them in two rows were a dozen children, the eldest must have been about sixteen, the youngest three or four. I also noticed a couple of babies held in their mothers' arms in the row on either side of the elderly couple.

I was about to ask Dr Eichler if this was his family when he turned to Dr Ephraim and said, 'Alright, you can take the bandage off now.'

Dr. Ephraim began carefully to unwrap the bandage, taking care that none of it was stuck to my head. I noticed that there was a lot of dried blood on the bandage. Eventually it was all off.

'Shall I leave the plaster on over the cut?'

'Yes, yes, that's alright.'

He led me over to the x-ray equipment.

'Lay down on this.' He indicated the padded bench under the x-ray machine. 'Lay on your right side.'

I maneuvered myself with difficulty into position, it was difficult because of my damaged leg and the other bruises on my body.

He positioned the machine over the left hand side of my head and gently moved my head with his hand. I noticed some numbers tattooed on his left forearm.

'Now keep still.'

He beckoned to Dr Ephraim to follow him out the door.

There was a brief buzzing sound and they re-entered.

'Now lay on your back.'

He repeated the process until all sides of my head were x-rayed.

'Good, you can sit up now.'

I sat up. Dr Eichler turned to Dr Ephraim, 'I'll let you have the results in an hour.'

As I was about to leave I went over to the photograph on the filing cabinet. 'Is this your family?'

Dr Eichler nodded.

'Where are they now, are they here with you?' He didn't reply but went back to his desk.

Dr Ephraim took me by the arm, 'Come along, let's get back to the others, I need to change your dressing.'

As he led me from the room I turned to look back at Dr Eichler, he was seated again at his desk with his head bowed.

We walked down the corridor.

'Is he alright, he doesn't look well?'

Ephraim walked on in silence until we were nearly back at the ward, then, 'What you should know is that Dr Eichler was in Auschwitz in the last months before it was liberated. When he went there so did his whole family, you saw them in that photograph . . . they were all gassed and went to the ovens, all except him. He somehow survived . . . perhaps because he was a doctor, or maybe just luck. He has never got over it, he feels a terrible guilt because he survived and they didn't. That's why he didn't answer you.'

I felt terrible, terrible because I had been so tactless, asking him questions about his family.

'Oh I'm so sorry, what a fool I was, how could I have been so clumsy?'

'It's not your fault, you didn't know.'

When we reached the ward Tami was still there, talking to Chaim. There was no sign of Arella. Chaim turned to me when I came in.

'I hear you are better, I'm really pleased to hear this, you didn't look too good last night.'

'Actually I didn't feel too good.'

Dr Ephraim felt the need to comment, 'His blood pressure's good, he doesn't seem to have a temperature, I've had him x-rayed, we just need to wait for the result in about an hour.'

Chaim looked pleased, 'Sounds like our new medical facility has been a success for our first patient'

I was beginning to feel rather uncomfortable, everybody else was fully dressed and I was still in my hospital robe.

'Umm . . . I'd like to get dressed.'

Tami said, 'I've got some clean clothes for you, I'll go and get them.'

While she was gone I had a conversation with Chaim. It seemed that he had come to Israel after the 1947-48 War, he was from New York. When he arrived in 1950 he was only 22. He was a very enterprising young man and soon found a niche for himself at this kibbutz. Initially he had been an assistant to the then head of the kibbutz, and had shown himself to be a very good organiser. The head of the kibbutz grew to rely on him and when he decided to retire it was almost a natural process for Chaim to take his place.

Once in charge Chaim showed himself to be not only a good organiser but also an innovator. He had some very good ideas about the kibbutzim, particularly this one, he saw them as becoming self sufficient, not only from an agricultural point of view, but also from a manufacturing point of view.

While he was explaining all this to me Tami had returned with a small pile of clean clothes.

'The T-shirt you were wearing was covered in dried blood, I had to throw it in the garbage. The shorts also had a few bloodstains which I have tried to wash out, they'll do for now but as soon as we get to Haifa we'll buy some more shorts and T-shirts.'

'Thank you.'

Chaim told Tami that she should bring me to his office when I was ready. He turned to me, 'Then, when you're OK I'll show you round.'

'Thank you, I'll look forward to it.'

After he left, Tami said, 'Are you OK? Are you sure you are up to being shown around

'Yes, yes, I'm fine.'

'Your scooter's been repaired in the workshop here, they say it wasn't badly damaged.'

'Well that's good.'

I got dressed, with some difficulty, largely because my left arm and shoulder still hurt. As I was finishing Dr Ephraim came in.

'Good news, the X-Ray showed no fractures, so you are all right. However you should take it easy, you did have concussion.'

'Yes I will.'

Dr Fischer was here talking to Chaim, I told him about the x-ray, he's very pleased.'

I turned to Tami, 'Can we go over there now? I'd like to thank him.'

It wasn't far, in fact it was in the next building. Dr Fischer was there with Arella. He greeted me warmly, 'I see you're better already, you've been in good hands here.'

'Yes I know, but I must thank you both for your kindness and the fact you rescued me and brought me here. Arella has been particularly good, staying up nearly all night with me.'

'I told you she was an angel.'

Arella looked pleased, 'I'm a nurse, that's what we're trained to do.'

Dr Fischer looked at the left side of my face.

'We should change the dressing on the stitches.'

Dr Ephraim nodded, 'I'll take care of it.'

'Arella and I need to get on our way back to Tel Aviv, so we'll be leaving.'

He shook my hand, 'I'm glad you were not more seriously injured. If you're staying in Haifa, leave the stitches in for another four or five days, then go to the Accident and Emergency at the Rambam hospital and have them removed. You can mention my name, they know me well there. Take care.'

As she was leaving Arella said 'Don't forget to get in touch with me in London, I'll be there in four weeks' time, here is an address for me and a telephone number. I'll be staying with friends there.' She handed me a piece of paper and lightly kissed me on the cheek before she left.

Tami, who had watched this, frowned and muttered something to herself. It was in Hebrew and sounded like an imprecation. I could see by her face that she was not pleased by what Arella had said, or the kiss on the cheek.

Dr Ephraim turned to me, 'Come, I'll change that dressing.' He started to lead me out of the room.

Chaim called out just as I was leaving, 'Come back here afterwards and I'll give you the guided tour.'

'Yes of course.'

Tami stayed there with him.

Dr Ephraim led me to his office again. After carefully removing the dressing he examined the wound on the side of my face and head.

'That's healing nicely, you're a good healer, and the stitches are holding it together well. You'll have a scar of course, but it should be quite neat. Tell the girls it's a duelling scar, they'll love it.'

We made our way back to Chaim's office, Tami was still there.

'I think he's recovering very well, as long as he doesn't overdo it he should be fit to leave,' said Dr Ephraim.

'Good, but I want first to show him what we are doing here and how we've developed from being just subsistence farmers to a profit making organisation. Then when he goes back to England he can tell everyone how well we're doing.'

Dr Ephraim turned to me, 'Well I'll leave you in Chaim's care, be careful he doesn't exhaust you with his enthusiasm.'

He shook my hand and wished me well and left, but not before I had thanked him for his care and attention.

So Tami and I set off with Chaim, on what was an exhausting tour of the kibbutz. I took my camera with me. There was no point in taking my sketchbook as I knew that I wouldn't have time to do any drawings.

First he took us to see the areas of cultivation, mainly of citrus, like oranges, lemons and grapefruit, but also avocados and other vegetables. I asked him how large these areas were, thinking in terms of acreage.

'Altogether? About 50 square dunams.'

'Dunams?'

'Yes, it's the form of measurement here, rather like acreage. One dunam is approximately 1200 yards, so if you square 50 dunams that's just over 12 acres.'

He then took us on to the cow sheds and the dairy.

'This is where Tami worked, didn't you?'

'Yes I was one of the ones who milked the cows by hand, I had permanently sore hands and also got kicked a few times.'

'Yes, that's all changed now, we have mechanical milking machines installed.'

'Now you tell me.'

After that we went to the hen house. It was vast and noisy.

'How many birds here?'

'About 1200.

In the next shed there were turkeys.

We've only got about 500 at the moment, but with the help of Granot we hope to expand, both the number of chickens as well as the turkeys.'

'Granot?'

'Yes, Granot Central Cooperative Ltd.'

'What does it do?'

'Well it encourages farmers to join forces so they can reap the fruits of their labours on a larger scale. It serves as a central purchasing and marketing agency for a number of kibbutzim. It's very successful. It was one I tried to get this kibbutz to join when I first came here. It wasn't until we split with the other group that we succeeded.'

'Split with another group?'

'Yes, sorry I should have explained all that before. When I first came here there was a great deal of politics going on. Basically it was two groups, one was extremely left wing, in fact it was a communist group with strong leanings to the Marxist-Leninist philosophy. The other group, this one, was more liberal, inclined towards a left leaning liberal democrat philosophy. There were tremendous arguments and bad feeling. Eventually, in 1952, it was decided to split. The other group, the Marxist-Leninist lot, moved to another site, a few kilometres up the road towards Haifa.

He then took us to a large shed which contained a group of men. There was quite a lot of machinery around and some of the people there were working with them.

'These are our engineers, they are involved in designing new agricultural machinery as well as other projects.'

He introduced us to a large man with a ginger beard with flecks of grey, called Alexi.

'Alexi was originally from Russia, he fought with the Russian army during the war, was taken prisoner by the Germans and almost transported to a concentration camp. The camp they were in was liberated by the Americans. He was an engineer in Russia, helping to design tanks for the military. Now he is in charge of the tractor repair section here and is helping to design additions to Caterpillar bulldozers.'

I was impressed. 'You must be happy to be here?'

He nodded, 'Yes I am, although I would be happier if I had my family here.'

He spoke English very well, with a slight American accent

'Where are they?'

'They're still in Russia, I cannot get the permission for them to leave. The government want me to come back, so they can put me in prison, or worse.'

'Why prison?'

He shrugged, 'It seems to be the fate of all soldiers who were captured, Stalin would often have them executed immediately on their return.'

I found this very disturbing, and would have continued to talk to him but Chaim was showing signs of impatience, he obviously wanted to show me round more.

'Can I see some of the designs for the bulldozer?'

He led me over to a drawing board, it was covered in plans, elevations, details and rough sketches.

After stacking some of them on another table, Alexi revealed what I assumed was the initial plan and elevation. It was very impressive, the blade was at least fifteen feet across, it was a humped tracked vehicle, the engine appeared to be huge as well. The drawings also indicated protective armour round the driver and presumably where the commander sat.

'That's enormous, you could push a house down with that! Who would want something so big?'

'The military, they import these Caterpillar bulldozers from the States and want them modified.

'What can they want them for?'

'I don't know, building defences I suppose.'

Chaim was showing increasing signs of impatience, I knew he wanted us to move on. I hastily took some photographs of the whole area as well as a few surreptitious ones of the drawings for the bulldozer modifications, whilst Chaim and Alexi had their backs turned.

From there we went to another building which housed scientists, involved in a variety of projects, from developing plastics to pharmaceutical products.

By this time I was in some pain, I was limping badly because of the damage to my left leg, and I was beginning to flag. I didn't say anything but Tami who had noticed called out to Chaim, 'I think we should call a halt, I think Christopher is in pain.'

Chaim turned to me. 'Oh Christopher, I'm sorry, I get so carried away by what we are doing here.' He looked at his watch, 'Well it's nearly lunchtime anyway, time passes so fast.'

He led the way to a long, low building, quite close to where we were. Once inside I could see it was a communal dining room, with long trestle tables and benches both sides. At the far end was what seemed to be a serving area, with four women ranged behind it. There were already about a dozen people eating and talking. They were grouped together at one end, talking noisily together.

'Put your stuff here.' he indicated one of the tables, 'I have to go back to the office for a while, but Tami will look after you she's been here before, I'll join you later.' With that he hurried off.

We sat down where he suggested, I was suddenly feeling very tired and in pain.

Tami sat next to me and put her arm round my shoulders. 'You stay here and I'll get us something to eat, I'm famished.' She kissed my right ear, 'Don't move I'll be right back.'

While Tami was getting our food I looked around the room. It was very simple, the only furniture being the trestle tables and long benches. The only picture on the wall was a large framed photograph of who I assumed was Ben Gurion. There were central hanging light fitments with fluorescent tubes. The whole effect was austere to say the least.

Tami started to return with a tray of food, several people at the table which was already occupied called out to her. She stopped for a moment and had brief conversations with them before continuing towards me. She was smiling when she arrived.

'Some of those people were here when I was, they are more or less permanent residents.'

She smiled again, 'it's nice to be remembered.'

'Who could forget you!'

We began eating, I realised that I was very hungry. I hadn't eaten since breakfast the previous day.

'Let me ask you something.'

She waited expectantly.

'What was that word you said when Arella was saying goodbye?'

She looked uncomfortable. 'What word?'

'I don't know, it was in Hebrew.' I made an effort to do a phonetic version.

This made her laugh, then she said it properly in Hebrew.

'So what does it mean?'

She again looked uncomfortable, then said, 'Bitch!'

'Why did you say that?'

'Oh come on Christopher, couldn't you see? She was coming on to you! She fancies you! All that "Don't forget to get in touch with me . . . I'll be in London in four weeks' time!" . . . I'm sorry, it was just the idea that in four weeks' time you could be meeting up with her in London . . . and . . . and I'll be here and may never see you again.'

This last was delivered with tears in her voice.

I reached across the table and held her hands. 'Tami, I'm not interested in meeting Arella, I only want to meet you again . . . we'll work something out.'

'Will we?'

Before I could reply, we were interrupted by a man who came up from the other table.

He was a tall, with short cropped blondish hair. He greeted Tami warmly, kissing her on both cheeks. He glanced at me curiously and said something to Tami in Hebrew. She laughed and replied.

'What did he say?'

'He wanted to know if I had been beating you up, I told him you had been in an accident.'

He extended his hand, 'My name's Amos, you are British?'

'Yes . . . and you're American? My name's Christopher.'

'Nearly right . . . I'm Canadian.'

'I'm sorry.'

'Don't be sorry, I like being Canadian.' he sat down.

'What happened?'

'I got crowded off the road by a truck.'

'What were you driving?'

'A scooter.'

'He burst out laughing, then put his hand over his mouth.'

'I'm sorry, I shouldn't laugh . . . the idea of someone driving a scooter on the main Tel Aviv Haifa road seems to be asking for trouble.'

'Well I was leading him on my scooter,' Tami protested.

'Well then you're both mad. So what are you doing here?

Tami explained about the doctor seeing the accident and bringing us here, where I had been cared for in their new medical centre.

'Who was the doctor?'

'The one who picked us up? Dr Fischer.'

'Oh he's a good guy, he often acts as a locum here when Ephraim is away.'

At that moment Chaim returned. 'Hi, sorry I was busy in the office, it's one of the problems about being an administrator.'

He turned to Amos, 'I see you're still carrying a torch for Tami.'

'No, I realise there's no hope for me, but I still love her.' He looked teasingly at her.

Tami blushed, 'Stop that! You're embarrassing me.'

Amos got to his feet. He grinned, 'Remember me, I'm always here, waiting for you.' He blew her a kiss and headed back to the other table.

Tami was looking quietly furious.

'I wish he'd stop that, it's not funny anymore.'

'Don't worry about it, you haven't been here for over two years.'

He turned to me, 'How are you feeling Christopher?'

'Better, I just needed a break. I also realised that I hadn't eaten since early yesterday morning.'

'How was the food?'

'Very good.'

'Good. I've been thinking . . . I've shown you a lot of what we are doing here, there are other things we could skip, but I'd like to show you the school before we finish, so when you're ready we'll set off.'

I looked across at Tami, she nodded.

As soon as I got up I realised that my leg was getting very stiff. I did my best to conceal it. Fortunately it wasn't far to the building which housed the school. Not only did it contain the school, with its three levels, but it also contained a childcare unit, taking care of the children of the workers in the fields and other sections. It was all very efficient and well run, I couldn't help being impressed, and saying so.

Chaim looked pleased, 'We think we have made great advances here, but we still have much to do.'

'I would like to spend some time taking photographs and maybe some quick sketches,' I said.

'Go ahead. I won't come with you, I have quite a lot to do at the office. Tami can take you round, maybe I could see some of your work this evening. You are going to stay another night?'

'If you don't mind?'

'Please . . . you are welcome.'

Tami and I set off on our own tour. I was determined to do it although I really felt quite a lot of pain. However I would stop at intervals, in order to do quick sketches, or take photographs, and these brief respites helped a lot. Tami spent her time talking with the people we met. She seemed to have a natural ability to draw them out.

By the end of the afternoon I felt that I had managed to do quite a lot. I was now getting very tired and was limping badly.

'OK, I'm done, let's go back to Chaim's.'

She put her arm round my waist as we walked.

'Where will we sleep tonight? I hope not in a hospital bed.'

'No, they have a couple of guest rooms. Quite adequate for us I think, though they may only have a couple of single beds.' She turned to me.

'We'll manage though, won't we?'

When we got back to Chaim's office he was still busy. He turned to the young woman working with him.

'Rachel, would you take Tami and Christopher to one of our guest rooms?'

He turned to us, 'I'll be here for a bit, I'll get someone to bring your bags and stuff. Later, when I finish here I'll come and collect you and we can go and have supper.'

The room was small, and as Tami had predicted, there were only two single beds. Tami eyed them, 'I guess we can put two together.'

'Sorry, they don't seem to recognise that some couples like to sleep together yet.' Rachael said.

'Don't worry, we'll figure it out.'

Rachel left, after promising to have our bags sent over.

I laid down on one of the beds.

'It's the same size as the one in Tel Aviv.'

Tami carefully laid down next to me, 'Maybe we can make it work, but I must be careful of your left side.' She put her arm across my chest and rested her head on my shoulder. 'No sex though, it may hurt you.'

'What!'

We must have both dozed off because the next thing I knew was someone knocking on the door. Tami got up immediately and went to the door, 'Who is it?'

'It's Chaim.'

She let him in, 'Sorry, we must have dozed off.'

'I'm not surprised, you must have had a rather sleepless night. Why don't you come over to the canteen when you're ready, I'll be there and I'll keep a place for you.'

Someone had brought our bags and left them outside. We got ourselves together and went over to the canteen where Chaim was already ensconced at a table with several other people. There were two empty seats, which he had obviously saved for us. We went to the food counter and returned with trays of food.

Chaim introduced us to some of the people at the table. 'This is Avi, he's the agricultural supervisor, in charge of all the crop production.'

Avi was a tall man with a long beard flecked with grey. He shook hands, his hands were large and very strong, I noticed that there was a number of cuts and abrasions on them, inevitable I suppose with the work he did. He had kind eyes with webs of lines in the outside corners of his eyes, where he must smile a lot in the sun. 'I saw you in the distance this afternoon, sitting drawing, you are a famous artist from London I hear.'

I couldn't help laughing. 'Please,' I said, 'I'm only a student.'

He looked at me doubtfully, 'That's not what I hear.'

Tami said, 'Why don't you show them some of your drawings?'

'They're back in the room.'

'I'll go and get them.'

She got up and went off to fetch my sketchbook. I hoped she would remember that I had stuffed my bag under the bed, as far back as I could push it.

One of the other men at the table was Alexi, who I had met at the engineering shop. There were two more men in that group who I was also introduced to, one was called Mordechai and the other was called Yuri, another refugee from Russia I supposed. I didn't find out what they did before Tami returned with my bag.

She was obviously upset about something. She gave me my bag and sat down.

'Are you OK?'

She frowned, 'Not really . . . when I got to the room there was a man, who I'd never seen before, rummaging about in our things.'

Chaim overheard this. 'A man, what did he look like?'

'I didn't get a good look at him, he pushed past me and ran off . . . all I remember is that he had red hair.'

'Did you lock the door before you came here?'

'Yes of course.'

Chaim got up, 'I need to go to the office.' He went off.

Alexi looked concerned, 'Was anything taken?'

'Not as far as I could see, we don't have much anyway.'

'Well that's good.'

'Maybe we could see some of your drawings now?' asked Avi.

I rummaged in my bag and pulled out my sketchbook. The camera was there, to my relief, and as far as I could feel, all my film. Obviously my red headed friend had not had time to find it.

As my sketchbook was passed around, with various expressions of approval, by all the people at the table, I managed to eat my food. Tami picked at hers, I could see she was still troubled.

Chaim returned, 'Well nobody seems to know who that was, we'll keep an eye out for him though.'

He reached out for my sketchbook, 'Maybe I could look at your drawings now?'

'Of course.'

He went through every page, sometimes going back to look at some again. When he reached the ones I had done today, I explained to him that although they were just brief sketches there was enough information for me to work them up later. I showed him some of the earlier work to demonstrate. He seemed very impressed.

We sat and talked more about his plans for the kibbutz, how much they had developed it since he joined.

I asked him about how they had come by the land.

'The Palestinians just abandoned it and went to live in the Lebanon, they didn't seem to want it, so we took it over and used it much better.'

'Don't they want to come back?'

'Well they can't, our laws won't allow them.'

'What about their laws?'

'They don't have any.'

'So, are they paid compensation?'

'I don't know.'

I could see he was getting irritated. Somehow I couldn't leave it alone.

'I heard they were terrorised and driven out?'

'No! They left voluntarily . . . they didn't want to stay here anymore!'

I must stop this, I thought, otherwise he is going to ask us to leave. Tami was watching me anxiously.

'I'm sorry, I always ask a lot of questions, I'm just trying to get something right. Everybody will ask me a lot of of questions about what it is like here when I get back to England, now that I have been to Israel. Forgive me, I didn't mean to upset you.'

He seemed mollified by this.

We stayed talking both with Chaim and the others for quite a long time, Avi and Alexi were very enthusiastic about what they were doing and the kibbutzim movement in general. Tami was distracted during these conversations and after about half an hour said that she was going back to the room as she was feeling really tired. I said I would join her shortly.

Somehow the subject of the Palestinians came up again, not instigated by me. It was Avi who brought the subject up, I stayed well out of it as I didn't want another confrontation with Chaim. Avi was concerned about the plight of the Palestinians who had their land stolen and the refugees who were not allowed to return. Chaim flared up again and said they had left voluntarily, Mordechai agreed with him but Yurem supported Avi. It became a rather noisy discussion. Needless to say I tried to stay well out of it, although at one time Avi, remembering my early confrontation with Chaim, asked me what I thought about it. I rather weakly said,

'I'm afraid I'm really rather ignorant, I came to Israel not only to draw and paint but to understand about this new country and it's only by listening that I may find out, I have yet to speak to many Palestinians.'

'Don't bother,' snorted Chaim. 'They are an ignorant people, who lie and claim that we drove them out.'

'With justification,' said Avi.

There then ensued a very angry argument which at one point almost came to blows. It was about that time that I decided to leave and go back to the room where Tami was waiting. It was hardly noticed that I was leaving.

Tami was lying awake on the bed. I told her about the violent discussion which I had just witnessed.

'That's Israelis for you, nothing ever gets done or discussed with out loud, sometimes violent arguments.'

'Are you OK?'

'Not really, I'm still thinking about that red headed man who was going through our things.'

I decided to tell her about the experiences I had with a red headed man and the woman with the mole at the corner of her mouth, frequently turning up where I was, almost ever since I had been in Israel.

She listened in silence as I recounted the various times they had turned up unexpectedly.

'That doesn't sound like Mossad, they aren't usually as crass as that. Could be CIA though, they're pretty ham fisted. Using a red head is the sort of stupid thing they might do.'

I decided not to mention the other possibilities, SDECE and MI6, she might have started asking who they were.

'Why didnt you tell me about this before?'

'I thought you might think I was being paranoid.'

'A couple of times maybe, but not as many as you've told me. Come here and lie down next to me.'

I lay down carefully next to her. She rested her head on my shoulder. 'They obviously suspect you of something . . . what have you been up to?'

I was silent for at least a minute, until Tami said, 'Well?'

I had been hastily trying to construct a reasonably innocent version of what Simon and I had been up to.

'I suppose it stems from the last visit I had to Paris. Simon was living in an apartment mainly occupied by students. Like all students that I know, there was much argument and discussion just about every subject. One of the students was a Palestinian and he was very outspoken about what he saw as the persecution of the Palestinians by the Israelis. I was very outspoken in support of the Israelis. We had some of our discussions in a nearby café, much used by students. I said that as I had this invitation from New Horizons I would try and observe what was really happening here. I think our rather loud discussions may have been overheard by someone from one of the security services, hence these people who have been trailing me.'

'Why didn't you tell me?'

'Well I wasn't sure at first, as I said, I thought you would think I was being paranoid.'

'I suppose I would have been more upfront with you if I had known.'

'Yes, I'm sorry, but how was I to know?'

'It's alright, now I know, I might try and find out who they are.'

'How will you do that?'

'I've still got friends in the intelligence services.'

I found this somehow rather disturbing, but I decided not to question her.

'Come on,' she said. 'Take your clothes off and get into bed.'

I did as she said and clambered rather gingerly into bed with her. We arranged ourselves carefully. As I lay on my left side, the damaged one, I was able to caress her with my right, but little more than that. For the first time since we had become lovers we did not make love. She was soon asleep, but I lay there listening to her soft breathing and pondering on our recent conversation. 'Friends in the intelligence services', what did that mean? Eventually I too fell asleep.

Chapter 22

The next morning I woke feeling stiff and sore. As I eased myself out of the narrow bed, trying not to wake Tami, she murmured and reached out for me. I kissed her gently and told her I was going to the bathroom. She drifted back to sleep. I managed to slip a t-shirt on with a minimum of pain and opened the door and peeped out. There was no one in the corridor, I had noticed the bathroom was at one end. I made my way there. It was a bleak and utilitarian room, with a toilet, a sink and a shower. There was a small mirror over the sink.

I locked the door and went across to the sink and peered at myself in the mirror. I was a truly unprepossessing sight, the bruises on one side of my head were purple that was slowly turning yellow. The stitches enhanced the long red cut in my face. My head was partly shaved on the left hand side, and the left eye was partially closed and was black. To be quite honest I thought I looked horrible and couldn't understand why Tami wanted to be anywhere near me.

I washed myself carefully, trying to avoid the cuts, scrapes and bruises, without much success. When I was finished I looked for a towel and found there wasn't one. I ended using my t-shirt and had to put it on wet in order to make my way back to the room. I needn't have bothered, there was no one else in the building. Tami was awake now and watched me with amusement as I arrived and immediately stripped off the wet t-shirt, and stood there naked, allowing the already warm air to dry me.

'Whatever are you doing?'

I explained about the lack of a towel.

'Oh well,' she said, 'I'll manage without.' With that she got up, opened the door and went off to the bathroom completely naked.

When she returned I helped her dry herself with one of her used T-shirts. As always I found her body beautiful, and refrained with difficulty from trying to caress her.

'Let's get some breakfast then we can set off.'

I realised suddenly that I hadn't checked my scooter.

'Don't worry I checked it yesterday,' Tami said, 'It's fine, it was bit bent, but they fixed that, otherwise it's OK.'

We packed our meagre belongings, then went to the canteen. I took my shoulder bag with me, in the light of the intruder in our room yesterday.

There were very few people there. I checked my watch, it was just over 8.30, I guess most of the workers came in early, probably 6 to 6.30.

We managed to get some food, although there was distinctly less choice. There was no sign of Chaim, he probably ate much earlier as well.

We went back to the room and picked up the remains of our baggage, then headed off to Chaim's office.

Chaim was there, busy as usual. He greeted us warmly and seemed to have forgotten about our heated discussion the evening before.

I thanked him profusely for his kindness and for the medical treatment I had received. I volunteered to pay him something for the treatment as well as the hospitality. He shook his head and refused to hear of it.

'Perhaps though, you might spare us one of your paintings when you complete your collection. It would be nice to have one of here . . . just a small one would be good.'

'Of course, I'll do one specially.'

'Did you manage to find out who that man with the red hair is?' Tami asked.

Chaim shook his head, 'Not a trace.'

We shook hands with Chaim and thanked him again, I promised to contact him when the painting was finished. Then we headed for where my scooter had been repaired, Tami led the way.

Here we were greeted by a jolly fat man called Ariel.

'Well it was a bit bent when we brought it in, but we've fixed it OK. There are a few scratches but everything seems to be working now.'

He took us into his workshop, where there were other mechanics working on a variety of farm machinery and vehicles.

'Yours is the first scooter we've had in here, pity it wasn't more damaged, it would have been more interesting.'

'Sorry about that, I'll try harder next time.'

He laughed at that.

We asked him if we could pay him something, but he refused, saying that Chaim had said the kibbutz would absorb the cost.

'It's a new experience for us anyway.'

We bid him farewell, then I climbed with difficultly into the saddle, with Tami behind me I drove over to where her scooter was parked. We then reloaded our bags and set off, with Tami leading.

When we got to the gates we waited until the traffic cleared enough for us to slot in. While we were waiting I glanced over to the last hut, which was near the gate. Standing looking out of the window was the red haired man! As I caught sight of him he turned away and at the same time Tami, seeing a gap in the traffic, set off, so I had no choice but to follow her.

I kept close behind Tami, trying to make sure that no one slotted themselves in between us. Mostly I was successful, except for the occasional car. The road seemed not so busy today.

I was concentrating so much on keeping up with Tami that I hardly noticed the countryside we were passing through. Although I did catch some of the place names when they were conveniently both in Hebrew and English. Hadera, Scot Yam, Caesarea, then an area of what looked like reservoirs where a sign post said Ma'Agan. After that there was Nasholim, Ein Carmel, Ein Hod (where had I heard that before?) then Tirat Carmel. Finally we came into the outskirts of Haifa.

I was too busy trying to follow Tami as she headed towards where her friend's apartment was to note all the names of the streets. Eventually we drove along a modest dual carriageway then took a right turn down to Siderot Galin, then left a couple of blocks until she finally drew up on the corner of Hasharhal outside a tall apartment building. We parked our scooters, I stayed with them while Tami went to the front door of the building. She pressed the buzzer by the door, after a few moments a voice answered and after a brief exchange she came back and said, 'Ester is coming down, she lives on the top floor.'

After a few moments the door opened and a tall, lean woman came out, she had fair hair tied back and was about thirty years old. She came over to us and Tami introduced me, 'Christopher, this is my friend Ester, she was my commanding officer when I was in the IDF . . . in spite of that we became firm friends.'

Ester grinned, 'Yes, Tami forgave me for my occasional authoritarian moments and now we are out of our military service we find we have much in common. She shook my hand, I could not help noticing that she had a very powerful grip. Her voice had a strange, rather masculine sound to it.

She looked at me rather curiously, 'My goodness you've been in the wars?'

'Yes, I had an argument with a truck, and I lost.'

'He was driven off the road by an IDF truck, which didn't stop.'

Ester turned to Tami, 'Where did this happen?'

'Between Netanya and Hadera.'

Ester looked at me again, then, 'OK let's go up to the apartment and you can tell me the whole story.'

She grabbed Tami's bag and my clothes bag, she also made an attempt to take my shoulder bag, but I hung on to it. 'Come along, I'm afraid I'm on the top floor, there is a lift but it's never working. Anyway I wouldn't trust it, last time someone used it it stalled between two floors and we had to get the engineer from Jerusalem, it took about three hours. The poor girl in it had to pee on the floor in the end.' She laughed, 'She was hysterical when we finally got her out.'

She strode up the stairs with the bags, with us panting up after her. I realised that she was not so much lean as very fit, she was as strong and muscular as a man.

The apartment had a tiny terrace one side, which looked over to where the main port was. The front window looked down on to a small yacht basin and then out to sea. It had a fabulous view.

'What a wonderful view.'

'Yes, that's why I rented it, it's quite expensive but worth it.'

I was intrigued by her accent, Where are you from originally?'

'Originally? From Holland, my parents and I escaped to England just before war started, I was ten years old. We stayed in England until 1949 then we moved here.'

I did a quick calculation in my head. That made her thirty three, a little older than I first thought.

She showed us round the rest of the apartment. There was a main bedroom and a small bedroom, which was serving as a study with a tiny desk, two sets of filing drawers and a bookshelf with files and books. There was also a kitchen and bathroom and separate loo, and of course the main living-room. It was all painted white. The effect was to make it feel light and airy. There was very little other decoration, some framed photographs and one small painting of what looked like Haifa harbour. The furniture was minimal, a small sofa in the main room, with two matching arm chairs and a dining table with four chairs. The upholstery of the furniture was all an oatmeal colour, it was remarkably unfeminine, more like a bachelor's flat.

Ester asked us if we would like coffee, we both said yes. Tami went with her to the kitchen and I heard them having a conversation, mostly in Hebrew, though with frequent lapses into English. Tami was telling her about my accident, though she didn't mention that I thought it was deliberate. I stood looking down at the little yacht basin and gazing out to sea. Somewhere out there was Cyprus, where Simon had served in the army. Would I be going there?

Tami and Ester came in with a pot of coffee, some milk in a small jug and three mugs.

We sat and drank the coffee and chatted about where we were intending to go, under the guise of it being a 'familiarising' trip for me. Ester was very interested in the fact that I was an artist, and asked to see my sketchbook. It was beginning to look rather worn with all the handling that it had been through. I must try and limit the number of people I show it to. No more groups of people, only selected individuals. I got it out for her. She seemed very impressed with the finished work and I explained that the rough sketches would be worked up to the same level. I was beginning to get tired of this explanation.

I asked her what she did, the answer was rather surprising, 'I work for an American bank in Jerusalem.'

'But you live here?'

'Well I work in Jerusalem during the week and come back here at the weekends.'

'That must be expensive?'

'Not too bad, they are kind enough to give me a small relocation allowance and I use it to rent a one roomed flat in Jerusalem. I love it here and don't want to give up this place.'

'I don't want us to be in your way.'

'No it's fine, also I've been asked to go to New York for a couple of weeks, on some sort of course. It'll fit in perfectly.'

'When do you leave?'

'Well I need to go back to Jerusalem this evening for a couple of days, then I'm flying via London to New York.'

'Wow, that's exciting.'

'Yes it is, I'm so excited, especially as I have never been to America before.'

She was taking a train from the main station in Haifa, Bat Galim, down to Jerusalem. Apparently the journey only took an hour.

She asked me about London and where I was studying.

'How is London now . . . what a battering it took in the war.'

'It's still is rather battered, there was a huge amount of damage done in the air raids, especially in the financial area and the docks. Gradually though it's improving.

'I still want to go there again, even more than going to New York.'

'I want to go there too,' said Tami, 'Maybe we could go there together?'

We talked more about where we would like to travel. I confessed that up until now I had not travelled anywhere out of Britain. Neither it seemed had the two women, out of Israel.

After a while Ester said she needed to pack her bags and went off to the bedroom.

Tami looked at me, 'How are you feeling?'

'Much better, improving all the time.'

She came over and put her arms round me and kissed me.

'I was so worried about you.'

At that moment Ester came back. Seeing that Tami had her arms around me she apologised.

'Sorry, I just wanted to tell you that I've put clean sheets on the bed and two towels in the bathroom. Feel free to have anything in the 'fridge, I won't be back for nearly three weeks, so it will go off if you don't eat it.'

She went back to the bedroom to finish her packing. We went into the kitchen. Tami examined the contents of the 'fridge. 'Looks like we can use most of this, but I'll need to go to the shops tomorrow and get some things.'

At about 5.30pm Ester came back carrying two large suitcases. 'Phew!' she said, 'That took time.' She eyed the cases. 'I may have overdone it . . . but I have no idea what situations I may find myself in the US, both socially and work wise. I've never done this before.'

She looked at her watch, 'Well, I've got about an hour, how about a drink?' Without waiting for a reply she went off to the kitchen and came back with a bottle of white wine and three glasses. She poured us each a glass, and after raising hers she said 'Shalom'. We in turn raised ours.

Tami said, 'How are you getting to the station? I don't think we can manage these on our scooters.'

Ester laughed, 'No, I don't think so either. It's OK, a friend of mine has volunteered to drive me to the station. She'll be here about 6.30, it's all arranged.'

We talked some more about what we were hoping to do. It seemed at first that Tami was avoiding saying anything that might reveal what we were really doing. Then she said, 'We hope to see Shimon Tzabar while we are in Haifa, we understand that he lives here.'

Ester responded immediately, 'Oh I know Shimon, he's such a talented man, so clever, so creative, an artist, a writer and amazingly an expert on mycology.'

'Mycology?'

'Yes, the study of fungi, you know, mushrooms, toadstools amongst other things. He's so funny and outrageous sometimes, also an outspoken anti-Zionist. That's why I like him so much.'

'I don't suppose you know how we can get to meet him?'

'Yes of course, I've got his 'phone number, he lives not far from here. I'll give it to you.' She rummaged in her bag and produced a small address book. She read out a 'phone number, Tami hastily wrote it down.

'This is great, we didn't know where to begin.'

'Good, give him my love, tell him you are friends of mine.'

'There is someone else I hope to meet when I go to Jerusalem, Amos Keinan. I don't suppose you know where he is living in Jerusalem?'

'No I don't, but Shimon may know, but they are not exactly friends, Amos and Shimon. I hear he is a difficult and sometimes a downright rude man. Why do you want to meet him?'

I looked at Tami.

She didn't hesitate, 'Christopher has become one of us. He supports the existence of Israel, but is very unhappy about how the Zionists are treating the Palestinians.'

Well, I thought, is that me? I suppose it is.

'Good for you,' Ester said, 'Take that thinking back with you to England. Tami and I became friends because we think that. How will your paintings reflect this?'

'I haven't worked that out yet, maybe I'll pose groups of Palestinians standing in front of land stolen from them.'

'Well you'll never get an exhibition here.'

I didn't say anything.

'If you are going to Jerusalem and want somewhere to stay you can use my little one-room place. I'll give you a key.' She rummaged in her bag, then wrote down an address and gave it to Tami 'Here's the key, it's a spare, leave it with Tami if you leave before I get back.'

At that moment the buzzer sounded.

'Here's my lift.'

She went to the entry 'phone, 'Hi, I'm just coming down.'

'We'll help you with your bags.'

'It's OK.' Tami grabbed one of her cases, before Ester could get hold of it, and set off down the stairs. I went for the other one, but Ester got there first,

I ended up with only her shoulder bag. Actually I was rather relieved, with my limping leg and painful shoulder I wasn't much use.

Her friend was a statuesque blonde, probably not much older than me.

Ester introduced her as Monica.

We loaded the bags into the car.

She turned to us, 'Well have a nice time here, when you leave drop the keys with Mrs Richler in the ground floor apartment. She's a nice lady, if you want any information ask her.'

She kissed Tami warmly then came to me, hesitated, then, to my surprise, kissed me on both cheeks

'See you in London.'

'With me!' cried Tami.

They drove off.

We made our way back upstairs, took our bags into the main bedroom and hung our modest collection of clothes in the wardrobe, or placed them folded in the drawers. The bed I noticed was extra large, such a relief after our rather narrow experiences.

Tami sat down on the edge and bounced up and down, 'This is really nice.' She held out her arms to me, 'Come and lie down here with me.' I didn't need asking twice. We laid together on the cover. I began to caress her, but she didn't let me go too far. 'I'm sorry, but I've just begun my period, I'm a bit of a mess right now, it'll only last a couple of days. Sometimes I get bad cramps too, so if you find me doubled up, and groaning, just ignore it. Or maybe just rub my stomach gently.'

I found this clear description of what was happening rather refreshing. Most of the limited number of girls I had previous experience with the subject was not discussed in such detail. Just, 'I've got the curse, sorry.'

We lay wrapped around each other, and after awhile we must have drifted off to sleep. When I woke it was beginning to get dark. Tami was still asleep. I lay listening to her quiet breathing. At moments like this I really realised that I was in love with her. I wanted these moments to go on forever.

Quite soon she stirred and turned her head to see if I was awake. 'We must have needed that, I feel quite refreshed.' We lay watching the light gradually fade. I suddenly remembered something. I told her about seeing the red headed man looking out of the window at the gate.

She was shocked, 'That means that Chaim knew he was there all the time.' She sat up, 'Maybe it is Mossad after all.' she thought for a moment, 'Chaim is American though, so it could be CIA.'

'Either way, it is still rather disturbing.'

'Let's get up.'

She went into the kitchen, and I heard her opening the 'fridge and various cupboards. I followed her in.

'She's got some stuff here we can use, but not enough to make a meal.' She thought for a moment, 'There's a café near here, I went there a couple of times with Ester last time I was here, it's near the yacht basin. Let's go there for now, I'll stock up a bit tomorrow.'

We made our way to the café, it was similar to Joseph's in Tel Aviv, pleasant and unpretentious.

After we had ordered we started to talk about what we should do whilst here. I wanted to find out more about what had happened here during the 1947-48 War. Tami said that she had some friends here who would know.

'We should see if we can get to meet Shimon Tzabar, he will have some stories about that time.'

'I also want to do some drawing and photographing.'

'Yes of course.'

'Sometime I should go to the Rambam hospital and have these stitches taken out.'

'Maybe next Tuesday?'

'OK.'

'You know it's Friday tomorrow, the start of Shabbat?'

I'd forgotten this. 'What are you going to do?'

'How do you mean?'

'Well what are you going to eat?'

She thought for a minute.

'Well there's no way I'm going to cook cholen, that's for sure, anyway, if you want to know I don't really like it, never have. You know we only follow the strict rules of Shabbat out of respect for my mother. Many people growing up in Israel nowadays do not practice the orthodox rules, the older generation like my mother still do. However I will call her tomorrow, and probably again on Saturday.'

'I'll get some food tomorrow to tide us over. I may fast during the day on Saturday.'

'In that case I'll do the same.'

'Why?'

'To keep you company.'

She reached her hand across the table and held mine.

'Why are you so nice to me?'

'Because . . . because . . . '

Why could I not say, 'Because I love you.'

She seemed not to notice the unfinished sentence. 'I need to see a couple of people while I'm in Haifa, one is a friend of my mother's the other is an old school friend.'

I seized the opportunity, 'While you're doing that I could go up to Acre.'

'Oh don't go without me, I want to go there too. I love old Acre, it's so like it used to be, mainly Arabic and so colourful.'

My heart sank. How was I going to get a chance to talk to Sayyid's brother?

Tami thought for a moment, 'I'll tell you what we can do, we can take a boat up there. Some of the boats from here regularly go there with supplies, or to pick things up. There's also a sort of water bus which goes there and back several times a day. Oh let's do that!'

She was as excited as a child by the whole idea of this. What else could I do except share her excitement. 'Yes that sounds great, let's do that.'

I thought I'll have to find a way to talk to Sayyid's brother on his own, when we get there.

'One of the other places I want to go to is Tantura.'

She wrinkled her brows, 'Tantura . . . Tantura, where is that?'

'I don't know exactly, somewhere quite close to Haifa, we may have passed it on the way.'

'I'll try and find out, I know someone I could ask.'

We talked a little about where else we might go. I also said I wanted to spend time in just Haifa itself.

By the time we got back to Ester's apartment it was getting quite late and we decided to go to bed. Tami went into the bathroom first. After she had finished I went in. When I came back into the bedroom Tami was sitting on the edge of the bed doubled over with pain. All she was wearing was a small pair of panties.

I sat down next to her, 'Are you getting cramps?'

She grimaced and nodded, 'Please try rubbing my tummy.'

She laid back on the bed. I lay down beside her and began gently to rub her stomach in a circular motion. After a while she said, 'That's really good, keep doing it . . . I'll have to keep you with me all the time, so you can do this when I need it. She turned her head and kissed me. After a time I realised she was going to sleep so I gradually stopped. I then must have also drifted off to sleep.

Next morning we were awake early. I got up first and after visiting the bathroom I went out onto the little terrace with my notebook and wrote down the events of the last three days, starting with being deliberately driven off the road by an IDF truck, being rescued by Dr. Fischer and Arella and taken to the kibbutz. How well I had been cared for there. Seeing how well the kibbutz had been developed and run by Chaim. Then Tami seeing the red-haired man searching our room. Me seeing him standing at the window. Later Tami coming to the conclusion that Chaim knew about him after all.

The journey to Haifa and arriving at Ester's apartment. Her giving us Shimon Tzabar's 'phone number and also offering us her one-room apartment in Jerusalem.

I was just finishing my notes when Tami appeared.

'Hi, would you like some coffee?'

'Yes please.'

I shut my notebook and followed her inside. She was already heating the coffee.

'There's some bread and butter, no fruit though, and no muesli. There are a couple of oranges, one each. After I've showered and dressed I'll go out and get some supplies.'

'Shall I come with you?'

'No it's OK, it's just round the corner.'

'How are you feeling?'

She made the hand gesture which indicated, not bad, but not good either. 'It'll pass after a couple of days. How about you, how's your leg and arm?'

'Getting better all the time.' Which was true.

She looked at me, 'You still look a serious mess though, black eye, half your head shaved, grazes, stitches . . . good job I love you.' She laughed and blew me a kiss.

We drank the coffee, and ate the bread and oranges.

'I'm going to the bathroom, do you need it?'

'No I'm OK.'

She went off. I cleared up and washed the cups and plates. I then took my sketchbook and went out onto the little terrace, looking down on the main harbour and started a drawing.

Eventually Tami appeared, wearing the little cotton dress and carrying a bag. 'I'm off, down to the store. Anything you need?'

'Nothing in particular, are you sure you don't want me to come with you?'

'No, no, it's only round the corner, I'll be back in half an hour.'

I settled down to continue my drawing. I should have gone with her even if it was just to see if my leg was getting better. Certainly my arm was, I had been trying it out ever since I'd got up.

She arrived back, carrying two large bags with supplies.

'This should last us a week.'

She began unpacking the supplies and putting them in cupboards and the 'fridge.

'By the way I saw that man you met on the 'plane.'

Which man?'

'The man you said helped you on the flight and when you arrived.'

'Jacob!'

'That's the man.'

'Did he see you?'

'Don't think so, he was walking on the other side of the road.'

That's all I need, I thought, Jakob and the red haired man. The next person probably will be the woman with the mole.

'Simon thinks he's CIA.'

She paused what she was doing, 'My God, are they all after you?'

'Seems like it.'

'Now I'm worried about you.'

'Well I'm sort of used to it, it's been going on since I first arrived.'

'I wish you'd told me earlier, I could have tried to find out who was doing it.'

'How?'

'Well I still have friends in the intelligence service.' She could see I was concerned about this, 'Don't worry, the people I'll speak to are all sympathetic to what we feel about the way we are treating the Palestinians, they will tell me the truth.'

I had no option but to believe her. 'OK, but it's already happening, there's not much we can do about it.'

'Well I may be able to find out if you are in any real danger, or whether it's a routine surveillance. After all that was a pretty nasty accident you had, and it could have been much worse.'

'I guess you're right.'

'I'll make some 'phone calls this morning.'

'Well I want to go out and walk around a bit, see if my leg is getting better.'

'OK, I'll stay here and make some calls. Fortunately Ester has a 'phone here, she also left a spare key.'

She gave it to me.

I gathered up my stuff, put my sketchbook back in my shoulder bag, as well as my notebook.

'I'll see you later.'

I set off down the stairs. There was no doubt I was feeling much better and my leg was less stiff. I decided to make my way down to the yacht basin. I kept a wary eye out for Jakob, or any other of the surveillance team.

It was actually much more than a yacht basin, there were some navy patrol boats tied up there, and a rather larger passenger boat, as well as a number of regular yachts and a couple of large motor yachts, millionaire's stuff, with a permanent crew living on board. I was examining one of them, *Aphrodite*, with some interest, when one of the crew, leaning over the side, called out to me.'

'Hey are you English?'

'Yes.'

'Want to come aboard?'

'That would be great.' There was a small gangplank leading up to the side, I went up it carefully.

He was about my age, with blue eyes and sandy hair. He was wearing white shorts and a white top, knee length white socks and deck shoes. He was very tanned. He held out his hand.

'Hi, I'm Robert.'

'Christopher.'

He was looking at my face, 'Looks like you've had a rough time?'

'I had an argument with a truck, he won!'

While we were talking another man and a young woman appeared. They were also clad in white, the young woman was wearing a short skirt, the other man, who seemed older wore shorts like Robert. They were obviously the crew. I was introduced to them. The older man was John and the young woman Bryony. They were friendly and cheerful. John it seemed was the captain. They told me that there were two more of them, another man and another young woman, they were getting some supplies.

They asked me if I would like some coffee, when I said yes they led me down inside. I was amazed at the luxury of the interior. Everything was sleek and modern. We sat and talked, it seemed that they were all English, except for John who was Scots and the man who was out getting supplies, he was Irish. It seemed that the owner was a Greek millionaire, who lived mainly in Cyprus, but did a lot of business in Israel.

Bryony said 'So we go backwards and forwards to Cyprus most of the time, though we get an occasional trip back to the UK. Once we went to Istanbul, that was interesting. There was some talk at one time of going to New York. I'm not sure if I want to cross the Atlantic in this.'

While she was talking the other two returned with the supplies, and I was introduced. 'This is Tom and Sarah. Tom is our deputy captain, I suppose if this was the navy he'd be First Lieutenant. We call him 'Thumb'.'

'Thumb?'

'Yeah . . . you know, Tom Thumb! Look at him, he's a midget!'

Tom grinned, in a good natured way. He was very short.

'And Sarah is our medic.'

She smiled, 'Well I'm a little bit more that, I have a ship's master's certificate, so if the occasion arises I can take care of the ship and order this rabble about, but I'm also a State Registered Nurse.'

She looked at my face, 'Looks like you've had a rough time recently.'

I was tired of telling my story about having an argument with a truck, I just said, 'I had an accident.'

'Looks like you were lucky to survive. Let me have a look at it.' She took my head with her hands and turned it from side to side. Her hands were gentle and cool.

'Nasty cut, still it's been well stitched, you'll need those out in a couple of days.'

'Yes the doctor who did it said to go to the Rambam hospital.'

'OK that's good, but if we are still here I'll take them out for you . . . if you like.'

I stayed talking for about an hour. Then, feeling I'd been out for quite a long time, I told them I was really looking for some areas to paint and I needed to get on with it.

I asked them for directions to the main port.

'It's quite a long way from here. Have you any transport?'

'Yes I've a scooter, it's parked back where I'm staying.'

The directions they then gave were actually rather confusing, largely because each of them had a different idea of how to get there. I thanked them politely but I had already made up my mind to get directions from Tami, who I knew was very familiar with Haifa.

I set off back to the apartment. While I was walking I thought about the fact that they seemed to make regular trips to and from Cyprus. Maybe if I really needed to get out of here in a hurry I might be able to get a lift with them. I would still go to Acre and link up with Sayyid's brother. This would give me two options. When I got back to the apartment building I let myself in with the key, which Tami had given me.

Tami was there, talking to a young man about her age. She introduced me to him, 'This is Avi, I worked with him when I was in the IDF. Now he's with Shin Beth the internal intelligence ministry.

I shook hands with him.

'I've been talking to him about you feeling you are under surveillance, he's going to look into it.'

I must have looked alarmed.

'It's alright, we're old friends, he's one of us, he thinks like we do about the terrible treatment of the Palestinians. He'll be very discreet.'

'Well,' Avi said, 'I can certainly find out if it's Mossad, or who else it might be. I can also find out if Mossad is aware of any other foreign intelligence agencies which maybe operating in the country. They won't like that if there are any.'

He turned to Tami, 'How long are you going to be in Haifa?'

'At least a week, maybe more.'

I was quite surprised to hear this, but then I realised that what with going to Acre, me having my stitches out at the Rambam hospital, finding out more about what happened in Haifa during the Civil War in 1947, also finding out what actually happened at Tantura. All this would certainly take a week.

Avi nodded, 'OK, I'll get back to you in a few days.'

He turned to me, 'Tami tells me that you are a wonderful artist.'

'She exaggerates I'm afraid.'

'I think not, she is not inclined to exaggerate. When we have time maybe I could see some of your work.'

'Of course.'

He turned again to Tami, 'I have to go.' He kissed her on both cheeks, then turned to me and held out his hand, 'Goodbye for now, I hope to see you later in the week. Tami went to the door of the apartment with him. 'See you when you get back.'

She turned to me, 'He's a good guy, I trust him. He'll find out who is after you and why.'

I told her about meeting up with the people on the motor yacht, and that they were all British. She seemed pleased for me.

'That's nice. I see you're walking much better already.'

I had decided not to mention to her about the fact that they made regular trips to and from Cyprus, and that was an option when I left Israel. We decided to eat in before going anywhere else.

While we were eating Tami told me she had enquired about boats going from Haifa to Acre.

'There's quite a large ferryboat that does the trip about four times a day, but I thought it would be fun to get one of those Arab caiques to take us. Tomorrow is Shabbat as you know and I'm sure there would one available. So let's do that.'

This was earlier than I had intended, but why not?

'OK, let's do that, sounds good.'

After we finished our meal and cleared up, Tami said that she would take me on a guided tour of the rest of Haifa. We went downstairs and I clambered onto the back of her scooter.

Tami plainly knew her way around. We worked our way down through side streets until we reached a main road, HaAliya Hashniya, this took us along towards the main port, past the Rambam hospital, which Tami indicated on our left. It seemed to be a big sprawling site. I made a note of this as I intended to go there in a couple of days.

We reached the main port area quite quickly. It was a much larger than Jaffa and crowded with large ships, tankers, freighters, passenger boats, ferries. There were also Israeli navy ships and several fast patrol boats.

There was a breakwater about three quarters of a mile long, which sheltered the port. We parked the scooter nearby and walked a little way along it and found somewhere to sit. I asked Tami about the history of the port. She, as with her description of the history of Jaffa, was very well informed. As before, when she had given me a history of Jaffa, I was deeply impressed, and I told her so.

She smiled, 'I love history, maybe I'll become an historian.'

'How about current history?'

She looked serious, 'It's too close now, I'll have to wait a few years.'

We walked further along the breakwater. It was busy with cargo ships.

'Well it's certainly booming here. Where are the Arabs?'

Tami walked in silence for a while, I could tell she was going to tell me things which would illustrate further iniquities perpetrated by the Zionist forces on the Palestinians.

'It's a tragic story, similar to Jaffa. I'll tell you later, when we're back at the apartment. Right now I'm going to take you to an area where many of the remaining Palestinians live, it's called Wadi al Nisnas.'

'Sounds a long way.'

'No . . . no, it's a suburb.'

We started walking back to where we had left the scooter. We then made our way to the suburb known as Wadi al Nisnas through a series of minor roads. Tami had plainly been here before. When we reached what I assumed was the area, although there was no sign to indicate this that I could see, Tami parked the scooter and we started walking.

The area consisted of densely packed houses and shops, with narrow alleyways winding their way through. Everything seemed in various degrees of disrepair. There were many ruined buildings left over from the 1948 war, fifteen years before. In spite of this there was a teeming life here. It was particularly lively as there was some sort of street festival in progress. We wandered through the streets and alleyways. There were a number of Israeli soldiers mingling with the crowd. They all carried Uzis. In spite of that they seemed to be happily enjoying the atmosphere of the festival.

'Let's find somewhere to eat,' said Tami.

We found what looked like a rather nice restaurant at the corner of what could be the main square. We sat down and soon a young boy came and asked us what we would like. Tami ordered something for both of us. He brought us some hot tea. Tami spoke to him in Arabic. The boy replied at length.

Tami turned to me, 'I asked what the festival was about. He explained that it was Eid al-Fitr-, which celebrates the end of Ramadan. Of course . . . I should have known that.'

'Ramadan?'

'Ramadan is one of the principal Muslim religious periods. It is a period of fasting. For 29 to 30 days they fast from sunrise to sunset, they do not eat or drink or have sexual intercourse during the day. After sunset they break their fast. She thought a moment. During the fasting period women who are menstruating are excused, so I'm OK.'

At that moment, as if on cue, the food arrived.

'Do they mind having to serve us food?'

She laughed, 'Nothing stops a Muslim from earning money. Anyway we're infidels and will go to hell anyway, so let us eat. Also Ramadan is over now.

It wasn't a meal in the accepted sense, it was a collection of small dishes, the ubiquitous humus and pita, some pickled vegetables, baba ghanouj, tabouleh, raw vegetables and taramasalata. Tami spoke again to the boy serving.

Before he came back she explained to me that all the little dishes were under the collective heading 'meze'.

'They're usually served with beer or wine, I've just ordered a bottle of wine.' As if prompted, the boy appeared with the wine. Tami examined the bottle before it was opened, she nodded and the boy produced a corkscrew and opened it. He poured some and Tami sniffed it, then tasted it, she nodded again and the wine was poured into both our glasses. I was astonished by this performance.

'What was that about?'

'It's a very fine Lebanese wine.' She showed me the label, it was from a Lebanese vineyard called Ksara. 'Taste it.'

I dutifully tasted it. To be quite honest my taste in wine had hardly begun. So far I had drunk whatever was put in front of me. Also all the wine I had drunk since Paris to here, was white wine, this was red. It was definitely different. How to describe it? Well it seemed softer . . . smoother . . . mellower, it left a nice after taste

Tami was looking at me expectantly.

'Mmm . . .' I nodded. She laughed, 'Is that approval?'

'Yes, I suppose it is.'

She laughed again, then leant forward and took my hand and looked into my face seriously for a minute, then . . .

'I love you . . . please don't leave me.' She had tears in her eyes.

I kissed her hand and shook my head. What did I mean? No I won't leave you? Or no I can't stay?

She looked at me for a little longer, then, 'Come, let's eat and drink . . . for tomorrow we die.' This last was said with a grin.

We ate from the little dishes, and drank the mellow wine. Something had passed between us.

Later we walked, hand in hand, through the souk, we were communicating, without speech, I could feel it. We were closer than we had ever been. All the colours and textures of the souk seemed to envelope us.

Eventually we walked back to where we had left the scooter

'Let's go back to the apartment.' I nodded. In truth I was still hurting and beginning to limp again.

When we got to the apartment I could see that Tami was having cramps, I made her lie down on the bed while I made some tea and brought it in, then laid down beside her. She snuggled up to me for a while.

Eventually she sat up and reached for her tea.

'OK I feel better.'

'You were going to tell me about the Arab people and Haifa.'

'Its not a pretty story. At the end of the 1947-1948 War the Arabs were largely driven out of Haifa by violence and threats. Loudspeaker vans toured the city ordering all Palestinians to leave. Boatloads of them left for the Lebanon and Egypt and now 90 per cent of the population is Jewish, only 10 per cent of Arab people are left. Not only that, the Israeli forces cleared out all the Arabs from the surrounding villages like Kafr Saba, Qaqun, Qalansuwa and Tantura. A lot of this was carried out by the Alexandroni Brigade.'

'Wasn't your father in the Alexandroni Brigade?'

She hesitated, 'Yes he was . . . I've frequently asked him if he was involved in this . . . he refuses to talk about it.'

'I'd like to go and visit these villages, particularly Tantura.'

'Why?'

'I heard bad things happened there.'

Tami suddenly remembered something, 'I need to call Shimon Tzabar, see if we can meet him. Maybe we can do it on Monday.'

She found the piece of paper she had written the number that Ester had given her. She dialed the number and waited, it rang for a long time and she was about to give up when it was answered. She spoke in Hebrew to someone, then waited, 'That was his wife,' she explained to me, 'She's gone to get him.'

He must have come to the 'phone because she lapsed back into Hebrew, I heard the words 'English artist', after a while she nodded, said a few more words then hung up.

She came back to the bed, and sat cross-legged, 'He says he would like to meet you. He asked if we could come tomorrow evening after Shabbat is finished, as he is going away on Sunday and won't be back for two weeks. I said yes . . . is that OK?'

'Yes that's OK, maybe instead of going to Acre we could spend the day visiting some of those villages?'

She nodded, 'Don't forget I'm trying to fast tomorrow.'

I hadn't forgotten that I had also decided to fast with her.

We didn't do much after that, we lazed around in Ester's apartment, Tami called her mother, I continued my drawing looking down on the main harbour. Tami told me that her mother had asked after me and when she had told her about my accident, her mother had immediately wanted to come to Haifa to look after me. Tami had great difficulty in convincing her that I was all right and recovering nicely.

Later Tami prepared a meal and after we had eaten we sat out on the little terrace, looking down on the lights of Haifa.

'That's the first Shabbat meal I've had which wasn't cholen. I don't know what my mother would say.'

'Will you tell her?'

'I think she's probably guessed, after all I'm not in a position to make cholen here, even if I wanted to.'

We went to bed early. I slept with my arm around her.

Chapter 23

As usual I woke early, Tami slept on. My leg was still quite stiff but it was improving all the time. I went out and sat on the terrace, watching the sunrise. This was a beautiful time of day, still quite cool, before the sun strengthened. There was a slight mistiness which dissipated soon after the sun rose. There was activity down at the main harbour, a large tanker was manoeuvering its way out, while another stood off, before taking its place.

I felt wonderfully peaceful. My relationship with Tami was now so strong that I couldn't bear to think of us parting. Could I stay here? What if we married? How would I make a living? These were just passing thoughts, though I knew that inevitably I would go back to England, go back to my life there. Perhaps I might be able to return, or Tami could come to England.

Tami interrupted these musings; she held a glass of water in each hand. She handed one to me, 'Good morning . . . here's breakfast.'

Yes of course, we were fasting today, at least until the evening, when Shabbat ended.

'No coffee?'

She shook her head.

'No orange juice?'

'Absolutely not.'

I laughed and kissed her.

'There is good news though . . . I've finished my period.'

'Oh wow, well . . . '

'Let's wait until this evening.'

I nodded obediently, although I was disappointed.

'So, how shall we plan our day?'

'Let's try and visit some of the Carmel villages and others nearby. You want particularly to go to Tantura.'

I nodded, 'Let's do that one first.'

'Right I'm going to have a shower, then I'll call my mother.'

She went off and I continued with my sketch until she re-emerged.

Later, after she had spoken to her mother, who apparently had asked several times about how I was, we took my scooter and headed down to where Tantura had been. It was about 24 miles south of Haifa. There was a new car park when we arrived there. It seemed that this area was being turned into a seaside resort. We asked if there were any remains of the original town. Some people had never heard of it, they were mostly people who had arrived, others just pointed at some slabs of stone just being absorbed back into landscape. There were one or two buildings which had been occupied by the Israeli authorities. Tami asked one of the occupants if there was any more of the original town, he just pointed at the car park and said this was it. No one talked about what had happened here, maybe no one knew. I took some photographs of the ruins and did a couple of sketches. We walked along the beach, it had obviously been a lovely place. There was much activity by the Israeli authorities to turn it into a resort. In the end we decided to try and visit some of the other areas.

We headed back to Haifa. Initially we were going to examine some of the villages around Haifa, to see how they had survived the attacks during the 1947-48 War, but Tami had decided that she would ask down in Wadi al Nisnas if anyone knew about what had happened in Tantura. We went to the restaurant where we had our meze and the wine from the Levantine. We broke our promise and ordered coffee, it seemed churlish to just sit there and only have water. The young man who had served us was still there. Tami asked him if he knew anyone who had a history of what had happened at Tantura. He didn't seem to know anything himself, he did not know where Tantura was even. He said he would ask his father who might know. We drank our coffee and after a little while his father came to see us. He was about 40 years old and had been in Nisnas when the Israelis came. He spoke English well, as did many of the people who had been educated when the British were here. He was getting rather grey and had a beard, all though he was still relatively young. He told us that he had heard bad things about Tantura, when the Israelis came.

He knew of a man who had collected stories about what had happened when the war was on. He would have some stories to tell about Tantura he was sure. He lived up the road toward Acre, about six miles, in a small village. His name was Fadir. We should ask at the café.

We set off up the road toward Acre. It didn't take long and we soon found ourselves in the village. There were three cafés: we tried the largest one, they didn't know of Fakir, we then tried the smallest. The young man who came to wait on us asked who we were. Tami explained that she was Israeli but I was from England, we wanted to hear what had happened in Tantura. He looked at her rather doubtfully, she was Israeli.

'Its alright, we want to tell them in England how bad the Israelis are to the Palestinians, this is why my friend has come from London, he is an artist.'

The young man went off, presumably to find Fakir.

When he came back he had a man who was about 45 and another man who was probably in his late 70s. The younger man, who bore some resemblance to the one who had served us, and might be either his father or elder brother, spoke to us first, his English was good.

'Why do you want to talk to my uncle?'

'My friend here is English, he has come to find out what has happened to the Palestinians under the Israelis. Although I am Israeli I belong to a group of us who are very against the Zionist government and what they are doing to your people. My friend here, when he goes back to England, will do his best to reveal it to the people there.

This man, who was called Said, translated this to the older man. The man replied in Arabic.

'Yes, he says that he will tell us some stories.'

He then began to tell us stories, which he had collected from many different sources. I listened as carefully as I could, making notes in my notebook. I tried to write down the names of the people. They were nearly all dreadful stories.

We stayed there for a couple of hours. We were offered food, but Tami explained that we were fasting, which they accepted quite regularly, they did offer us tea, which we did accept. I wrote down everything I could, trying to get the names right. Tami did her best to help me. I would try and get them in some order later on.

When we left there it was 4.30 in the afternoon. I drove us back to Ester's flat. We decided not to do any more, we were both tired and exhausted by some of the things we had heard. We had a couple of hours before we needed to go to visit Shimon. I sat out on the terrace and tried to put some of this in order.

The stories were almost too difficult to write down. One man said that he had been led away with others, but had later come back on his own. A Jewish soldier said, 'Anyone here who speaks Hebrew?' This man said that he did, the Jewish soldier said. 'Watch how they die, then go and tell the others.' They lined up all the others and shot them dead.

A bus arrived with Palestinian prisoners, the men were suffering with thirst, they let them down to drink from the only water faucet, because they were so thirsty there was a real crush to get to the tap, and the soldiers opened fire on them and blood was mixed with the water. Tens of men fell before our eyes.

Another man heard a young man crying, a Jewish soldier asked him why he was crying, he said, 'My two brothers have been killed, my mother has only me now, the Jewish soldier said, 'What use is your life then.' And he shot him.

One young man was promised his life if he surrendered, but they shot him when he gave his rifle to them.

Female soldiers searched the women and took all their jewellery, which they put in a soldier's helmet. They didn't give it back.

On the beach the soldiers led groups of men away and you could hear gunfire after each departure. Towards noon we were led on foot to an orchard on the east of the village, there were bodies piled on a cart, pulled by men of Tantura, who emptied the cargo into a big pit. On the road, near the railroad tracks, other bodies were scattered about. One person saw the bodies of seven young people, a woman started to scream, but a burst of gunfire silenced her for good.

In their search for gold they even went through the swaddling clothes of our infants, when a little girl tarried in taking her earring off, a woman soldier ripped it off and the little one began to bleed.

A woman returning from the fields with a bundle of wheat on her head to feed her children was run down by a truck driven by a female soldier. A woman who saw the accident tried to remove the body from the road, another vehicle barreled towards her, missed her but ran over the dead woman a second time. Several of the accounts said that at least 200 men had been massacred. There were many more stories.

I was overwhelmed by the stark dreadfulness of what I read, I didn't know how to put it in any order, and it was all just horrible.

Tami came out at one point. She was as devastated as I was. There was also the fact that her father had been with the Alexdroni at that time. We talked about it, she was determined to find out if he had been there.

It was getting late, soon we would be going to see Shimon Tzabar.

Tami put on her cotton dress and sandals. I put on a clean shirt and my trousers, as well as my reasonable shoes. He did live quite close by. We could have walked it I suppose, instead I took the scooter. We arrived at 7pm. He had an apartment in a new block, some way from the sea. I don't know why we dressed up, he was wearing a short sleeved shirt and jeans, with nothing on his feet. His wife was slightly less casual.

He was immediately friendly. He asked after Ester, then he took me through to see his studio. I was very taken by his drawings. He was putting together a book on mycological drawings. I had never met anyone who studied mushrooms and toadstools.

I expressed my ignorance of mycology.

'Well I learned the hard way, I ate a bad one and ended up in hospital. They are fascinating though.'

There were lots of very interesting things, including articles written for *Haaretz*, the main Israeli newspaper, some in English, as well as cartoons of a political nature.

'I gather you are not very fond of the Zionist movement.'

He snorted, 'You can say that again. Tell me what you are doing here.'

I told him how I was here working for New Horizons, trying to show how the country was developing now it was Israeli. I wasn't sure how much Tami had told them about our feelings about the treatment of the Palestinians by Israel.

'Yes we have already come a long way. May I see some of your drawings?'

I passed him my main sketchbook, and as he was looking through it I went over to look at more of his work. I could see from some of his articles in English that he was very acerbic about the government.

'It seems you have been looking at some of the things we have done to these people.'

'Yes, Tami and I have found out many things, which maybe others do not know.'

'Don't think that we were the only ones who were guilty of massacres.'

'Yes but it seems that Israel were deliberately driving these people out of the country. Now it's all over can these people come back to their villages?'

'No . . . that is the tragedy.'

I realised that I was being very overt with him. I was making it plain that whatever had happened here, Israel was determined to hold on to most of the country, including much of what had been Palestine.

'You fought in the war?'

'Of course, in fact I fought with all the branches of our army, the Stern Gang, Irgun Zwei Leumi and the Haganah, against the Jordanians, the Syrians, the Iraqis and of course the British.'

'So you don't think much of us.'

'You were so incompetent, you made promises that you couldn't keep, you encouraged us and then tried to exclude us. You talked with the Palestinians, the Jordanians, and all the others, as well as us. At one point in 1944 the Stern Gang sent people to Britain to assassinate Churchill and the Foreign Secretary, Ernest Bevin, when he began to try to avoid Israel being here. There was no end to your perfidy. I must admit though I went off the Stern Gang at that point.'

'And now?'

'Funnily enough, now that you are no longer messing about here, and seem to be losing your empire, I have begun to find that there are many qualities which you do posses, that I quite like.

'Well thank you!'

He laughed, 'Sorry, I seem to have been giving you a hard time, which you are too young to deserve. Come, let's go and join the others.'

He put his hand on my shoulders in the most friendly way.

His wife had produced a sort of meze, Shimon pulled out a couple of bottles of white wine. We were very hungry and enjoyed the food and the wine. Shimon was a wonderful host and entertained us with many scurrilous stories about the government and other Israeli leaders.

We told him about visiting Tantura and finding out about some of the things that happened there.

'Yes I know about Tantura.' He thought for a moment.

'If you really want to find out about what happened in many villages you should visit Walid Khalidi in Beirut, he is collating all these things.'

'I'm not sure that New Horizons would approve my funds for doing that.'

He laughed at that. 'Yes you are right.' He turned to Tami, 'You could do that though.'

She nodded, 'Yes I'll try.'

We stayed a couple of hours. When we were leaving Shimon said to me,

'Let me have an address, when I come to London I'd like to get in touch with you.'

I gave him my parents' address, as he was not sure when he would be coming to London.

We went back to Ester's apartment.

Visiting Shimon made us both pleased, and I hoped he would come to London. We went to bed quite early. Now Tami had finished her period we could make up for the time we had missed.

In the morning we made our way down early to the area where the fishing boats were. Most of them went out at night, during the day they were mostly empty, or with the fishermen mending nets or their boats. There was one called *Olympic*, in English, which for some reason Tami liked. The owner was painting the area where the steering was. Tami greeted him in Arabic, he replied in English. She asked him if he would like to take us to Acre.

'You pay me?'

'Yes of course, and we'll pay you extra if you'll stay there until the afternoon.'

They agreed on a sum and we clambered aboard. He told us not to sit near the steering area, as it was still drying from the new paint.

Tami loved being on the boat in the early morning sun. It seemed to be going straight towards it. We sat together with our arms around one another. It was very nice, warm but not yet hot. Tami turned to the fisherman, 'What's your name?'

'Ali. Ali al-Hijazi.'

She asked him about where he came from. It appeared that he was from north of Acre.

His English was good, again probably due to the British schools.

'Why did you come here?'

He looked at her, 'You are Israeli?'

She nodded. He looked at me.

'I'm English, I'm an artist visiting here.'

'He's recording what has happened here since the Nakba.' Tami said. 'He wants to explain to the English how badly the Israelis have been treating you.'

'So you know about the Nakba?'

I nodded, 'I do now, I want to explain it to the British people.'

'Tell them . . . this is what they left us with.'

Yes I thought, he is right, us, the French and the Americans.

'I'm sorry, and now I want to show what has happened.'

'It won't change anything, but maybe people will be more critical of the Israelis.'

'This is what I hope.'

At first I had thought that he wouldn't forgive me for being English, but now he became more friendly. It seemed that he, like other fishermen, had come to base himself in Haifa.

'I miss my village, but The Israelis destroyed it, leaving the ruined mosque and the remains of the head man's house.'

'Where are the people?'

'Mostly in Lebanon, it's all Israeli now, before there were no Israelis in the village, now they are all Israelis living on our land.'

Another tragedy, I thought, living on their land and refusing to allow the people to return.

We landed at a small quayside, away from the main port. We asked if he knew a café called the Salome, he pointed to the end of the buildings.

'It's there, I know it well, Faisal owns it. I may see you there later, I've got some friends to see first.'

'Why are we going there.' Tami asked.

I realized I had not told her about Sayyd in Paris. 'I met a man in Paris whose brother owns this café, he asked me to visit him. Sorry I should have told you.'

We made our way to the café, a boy of about fourteen was laying out the tables. We asked him if Faisal was there.

'He's my father, he's gone to get some supplies, he should be back in about half an hour. Would you like something?' We ordered tea.

The boy asked us if we wanted anything else. When we said we wouldn't have anything now he went out to the kitchen.

When he came back he said that his sister would bring it. Then he continued to lay the tables.

'What's your name?'

I rather liked the way Tami immediately started making friends, usually asking their names.

'Assef.'

'You speak English very well.'

'That's my father, he insists we all speak English, especially now that all the Americans have started coming here.'

A young girl came with the tea. Tami tried talking to her, she only responded in Arabic, she was plainly very shy.

After she had gone Assef came over. 'That was my sister, don't tell my father, he still believes that women should stay out of sight. I'll get into trouble if he hears that I got her to bring out the tea, I just think we should be more modern.'

Tami agreed, 'You are right, women should be part of our society, my father would also like to control me.'

Without much success I would say.

At that moment Faisal appeared, I recognised him immediately, he was an older version of Sayyid, with a grey beard.

I stood up, 'Hello, I'm Christopher, I met your brother in Paris.'

He beamed and came forward and embraced me, 'Salaam aleicum.'

'Aleicum Salaam.'

'I've been expecting you, my brother wrote and told me. How is he?'

'He looked very well to me. He shares an apartment with a friend of mine and others in Paris.'

'Yes, yes, Simon isn't it. Where is Simon?'

'He's down in Gaza, working with the Palestine observation people.'

He glanced every now and then at Tami.

'Tami is my interpreter.'

Tami was talking with Assef, they seemed to be getting on well together, speaking in English and Arabic.

I turned away from them and said quietly, 'She is very much on our side, she belongs to an Israeli organisation which completely disapproves of what the Zionist governments are doing to the Palestinians.'

'Good.' He said, 'We need more like her.'

'Tami, this Faisal.'

She got up and came over to us, 'Salaam aleicum.'

'Salaam, salaam aleicum. You speak Arabic?'

Tami replied in Arabic. Assef came over as well and asked something in Arabic.

Faisal looked at her, 'Do you want to do that?' in English.

'Yes, that would be nice.'

She turned to me, 'Assef wants to show me more of Acre and take me to see the mosque, is that alright with you?'

'Yes that would be good, I can stay and talk with Faisal.'

'Come,' said Faisal. 'Have something to eat before you go.'

I was relieved about this idea, it meant I could talk to Faisal about how to get out of here. It wasn't that I wanted to conceal things from Tami, it was just that I wanted to keep any plans for my final escape as quiet as possible.

We had some breakfast, then Tami and Assef set off together. Just as they were leaving, Faisal said in English, 'Be back for lunchtime.'

When we were alone I asked Faisal about getting out of here if I had to.

'I've made friends on a cruise yacht in Haifa. I may get a lift with them to Cyprus as they go there frequently. It's just that they may not be there when I need to go.'

'Then come here, I could find you a way out in a couple of days.'

I stayed talking with him about Sayyid in Paris. I also described Paris. He listened intently.

'He's so lucky to be there. We can never leave here, they will never let us return. We are prisoners in our own country.'

That's true I thought, they are just prisoners in their own country.

Assaf and Tami returned just before noon and he began immediately to help his father. Tami and I went for a walk along the front.

'I like this area, I'd rather live here than Haifa, or Tel Aviv . . . in this part, which is the old name 'Akko', it's the older city. I like it here.'

We sat on a wall and watched the small ships come and go. She put her arm around me.

'Where will we live Christopher?'

'Between here and London. I'll sell my paintings and people will buy your books.'

And we will love each other forever, along with our four children. Kiss me Christopher and tell me it's true.'

I kissed her and told her it would be true, but I knew it wouldn't be like that.

We made our way back to Faisal's. We had a nice meal and drank some wine and sat out in the sun.

About 4 o'clock we said our goodbyes. Assaf decided to accompany us to Ali's boat, he and Tami plainly liked each other. We found Ali; Assaf knew him and they greeted each other warmly.

We got on the caique, Ali called out in Arabic as we left.

'What did he say?'

'He said come again soon.'

We got back to Haifa and walked back to the apartment. Tami put the radio on. It was in Hebrew, I was going out onto the terrace when I realised she was listening with close attention. I started to say something but she held her hand up for me to stop. She was listening to something serious.

'My god, my god . . . there's been a bomb in the market in Jaffa . . . my mother always goes there on Sundays.'

She grabbed the 'phone and dialed. After a moment or two she started talking in Hebrew. She talked some more then hung up.

'That was my brother, they have just heard about it, he is going to get in touch with the authorities and find out who has been injured.'

She went back to the radio, it had gone on to other subjects.

I didn't know what to do, she was obviously just trying to hear.

The 'phone rang. 'Yes . . . ?'

She listened, then checked her watch and said something. She turned to me, 'I'm going to have to go back to Tel Aviv, I think my mother has been injured.' She went back to the 'phone and finished her conversation.

She was plainly very anxious. 'My brother has got hold of my father and he has gone to the hospital, I must go down there.' She looked at me anxiously, 'Will you be alright here?'

'Yes of course, there is a lot I can do from here, I'll manage OK. You can call me and tell me what's happening.'

She sorted out some clothes and put them in her knapsack. She turned to me, 'I'm so sorry, but it's my mother, I'm really anxious.'

She put her arms around me, 'Don't forget me, I'll call you and tell you what is happening.' She kissed me passionately. I went downstairs with her and waved as she drove off. I looked at my watch, it was about 7pm, she should be there by 8.30.

I didn't hear anything for the rest of the evening. I went to bed about 11pm, and after worrying about Tami I snuggled down in the bed and rolled over to her side, I could make out her perfume in the bed. About 2am the 'phone rang, I got up and went into the other room and picked it up, it was Tami.

'My mother's in hospital, she and several others were injured, three people are dead. Her legs were badly damaged, she may lose one of them.'

She delivered all this in a flat monotone as if it was a news broadcast. Then she started to cry. 'Why did they do this . . . why . . . she's never harmed anyone.'

'Shall I come back? I can be there in two hours.'

'No, no, I'm at home at the moment, but I'll be going into the hospital when it's light, I'll keep calling you.'

'I'm so sorry for you.'

'It's so awful, what's she done?'

There was nothing I could do. I went back to bed and with difficulty fell asleep.

The next day I got up and after breakfast I started to add all this to my journal as well as our trip to Acre. I looked at my face in the mirror, maybe it was time to have the stitches out. I worked out a way to get to the Rambam hospital, it was not that far.

There was no message from Tami, she must still be at the hospital. I was filled with shock about what had happened. She was right, what had her mother done? The trouble is what had all those innocent women in the villages and towns done when they were killed, raped and driven out in the war, and refused re-admittance to their country. It was not the time to discuss this with Tami, but it was behind all that was happening and what would go on happening until it was resolved.

About 11am I set off for the Rambam hospital, it was quite easy to find. I drove into the concourse and found somewhere to park. I went into the main entrance and was directed to the outpatient area. I explained that I was there to have some stitches out and was directed to where I could wait for someone to attend to me. While I was waiting I picked up one of the brochures on the hospital. I found out that it had been built in 1938 under the British Mandate. It was an impressive series of buildings designed I found out by Erich Mendelsohn, a Bauhaus architect. It was known as the British Hospital. After the war of 1947-48, when it became Israel, the name was changed to Rambam. The name Rambam was derived from a Jewish philosopher, Mosheh ben Maimon, who existed in the twelfth century. His name, Rabbi Moshen ben Maimon, was the source of the name. Well that was useful, I'd never have been able to work that out. There was a new School of Medicine just opened, presided over by a Dr Gutman.

There was an Arab man cleaning the floor nearby. I watched him. Every now and then someone would ask him for directions, mostly they were Americans. He answered in very good English. I was thinking of talking to him myself but then I was called. I was directed to a door at one side, it was open, inside was a nurse, she said she would remove the stitches. I mentioned that they were put in by Dr Fischer. She smiled at that.

'He's a good man.'

I explained how I had an accident and he and Arella came to my rescue. The wound was clean and she deftly removed the stitches. 'Take care of this, the red colour will fade and you'll have a white scar.'

When I went outside I saw the cleaner sitting on a bench smoking. I sat down beside him.

'You speak very good English.'

He looked at me, 'Well I was educated in England.'

I asked him his name.

'Aaron.'

'Why were you there?'

'My father was a medical consultant and had been invited to London to work at one of the hospitals. We were there for five years and I went to school there. Then we came back here.'

'Where is your father?'

'Dead.' He threw his cigarette away.

I knew what I was going to hear, but I asked him anyway, 'How did he die?'

He looked round at the hospital, 'These bastards killed him.'

'Where are you from?'

'Safsaf.'

'Where is that?'

It's about 30 km from Acre, just south of the Lebanese border.'

'What happened?'

'I was living here with my father in Haifa. He went back to the village to visit his mother. The IDF attacked the village, they took 52 men, including my father, handcuffed them, then shot them in front of their families, throwing the bodies into a well. They took four women, ostensibly to gather water, but in reality to rape them, one of them was my fourteen-year-old cousin. Then they killed them.'

'Later I found out that the man in charge went on to carry out similar operations in Palestinian villages around this area. The main commander was Yigal Allon, but he used one of his officers, Yoshe Kalman, to carry out the raids. He was known for his operation against Khisas. This area has some of the best land and he saw it as a good place to get rid of the owners so the Israelis could steal the land, which as you see they have all done. One day I will kill him.'

I was aghast at this story and asked if he could repeat the names so I could write them down.

He looked at me, 'Where are you from?'

'England, I'm an artist, I came here to record many of these events.'

'Will you tell them this story?'

'Yes of course, along with others.'

'I wanted to become a doctor as well, now the only job I can get is what you saw me doing.'

'What other villages were they?'

'A lot of them are now Israeli settlements, so they often have different names. Here are some though, if you can find them. Quaymun, Guira, Arab al-Khiyat, Husainynyiyya, Kirad alGanimmi. They were attacked in the same way, who knows how many were killed and women raped. They were stealing our land.'

I asked him to repeat the names of these villages, and did my best to write them down.

All this again distressed me. I decided to try and find them and see what was left. I went back to the apartment. I made some lunch from some of the things that Tami had purchased. After I finished I got out the map and tried to work out my next move. I needed about three days to go to see the villages and Safsaf. Then I wanted to go to Deir Yasin, although I knew that it had been largely demolished, and was quite a long way from here. It was close to Jerusalem, I thought I might spend a night in Jerusalem and if possible meet up with Jakob Steinhardt and go to the Bezalell School. I didn't want to do it until I had spoken to Tami, I wanted to make sure she knew where I'd be.

I made another trip to the yacht basin and talked with my friends on the motor yacht. I noticed that they had a 'phone on board. I asked if they had ever taken passengers across with them to Cyprus.

'Yes, we occasionally have friends of the owners, and a couple of times someone we knew. He is quite generous about this, we just have to tell him.'

'I wonder if I could make the trip with you?'

'Sure, take the 'phone number and give us a call.'

During the afternoon I continued with the drawing I had been doing from the terrace. I was impatient to hear from Tami, as I wanted to get on with my trip. It was 6.30 before she called.

She was in tears, 'They're going to cut off her left leg below the knee. They'll be able to repair her right leg, although she will always walk with difficulty. Why . . . why, what did she do . . . why is she being punished?'

'Shall I come back?'

'No, I'm dividing my time with going to the hospital and being at home to look after the others. My father spends the whole time at the hospital. I wouldn't be able to see you.'

I told her my plan about going later in the week to Deir Yasin and then on to Jerusalem, and staying one night in Ester's one roomed flat. Trying to get hold of Jakob Steinhardt and seeing the Bezalell School. I would try and call her from a pay phone when I was there.

'I'm also going to Dawaymeh, then Beersheba, on the way I'll get as close to Dimona as I can. After that I'll head for Tel Aviv. So I'll be travelling until later in the week.

I'll call you whenever I can.' 'I'm so sorry about what's happened . . . I wish I could see you.'

'Yes I want to see you too, but it's a bad time now.'

'After I finish at Jerusalem I'm going to come to Tel Aviv for a night, then head back up to Haifa the next day. Maybe I could see you then.'

'Yes, yes . . . let's try then, I really want to see you.'

I was seriously shocked by what had happened to her mother and could only imagine how it was affecting Tami.

During the next few days I visited the areas mentioned by Aaron, starting with Safsaf. In many ways there was not much to see, ruined buildings, some just rubble, gradually disappearing back into the ground. All the land was being farmed by Jewish people. Many knew little or nothing about what had happened here. They came from many different countries and just saw the land as theirs to cultivate. I mentioned some of the history to them, they either did not believe it, or were very resentful of me even suggesting it, while others knew about it and didn't care. 'Let them go back to the desert.' was their usual response.

Over the next two days I did my best to cover the other villages he had mentioned. The stories were just the same and the villages were now just rubble. There were no Palestinians. I asked a couple of people if the original owners had been compensated for their property.

'They went away and left their property, now it's ours.'

There was general contempt for the Palestinians. I was deeply depressed by all of this. I took many photographs and did a number of quick sketches, to work on later.

I managed to have two more conversations with Tami. She was now running the household as well as visiting the hospital. Her father came home although he still went to the hospital every day.

On the Friday I set off for Deir Yasin. I took my remaining clothes and toiletries, in case I stayed away longer. It was a long journey over the central area and then down the east side of Palestine near the border with Jordan. There were Palestinian villages and towns on the way; I was tempted to stop but I wanted to see Deir Yasin and then make the journey into Jerusalem.

When I was near Deir Yasin I asked the way. Some did not know what I was talking about, but I found a man who said that it was now known as Givat Shaul Bet. It was already becoming part of Jerusalem and being turned into an industrial area. There was little trace of any village. I thought of all those children that had been clubbed to death in the roads.

So much I thought for the site of one of the worst massacres, an industrial area.

I made my way into Jerusalem. It was plainly growing all the time. I found the street, after asking several times, where Ester had her room. It was in a small rise of apartments and her room was on the sixth floor, at the top. It was a simple room with a view of more buildings across the street. There was one room with a bed, a small sofa and a little table with two chairs, on the wall was one picture, a reproduction of a Kandinsky. There was a tiny bathroom with a shower, and an equally tiny kitchen, with a two burner stove and a microwave, there was also a small 'fridge. Surprisingly again I found a telephone. It was a good time to call Tami.

'My mother is having an operation tomorrow. She is being very brave about it. I'm so sad for her, she is making jokes about it, "I'll be like one of those pirates" she keeps saying. I know she is dreading it though.'

'Please give her my love.'

'I will, she always asks about you, "Is he eating enough . . . how is he managing without you".'

I was overwhelmed with her kindness.

I gave her the number here, but told her that it would be only one more night, unless I discovered something else to do. In truth I would have liked to stay at least a week, how many more chances would I have to visit this ancient city?

Chapter 24

There was nothing to eat in the 'fridge, just a half empty bottle of vodka and a bottle of what looked like champagne, and three diseased-looking lemons.

I remembered that I had passed some shops and stores just round the corner. I was in fact hungry, as I hadn't stopped for something to eat the whole way.

I made my way downstairs, there was no lift. Then round to the shops. There was a small store, where I bought some oranges, bread, butter, instant coffee and a cereal brand, as there was no evidence of muesli. There were two cafés, I went in one. I had an omelette with a salad, they also had some wine, and I had coffee afterwards. There was a shop selling papers and books, I bought a road map of Jerusalem. It was early evening when I went back to the room and very soon it was dark. I looked up Jakob Steinhardt's number in my notebook and called him. He was in.

'Jakob, I don't know if you remember me, but I met you at New Horizons, my name is Christopher.'

'Yes of course, you're the new Canaletto.'

'I wish. I'm here in Jerusalem, I was wondering if we could meet up.'

'Yes, yes, I said I'd take you to the Bezalell School. Where are you?'

I gave him the name of the road I was in.

'Oh that's not far, come to the college about 10am, I'll meet you in the lobby.' He gave me directions from where I was.

I spent the evening writing my notes and looking at some of the more recent drawings.

I went to bed quite early, I was very tired after all that driving. I lay awake for a while, then drifted off. I had a dream that I was living with Tami in a town by the sea, in England, but not where I grew up. I was painting, she was writing, there were children running in and out, were they ours? Then suddenly it wasn't Tami, it was Sylvia. I was completely confused. Sylvia kept saying 'we must go back to Israel'.

I woke early, it was just getting light. I got up and showered. Then I washed my underwear and a t-shirt. I had clothes for today but I would need these tomorrow.

I decided to take a walk before I had breakfast. I walked north up the road until I reached a crossing, the road across was called 'HaRev Schmuel Baruch'. I crossed over and continued walking until I reached a market area called 'Yehuda Market'. Interesting I thought, I live on Yehuda Tel Aviv. It was not really a 'souk', as it had been in Tel Aviv. It was I suppose more civilized, with small shops and a quantity of barrows. I preferred the 'souk' in Tel Aviv. I walked around a bit, then headed back to the room.

I had some breakfast, some of the local cereal brand, too sweet really. I put orange juice on it, should have got some milk. The orange juice was OK, although she didn't have a proper squeezer. I had some bread and butter and instant coffee.

About 9.30 I set off for the Bezalell School of Art and Design. I had checked it out on the map and decided to walk there. I was there about 9.50. At first sight it was not very remarkable, the entrance was in a long low area of buildings.

I went inside, where there was a sort of waiting area with chairs and a low table, with some brochures about the college. I began reading one of these. It was indeed a very interesting brochure, it plainly covered most of the courses we had at the Royal College. Just after 10.00 Jakob turned up.

'Hello again.' He shook my hand. 'Let's go and have a coffee first.'

He lead me to a large café area. The coffee was good, distinctly better than the instant stuff I had with my breakfast. Jakob began to explain the various departments the college had, and how they were in the process of having a new building erected to contain all these elements. He then took me on a grand tour of what they had. I was of course interested in the painting department, but there were many other areas, which I found fascinating. The tour took most of the morning, then Jakob insisted on buying me lunch in the canteen, which was also very good.

'Where are you going after this?'

'I want to go to Beersheba, then back on to Tel Aviv. I need to see Tami.'

'Oh God yes, her mother was injured in that bombing, how is she?'

'According to Tami they're going to remove her left leg below the knee.'

He was shattered by this information. 'How could they do that to someone so innocent?' He said something in Hebrew.

'Sorry, I didn't hear you.'

'It's nothing'

After lunch he said that he needed to go as he had another appointment. He didn't ask me to his studio. I asked him if there was a gallery in Jerusalem that I might visit.

'Yes, the Safryia Gallery, I'll tell you where it is.' He gave me directions.

I thanked him very much for showing me the Bezalell School.

'I look forward to your exhibition, let me know when it will happen.' He let me have one of his cards. It had his address in Hebrew on one side, and in English on the other.

I made my way to the gallery, it was on King David Street, not far from a Park called the Gozian Gardens. It was entirely showing Jewish artists. Apparently it had been in existence since 1935, sometime before Israel was formed.

I spent some time there. There were some very interesting artists. I tried to think of Jewish artists, Mark Chagall, Amadeo Modigliani, a new artist emerging from the United States, Mark Rothko. Who else was there? My problem was that I very seldom thought of people by their religion or beliefs, it didn't seem important to me, just their art. However I suppose the faith of many of the Renaissance artists was Catholic. Anyway there was a prodigious collection here. A lot of the work was very interesting, I could see why this was a gallery devoted to them. I stayed in the gallery until 5.30. After that I went back to the room and called Tami about 6.00pm. She had returned from the hospital, her mother had had the operation and was still sedated. Tami was going back there shortly.

I asked her if she knew anywhere I could stay in Dimona for a night.

'There was a cheap place on Aliya, it was an army camp once but now is a sort of hotel. It largely consisted of shacks with rooms in. I don't know if it's still there. Otherwise you may have to go to Beersheba.'

'The day after tomorrow I'll be back in Tel Aviv, I'll call you, it maybe about this time in the afternoon.'

'Oh yes, please call, we must get together, I want so much to see you.'

I decided to take myself to that café again and have a meal, my own effort here would be pretty miserable.

That evening I added to my notes. I realised too that I had not had time to find that other journalist, Amos Keinan. Without Tami I was a bit lost.

Chapter 25

The next morning I looked up the famous sights in Jerusalem, the Dome of the Rock, the Wailing Wall and other places. I had not visited the old city either. As a tourist I was a failure. I hesitated, should I stay another day? I was not really here as a tourist, I was here to do a job. Although it would have been nice, spending my time doing this it was not what I was really here for. I decided to head off for Dawaymeh.

I looked at my map, I knew roughly where it was but had no idea how to get there. It seemed to me that if I headed northwest from Jerusalem until I reached a main road with the number 6, then went south on this until I reached a turning to the left at Pethayia to Kamel Josef, I would be nearly there. There was a way by small internal roads, but I was sure I would get lost. I filled up with petrol and headed off. It was quite a long trip to Route 6, then to Pethayia and finally the area called Kamel Josef. This seemed to be a small farming village. There was a café I was pleased to see, as I was starving. The man who ran it did not seem to have much English, but there was another man eating there who did.

'I wonder if you could direct me to Dawaymeh?'

He looked at me with surprise, 'It doesn't exist anymore, why do you want to go there?

This was going to be difficult.

'Well you see I have been asked to travel round the country and record how well the country is coming on, now that it is Israel again. Someone mentioned that I should try and visit it.'

He looked at me with some suspicion. 'It was destroyed during the war of 1947-48. Who are these people who asked you?'

I produced my rather worn letter from new Horizons in Hebrew.

He read it. 'Yes well, they obviously regard you as an artist, I'm just a bit surprised they suggested Dawaymeh, it's really a heap of stones now.'

He gave me some directions, 'What sort of car do you have?'

'A scooter.'

He laughed, 'I'll guess you'll be OK, probably better than a car, the roads are very rough there.'

I thanked him for his help and after the meal I set off following his directions to Dawaymeh. He was right about the roads, in fact they were at times little more than tracks. There were no real villages, just occasional gatherings of dwellings, a few houses at a time. They were obviously lived in by people doing subsistence living on the land, a few sheep and goats. I saw houses with chickens and small holdings. Eventually these ran out. It had become increasingly steep as well, raising itself to an almost mountainous area. I was worrying about the tyres on the scooter, the last thing I needed out here in these wilds was a puncture.

I eventually arrived at where the village must have been. It was true, there were really nothing but stones and rubble here. I walked around, trying to imagine it with houses standing, it was very hard. I found an area which looked like the cemetery. Some of the stones had inscriptions in Arabic, there were two that had the fading images in photographs, sheltering under a larger stone, a ruined house or a building of some sort. It was infinitely depressing. The tragedy and cruelty that had taken place here, the dead people and the children with their heads broken as in Deir Yasin. It was all fading into the dust. No wonder some Israeli politician had likened this to the acts of the Nazis.

I took some photographs again, and managed a few sketches. In truth I didn't want to stay any longer, and soon headed back, guiding the scooter around the worst of the damaged roads and paths. I passed through Kamel Josef without stopping and found my way back to Route 6. Once I got there I wasn't sure which way to turn. I wanted to go to Dimona, but it was a long way from here. If I turned left I could head down to Beersheba, or I could miss it out and head up to Tel Aviv. I thought about it and then decided to head for Beersheba. I'd really got this wrong, I should have gone to Dimona first, then, via Beersheba, to Dawaymeh. I'd given myself another day of travelling.

It was nearly dark when I got to Beersheba. I went to a café there and asked the proprietor, who spoke English, if he knew of a place I could stay for a night.

'Just for a night?'

'Yes, I'm on my way to the Dead Sea, then up to Jerusalem.'

He gave me an address nearby.

It was a small house, set back behind a tiny garden. The woman who owned it was in her sixties. Her husband had died about five years before, and she rented out this one room at the back of the house. Her English was very good, her father, who had been a doctor, went to England to study and she had been educated for three years in the local school. She showed me the room, which was very small, but all I needed. There was a shower out at the back. I thanked her and said that was fine. We had some conversation, her English, although very good, had a sort of Somerset ring to it. It seemed that her father had been studying at the local hospital in Bristol. I told her that I knew Bristol very well, as my parents came from there. She was delighted to hear my memory of it.

I slept very well, my journey the previous day had been exhausting. I paid the woman and thanked her for her hospitality. I found a public 'phone booth and called Tami, fortunately she was in.

'Tami I'm in Beersheba, just about to go to Dimona. I screwed up yesterday, I went to Dawaymeh first, I shouldn't have done it that way round it means I'm coming a day later.'

'Oh I'm sorry. There's news here, New Horizons has shut down, there's a sort of police notice on the front door. I can't get hold of Yurem. I don't understand what's happened.'

'I wonder what that's about?

How's your mother?'

'Considering, she's much improved. One of the other people has now died.'

'That's terrible.'

'Please come back soon.'

I said I'd try and call her this evening, from Dimona.

I set off to Dimona about 10.30. It was a long trip, the scooter was doing well, although it had been suffering yesterday. I was as brown as a berry, although I had been wearing the cap that Tami had given me, my arms and legs were red and going even more brown. I tried to keep sun away from my face, but it was inevitable that I got some. As I was approaching Dimona I saw on my right a series of buildings, set back off the road, there was a gate with two armed soldiers and close by what looked like a guardroom. There was a tall wire fence all the way round the area. Just after I passed it I saw an area where trucks had pulled off the road and gone towards the wire fencing further in.

I went into Dimona and found the hotel which Tami had mentioned. She was right it still looked like a camp. I rented a room in one of the buildings and put my stuff in there. There seemed to be a few other people staying. I needed a shower. I found them outside in the yard. There were no cubicles, just a line of them with rather skimpy curtains in front of them. I stripped off and went inside one of them at the end. At first I seemed to be on my own, then I heard voices and a group of other people came in and ran the other showers, the water in mine gradually diminished, until it was just a trickle. I had more or less finished, when I left I passed the other cubicles with their skimpy curtains and found there were men and women in them. It was a seriously a communal affair.

I decided to take a walk later in the afternoon, mainly to ascertain how long it would take to get to the nuclear site. I was careful not to go too close to it. I reckoned it would take me about half an hour.

I found somewhere to have a meal. While I was having it I started to contemplate what I was going to do. This was going to be the most dangerous trip I was going to make. If I screwed up I would be in serious danger. What I needed was a photograph of the front of it. Thank God I had Andy's camera, with its long lens.

I found a pay 'phone. I was getting seriously short of small change. Tami was at home. 'I'm in Dimora, I'll be here until tomorrow, then I'll head back.'

'Oh yes please, it's getting very strange here, New Horizons is still closed, nobody knows what has happened. I still can't find Yurem. That friend Avi I knew in the army is trying to get in touch with me. Please come back as soon as you can.'

I decided to wait until midnight before I made my move to the site. I'd leave my scooter here and walk the whole way.

There was a half moon, and when it was out it gave sufficient light to see very well, but there were a lot of clouds scudding by. I walked towards the site, there was no traffic, this road was deserted at that time, not that there had been much traffic during the day.

The only lights at the site were some at the guardroom at the entrance and the main building, which was about 200 yds back from the road. When I reached the area where I had seen tyre tracks, I turned off the road and followed the gulley they had made. It became quite cloudy and I nearly lost my way. Eventually I reached the fence. It was plain that quite a large area had been taken out, although it had been replaced. By searching around I found a couple of areas where there was quite a gap at the bottom. Looking around in the scrub I found some sturdy twigs and managed to prop up the wire sufficiently for me to ease myself underneath. I started to move cautiously towards the building, crouching down as much as I could. The building also had another wire fence around it. When I was about 30 yards away I got the camera, which I had slung round my neck, ready to line up on the building. With Andy's long lens, it was perfect to get the whole building. As I took the photographs I managed to inch my way forward, so that in the end I was able to take a whole picture of just the notice board outside. This was covered by a sign in Hebrew.

I had just finished taking the shots when there was a noise behind me, turning my head I saw a vehicle being let in through the gate. Its headlights were on and I ducked down as much as I could as it drove towards me. I was suddenly terrified, if they spotted me I would have no chance. There was a deep depression where I was, probably made by the construction vehicles when they were here. I crouched down in this and literally prayed. The vehicle passed me without any sign and went up to the main entrance. A guard appeared and opened the gate. I wondered where he been while I was taking the photographs. I was lucky he'd not spotted me.

Two men in uniform got out of the vehicle, judging by the way they were saluted, they were quite senior officers. They disappeared into the building. I began to work my way back to the outer fence. There was a burst of activity. I dropped down and started to crawl to towards where I came in. A searchlight on the roof of the building came to life and began to scan the area. I reached the fence, had difficulty finding the spot where I had come through. The searchlight was sweeping towards me, I just found it in time. I caught the back of my left arm in the wire as I went through, I painfully detached it. There were soldiers criss-crossing the area inside. I crawled further into the scrub, until I was distant enough to raise myself to a crouch. As soon as I was far enough away I started to make my way to the road. Looking back, I saw they had found the area where I had exited. I followed the road, keeping to one side, in case I had to duck down in the scrub again.

Eventually I got back to the hotel and let myself in, trying to be as quiet apossible. I examined my arm, it had a nasty tear in it and was bleeding. I didn't have any band-aids. I made a pad for it with one of my handkerchiefs. Well I thought, at least I've got the photographs. I looked at my watch, it was nearly 2.30. I went to bed and fell asleep immediately.

In spite of this I was awake at 7am. When I checked out the man behind the desk told me that they had a visit from the IDF, someone had been spotted in the compound up the road and they were trying to find out who it was. They had searched the other hotels and not found anybody. They were running out of steam. They thought of searching this hotel but he told them he only had six people, a group of tourists. They decided it wasn't worth it. He thought they were glad to give up and go back to their camp.

'What is that place up the road?'

'It's some sort of research, nobody knows what it's about, and they don't encourage questions. I think it's some sort chemical warfare, you know, gases and things.'

I paid my bill, which was very small, and headed off to Beersheba. As I passed the site I noted that there were many more soldiers around, not only on the main gate, but patrolling around inside.

It took me sometime to get to Beersheba. I thought of stopping for a coffee there but then decided to go on to Rahat. I found a café in Rahat with some shade, it was unbearably hot out there. The scooter was looking very dusty, I had taken it on some long journeys. It had done well, maybe I should return it back in Tel Aviv and get a more recent one, this one needed some servicing.

I set off again and decided I would make the whole journey back to Tel Aviv. That meant I would be back in Tel Aviv about 3.30 to 4.00 pm. I'd call Tami when I got in. There were many places I should have stopped to see, but now I was really anxious to get back.

Chapter 26

It was almost a relief to be on Yehuda, I seemed to have been doing a lightning tour of Israel. When I let myself in there was an envelope on the floor, I carried it upstairs to the apartment. When I looked at the writing on the envelope I saw it was Simon's. There was a message saying that he needed to talk to me tomorrow, it was urgent. He would see me at the café by the sea about 3pm. I was surprised that he had written after all his concerns about security. Also I was surprised that he knew I was back.

After I had cleaned up I went to the 'phone booth and called Tami. She was delighted that I was back in Tel Aviv. She would come after the hospital at about 9pm.

I went to the store and bought a few things to eat, as well as some band-aids. Back in the flat I dressed the wound on the back of my arm. I then sat down and recorded my memories of the last few days, in particular the event at Dimona. I had no idea what was written on the signpost, I would have to find a way of getting it translated when I was back in London.

Tami arrived at 9.00pm, we literally threw ourselves into each others' arms. We made love almost immediately. After, she examined me carefully and asked what the mark on my arm was. I told her what I had done. She was horrified, 'My God, if they had caught you there would have been so much trouble.'

She laid on her back, looking at the ceiling. 'I'm afraid I can't spend the night, I need to get back and take care of things. Now my mother is in hospital I have become mother. The children need looking after, and my father, although capable in many things, does not know how to cook. So I'm in charge.'

She turned to me, resting her head on my shoulder. 'We will get together in the end, won't we?

'Yes, we will.'

When she left I walked downstairs with her. She kissed me again, 'I'll see you tomorrow.'

I slept badly that night. My head was full of the things I had done and full of the things that I had not done. Now that New Horizons seemed to be shut I was not sure how long my money would last. I wonder what happened there. I had dreams about Tami and dreams about Sylvia, both mixed in my head. I wonder what Simon was going to tell me.

I woke early and went out and did my exercises on the terrace. It was so long since I had done any I was full of aches and pains afterwards. I decided I would go and see Hamid. Maybe he might know what was going on.

About 10am I set off to Jaffa. I showed my passport and headed down to Hamid's. When I got there I first thought I was in the wrong street, it looked different. Then I realised, Hamid's house had gone, there was just a pile of rubble. In front of where the house had been were the remnants of furniture, everything smashed or broken. Nearby there had been a fire, when I poked about in the remains I saw that they were Hamid's paintings. I was aghast at this sight. A young boy who had been watching, said something to me in Arabic, he made a gesture with his hands, as if showing me what had happened. When he saw that I did not understand he picked up a twig and drew something in the dust.

I looked at what he had drawn, it was a crude drawing of something like a tractor. I realised what it was. It was one of those machines which I had seen drawings of at the workshop in the kibbutz I'd been to. So that was what they were for.

There was no one I could ask, the boy didn't speak English. I made a gesture with my hands, 'Hamid . . .' He understood and showed me his hands as if they were bound together, and waved into the distance.

I was distraught, I gazed at the ruin, where were the others? Under a piece of rubble I saw a scrap of paper, I bent down and picked it up. It was covered in dust, I did my best to clean it and there was the drawing I had done of Saba. I felt tears coming, but managed to control it. I showed it to the boy. He nodded, 'Saba'. I made a gesture with my hands, like where . . . ?

He waved his hands, they had obviously been taken away.

I photographed the rubble and the fire. This was what the Israelis were doing to the Palestinians.

I drove back to the flat. I got out my notebook and recorded what I had seen and tucked the drawing of Saba in with it.

This was a tragedy, I could hardly bear to think about it, where would she be, what refugee camp was she in, what country for that matter.

About 2.30 I went down to the café on the beach. I sat there drinking a glass of wine and pondering what to do next. Simon arrived promptly at 3.00pm. He was shocked at my appearance. 'What happened to you?'

I explained about the IDF truck driving me off the road and being taken to a kibbutz. Later how Tami and I went to Haifa and what we had found out about Tantura. I described our trip to Acre and meeting Sayyd's brother, and how we had discussed a route out that way. Then I gave him the shocking news about Tami's mother. How I was now operating on my own.

I also explained about my trip to from Haifa to Jerusalem and then to Dawaymeh. How then I had gone to Beersheba and then down to Dimona.

'Did you know that someone broke into Dimona about the time you were there?'

'That was me.'

'That was you?'

'Yes.'

He looked at me in astonishment. 'How did you get in?'

I explained it to him, and told him about the photographs I had taken.

'My God that was good.'

'Yes I guess it was my only chance.'

'Wow, that was the best thing you could do . . . great! Now I know why we are in trouble. We have to go, they are really after us. I'm going back to Gaza and leaving via Egypt. How are you going?'

I was shocked by this, "Do we have to go?'

'No question.'

I thought about leaving, this was not the way I expected it to happen.

I told him about the motor yacht, and if I couldn't get out that way, there was also Sayyid's brother.

Simon went back to talking about the explosion at the souk.

'Let me tell you something I heard about that. The explosion was only in the area used by the Arab people, it was nowhere near the ones used by the Israeli people.'

I hadn't thought about this. 'You think it might have been a setup?'

'Maybe.'

'I don't want to go yet?'

'If you don't go you'll be arrested and none of the material will get out.'

I told him about what had happened to Hamid's house.

'I heard that some houses had been demolished in the Arab areas, I never thought it would be his house. That's terrible.'

We sat in silence for a while, then Simon said, 'I'm sorry, we really have to go, otherwise you in particular will be arrested. Now that New Horizons has been shut down and all the rest of it, it's getting dangerous. I'm going back to Gaza to start to make my way out via Egypt. You'd better get out via the motor-yacht or Sayyid's brother. What about Tami?'

'She can't leave, she's taking care of her family.'

'OK I'm going to go, I need to get back to Gaza. I'm going to head for Paris, when you are back come across there as soon as you can.'

I walked with him to the bus stop.

When we saw the bus coming he said, 'This has been an adventure, you've done wonderfully well, I'm so pleased you were here. See you in Paris.' He got on the bus and waved as it went away.

I was seriously depressed at having to leave. I went to the 'phone and called the number of the yacht. Sarah answered.

'I wonder if you can take me on your next trip to Cyprus.'

'We are leaving tomorrow morning, can you get here by 10?'

'Yes, I can do that.'

'OK I'll tell the owner, I'm sure it will be alright.'

I went back to the flat and sorted out the things I could take. I'd dump the suitcase, and some of my clothes and travel as lightly as possible. Tami was coming about 9pm. I had to tell her.

When Tami arrived I could see that she was exhausted. She slumped in a chair in the kitchen.

'I'm sorry, being mother and spending time at the hospital is exhausting. I don't know how my mother managed it.'

'Let's go out on the terrace.'

We stood looking down on Yehuda, the evening traffic was quite noisy.

'I need to talk to you.'

I held her hands and kissed her.

'What do you want to tell me?'

'Tami, I'm going to have to leave.' I told her what Simon had said. There was no point in trying to conceal what we had been doing here.

She listened in silence. When I was finished she said, 'When will you leave?'

'Tomorrow.'

She stood, gazing out towards the sea. She said nothing for a few moments.

Then, 'I knew this was going to happen . . . I said it would . . . it was all a dream.'

She turned and looked at me, 'Tell me it was a dream.'

'No it is not a dream, I love you, I didn't mean to, but I do.'

She held me again with her gaze, 'Come, let's make love.'

One more time in that little bed, we made love, there was passion and agony.

After, we lay gazing at the lights on the ceiling. Tami said. 'I love you, and I'm in despair. How can we go on, I have to be here because of my mother. You may never be allowed back into the country, I cannot leave it, certainly not for a very long time.' She laid her head against my shoulder, I could feel her tears, she cried silently.

After a while she got up and went to the bathroom. When she emerged she began to dress. I got up too.

'We must write.' I said.

'Yes, we must write.'

When she was ready I prepared to go downstairs with her.

'No, don't come with me. Let me go.' She kissed me once and set off.

I went out on the terrace and watched her drive away. I was filled with a terrible sadness.

I slept badly and found myself wide-awake at 5am. I got up and after showering and shaving I checked all the things I was going to take.

About 7.15 I was downstairs and loaded my stuff on to the scooter and set off for Haifa. The road was still relatively clear and I made good time.

I turned off the main road and made my way down to where Tantura had been. The car park was empty at that time of day. I parked the scooter in the corner where the trees were, hoping that they would shelter it from the sun for most of the day. I took out my shoulder bag with the sketchbooks, notebooks and camera, as well as two changes of underwear and two T-shirts and another pair of shorts, and the trousers. Hopefully these would last me until I could find somewhere to wash my clothes.

I walked back up to the main road. I needed to get into Haifa as soon as I could, before the motor yacht set off for Cyprus. I stood by the main road, in a spot where I could step back into the shadow of a couple of palm trees. The traffic was building up for the early morning rush hour to Haifa. I needed to hitchhike, but I wanted to avoid any vehicles which might be police or IDF.

Just along the road were a couple of other people, obviously intent on hitch-hiking, a young man about my age and a girl. If anyone stopped for them I would be next. I had noted that hitchhiking was a way of life for young people here. Most of them were doing their military service. Sometimes they would have their uniforms on, a guarantee that someone would stop for them. Some even carried their Uzi's. This couple didn't have uniforms on, they may have completed their service.

Quite soon a battered Ford pick-up stopped for them, and after a brief conversation with the driver they clambered into the back.

I started to watch for the next vehicle to come along, when I suddenly realised that the pick-up was slowing down as it approached me. It drew alongside, the driver's window was down, he looked at me, obviously wanting to know where I was going.

'Haifa?'

He nodded, and jerked his thumb back, indicating that I should join the other two. I clambered in the back, the young man gave me a hand, the girl watched.

As soon as I was settled the pick-up started. The young man said something to me in Hebrew.

I made the open-handed gesture, meaning I didn't understand.

'I'm American, I don't speak Hebrew.'

He smiled, 'That's OK, I speak American, my father's from New York. My name's Ariel, this is Sabra,' he indicated the girl. 'What are you doing here?'

'I'm on a long vacation from university, just travelling around.'

'Funny, you don't sound very American, more like a Brit.'

'Yeah well my father's a Brit originally.'

He seemed satisfied with this explanation. Before he could ask any more questions about me I quickly asked him one.

'Have you done your service in the IDF?'

'Not yet, I've had a deferment as I was studying, next month I join up.'

'Wow, that means three years!'

'I know, but I'm hoping to become an army doctor, I've been studying medicine. She's done hers though. He indicated Sabra.'

I turned to her, 'What did you do?'

She hesitated and looked at Ariel.

'She doesn't speak English very well.' He said something to her in Hebrew.

'Ah . . . I was . . . paratrooper.'

Blimey I thought, she only looks about eighteen. I thought of the eighteen year olds I knew back in England, no way!

We were penetrating the outskirts of Haifa.

'Where do you want to be dropped?'

'Umm . . . somewhere near the yacht basin.'

Ariel leant over the side and shouted something to the driver.

He dropped me off very close to where we had been staying. I thanked him in English. I know he didn't understand but I think he got the idea. They drove off and I waved to them and they waved back.

I hoped my rather thin story about being an American, with an English father was enough, but probably not. If they were questioned it wouldn't take too long to figure out who I was. Let's hope that wouldn't happen too soon.

When I got to the yacht basin there was no sign of the *Aphrodite*. There were a couple of other motor yachts, as well as the usual collection of caiques and fishing boats. I saw a man from one of the other motor yachts coming down the gangplank. When he reached the quayside I went over to him, 'Do you know if the *Aphrodite* has left?'

'Yes mate, they left about an hour ago, their boss man came early and wanted to leave immediately.' He too it seemed was English, with a strong Cockney accident.

He looked at me, 'Are you Christopher?'

'Yes'

'That woman, their medic, said if you turned up, that she was sorry, but they'd be back in a couple of days.'

Too late for me I thought. I thanked him.

I walked along the quayside to where the smaller boats were. I hoped to find Ali and his caique, maybe he would ferry me across to Acre. He too was not there.

What should I do? I didn't want to take one of the ferries or the bus, as I was sure that the police would spot me. I could try hitchhiking again I suppose.

There was a small Arab café on the quayside, I went and sat there and ordered a coffee. It was near where all the small boats were, so I could look out and see if Ali turned up.

After a while the café owner came out, there were few people sitting outside. He saw me sitting there with my shoulder bag beside me.

'Are you waiting for the ferry?'

I shook my head, 'I was waiting to see if one of the caique owners turned up, I prefer to go on one of those.'

'What's the name of the man you are waiting to see?' His English was very good.

'Ali.'

'I know three Ali caique owners, what does he look like?

I did my best to describe him.

'Does he have beard?'

I shook my head.

'OK that's Ali-al-Hijazi, he's the only one without a beard. His wife is sick, he had to take her to hospital.'

I must have looked rather crestfallen, so he said, 'Do you want someone to take you there?'

'Yes please.'

'My son will do it, he's got a fast boat.'

'I'll pay him of course.'

'What time will you come back?'

I hesitated, I didn't know him, should I tell him that I wouldn't be coming back?'

'I'm going to stay there for a while, maybe several days.'

'I have a good friend there, he runs a café like this, on the quayside at Acre, his name is Faisal, we were at school together.'

'What's the name of his café?'

'Salome, if you go there give him my best regards, tell him it's time he came over here to see me.'

'What's your name?'

'Azad.'

'And your son?'

'Fahad.'

As if summoned a young man appeared in the doorway of the café, drying his hands on small towel. He said something to Azad in Arabic.

Azad turned to me, 'This is my son, Fahad, he's just been fixing the waste pipe in the kitchen sink. He's a good boy and very practical, he can do anything, I'd be lost without him.'

He turned to his son and said something in Arabic, the young man came over and shook my hand, 'Salaam aleicum. My father says you want to go to Acre, I will take you there in my boat.' Like his father his English was very good.

'Thank you, I will pay you of course.'

He nodded, 'I have just a couple of things to do here then we'll go.' He went back indoors.

Azad stayed talking with me, he asked me where I was from, without thinking I told him that I was from England.

'Why are you here?'

I hesitated, then, 'I'm an artist, I've been recording what I see here.'

He nodded, 'I would love to go to England, when the British were here they did a lot of good, built schools, railways and hospitals. I went to school here in Haifa, there were British teachers. That was where I learned to speak English. When I left school I worked with the army as an interpreter, they were good to me. Then the Israelis came and it was bloodshed and terror, many people I knew were either killed or forced to go into refugee camps in the Lebanon, Jordan or Egypt, never to return. I lost many members of my family, a few of us have survived.'

I told him that was a story I had been hearing frequently during my recent travels around the country.

Fahad appeared, 'I'm ready to go, are you ready?'

'Yes, I'm ready.' I held out my hand to Azad, 'I hope we meet again, thank you for suggesting that Fahad could take me. I'll give your regards to Faisal.'

'Yes do go to him, he will help you if you are in trouble.'

I was surprised at this comment, 'How do you mean?'

'My friend, we hear things, we have friends everywhere, news travels fast. I have been told to look out for you. I knew Faisal's brother, Sayyid.'

He turned to Fahad and spoke to him rapidly in Arabic, glancing at me.

He turned back to me, 'You should go now, the Israeli police are looking for you, should they ask I've never heard of you.'

I started to say something, but he held up his hand, 'Go, go . . . '

Fahad led me across the quayside. I had been expecting another caique, so I was surprised to find that Fahad's boat was a rather fast looking motor-launch.

He saw that I was looking at it with surprise, 'Yes it's not a caique like Ali's. My father saw that we would be getting an increasing number of American tourists, many of whom would like to water-ski, so he encouraged me to make this investment.'

'So do you get many water-skiers?'

'Enough, and it's increasing every year.'

I scrambled aboard. Fahad untied the boat and started the engine. He guided us clear of the other boats, which were tied up along the quayside. Once we were clear he opened the engine up and we increased speed dramatically and roared across the bay towards Acre. I sat upfront next to Fahad, exhilarated by the speed and the spray. It was impossible to have a proper conversation with the roaring of the engine so I just wallowed in the sensation.

It took nearly twenty minutes before Fahad slowed and guided us towards the quayside at Acre. He didn't pull into the main harbour area but a smaller quayside to the west, it was in fact where Faisal's café was, where I had been before. When we reached there he helped me clamber ashore and passed out my bags.

'I'm not going to stay, I still have to finish the work on the kitchen. You'll find Faisal's café just along there.' He nodded towards the end of the quayside, 'Though I expect you knew that already.'

It seemed that I had not been as invisible as I thought.

'I need to pay you for the trip!'

He shook his head, 'My father told me that there is no charge and he wishes you well on the journey. He hopes you will take word of the plight of the Palestinian people back to England.'

'Tell him, I certainly will, and thank him for me.'

He waved, and turned away. Again as soon as he was clear he opened the throttle and I watched him roaring off in the direction of Haifa.

I made my way along the quayside, towards the Salome. I kept my eye out for any police or military, but this area, which was largely Arabic, seemed clear.

I looked at my watch, it was nearly noon, lunchtime, a good time to arrive.

I approached the Salome. There were a few people already seated outside. As I got closer I suddenly saw a figure I knew, Jacob! Fortunately he was facing the other way, before he could turn and see me I hastily dived down the nearest alleyway. 'Damn!' I thought, what am I going to do now?

I walked deeper into the ancient alleyways, heading towards the little souk I remembered. When I was nearly there I spotted a small café tucked in a corner. I sat down and ordered a coffee. Maybe if I waited an hour Jacob might have left Faisal's. I didn't want to go anywhere near it though, in case he spotted me.

I was hungry, I hadn't eaten anything since last evening. I'd hoped to eat at Faisal's but at the moment I couldn't go there.

I was just making up my mind what to do. The café I was sitting at was plainly only offering snacks, and I was wondering if I should move on and find another place, when I heard someone calling me. 'Christopher . . . Christopher!'

I looked up . . . there was Faisal's son Assaf waving to me from the other side of the little square I was in, he came across to me. He was carrying two heavy bags and was obviously on his way back from the souk, doubtless with supplies for his father.

He was smiling broadly, 'What you doing here?'

'Sit down for a moment, I want you to do something for me.'

He sat down, with some relief, the bags were obviously very heavy. I asked him if he would like a coffee, but he shook his head.

'I was on my way to see your father but there's a man there I want to avoid.'

'Is he an American?'

'Yes.'

'I know who you mean, he has been coming to the café the last three days. He's been asking a lot of questions, he asked my father if he knew of you, my father told him that he'd never heard of you, I don't think this man believed him. My father doesn't like him. He usually stays about an hour.'

'When you get back to your father's, see if he is still there, if he's gone maybe you could come back and let me know.'

He nodded, 'Yes I will,' he looked round, 'Where is Tami?'

'She had to go back to Tel Aviv, she had bad news . . . her mother was badly injured in that bomb explosion in the souk.'

His face clouded, 'That's terrible for Tami . . . she is such a nice woman . . . so sympathetic.'

He got up, 'I'll come back as soon as he's gone.'

'Please tell your father that I badly need help.'

He nodded, he understood what that meant.

After he'd gone I sat thinking about what he had said. They were plainly closing in on us. I hoped that Simon had got back to Gaza alright.

I didn't have to wait long, Assaf came hurrying back. 'It's OK, he's gone, said something about getting the ferry back to Haifa.'

I followed him back. Before I went out on the quayside I peered round cautiously, there was no sign of Jacob. I slipped into Faisal's café, he greeted me with the traditional hug and a kiss on both cheeks, 'Salaam aleicum.'

He looked at my scar, 'How is your face?'

'It's OK, it's healing gradually.'

I told him about Simon's warnings, that we had to get out of here, and I told him that I'd hoped to go on the motor yacht from Haifa, but it had already left this morning.

He thought for a moment, 'You'll need to stay here a couple of days while I get something organised.'

He showed me the yard at the back of his café, in the corner there was a clean dry storeroom. 'Leave your bags, I'll put a bed in here later.'

I went back inside with him, he asked, 'Have you eaten?' I confessed that I hadn't. 'Sit here and I'll get you some food.' He indicated a small table in the corner of the café. 'Best not to eat outside, you might be spotted.'

Faisal's daughter, Erina, brought the food to the table, she was older than Saba, probably thirteen or fourteen, but quite different in temperament, she was shy and hardly spoke, and kept her eyes cast down. I knew she spoke some English, but I couldn't draw her out. I thought with sadness about Saba, where was she now? Where was Hamid?

'Hello Erina.'

I thought at first she wasn't going to reply, but then she raised her eyes and said rather hesitantly, 'Hello.' She then continued to look at me. I could see she was examining the scar on the side of my face, from the accident I'd had two weeks before. She then did something rather surprising, she reached out and touched my face. 'Poor you . . . poor face.' She quickly dropped her hand and blushed, her eyes cast down.

I reached out and held her hand, 'It's alright Erina, it's gradually healing.'

She pulled her hand back and still blushing, went back to the kitchen.

After I'd eaten I went to the window of the café and looked out. There was no sign of Jacob. Neither was there any of Faisal. Assaf seemed to be taking care of whatever customers were there. I realised I couldn't just stay indoors for two days. Maybe if I went out and took myself to places away from this café it wouldn't incriminate Faisal if someone did spot me.

When Assaf came inside I told him this.

'I'll show you the way out at the back, you can use that to come and go.'

There was a small door in the wall behind the storeroom in the yard. This let out to a narrow alleyway. It was obvious that the other shops along the quayside also had rear entrances there.

I told Assaf that I would be gone a couple of hours and to tell Faisal. Taking my sketchbook, I went out the back door and worked my way up through the alleyways to the higher ground. I found a place I could sit in the shade and draw.

While I was drawing I thought about Tami and our last conversation together. Would I ever see her again? When I was back in London I would write to her. That's if I made it back there! I wondered what plans Faisal was making to get me out of here unscathed.

I worked at the drawing for a couple of hours, then, glancing at my watch I packed my stuff up and made my way down to Faisal's café.

Faisal had returned, he had another man with him.

'Christopher, this is Faraz, he has a fishing boat and is going to take you to Cyprus.'

Faraz held out his hand, 'Salaam aleicum.'

'Salaam aleicum.'

Faraz was short and stocky with curly black hair, judging by his arms and the hair peeping from the neck of his shirt, was probably covered by this dark curly hair all over. His grip was firm and strong.

He said something rapidly in Arabic. Faisal translated.'Faraz doesn't speak English . . . maybe a few words. What he says is that it is quite dangerous at the beginning, they have to watch out for Israeli patrol boats. Sometimes they come alongside and shine their searchlights at the boat and check who's on board, he'll need to dress you like a fisherman, so you'll look part of the crew. Sometimes they come aboard and check papers, not always though, let's hope we'll be lucky. He may be able to borrow someone's papers. Once the patrol boat has gone away they switch their lights off and head out to sea with the engine running quietly, as soon as they're clear they'll speed up.

'How long will it take?'

He asked Faraz, who replied at length in Arabic.

'It will take all night and most of the next day. Depending on the weather, they'll wait until its dark before going in close to the Cypriot shore, to avoid any chance of being spotted. They'll drop you near Salamis, which is not far from Famagusta.

Faraz said something else.

'He thinks you shouldn't shave for a couple of days.'

So, it looks like I'll be here for a couple of days. Well it should be an opportunity to do more drawings round Acre.

Faraz shook my hand again and departed.

I turned to Faisal, 'How much should I pay him?'

'Well the main cost is the fuel, maybe £25 Israeli. There is also their loss of fishing time, though they'll probably do some on the way back, and of course the risk they're taking. Say £35 Israeli altogether?'

That seemed absurdly reasonable, and still left me plenty to pay for my airfare from Cyprus to London. I resolved to give him £50 Israeli.

I was anxious to get on my way out of Israel, I felt increasingly vulnerable. I wondered how Simon was doing. He had talked of maybe trying to get out via Egypt.

During the following two days I made several journeys out the back entrance, then through the alleyways to various vantage points where I could do more drawings. I also brought my notes up to date in the evenings. Faisal continued to feed me and refused any payment. 'It's for my brother in Paris.' He would say.

Erina continued to wait on me and began to lose her shyness. I found out that she spoke more English than I originally thought. She asked me if I would be seeing her uncle, Sayyd, in Paris. I said that I would be going there after I got back to England.

'I was very young when he left and just remember what he looked like. He writes to me and tells me about Paris. I long to go there.'

On the second day, after I had been out doing some sketches in the souk, I went back to Faisal's and again was brought some food by Erina. She sat by me while I ate and began to ask me questions about London and England. She was entranced by my stories and description of places I had been to in London.

I asked if I could draw her. At first she shook her head but when I persisted she said she would go and ask her father if it was alright. When she came back Faisal was with her, he seemed pleased that I wanted to draw her and asked if he could have it when I finished. I said yes, but I would like to do two so I could keep one.

In many ways Erina was easier to draw than Saba had been. She sat perfectly still, she didn't bounce up and down, nor did she talk or make faces. She did not have the sparkling intelligence in her eyes that Saba had, but her eyes were beautiful, with a sort of gravity and calmness. I supposed she resembled her mother, although I had no reference for this, as there seemed to be no photographs of her.

I worked away and after an hour I had two sketches of her. I must admit that I decided to keep what I thought was the best one. I showed them to Erina, who like Saba, gazed at them with interest and pleasure.

'Am I really like this?'

'Yes, you can keep this one.'

I gave her the one I least favoured, and she seemed very happy. She went off to show her father.

Faisal came back with her, he was very pleased also, 'That's very good, it's so like her, she looks just like her poor mother.' He looked very sad for a few moments.

Like Saba, Erina couldn't stop looking at the drawing, somehow entranced with that image of herself, she kept asking if that was really how she looked, and I kept reassuring her that indeed it was.

Faraz came later with one of the white caps that many Arabs favoured, and a long loose white garment and a chequered blue and white piece of cloth, which many Arabs wore on their heads, held down by a black head rope, when they were in the hot sun, called a 'kuffiyeh'. Otherwise they wore it round their necks or wrapped round the lower part of their faces. He had borrowed them from one of his friends, so they were quite grubby, which I suppose made them more authentic.

Faraz explained that we would start the next evening, he would come and collect me from Faisal's at about 9pm. I should have the kuffieh on, and the loose white robe. So at last the possibility of leaving Israel was coming closer. I tried not to think what would happen to me if the Israelis intercepted the boat.

I wondered about my shoulder bag. It would look rather odd with my Arab dress carrying a shoulder bag. Erina solved the problem. She brought me what looked like a shawl, then wrapped the shoulder bag in it and knotted it. It looked quite innocuous this way.

I found it difficult to sleep that night, my mind was filled with the journey ahead. First we had to get clear of Israel and all its associated hazards, then tackle the long journey to Cyprus; I prayed we'd have good weather. Once we arrived in Cyprus I would have to make my way to Nicosia and the airport, hoping I could get a ticket to London on the earliest flight, and finally hoping that they wouldn't question me about my arrival.

The next day, as I had nearly a day before we set off, I decided to try and get a bit more drawing done in Acre. I wanted to go to the souk again, it was so interesting, like the one in Jaffa, so full of colour and texture.

Erina offered to wash my clothes. There wasn't much as I couldn't carry much with me. It was very kind of her though and I thanked her.

'I'm a woman, that's what we do.'

I was interested that a thirteen year old would describe herself as a woman, that she had already assigned herself to that role.

Drawing in the souk was a sufficient distraction from my concern about the journey. Time passed so quickly that looking at my watch I was surprised to see that it was already late afternoon.

When I returned to Faisal's my clothes were dry and neatly folded on my bed. I found Erina in the kitchen preparing food. I thanked her for the clothes and she looked pleased. She said, 'If you were here all the time I would always wash your clothes.' She then blushed and hid her face.

Later she brought me a meal, my last one there I supposed. She sat beside me and watched me eat. She didn't say anything until I had finished. Then, 'I wish you weren't going . . . I shall miss you.'

About 8pm I dressed myself up in the robe and put on the kuffiyeh. I glanced in the mirror, I looked quite convincing. I took the kuffiyeh off and put the white cap on. This looked good as well. I hope I was convincing enough to fool anyone on a patrol boat.

At 9pm Faraz came for me. He eyed me approvingly, 'Good.' He said.

I said goodbye to Faisal, embracing him and thanking him, assuring him I would give Sayyd his greetings, then Assaf, thanking him too for his help. Erina hung back, I took her hand, 'Goodbye Erina, thank you for looking after me.' She looked at me, her eyes filled with tears and she turned her head away and let go of my hand. She muttered something in Arabic.

Faisal translated, 'She said, "Go safely, I'll pray to Allah for your safety."'

So I left them and followed Faraz down the quayside to the fishing boat. It was much larger than I expected. Although it plainly had sails it was also motorised and had a cabin at the back where the steering wheel was. I was rather relieved by this as I had expected it to be rather like a dhow.

I clambered aboard, where there were already three crew. I wasn't introduced but they smiled at me and made me welcome.

It was beginning to get dark and there was preparation for departure. Faraz shouted instructions and we cast off. We then headed out to sea.

Very soon it was completely dark, Faraz had switched on their navigation lights. There were other fishing boats dotted about the sea nearby. Many had already cast their nets. Every now and then an Israeli patrol boat would come by, shining its searchlight on the fishing boats. One began to approach us,

Faraz barked some instructions and the crew began to open out the nets. Faraz indicated that I should join in. I grabbed a piece of the net and with the other three began to cast it over the side. The patrol boat came close and shone its searchlight. I bent my head and busied myself with the net. After what seemed an unbearably long time, the patrol boat switched of its searchlight and moved away. I breathed a sigh of relief. It wasn't over yet though, the patrol boat continued to circle around the little fishing fleet, shining its light on one fishing boat after another for another hour, occasionally getting close and on occasion actually boarding one. Eventually it moved off. As soon as it looked like it wasn't coming back we moved further out, pulling in our nets. Finally Faraz switched off our navigation lights until he judged that we were well clear of Israeli waters. Then he increased speed and we headed off to Cyprus. After tidying away the nets I and the other members of the crew settled down for the long journey. One of them relieved Faraz at the wheel and he came forward and sat down next to me.

One of the other fishermen, called Haleef, spoke quite good English and with Haleef's help Faraz began asking me questions.

He asked me why the Israeli authorities were after me. I did my best to explain what I had been up to, the subterfuge that I was here to praise the progress of the Israelis, whilst recording how they were stealing more land and the dreadful things they had done during the period of the Nakbar. How I was going to find a way of broadcasting this information when I was back in England. How Mossad and the others had been trailing me since I first arrived here and how in the end they had decided to arrest me, which is why I had to leave this way.

Haleef did his best to interpret this and Faraz listened intently, nodding occasionally. Finally he patted me on my shoulder and rose to go back to the steering. He said something, which Haleef interpreted back to me.

'He said that you must tell the world about what the Israelis are doing to the Palestinians. He also said "try and get some sleep, it's a long journey".'

I settled down as best I could, on the pile of nets, which smelt strongly of fish. It began to get much colder and I was grateful for the long robe, which I wrapped around me. I did sleep fitfully, but woke every time they changed watch. It was a beautiful starlit night fortunately, and relatively calm.

Around about 5 am the sky began to lighten. We were in the open, with no land in sight. Occasionally a large ship would pass by in the distance, usually tankers heading for one of the oil terminals, but there were also freighters and what looked like small passenger boats.

The sea became rougher and we began to pitch and roll. Fortunately I didn't seem to suffer from seasickness, although I noted that one of the younger crew was throwing up over the side frequently. After a while the sea calmed down again.

Towards the end of the afternoon we saw land in the distance.

'That's Cyprus.' said Haleef.

Faraz came towards me and said something which Haleef interpreted.

'He says that we must keep well outside the national Cypriot limits until it gets dark, then we will go closer in and work our way to the area where we will drop you off.'

So we alternately sailed up and down the coast, keeping in international waters. I was able to see a lot of the coastline, as well as getting a sense of the landscape, which seemed to vary from quite green to very arid. Not so dissimilar from the Israeli/Palestine coast, which I had left. Then we would sometimes just drift. The crew was in a happy mood, having it seemed a welcome break from the hard work of fishing.

Eventually it began to get dark and we started to move cautiously toward the shore. There didn't seem to be any patrol boats cruising up and down, but nevertheless Faraz was being very careful. Again it was a beautiful starlit night with a quarter moon rising.

At 11pm we moved in very close to the shore. Lights twinkled from what looked like a small village.

'That's Salamis,' Haleef said. 'We're going to drop you off a little way along the shore. You should try and find somewhere to sleep. Then in the morning you can walk to Famagusta. There should be a bus from there to Nicosia, where the airport is.

I took off the white robe and the kuffiyeh and handed them to Faraz. I also unwrapped my shoulder bag and handed the shawl to him, 'This belongs to Erina.' He nodded.

I then got out my money and gave him £75 Israeli. It was all that was left of my Israeli money. He seemed very pleased.

He moved in as close as he could to the shallow beach that I could just see in the light from the stars and the quarter moon. When he was nearly in danger of grounding he stopped. I slipped over the side, the water came up to my waist, but there was a slight swell so sometimes it came up to my chest. Haleef handed me my shoulder bag, I balanced it on my head, holding it steady with my left hand, I didn't want my sketchbooks and camera to get wet. I started wading towards the little beach. As it became shallower it was easier to walk. I finally stood clear of the water and turned, Faraz's boat was still there. I waved to them and they all waved back. Slowly the boat backed away, turned and steadily moved away. I watched until it was swallowed up in darkness.

I looked around. So here I was in Cyprus. This was where Simon had spent a year and a half of his military service. It hardly seemed different from the landscape of Palestine.

I made my way along to a small cove where the beach broadened out. My eyes were now accustomed to the light provided by the stars and the quarter moon. I needed to find somewhere to sleep. In a corner of the cove I saw what looked like a small hut, probably used by people changing. I went up to it, the door was shut but when I turned the handle, it opened. I felt for a light switch, but there wasn't one. Leaving the door wide open I managed to see a little inside the hut. There was a long bench of slatted wood in the middle of the room, presumably for people to put their clothes on while they were changing. I put my shoulder bag down on it and went back outside.

I walked down to the water's edge and stood looking out to sea. The sky was still clear and speckled with bright shining stars, the quarter moon was even brighter. I gazed out to sea, somewhere over there was Palestine, I felt a huge sense of relief that here I was, standing safely in another country. There was still more of my journey to make but now that I had escaped the clutches of the Zionists I felt optimistic about the rest of the journey.

I made my way back to the little changing hut. There was the consistent sound of the cicadas, mingled with the susurrus of the gently lapping waves. I used my shoulder bag as a pillow, moving the T-shirts and other soft stuff to rest my head on, taking the camera out and putting it with my sketchbooks and notebooks under the bench. My clothes were wet from wading ashore, so I changed into my remaining dry stuff. I lay down and let my mind wander about the last few days. My farewell to Tami, deeply moving as it was, held the promise of something in the future. My last conversation with Simon had made me confident that he would find his way out via Egypt. How New Horizons had simply shut down, for no apparent reason. I felt again my sadness at the destruction of Hamid's house and the disappearance of the family and most particularly Saba. Gradually I fell into a restless sleep.

Chapter 27

When I woke there were the beginnings of daylight filtering through the door. I stood up, feeling stiff from my hard bed, and made my way down to the water's edge. I looked around, there was no one in sight, and all was quiet. I quickly slipped off my clothes and plunged into the warm sea. I swam out a little way, then, rolled onto my back. The sky was lightening; I wallowed in the warm water then rolled over again. Peering down I could make out shapes, some of them quite long, on the sea floor. I dived down to examine them. I was astonished to see the necks of amphorae jutting out of the sand, I tried pulling one up, but it wouldn't budge. The longer shapes were columns, lying on their sides, their Ionic capitals very evident. I returned to the surface and after recovering my breath made several more dives. It seemed there were parts of a temple lying here under water. Eventually I returned to the shore and sat on the beach, warming myself in the rising sun.

After a while I began to hear more activity from the village, the syncopated sound of a herd of sheep or goats with the bells around their necks, moving along some road nearby. I hastily put on my clothes and repacked my shoulder bag with the camera and sketchbooks and made my way up to the road, just in time to see a herd of sheep and goats disappearing round a corner.

I made my way through the village where there were increasing signs of activity. Women sweeping doorsteps, or hanging bedding out of windows, a bakery with its doors open and the delicious smell of freshly baked bread wafting in the morning air. I had thought that with the recent conflict, as an obviously British person, I would be regarded with resentment, if not downright hostility. This turned out to be quite untrue, various people greeted me with calls of, 'Calle mera', 'Yassou' or 'Tikanis'. All of which I assumed were early morning greetings. So I replied with a conventional 'Good morning' in English, smiling and waving cheerfully, which was reciprocated equally with smiles and waves. I assumed that I was walking in the right direction for Famagusta, although at one point to verify this I pointed along the road to where I was heading, and asked, 'Famagusta?' I was somewhat confused by the response, 'Ney!' which was accompanied by vigorous nodding, I proceeded on, until I came into the outskirts of what I assumed was Famagusta. I found myself near the harbour; there were many signs still in English. One of which seemed to point to something called Othello's Tower. I wondered if this was the real site of Shakespeare's play.

Again I passed a baker's with its concomitant aromas and realised that I was ravenously hungry. I hadn't eaten since the meal Erina had made for me the evening before last. I had no Cypriot money, I looked around for a bank, although it was too early for one to be open. As I was still near the port I found a cambio, which seemed to be the universal term for a money changer, it was just opening. I was concerned about the amount of English money I had left. I wanted to make sure there was enough for my airfare. I rummaged in my pockets and found a £10 Israeli note which I had overlooked when I paid Faraz. I changed that and it gave me sufficient money I hoped, to buy breakfast, and maybe enough for my bus fare to Nicosia. If not I was sure I could hitchhike, my favourite form of travel.

I found a small café where I was able to order a recognisably English breakfast. Plainly after a long occupation by the British there were many traces left. After all Cyprus had only had independence for three years.

Feeling considerably better I decided to explore Famagusta a little. This part was relatively ordinary and modern. There was a nice sandy beach, which stretched for about half a mile. I resisted the temptation to have another swim and wandered further into the town.

There were various bars and small restaurants, also a couple of buildings, which had obviously been clubs in the heyday of the British occupation. They were abandoned now, their signs faded and slipping. One was called 'The Spitfire' another 'The Ambassador'. They had probably been created at the peak of the Second World War, when the island was packed with troops in transit to the battle zones of north Africa.

Further on I saw signs pointing to the 'Old City'. Simon had said very little about Cyprus, but he had mentioned this part of Famagusta, indeed some of the drawings I had seen in the sketchbook he had snatched away from me were of the old city of Famagusta. I was determined to see it before I set off for Nicosia.

It was in fact a walled city, within the environs of Famagusta, and I passed through the arched entryway. It was another world inside. Peopled mainly by figures in Muslim dress, there was a mosque, with its towering minaret. I climbed up onto the perimeter wall, which circumnavigated the city and gave me a good view looking down. I recognised some of the points of view that Simon had sketched. I was tempted to sit and do some drawings of my own, but time was running out and I needed to get to Nicosia and try to get on the next flight to London. I did take some photographs though, to show Simon when we got back.

The old city was not far from the beginning of the road to Nicosia. I decided to try my luck at hitchhiking. I stood on a corner in the shade of a eucalyptus tree. I didn't have to wait long, a car drew up alongside me and a cheerful fair haired young man leant across and opened the passenger door, I climbed in.

'Where you going?'

'Nicosia.'

'I'm only going as far as 4 mile point. I'll drop you off there, then it's a straight road to Nicosia, you shouldn't have much trouble getting another lift.'

He was interested in what I was doing in Cyprus. I said I was only here for a few days, passing through on my way back to England. I told him I had been in Israel and Palestine, recording as much as I could of the establishment of Israel. It seemed harmless to tell him. Fortunately he didn't ask me how I had got here.

I was also interested in what he was doing here in Cyprus, he was obviously British and had the manner of someone who had some authority. So I asked him.

'I'm a Lieutenant in the Army, at 2 Wireless Regiment, or Ayios Nikolaos as it's known locally.'

So I thought, this is Simon's camp I'm about to see. It still exists.

'I'm sorry, I thought Cyprus just won its independence from us, how come we still have British Army here?'

'Yes that's true, but we are still allowed a base here. It comes under what is called 'The British Sovereign Base Area of Dhekelia in Cyprus.' It was agreed in the 'Treaty of Establishment' when Cyprus became independent in 1960. Britain insisted on retaining this military base because of its strategic importance at this end of the Mediterranean.

'Wow, I didn't know all that.'

'Why should you know all that, if you didn't do military service here.'

'I have a friend who did.'

'When?'

'1957 to 1959.'

'I came here in 1959. What's his name?'

'Simon Kennedy, he was attached to the Intelligence Corps and posted to Egypt.'

I was beginning to feel uncomfortable, revealing stuff about Simon.

We were approaching a small roundabout. On either side appeared to be a military camp. He pulled into the side of the road. 'This is where I drop you off, we are at 4 mile point, that's the camp.'

There was a sign proclaiming it was '2 Wireless Regiment, Royal Corps of Signals' to prove it.

He was silent for a moment, then, 'I remember your friend . . . he got into some trouble . . . where is he now?'

This was getting too close.

'I don't know, he dropped out, went to live abroad, searching for his soul I think.'

He was thoughtful again. 'If you do hear from him, tell him to get in touch, I know people who would like to talk to him.'

He held out his hand, my name's Harper, Barry Harper, I'll be based here for at least another year.'

'Christopher,' I said, and shook his hand.'

He leant across and opened the door for me, and I clambered out.

'Don't forget, tell him to get in touch.'

Like hell I thought.

He drove off round the roundabout to the right. A sentry raised a barrier and saluted him as he went by.

I stood for a while, gazing across at the camp. There was a guardroom by the barrier on the left and a nondescript collection of Nissen huts on the right. In the distance was a larger building with another guard at its gate. The whole camp bristled with aerials, some appeared to be at least 80 feet high. Even without the sign this was plainly some sort of 'listening' post. Signals intelligence I remembered Simon saying. It was strange to see the place he had spent most of his time in the army, without him being here. I couldn't wait to tell him when we got back.

Eventually I walked on, beyond the roundabout, and took a position at the side of the road. There was no shade here and I hoped a lift would come soon. After about ten minutes a battered pickup came along, there were some farming implements in the back. The driver opened the door for me, 'Nicosia?'

He shook his head but added, 'Angastina . . . maybe halfway?

Well, as long as it's going in the right direction, why not.

'OK,' I said and clambered in.

He was a big jolly man with a large black moustache, which looked almost as if it had been stuck on; he was a farmer, probably about fifty. His English was quite good and he kept up a garrulous chatter as he drove. He said he was pleased that the war of independence was now over, 'Now we can be friends,' he said. He said that he never supported the killing of British soldiers. He shook his head and said that he had two sons, who wanted to be involved in the war, but he had made it clear to them, that if they did, he would no longer allow them to live in their home.

'Mind you,' he said, 'You made it difficult for us to love you, with all those imprisonments and sending Makarios into exile.'

I thought about what Simon had been involved in.

He chatted on about the new Cyprus government, how he thought it was weak about the farming economy. He talked about his two daughters and their prospects of getting husbands. At one point he more or less asked me if I would be interested in meeting the eldest one, who had just turned eighteen. He told me his name, Andreas, and asked me mine, then insisted on calling me 'Christos'. Surprisingly soon we arrived at where he had to turn off the main road, to go to his village. He asked me again if I'd like to meet his daughters, and I politely refused, saying I had to catch a 'plane, but maybe if I came back again.

I clambered out and he waved as he drove off with a farewell,

'Adio Christos . . . Sto Callo!'

I waved and said 'Goodbye Andreas, and thank you!'

I waited quite a long time for my next lift. Fortunately there was a eucalyptus tree by the road and I was able to stand in its shadow.

Eventually a small green car came along and stopped for me. The driver was a rather dour Scotsman, and at first I thought he was would be rather taciturn, but quite soon he warmed up and talked about what he was doing here. His name, rather unoriginally, was Angus. It appeared that he was an engineer, a water engineer, something I had never heard of. His responsibility was to the British military installations in Cyprus, mainly Dhekelia, which would have also included Simon's camp. He traveled around the various camps, ensuring that their water supply was pure and the systems functioning properly.

He asked me where I was heading and when I said I was on my way to Nicosia airport, as I hoped to get a flight back to London today.

'You're in luck laddie, that's where I'm heading. You know the airport is still a British military base, so you get a choice of international airlines or Vulcan bombers.'

Angus chuckled, he obviously found it rather amusing.

'It's Monday, I think BEA have a flight at 4.30, nonstop to London, should get you there about 6.30, given the time difference. It's not usually crowded.'

I thought about what Simon had told me. How the RAF would send a Vampire jet across the Black Sea to tease the Russians and get them to light up their radar systems, so they could DF them. This was a term for direction finding, it enabled the listeners to focus up on it from two points, thus finding its exact location.

I looked at my watch, it was about 12.15 so I had plenty of time. We came into the outskirts of Nicosia. I was quite taken by the random style of the architecture, no building was like another. There were also no buildings more than three stories high. We reached what seemed like a central point. There was one quite large building, which had obviously been burned some time before. It was derelict and the roof was gone. Looking up through the first floor windows I could see the sky. No attempt had been made to repair it. Angus noticed that I was staring at it.

'Aye, that was the British Institute, it was burned back in 1955, one of the first casualties of the war of independence. Nothing has been done about it, it's a monument to their rejection of British culture.'

'British Institute? What did it do?'

'Oh it had a good lending library, a place for exhibitions of art, a small concert hall and a large collection of records, all destroyed. They had fun burning the books and smashing the records, as well as setting fire to the building. I think they regretted it afterwards.'

We drove further on and at one point he pointed to a road, which headed north from the centre.

'See that road, it's Ledra Street, goes all the way to the Kyrenee Gate, then heads for Kyrenia. During the troubles, it became known as 'Murder Mile'. Many British soldiers were shot in the back regularly as they walked down there. Nice don't you think?'

It seemed to me that he was rather bitter about the Cypriots at that time.

'Well that's the end of your short tour of the trouble spots of Nicosia! Let's head for the airport.'

He lapsed into taciturn silence until we got to the airport. Just before he dropped me off he said.

'A son of one of my friends was shot in Ledra Street, it always puts me in a bad mood when I pass by. He was a lovely boy.'

He drew up outside a large Nissen hut,

'Anyway, here we are at beautiful Lakatamia airport.'

I gazed at the Nissen hut with astonishment. Up to now my only experience of airports were London's Heathrow, Paris's Orly and Tel Aviv's Lod airports. They were probably not the most sophisticated airports in the world but . . . a Nissen hut!

'What's this?'

Angus laughed, 'Yes, a bit primitive, what you must realise is that this has been primarily used for military purposes. It's only had a civilian usage in the last two or three years.'

He pointed up the road, where there was a busy building site. 'That's going to be the new terminal in a couple of years. Until then, this is it. You'll be OK, all the civilian airlines have desks in there.'

He held out his hand. 'Have a nice journey, nice to meet you.' He shook my hand.

I clambered out and with a wave he drove off.

I went into the large Nissen hut, it seemed to contain desks for half a dozen airlines. I spotted one that said BEA. There was a young woman in a stewardess uniform doing something behind the desk. She looked up as I approached.

'Sorry, you're too early for check-in.'

'Well actually I wanted to find out if I could purchase a ticket for the next flight to London.'

She frowned, 'Usually people purchase their tickets at the office in Nicosia.'

'I didn't know that, I'm just passing through. I wondered if I could do it here?'

She frowned again, 'I don't deal with that side, you may have to go back to Nicosia.'

'Oh lord, I'm a bit short of money, I had hoped that there was somewhere here.'

She looked at me, her manner softened, 'Let me enquire.'

She picked up the 'phone and dialed a number. 'I've got someone here, who wants to purchase a ticket . . . yes I know, I told him that . . . well he's a bit short of money . . . just about got enough for the flight' she looked at me enquiringly, I nodded. 'If he has to go back to Nicosia . . . '

There was a pause, then 'OK thanks, I'll send him over.'

'Well you're in luck, there's someone here who's authorised to sell you a ticket, this is where you go.'

She proceeded to direct me to an office building nearby.

I thanked her profusely and she managed to produce quite an attractive smile.

'See you later at check-in.'

I made my way to the office, which was quite nearby. It was in a plain brick building, three stories high, and the office was on the top floor. It was now the hottest time of the day, and I panted my way up the stairs. When I reached the top floor I saw there were three offices there, the third door, the furthest, was marked BEA, underneath in smaller letters, it also said Cypriot Airline. I knocked on the door.

'Come.'

I went in, there were two desks, one had a sign saying BEA the other Cypriot Airlines, and both had women behind the desks. There was also a man bending over the BEA desk, pointing something out to the woman, He was a thin, rather officious looking man with balding hair and a small moustache.

He looked up as I came through the door.

'Yes?'

'Umm . . . I want to buy a ticket.'

'Oh yes, you're the man who didn't get a ticket in Nicosia.'

'Yes I'm afraid so, I didn't know . . . I thought I could get it here.'

He scowled, 'Well don't do it again. He turned to the woman, 'Make him out a ticket.' He turned to me, 'Single?'

'Yes I'm on my own.'

He made an impatient noise, 'I mean, you don't want a return do you?'

'No, I don't want a return.'

What's with these people, they're always scowling and grumping. What happened to customer service?'

The woman made out the ticket and I waited with bated breath for how much it was.

'That'll be £45.'

I heaved a sigh of relief, I just had enough, with £5 left. I fished in my bag for the money. He eyed it with distaste.

'Don't you have a cheque?'

'No, sorry.'

He made more disagreeable noises, then reluctantly took the cash.

I was just able to say 'Thank you.' Then I left, clutching my ticket.

I went back to the big Nissen hut. Miss charm school was nowhere in sight. I looked at my watch, it was 2.15. I also checked the departure board. The flight was scheduled to leave at 4.30, Angus was right. I looked around for somewhere to sit and wait. Down the end there seemed to be a waiting area, with what looked like a small bar.

I made my way down there and sat down. I wondered if I might use a little of my £5 to buy myself a drink. There was a man behind the bar, putting out bottles and glasses. I went up to the bar, 'Are you open?'

'Nearly there mate, give me a few minutes, just finishing up. What would you like?'

'Do you have a light ale?'

'Pint or half?'

'Half will do, maybe I'll have the other half later.'

'Right you are, I'll bring it over.'

It was really nice to have someone cheerful, after my experience with the airline staff.

I sat down again, by the window. Looking out I had an uninterrupted view across the airport. There were various commercial airline 'planes, I saw BEA and Cypriot Airlines nearby.

Further away I saw three Vampire jets parked in a neat row. In the far distance there brooded a Vulcan bomber. It was attended by a group of what I assumed were mechanics. There was something very sinister about it. I thought of the fact that it carried nuclear warheads.

The cheerful bartender arrived with my half of light ale.

'Admiring the view?'

'Yes I was just wondering about the Vulcan bomber and what it carries.'

'Yes they're not usually here, they're normally stationed at RAF Akrotiri. This one developed some mechanical fault and had to land here. They're working on it.'

Yet another English person still here, which intrigued me.

'Did you come from England to work here?'

'No I was in the services here and I married a Cypriot girl, so I'm here to stay.'

'That couldn't have been easy when the troubles were on.'

'Yeah well, I wasn't in an infantry regiment, so nobody asked me to shoot anyone. I was a clerk in an office. It was harder for my wife, but it's all fine now.'

He went back behind the bar.

I was at a loss, I hadn't anything to read. I didn't think I should do any drawing out the window, I was sure they wouldn't like it.

There was a sort of coffee table in the middle, with some magazines scattered around. I went over to it. There were three Greek magazines, a couple of French magazines, an Italian magazine, and two English magazines.

I picked them up. One was 'Horse and Hounds' another was 'House and Garden.'

I looked at the dates. 'House and Garden' was dated June 1959. 'Horse and Hounds' was dated 1956.

Great I thought, just what I wanted.'

I took the Italian magazine, it was a fashion publication, and at least it had some beautiful women in it. Browsing through it I suddenly thought of Tami and I experienced a terrible longing for her. I felt the pain of our parting, both of us expressing a determination that we would meet again. Our last, clutching, love making. There was so much happening there: Israel was revealing it's more expansionist mode, the Palestinians were showing more signs of unrest, there was a new generation coming. I thought of Saba saying that she would shoot Israelis when she grew up, and Tami's young brother, who seemed to think it natural to shoot Arabs. There was war coming.

I supposed in time I wouldn't care so much, but now I felt it like a physical pain.

My thoughts were interrupted by an announcement,

'Will passengers for BEA flight number 128 proceed to immigration.'

I checked my ticket to see if it was my flight, it was. I got up and asked the guy behind the bar where immigration was.

'Customs and immigration are in the next hut.'

I made my way there, one man sat in a glass booth, he beckoned me forward. I went to the desk with some trepidation. He looked through the pages.

'You don't have an arrival stamp?'

'I came on a private motor yacht from Haifa. When we got to Famagusta an immigration man came on board and checked the crew's passports, then just waved us on. He must have thought I was one of the crew, they do a regular trip to and from Haifa, so I suppose he was used to them. They just offered me a lift from Haifa. I didn't think about a stamp.'

He muttered something in Greek, then for my benefit he said in English, 'They're lazy down there, he should have stamped all their passports even if they are there for one day.'

He said something else in Greek, which I assumed was not very complimentary about the Famagusta immigration staff, then stamped my passport and waved me on.

I heaved a sigh of relief and went through to the customs area. They also simply waved me on, it was obvious that they were only interested in incoming passengers.

I got to the departure area and I was surprised to see there was a large number of passengers already there. I supposed that they were seasoned travellers who bought their tickets beforehand and knew to go to the departure area when they arrived.

I found a seat near the window. I looked at my watch and was surprised to see it was already 3.15. I looked around for something to read. There didn't seem to be any magazines. The man opposite me had a newspaper on the seat beside him.

'Excuse me, have you finished with that paper?'

'Not really, but if you'd like to read it until we take off you're welcome. It is a couple of days old though.' He passed it to me and I thanked him.

I was surprised to see that it was the Manchester Guardian, I didn't think what I regarded as a minor broadsheet would have got as far as Cyprus.

I'm not much of a newspaper reader normally, but I was thirsty for the news. I looked for domestic information at first. There was plenty of news. The Beatles had come out with their second single, 'Please, please me'. Profumo had resigned after it was revealed that he had an affair with Christine Keeler. A gang of train robbers had held up a mail train and robbed it of two million pounds. It was officially revealed that the winter of 1962/63 was the coldest on record. Harold Philby had been confirmed as the third man.

Moving on to foreign news, John Kennedy, President of the United States made a speech in beleaguered Berlin, saying 'Ich bin eine Berliner'. Martin Luther King had been arrested in the United States. There was more trouble between the Israelis and the Palestinians. Some people had been killed by the Israelis. Jomo Kenyatta had been confirmed as prime minister of Kenya.

I was so absorbed by reading this paper that I missed the call to board the aircraft, it was only when the man asked for his paper back that I realised. In spite of this I managed to be one of the first on board, and quickly found myself a window seat on the right hand side. I forgot to enquire what make of 'plane this was. It was definitely a sleek new jet. I wondered if it was an American Boeing. Other passengers came aboard, I hoped that a couple would not occupy the two other seats. Eventually a young dark haired woman paused by the row.

'Is someone sitting here? She indicated the aisle seat.

'No, no . . . please take it.'

She put her bag in the overhead locker. I was still clutching mine, almost as if I feared someone would snatch it away.

'Do you want me to put your bag in the locker as well?'

The young woman was smiling at me as she asked.

'No thank you . . . I need it with me as I have some things to write.'

The 'plane gradually filled, but there were still some empty seats. Fortunately no one asked to take the middle seat. The doors shut and one of the hostesses demonstrated the safety routine. I put my bag on the floor by my leg. The whining sound of the engine startup began. The plane began to taxi to the end of the runway, where we sat for several minutes. Then the engine note increased until the whole 'plane trembled. Suddenly we began to move forward, rapidly increasing speed, the airport buildings flashed past us, the moment came when I felt sure that it was not going to make it. Suddenly the rumbling of the undercarriage reached a crescendo then ceased, and we were flying. Up into the bright blue sky, there were no clouds at all. Gradually the whole island appeared, as we circled before heading west. I remembered how I saw the island first, en route to Israel. That seemed a long time ago, although it was only a few weeks. So much had happened in that time.

When the seatbelt sign was switched off I got up my bag and took out my notebook and the main sketchbook. I pulled down the little table on the back of the seat in front of me. It was really only big enough for the notebook. I placed the sketchbook on the empty seat beside me. The young woman had already placed a neatly folded light jacket on her side of the seat. I asked her if it was OK if I put my sketchbook there.

'Of course.'

I began to go through my notes. I had not added anything since Simon had said that it was time to leave, Mossad were on to us. I set about bringing them up to date. I began with the last meeting with Simon and his urgent warning that we should get out while we could. He was going to drive back to Gaza and get out via Egypt. I went to see Hamid, and the shock of what I found. My meeting with Tami and our last, passionate love making. Then that early morning drive to Haifa and finding that the motor yacht had sailed. Getting to Acre and the wait for three days before the hazardous journey to Cyprus, the landing near Salamis, swimming in the dawn light and seeing the remains of the city on the bed of the sea floor. The journey hitchhiking, the lieutenant who remembered Simon and wanted to know his whereabouts, the friendliness of Andreas, my next lift, until finally the last one, with Angus. Now I was sitting on the 'plane having survived the hazard of the immigration process.

All this took some time before I shut my notebook. I sat back as the stewardess came along with a drinks trolley and I asked for some white wine. The young woman did the same.

'This is the best part of flying,' she said and raised her glass to me.

'Yes, that and coming up through clouds to the sunny uplands.'

'That's nice . . . are you a writer?'

'No, no . . . I'm an artist . . . a painter.'

'Oh . . . you were so busy writing I thought you were a writer.'

'No, I was just getting my travel notes up to date.'

'May I look at your sketchbook?'

I hesitated, I didn't know this woman and I was not certain I wanted anyone new looking at it, I was nearly home and I didn't want to raise anyone's curiosity.

She saw my hesitation, 'I'm sorry, it's rude of me to ask, I am fascinated though by anyone who can draw and paint, I'm so unable to do it myself.'

It seemed churlish to refuse her, 'OK, they are just sketches though, some are unfinished, I'll be working on them and using them as a source for paintings.'

She picked it up and opened it, and became immediately absorbed in each page. I sipped my wine, resting my head against the window. We must have passed Athens and were crossing the toe of Italy. I could just see Sicily to the south.

'These are wonderful.' She finally said, 'Where were you?'

'Israel.'

'Why did you go there?'

I didn't want to tell her the whole thing about New Horizons.

'I was just curious, and I had the opportunity to go there during the long summer vacation.'

'Are you at university?'

'Royal College.'

'You must be very talented.'

I shook my head, 'Not really.'

'I'd love to read your journal.'

'Sorry, it's private.'

I was getting tired of this conversation, I really felt like going to sleep, not having had much the last two nights. On the other hand I didn't want to miss the meal, as I was still hungry. Fortunately she decided to go to the loo before the meal trolley arrived, and got up and headed to one of the ones at the back of the 'plane.

I decided to appear to be asleep when she came back, intending to wake up when the trolley arrived. I shut my eyes and leant against the side of the seat.

Next thing I knew was that someone was nudging me.

'Wake up sir, we're coming in to land.'

It was the stewardess. 'Please straighten your seat and fasten your seat belt.'

I looked across at my companion.

'I missed the meal.'

'Yes, you were fast asleep when I came back, I didn't like to disturb you.'

I looked on the seat between us, my bag wasn't there!

'Where's my bag?'

'Oh I put up in the overhead locker, the stewardess wanted to take it.'

Shit! I thought, I hope she hasn't been reading my notes. I looked out the window and saw the outskirts of London coming into view. A great sense of relief swept over me. At last I was back. I watched, as each suburb unraveled below me, then the Thames, winding its way west, passing over what I assumed was Richmond Park. The 'plane reducing height until we seemed to be brushing the rooftops, crossing a main road the runway came into view, we seemed to hover over it then with a slight bump we touched down. The flaps came down and the brakes were applied as we rushed past buildings and parked aircraft. Until at last we slowed to what seemed like a walking pace and turned off the main runway, heading for a parking bay, a man with what looked like large table tennis bats guided us to a standstill. The seat belt light went off and people rose to their feet, grappling for hand luggage in the overhead lockers. The young woman got up and handed me down my bag, before retrieving hers.

'I have a confession to make, I did take a peek at your notes . . . I thought they were very interesting and rather sad in the end, it's a love story really.'

Before I could say anything she joined the queue of people exiting, I tried to catch up with her but I couldn't get past the other people. When I reached the exit and started down the steps I saw her at the bottom, talking to a man. Before I reached the bottom she got into a car, which was parked nearby, and they drove off.

I got on the bus and sat down. I looked inside my bag, everything seemed to be there. I was quietly furious that she had the temerity to read my notes, also I realised I had not asked her name or what she was doing in Cyprus. Why was she picked up as soon as she got off the 'plane and driven off with that man? There was something odd about all that. I was still infected by Simon's paranoia about the security services.

We arrived at the terminal building and I joined the crowd entering. I looked around everywhere to see if I could spot her, but there was no sign of her.

I went through immigration without trouble, just a cursory glance at my British passport. There was no luggage to collect so I went straight to customs, where, seeing that I only had a shoulder bag, they just waved me through. With relief I exited on to the main concourse and made my way to the bus which would take me to the London terminal.

Travelling up to west London through the suburbs of Hounslow and Isleworth I felt euphoric that I had managed to get back without being arrested and imprisoned, either by the Israelis or in Cyprus.

When we arrived at the terminal building on the Cromwell Road I made my way to South Kensington and caught a bus to Clapham and my flat.

Chapter 28

After I had put my bag down, I went to the bathroom and ran a bath. I looked in the mirror. What a sight I was! Three days' growth of beard, my unwashed hair sticking up all over the place, and the long red scar with stitch marks along the left side of my face. As well as all this I looked gaunt and drawn. Dear God, what was my mother going to think?

Before I did anything else I climbed into the bath and lay there wallowing gratefully in the hot water. For the moment I no longer wanted to think about anything except the fact that I was back, and hopefully I would be seeing Simon soon, when we could compare our notes and presumably devise a plan of action.

After about twenty minutes, when I was in danger of falling asleep, I washed my hair then got out. After drying myself I examined my body, and was relieved to see that nearly all the bruising on my left side had faded. I then shaved carefully. Finally I looked reasonably presentable, though even thinner than I usually was. I knew I wouldn't fool my mother though. I must call her.

I found some change which I had left in a drawer, especially for 'phone calls, and went out to the nearby 'phone box.

My mother picked up immediately, 'Hello.'

'Hi mother, it's me, I'm back.'

There was a gasp, then, 'Oh thank God! I've been so worried . . . when are you coming down, or shall we come up?'

'No, it's OK, I just need to get myself together up here, then I'll come down on Friday, the day after tomorrow.'

'When did you get back?'

'I've just arrived, had a quick bath and came out to call you.'

'You must be exhausted.'

'No, it's all right, I slept on the 'plane. I'll call you Friday morning and tell you which train I'm on.'

'I'll meet you.'

'You don't need to mother, I'm quite grown up now. I'll get the bus from the station.'

'Are you sure?'

'Yes mother.'

'Call me collect on Friday morning, I can't wait to see you.'

I went back to the flat. It was now about 8.30 in the evening. If I wanted to get anything to eat I'd better go now. The nearby café usually shut at 10pm.

I hurried out, taking my notebook with me. The café was still open and I ordered fish and chips and a cup of strong tea. While I was eating I read my notebook. It was quite comprehensive, I wondered how it would compare with Simon's. There were a few small details I remembered, which I would insert. Also I wanted to add the final bit about the young woman on the 'plane. I had a second cup of tea, so nice after nothing but coffee and wine. Then I made my way back to the flat.

I must have been exhausted, I slept until nearly 9 o'clock in the morning. I lay for a while thinking about what I needed to do that day. I'd go first to the College and see if Andy was there and give him back his camera with many thanks. I needed to process the films. In the evening I would go to the theatre and tell them I was back and that I could relieve Andy on the coming Monday. Sometime during the day I would call Sylvia and tell her I was back. I slightly dreaded this, as I could not ignore her growing dependence on me. I was aching inside about Tami and didn't know how I could tell Sylvia about her.

I got up and went into the kitchen. I still looked a mess in the mirror, although a distinct improvement on what I had looked like when I got back. I shaved again, washed myself all over and got dressed. I left my notebooks and sketchbook in the flat, emptied the camera and put all the films in my shoulder bag. I then went and took the bus to South Kensington.

I think I was still in a state about my last few days. It had been such a blur: the sudden exit from Israel, my last time with Tami, the journey to Cyprus with the fishing boat. As I traveled up through London, crossing the river and eventually into South Kensington, I reflected that the previous day I had looked down on the river from way up there in the sky, just anxious to be back. I still was, but also there was still part of me back in Israel. That would pass, I supposed.

When I got to South Kensington I made my way to the underpass and came up opposite the entrance to the Royal College. It was all still there, unchanged, I would soon be back, unchanged . . . or would I?

I went into the College and made my way up until I was in the studio we used. There was no sign of Andy. I looked at my painting that I had been working on when I left. Somehow I was not keen to finish it. I wandered down to the desk where we usually checked in, there was no sign of Andy.

I left and went down to South Kensington and had a coffee in one of the coffee bar places. Should I call Sylvia? Maybe not until later in the afternoon, I would tell her that I was going down to see my parents and I would be back on Monday.

I took my films to a place that would process them. The facility at the College was not open and anyway I wanted them processed by a professional, I was afraid I might screw them up. They said they would have them by Monday. I decided not to go to the theatre until Monday. I thought of calling Paris, and talking to Claudine, I was pretty sure that Simon was coming to London first though. In the end I didn't, somehow I had become rather lost, I think I just needed to have some time out for a few days.

There was still some money in my savings account and I drew out enough to pay my train fare and give myself enough for a week. I walked down by the river, it always seemed rather peaceful there.

I had something to eat at one of the cafés on the Kings Road. It was called the Picasso and had been there for some years. Quite what it had to do with Picasso I was not quite sure, but it had a number of reproductions of nineteenth- and early twentieth-century French painters, including Picasso. Maybe Picasso came here when he visited London recently. I liked it anyway.

Eventually I went back to my flat and about 7pm I decided to call Sylvia. The person who answered the 'phone was a woman and I assumed it was Sylvia's mother, she had a foreign accent, though not as strong as her fathers.

'I wondered if I might speak to Sylvia.'

'Who is it?'

'Christopher, I'm just back from Israel.'

'Oh that's so good, she has not been well but I'm sure this will cheer her up.'

She went off to call her. There was a pause then I heard Sylvia.'

'Christopher . . . oh it's so good to hear you . . . so good . . . will you come and see me?'

'Yes Sylvia, but I must go and see my parents tomorrow, but I'll be back and can see you on Monday.'

'Oh yes, come and see me Monday . . . as early as you can. Are you alright?'

'Yes I'm fine, what about you?'

'I'm so glad you are back.'

I decided that I would tell her on Monday about the accident. We talked some more, then I left her saying I was very tired and I would see her on Monday.

I went back to my flat. The people who owned the flat were pleased to see me and we had some conversation about the trip. Then I went down to the basement and got out my notes again and began to add the extra pieces I remembered. Soon, though, I was back there again, wondering about Tami. I found a music programme on the radio and listened to a Brahms symphony. I went to bed quite early and slept through until 7am.

I called my mother about 10am and told her I was getting the 12.30 train to Bournemouth. I packed a few things in my now rather battered shoulder bag, including the sketchbooks and notebook. The journey, although the same as always, suddenly made me aware of the colour in England. I suppose because I grew up here I had taken the colour for granted, but now, having taken that time in Israel and in Cyprus I was aware of the difference. Those countries seemed to have a much narrower range of colours, whereas here there were so many more.

My mother didn't meet me and I took the bus. When I arrived at the front door my mother seemed to be already there waiting. She put her arms round me immediately, I was astonished at her response, we were not a very emotive family and this seemed surprising. I put the bags down and faced her as we walked to the kitchen. She took in my damaged face and rather thin look with shock.

'Oh my God, what has happened to you?'

'It's nothing really, I just had a crash on my scooter, it's already nearly cleared up.'

'Oh it's terrible, were you with Simon?'

'No we weren't together, he was in another part of Israel.'

'Oh when we heard about him I thought you might have been together!'

'What did you hear?'

She looked at me, I saw something in her face, suddenly I knew I was going to hear some terrible news.'

'He's dead Christopher . . . I thought you knew.'

We were in the kitchen, I sat down on the nearest chair. My mother looked at me with shock, realising that she had told me something which was the worst thing I could bear. She made a move towards me and without meaning to I brushed her away.

'I'm sorry. I just don't understand . . . I spoke to him five days ago. How did you hear?'

'His mother called, I was so afraid you were with him. I'm so sorry I didn't realize . . . '

Although Simon and I had discussed the possibility of danger to ourselves, somehow we never thought anything could happen. I was completely shocked.'What happened?'

'According to the Israelis he was killed in a car crash.'

He must have been on his way back to Gaza, after his meeting with me.

My mother made some tea, always a help she felt when one needed it.

'Tell me what you two were doing there.'

'It's complicated, I will tell you, but not right now. I'm going to my room, here's one of my sketchbooks for you to look at. I won't be long.'

I took my shoulder bag upstairs with me, leaving her looking through my sketchbook. I was terribly shaken by what I had heard, I needed a few minutes by myself. Everything was changed now, I needed to think about what I should do next. The loss of Simon was something I would have to bear always. I wondered what had happened to all his notes.

When I came downstairs my mother was still looking through my sketchbook.

'These are wonderful . . . what about some of these where you've just done short sketches.'

'I took a lot of photographs, I can work them up using some of them. Do you have Simon's mother's phone number, I must call her.'

She found the number for me and I went out in the hallway to call.

There was no one on the 'phone from next door.

I called his home number, after a moment or two she picked up the 'phone.

'Mrs. Kennedy, this is Christopher.'

There was a pause, then she said, 'Oh, I'm so glad you are back . . . your mother was so worried about you.'

'I've just arrived back . . . I have only just heard from my mother about Simon . . . I'm distraught.'

There was another pause, then, 'Maybe we could meet again and you could tell me about what you two were doing there.'

This was something I knew I had to do, but I dreaded it. 'Yes of course, I'm only down here until Sunday though.'

'Shall we meet tomorrow at 11am, the same café we met before.'

'Yes . . . yes that's fine.'

'I'll see you then.' Then she rang off. I stood there still holding the 'phone. Again I heard the sound as if someone was listening, but when I said that I was on the 'phone, there was no reply.

I went back to my room and took out my notebook. Although I had been concerned about the contents during my travels, I was apparently back safely in England. It was absurd to think of my parents betraying me but I felt that I needed to explain to them what we were doing there. Also I needed to talk about Tami and what had happened between us.

The news about Simon was so hard, I didn't know how I could manage. I needed time to think about it.

I heard my father come in downstairs. I waited a while to let my mother explain to him about how she had told me about Simon, and how I didn't know. I knew that I must go down and face them again.

My father was very good, he just said, 'I'm so pleased to see you back, and so sorry about Simon.' He put his arms around me. Again I was astonished by the familiarity of the gesture.

My mother made more tea and produced one of her cakes and we went into the living room.

I began to explain to them what Simon and I had been doing in Israel, how we had become concerned about the way the Israelis were behaving towards the Palestinians.

They found all this difficult, they still had the mind that the Israelis were being unnecessarily attacked by these 'terrorists'. I had to show them some of my notes about the way they had been treated. Even then they were still in doubts about what we had been doing.

Eventually I explained about my feelings for Tami. My mother was immediately interested.

'Will she becoming here?'

'I don't know.'

'Will you go back there then?'

I shook my head. 'It's difficult.'

I then had to explain about Simon telling me that that Mossad were after us, and we had to get out.

This really shocked my parents, the idea that their son was involved in some sort of dangerous activity in another country really disturbed them.

I was beginning to feel that I'd not been wise in giving my parents so much information, somehow I had involved them in it.

I decided to make it as light as possible.

'It's nothing really, he may have been wrong, they just don't want people prying around, I expect they just wanted to talk to us. Anyway, I had made friends with people who crewed an expensive yacht, owned by a man who lived in Cyprus, but did a lot of business in Israel, they took me across to Cyprus, and I came back that way.' I did not tell them about my hazardous journey on the fishing boat.

'Goodness you've done a lot of traveling.' For my mother, who had only been to Paris for a weekend, this was a lot of traveling.

Later, before supper, my father and I took a walk. We didn't go far, there was a pub about half a mile away and we decided to have a drink. My father very seldom drank, other than Christmas or some celebration. We sat together in a corner. I asked if they had any wine, the pub owner looked at me askance, sherry he suggested? I settled for a half of bitter and a scotch for my father.

'This business you and Simon were interested in, is it serious?'

'No, it was us looking for a cause I suppose. Don't worry about it.'

'Somehow I don't quite believe you.'

'Maybe it would be a good idea if you and mother didn't talk about it. We'll let it rest.'

My father's not stupid, he knew that I felt it was serious.

'I'll leave it to you, but take care of yourself though.'

I asked him about himself.

'It's good, the medication is working, and I just have to watch my diet and exercise.'

We went back home and had supper. Afterwards I sat with them and watched television for a while, then declaring myself still tired from my journey, I went to my room. I couldn't get to sleep, I read my notebooks again, taking myself back into Israel and my feelings about Tami. Eventually I went to sleep.

The next day I was up early and after breakfast I went down to the shed at the bottom of the garden. The documents were still there. I made a note of the address they were supposed to be sent to.

I went into town to be at the café in time to meet Simon's mother. This time I was there early and was already seated at a table when she arrived. I stood up and greeted her. She took one look at my scarred face and immediately asked how I was injured, I explained it to her, she listened intently.

'But you weren't with Simon.'

'No, Simon was mainly in Gaza, but we met up frequently.'

'So what were you doing there?'

'I was there with an arts club in Tel Aviv, called New Horizons, something which Simon organised for me. The idea was that I would travel around Israel doing drawings and photographs in order to produce an exhibition of work for them, showing how they were progressing as a new country.'

'And Simon was with Palestine Aid?'

'Yes.'

'When did you last see him?'

'I think it must have been the day he died. We had a meeting and agreed to meet up here or in Paris when we got back, Simon was going to leave via Egypt. I flew back via Cyprus.'

'Why Egypt?'

'Gaza was occupied by the Egyptians and it seemed easier for Simon to come through there.'

She sat for a while thinking about what I had told her. Somehow she was trying to come to terms with Simon's death.'

'Do you think he was killed deliberately?'

This question threw me entirely, the last thing I expected was her to doubt what we were doing there.

'Why do you say that?'

She looked at me quizzically.

'Christopher . . . you were Simon's friend, you knew how he was, how much he cared about people, he always needed a cause . . . I'm sure he and you were there, pursuing a cause.'

I must have looked embarrassed.

'Come on Christopher, what were you both doing?'

'Yes I suppose we were endeavouring to reveal something we felt was very wrong.' I had finally revealed it. In truth though I had not thought that he had been assassinated. This was a new idea, and perhaps she was right.

She looked at me for a moment, then reached out her hand and touched me.

'I'm sorry . . . your friend and my son are dead.'

Her eyes filled with tears and she bowed her head. 'I'm just so sad . . . forgive me.'

I suppose I had been close to how she was now, but not let it happen. Now I felt that I too was close to tears.

After a few moments she brought herself together.

'What will you do with what you have found out?'

'Simon had some ideas about trying to get it published.'

'Where is his material?'

'What he has done in Israel must still be there, the Israelis must have it.'

I was unsure about telling her about his original stuff, which was to do with Cyprus and Egypt. Somehow that was a different matter.

'Did you manage to get a lot of material information?.'

'Yes, I kept a very careful journal, and have brought back a lot of drawings and photographs.'

'What was Simon's idea about distributing it?'

'He had read a writer who did work for the Manchester Guardian.'

'Ah, I wondered why he read that paper, will you send your material to him?'

'Yes, I think so, I don't know anyone else.' I thought of telling her about Simon's time in Cyprus and Egypt. She had been very concerned about him the last time we met.

'You know the last time we met you told me about your concern for Simon after he came out of the army?'

'Yes.'

'Well some time later Simon told me about his time in Cyprus. He gave me his notes for that, which I am going to send as well.'

'I'd like to read them.'

'It shows why he was so upset. I am concerned that no one sees them except the writer he wants to have them, at the newspaper.'

'I would still like to see them.'

'People have been trying to find them.'

I told her about the burglary, also the one at June's. She was shocked about this.

'I see why you want to be so careful.'

'I'm going back to London on Sunday evening.'

'Well when you come back down, I'd like to see them before they go to the writer.'

'Yes I think you should read it.'

'Please keep in touch with me, I'll do anything to help.'

I was very impressed by her desire to help, it was not that my parents were against me, it was more that they didn't feel the way that I did, but Simon's mother was completely committed to helping.

She looked at me, as she had when she asked me to look after Simon.

'He was my son, I'll help you in every way I can.'

Once again she insisted on paying. As we said goodbye she held my hand for a moment.

'Take care of yourself.'

I decided to walk down to the sea before I went home. It wasn't raining, but there were a lot of clouds about. I stood and gazed out to sea. So different here than Jaffa, the sea was grey and waves were forming up and plowing towards the shore. In spite of this I thought of Tami and standing by the shore with her.

I walked through the pleasure gardens to get my bus back home. I hadn't used my scooter, preferring to travel on the bus and look out the window.

We had lunch together, and my parents asked how Mrs. Kennedy was. I explained that she wanted to hear from me about my time in Israel with Simon.

'I must call her.' My mother said, as we were finishing up and I was helping my mother with the dishes. She suddenly said, 'I know what I meant to tell you, June is having a baby.'

Apparently June had called when the news about Simon had come out, the local paper had printed a small article about it. She was concerned about me, somehow she knew that I was in Israel with him.

'I'm afraid I was a bit anxious about you when I spoke to her, maybe you could call her.'

Having a baby I thought, that could have been me, I was relieved that I'd avoided that.

After lunch I went for a walk, up to where the water mill was. I stood on the bridge and looked down at the water. There was a fish struggling to get up through the cascade, as I had seen before, maybe it was the same fish. Gazing down into the water was almost hypnotic, my mind drifted to my last meeting with Simon, and suddenly I began to cry, I cried so hard that if anyone had come by they would have thought I was in pain. Fortunately there was no one else around. Eventually I pulled myself together. I supposed it was always going to happen, and in a way it helped to relieve me of the tragedy.

I crossed over the bridge and went to walk in the fields, finding my way gradually to the woods. There was a large old house there, which had once been a minor stately home, it had now been turned into an agricultural college. I gazed at the windows. Some years before I had a girlfriend who lived with her parents in a converted Nissen hut near here. The local council were doing their best to build accommodation after the war, and had temporarily housed people in these. I had frequently gone out there to visit and sometimes walked this way at night on my way back home. The house had been deserted then and I would see the windows and imagine there were ghosts looking out at me. Now it all looked to be what it was, an agricultural college.

When I got back home I decided to call June. My mother had her new number.

This time there was someone calling from next door, so I had to wait for about half an hour. I was hoping that June would answer, I had never met her husband and felt that he may not be pleased that a previous boyfriend was calling. I was fortunate, June did answer.

'June, it's Christopher.'

'Oh good, thank goodness you are back, your mother was so worried about you.'

'Yes, I'm so shocked about Simon.'

'Do you want to talk about it?'

'Maybe in a while.'

'Are you going back to London?'

'Yes I'm going tomorrow afternoon.'

'When will you be down again?'

'In a couple of weeks.'

'If you can come on a weekday we could meet. Did your mother tell you? I'm going to have a baby.'

'Yes she did, I'm so pleased for you.'

'Thank you.'

'Let me call you when I'm coming, I'd like to see you pregnant.'

'I'm getting fat.'

We talked some more then, promising to call her when I was next down we hung up. I could tell that having a baby was somehow changing her. She was pleased to hear from me, but she didn't need me anymore. That was a relief.

On the Sunday I did my early morning tea for my parents and helped about the house. I was concerned about my notes and wondered whether I should take them back to London. In the end I decided to photograph every page, then leave the originals down here, hidden with the others. When I got back to London I would have them all printed out and go through them there.

I set off later in the afternoon on Sunday. My father had kept my scooter clean, in fact he'd bought a cover for it. I promised that I would drive carefully and waved goodbye.

Chapter 29

I got back to London quite quickly and after calling my parents to tell them that I was alright, I settled down to start working out the paintings I wanted to do based on my set sketches. The question was whether to do them as literal paintings, or make use of the idea that Tami had, which was to produce an amalgam of images, showing the growth of Israel and the destruction of Palestine. There were some images that I wanted to do literally, like the destruction of Abu Shushar. I worked out a progression of eight paintings, this would keep me occupied for some time, and I would think up others along the way. Quite a lot to do, but I looked forward to it. I listened to some more music then went to bed. I must buy some food tomorrow.

About 10am the next day I called Sylvia. She must have been near the 'phone as she picked up immediately.

'It's me.'

'Oh good, are you coming to see me?'

'Yes Sylvia, I'll see you in about an hour.'

'Great, I'll be here.'

'Sylvia, I had a little accident while I was there, nothing serious, just a small scar on my face.'

'But you are all right otherwise.'

'Yes, I'm fine.'

'Come as soon as you can.'

I gathered up my set sketches and set off for Sylvia's. I used my scooter as I had time, I wasn't rushing off to the theatre. It was good for me to do it as it gave me some more knowledge of driving in London.

As soon as I rang the doorbell Sylvia was there. She was dressed in the sort of clothes she wore at college, she was painfully thin. She gazed at me and a look of pain crossed her face.

'Oh Christopher, your poor face.'

She pulled me indoors and put her arms around me, then she ran her hand across my damaged cheek, before taking me into the living-room.

'Tell me what happened.'

'A truck came too close to me on the road to Haifa and drove me off the road and I crashed.'

'Did he stop?'

'No, I don't think he noticed, someone took me to a kibbutz there and they patched me up. They did a good job. It will gradually lose that red colour and you'll hardly notice.'

I decided not to tell her the whole saga.

'It looks terrible. I'm going to make some tea, come into the kitchen with me.'

I followed her into the kitchen.

'Where are your parents?'

'My mother's teaching and my father is working at the hospital. He passed his exams, so he is now a doctor here.' She made the tea. We sat at the little kitchen table.

'Poor Christopher, are you sure it will heal up?'

'Yes, it will be just a white line . . . I'll look like a gangster.'

She reached out again and touched my face, 'I really missed you so much. Thank you for the letters, you must have posted the last one just before your accident.'

'I have lots of sketches to show you.'

'Let's go up to my room when we finish the tea, where we can spread things out.' After she had cleared up, she led me up to her room.

She had been working on a painting, but as soon as we came in she took it down, and placed it face to the wall.

I laid my sketchbooks out on the table and Sylvia began to go through them, asking me questions.

'I see what you were doing, these are beautiful Christopher.'

I told her about the brief ones and the photographs I had taken to supplement them. In the back I had tucked the drawing I'd done of Saba.

'Who is she?'

I explained about Hamid and finding the drawing of Saba in the ruins. She listened intently. 'Poor child, where will she be?'

'Hopefully in a camp, maybe in the country, more likely though the Lebanon. I'll never know.'

'When will you get the photographs?'

'I'm picking them up today.'

'When can I see them?'

'I just need to put them in some sort of order, perhaps Wednesday.'

'Oh Christopher, you've done so well, in such a short space of time. Did you write any notes?'

'Yes a lot, but I need to sort them out as well.'

It suddenly occurred to me, maybe she didn't know about Simon.

'You remember my friend Simon.'

'Yes, the one I haven't met.'

'He's dead.'

She was suddenly shocked. It was as if she knew him.

'Oh my God.'

'It must have happened when I was on my way back, I didn't know and when I got home my mother said something about him and I asked . . . I'm sorry, I still haven't got used to it.'

'Oh Christopher, that is so tragic.' She could see the anguish in my face. Again she touched me.

'It's alright Sylvia, I will get used to it, but he will always be there in my mind.'

She put her arms around me again, suddenly I was the one being consoled.

I put my arm round her, she was so thin. 'How are you?'

She thought a bit, 'I wasn't too well after you had gone, but then I got your first letter and began to understand why you had gone, then the last one about two weeks ago. I knew what you were doing, I just wanted you back. Was it dangerous?'

'It didn't seem to be at first, but gradually I began to realise that it was. I'll tell you more things when I've sorted my notes out.'

I stayed for a while longer, I was pleased to see that she seemed better, although she was so much thinner. I must come again when her father was home. I asked her not to tell anyone about why I had been in Israel. We agreed to meet on Wednesday.

I went to the photography shop and collected the negatives, a number of contact sheets and small prints of the photographs. There was a café near by and I went in there to take a quick look at the photographs, while I had a coffee. They looked good.

Back at the flat I spent about an hour going through the photographs and filing them under the names of villages. I decided that I should start hiding this stuff away when I was not there. I found a place at the back of a kitchen cupboard, which had a loose board at the back. I took the drawing of Saba and put it on the wall.

I looked at my watch, it was four in the afternoon. I decided to go to the theatre early and see Andy there, also to tell them that I was back. I then went out to buy some food as there was literally nothing in the flat.

I went to the theatre just after 6 pm, the man at the stage door greeted me warmly and told me that Andy was already there. I went up to the stage where Andy was helping the stagehands put up some scenery. He saw me and came across.

'My God you've been in the wars, what happened?'

'Just a little accident with an army truck, which drove me off the road.'

'Look,' he said, 'I must just finish helping here and when the curtain goes up I can meet you in the pub. The lighting director's operating the switchboard tonight.'

The other stagehands saw me and waved. I went to the pub.

Andy turned up. 'How did you get on?'

'Pretty good, though I came back a bit earlier than I meant to. How was it here?'

'It was all right, I did screw up a couple of times, but I got better. When are you coming back?'

'The beginning of next week, if that's OK with you.'

'Good, that's fine, Susan will be pleased, she wants us to go camping before the holiday is over. It's your favourite play next, "Look Back in Anger", again.'

'Camping?'

'Yeah I know, I'm not sure about life in a tent. How was the camera?'

'It was great, I'll bring it in, will you be in the College tomorrow?'

'Yes, after 12 o' clock.'

He went back in at the interval and I left and took myself home.

The next day I started sorting out my notes early, as well as the sketches and drawings.

I called Sylvia first thing, and asked her if she would like to come to me in the afternoon. She had never been here before, I was afraid she might not want to come this way as it was quite far from where she lived.

'Yes that would be nice.'

I gave her instructions about which bus to take.

I went to the college later in the morning. Andy was already there, I gave him back the camera with many thanks.

I showed him some of the smaller prints and told him I would bring my sketches later in the week.

I then went back to the flat. I supposed I should have told Sylvia that I would pick her up, but I wasn't being very organised.

We had agreed that she would come at about 3pm. By 3.30 she had not arrived and I began to worry about her. She knew her way to college all right but I was not sure about anywhere else. About 3.40 she arrived. She was very apologetic, somehow she had got on the bus going the other way.

I showed her my little flat, which was not much compared with where she lived. She seemed to like it. I made her some tea, and then I sat her down at my kitchen table to look through the photographs. She was shocked by some of the images of ruined villages. In one photograph there was a picture of Tami, I'd forgotten she was there.

'Who's she?'

'That's Tami, she was my interpreter.'

'Oh I thought Tami was a young man.'

'Sorry, I should have told you, I wasn't thinking, it's a fairly common woman's name, she was very good, she spoke Israeli, Arabic and English.'

'Was she helpful?'

'Yes, in fact she was very helpful, I gradually realised that she shared much the same views that Simon and I had. Also she had done her military service in the Intelligence Corps. According to her there were many Israelis who shared the same views.'

I showed her some of my notes, I had chosen those which didn't have any evidence of Tami. The recent ones, which were my notes about Tantura struck her forcibly.

'This is like the Russians in my country.'

She looked away from me, lost in some thought. Then, she said, 'One day Christopher I have some things I need to tell you.'

She bent her head, at first I thought she was going to cry, but she didn't.

It was plain to me that she felt that she should tell me about what had happened to her with the soldiers. I debated whether I should tell her that her father had already revealed this to me, and decided not to.

I looked at my watch, it was nearly six o' clock.

'I'll run you home.'

'You don't need to.'

'No I'd like to, maybe I could meet your mother.'

When we set off I realised that she had probably not been on a scooter before.

'I think you should put your arms around me.' Part of me didn't want to ask her to do this, as my last experience of riding like that was with Tami, but it would have been unkind to her. She settled down and put her arms tentatively around me.

We set off, and as I drove she held on to me much more tightly, it was strange having her hold me, she was so physically different from Tami.

It was the rush hour and it took some time to get to where they lived. Sylvia had a key and let us in. She called out and her mother answered from the kitchen.

'I brought Christopher to meet you.'

Her mother came out of the kitchen. She was quite tall with her hair cut short, probably late in her 40s. Her hair was going grey and she wore glasses but she was very good looking and I could see where Sylvia got her look.

'Hello, I'm very pleased to meet you, I have heard so much about you, both from Georgios and Sylvia.'

Her accent was there but less obvious than Georgios'.

'I'm very pleased to meet you too, you have always been working when I've been here before.'

'Let's have some tea and maybe you could tell us about your trip.'

We sat in the front room and I gave her a brief outline of my time in Israel. She asked quite stringent questions, the school teacher in her I suppose.

She looked at my face, 'You suffered some damage I see.'

I explained about the military truck. As I was finishing my story, Georgios returned home. He was very pleased to see me. He too looked at my face, indeed he examined it carefully.

'Very well stitched up, you were in good hands.'

We talked some more. I wanted to ask him more about Sylvia, but it was not a good time. When Sylvia and her mother were taking the tea things to the kitchen, I said to him that I wanted to talk to him about Sylvia on our own. He agreed, and said he would come to the pub next to the theatre the following Tuesday, before I started work.

I left shortly after that. There were still two weeks of the long vacation left and I wanted to get the information off to the journalist at the Manchester Guardian as soon as I could. I decided to go down again to my parents on the Friday again and pick up Simon's original notes. That evening I called Simon's mother and asked her if she could meet me on Saturday morning again. I also bought a Manchester Guardian, from this I found their 'phone number. I decided to call them the next day. I needed to earn some money soon, as I was running out of cash.

The next day, about 10am, I called the paper and asked about the journalist. It appeared that he did work for them as a freelance columnist; they would not give me his home 'phone number. I borrowed a 'phone book from my landlord and by dint of searching I found three people with that name in the Manchester area. I called the first one, it was not him, the second one was. I told him I had just returned from Israel, and I had some material which might interest him. He asked me to send it. I was getting closer.

I finished editing my journal adding the appropriate photographs. When I was back home I would go through Simon's documents for Cyprus and photograph them, so I had a record. The ones I had done of my notes for Israel were perfectly good. I hoped that by the middle of next week I would have everything in the post for the columnist. That evening I wrote a long letter to Tami, which I would send when I got back after the weekend. I also called my parents to say I would be down again.

Chapter 30

I left quite early Friday morning and arrived back home about 10.30. My mother was out shopping, but my father was in. We had a coffee and I then went down to the garden shed. I retrieved Simon's notes and took them to my room. Laying them out carefully on the table near the window I photographed each page, then I went through his sketchbook and I photographed all the relevant sketches. There were about six more drawings like the one I had seen in his sketchbook, before he took it away from me. Along with his notes it showed a powerful indictment of the Intelligent Corps FS.

My mother was back and I had lunch with them. Afterwards I called June and asked her if she would like to have tea with me in town. She knew a café in Winton, not far from where she was now living. We met up about 4.30 and had tea and cakes together. She was only three months pregnant and only just showing a slight bulge. She had put on a little weight, but it just made her look very good; I complimented her.

She asked me how I was settling back in London. I told her everything was good, that I had decided to go back to the theatre on Monday. She was curious to know why I was down so soon.

'I had a lot of things I wanted to take back to London, when I'm back at the theatre I really need to be there on Saturdays, so Sunday was the only day

I was free.' We talked for a while, she was plainly very happy with her new status. When we parted she kissed me, I could tell that there was no passion there anymore, just friendship.

The next day I went into the town, again on the bus. This time I was a little late and Simon's mother was already there. We had coffee and avoided any cakes, she did remark that there was something called croissants on the menu and asked me if I had ever had one.

'Yes, in my recent trips to Paris I did have them a couple of times, why don't you try one?'

She thought for a moment, then decided not, 'Maybe next time I come here.'

I handed her Simon's notes and sketchbook. 'I'm very concerned about these, can you make sure to keep them in a secure place. I've copied them, but I will need them back as if it becomes public they'll be required.'

She started to open his sketchbook, and then closed it again. 'I'll look through them and call you. You've read them and seen his sketches?'

I nodded. I told her about calling the Manchester Guardian and finding out that he was a freelance journalist, who did work for them. When they refused to give me his number I had found it through the directory, and called him.'

She looked at me with some respect, 'You've been doing very well.'

We talked some more then parted. She said she would call me as soon as she had read his notes. She kissed me on the cheek.

I walked up to the cliffs. It was a beautiful day and I sat on one of the seats looking out to sea. Considering how late in the summer it was, it was still warm. The Isle of Wight was clear and looking towards the Dorset coast I could make out the headland at the end of the Purbecks, jutting out into the sea. This all reminded me of my walks with Simon at the weekends. This made me very sad again, that period of our idyllic view of the future, our dreams of life as artists.

On Sunday I helped my mother with preparing lunch. I told her that Tami had endeavoured to teach me to cook, but in the end did it herself. I think she rather approved of that. I also told her that her mother was in hospital after the bomb-blast and had one of her legs removed, and Tami was staying to look after the family. My mother was deeply shocked.

There was a 'phone call from Simon's mother which she answered and I heard her offering her deepest condolences. After a conversation she called me to come to the 'phone.

Simon's mother spoke of her feelings for what she had seen in Simon's notes and sketches.

'You must get it published, it's very important.'

'Yes, I'm doing my best.'

'I know you are, he was so thorough, I'm proud of him, I wish I'd known this at the time, it's very sad . . . I can't tell him.'

'I'm going back to London this evening, be careful with that material, I'll take it off you next time I'm down.'

She said she would write to me.

Sunday afternoon I got my stuff together. I told my parents that I would not be down for several weeks. This term would be the beginning of my final year, I had much to do.

On the Monday I went through Simon's journal and put the photographs I had taken of his notebook in to be processed. The sketchbook was more or less complete in itself, but I selected any to do with the interrogations and made them separate. I called Sylvia and said I was back and we arranged to meet later in the week. I sent my letter off to Tami.

I arrived at the theatre later in the afternoon, Andy was there as they were doing the dress rehearsal and he wanted to show me what changes there were in the lighting schedule. Peter the lighting director was going to work on the switchboard for the first three nights. The stagehands were all pleased to see me and admired my scar.

I was pleased that it was 'Look Back in Anger' again. Although I had seen it many times I was still entertained by its acerbic humour, and laughed as much as any new audience.

On the Tuesday I picked up the photographs I had put in and went through sorting them out. I reckoned that by Thursday I would have them ready to be sent off to the journalist.

At 6.30 I went to the pub by the theatre. Sylvia's father was already there. He asked about my journey to Israel, although I knew he would have heard about it from Sylvia and her mother. He seemed impressed that I had managed so much in the time. I asked about Sylvia.

'Well she was very down after you departed but as soon as your letters arrived she brightened up, and as you can see now she seems much improved.

'Do you think she will improve?'

'I'm not sure . . . she seems much better, but . . . it seems very connected to you.'

This was not what I wanted to hear, it underlined my own anxieties. I needed to tell him about Tami.

'When I was in Israel I fell in love with a woman there, she is an Israeli but her sympathies were very much with what we were doing.'

He thought about this. 'I was afraid this might happen, I realised that you were not necessarily in love with Sylvia, but that you cared for her. Will you be going back to Israel?'

I shook my head, 'I can't.'

'Will she come here?'

'Right now I don't think she can.' I explained about the bomb in Jaffa's souk, and how her mother was badly injured, and how Tami was there, running the family.

'Maybe for now don't mention this to Sylvia, let's see how she'll improve. If she really gets stronger there might be a better time.'

'Yes, you are right. Please believe me, I am very fond of her.'

'I know this.'

We talked some more, then as both of us needed to go to work we parted, agreeing to meet at intervals to see how Sylvia was doing again.

On Thursday I had finished putting together the package and sent it registered to the correspondent in Manchester.

Chapter 31

I started going into College during the day. Andy went on his camping holiday. I began laying out the first painting I wanted to do. It was still vacation time for another week and a half, and my tutor was not in. Sylvia came in a couple of days and we had tea together in the Victoria and Albert café. She seemed much better and was already working up some ideas for her next painting.

I read the Guardian every day, in the hope of seeing material from my documents. Nothing occurred so I had to assume that it might take time to choose the right moment. The recent bombing in Jaffa market had led people to continue their sympathy for the Israelis, surrounded by 'wicked terrorists'.

Andy came back from his camping holiday looking fit and well. The weather had been good and he was very brown.

When we went for tea we would take Sylvia with us. She liked us being together, regarding us as her mentors, too grand a title for us, but we liked it.

The term started and Andy and I became very conscious of it being our last year. My tutor was very pleased with my sketches and came frequently to see how my paintings were progressing.

One day I was reading the Manchester Guardian when I saw a small article on the third page. The person who I had sent the package to had been killed in a car crash.

This crushed me, I called his number in Manchester, and there was no one there. I had no idea if he was married or not, nothing had been mentioned in the article. I was now at a loss, who should I send it to. Thank God it was only photographs, I still had the originals.

I called Simon's mother and told her about the article. She too was at a loss. I said I would try and find someone else who might help.

To be honest it was a very difficult time, I was trying to get my paintings together, mainly because I was anxious to get a reasonably good assessment for my College degree, as well as for their political content. I needed to find out more but I knew it might take time. I tried again to call the number in Manchester, to no effect. I wondered what happened to all that material I had sent. I should call the paper and see if anyone knew about it.

I had a letter from Tami, she was still distraught about what had happened to her mother, not surprisingly. Her mother would stay in hospital for at least another month. She had asked again how I was.

Towards the end of the second week of the term Sylvia saw that there was going to be a 'hop' the following week.

'Will you take me?'

'Yes of course.'

'Then we can dance and dance,' She was very excited.

Andy said he was coming too and bringing Susan.

It was a good hop, there were two groups playing and we all got up and danced. It went on quite late. Andy and Susan left, but Sylvia and I stayed on until the last number. We were both exhausted but it had been very good.

I had my scooter and Sylvia got on the back. She held on to me very tightly as I made my way back to where she lived. I hadn't realised how late it was, dawn was just beginning when I got there. I parked the scooter and walked with her to the front door. She stood on the step, 'Thank you, that was so good.'

She held out her arms to me and I went up to her, she held me very tightly and started to kiss me, pressing her body against me and kissing me with increasing passion. There was no doubt she was aroused, whatever had stopped her doing this before seemed to have disappeared, she suddenly wanted me.

I gently disengaged myself. 'It's late Sylvia, your parents will be concerned.'

'Let me come and see you tomorrow, at your flat.'

'I'll call you tomorrow.'

I drove off, when I got to the corner and looked back, she was still there watching, I waved to her and she waved back.

Chapter 32

Andy climbed the stairs to check in to the College. The man there said, 'There is a gentleman waiting for you.' He looked in the corner of the landing. A small man, about 50 years old, came forward as Andy approached.

'Andy?' he enquired.

'Yes, that's me.'

'I'm Sylvia's father.' He held out his hand. 'George is my name.' He had a strong accent, and it was difficult to make out the name. 'George,' he said again.

Andy shook his hand.

'I wonder if there is somewhere we could talk.' He looked at the stairs, there were students everywhere.

'Yes,' said Andy, 'let's go and have tea.'

He led the way through the back entrance to the Victoria and Albert Museum. When they reached the café he found a table. 'You stay here and I'll get us some tea.'

He returned with the tea and sat down.

'Yes, tell me how is Sylvia.'

'Well that's why I wanted to talk to you.' He stopped.

Andy looked enquiringly at him.

You and Christopher were very good friends with her, she always talked about how kind you both were to her.' He paused again, then said, 'I wonder if you could find time to see her.'

'Yes of course, where is she?'

'She is at home now, although she spent some time in a Psychiatric Hospital.'

'When did this happen?'

'When she heard of Christopher's death she had a complete nervous breakdown. At one time I feared she might kill herself. If you could come and see her, it may help her.'

'Yes of course.'

'She may not respond when you see her, she is sometimes so absent, as if she was in another world, but if you could, it might help.'

'It was a tragic accident, I believe Christopher had just taken her home, from the 'hop' we were at.'

'Yes that's right.'

'I enquired into that, there was a woman out early, taking her dog for a walk. She saw the first truck pull out suddenly from a side turning in front of him, he went straight into it. The truck didn't stop, he was in the road still alive, before she could do anything another truck came along and ran over him, then drove off. A young reporter put that in the paper. Later the woman was questioned, she seemed nervous and rather frightened, and denied everything. The reporter was fired from the newspaper.'

Sylvia's father looked at Andy, 'I know there is some mystery there.'

'Yes I did think so and I tried to pursue it with the police, they were not co-operative. The woman was plainly frightened and didn't want to discuss it with me. I have tried to find the young reporter, but he seems to have vanished.'

'I wonder if the young woman in Israel was told'

'Yes, her name was Tami. When Christopher's mother came up to clear his flat she found several letters from her, with her address. There was one, which arrived on the day he died; she told him that she was pregnant by him. Christopher's mother wrote to her, Tami was terribly upset hearing about Christopher's death. She and Tami wrote further letters to one another. Later, after the baby was born, Tami wrote to say that when the baby was one year old she would bring her to England to visit Christopher's parents. She had called her Saba.

'So maybe there is some consolation there.'

'Yes I suppose so, also Christopher's parents and Simon's mother have the material and drawings that he and Simon did and are looking into a way to publish it.

About the Author

Michael Seymour

Born - Southampton, England.

Grew up in Bournemouth, England.

Educated at Grammar School and Bournemouth College of Art.

2 Years Military Service, mainly in Cyprus and Egypt.

3 years at Royal Royal College of Art Painting School.

Worked as a 'paparazzo' in the '60's.

Then worked for 40 years as an Art Director and Production Designer in the Movies Nominated for an Oscar on 'Alien'.

Lived for 14 years in Los Angeles.

Awarded British Academy award for Art Direction on 'Alien'.

Photographic exhibitions in Los Angelis, New York and National Portrait Gallery in London.

22 of his photographs in the National Portrait Gallery Archives. In London.

Current exhibition of Pauline Boty in London.

Currently living in London and working on his next book.

Lightning Source UK Ltd.
Milton Keynes UK
UKOW05f0613130813

215249UK00002B/76/P